Peter Seabrook

Good Food Gardening

photographs by Michael Warren

Cookery by Pamela Dotter

Cookery editor of Family Circle Magazine

BOOK CLUB ASSOCIATES, LONDON

Contents

This edition published 1983 by
Book Club Associates
By arrangement with Elm Tree Books

Text copyright © 1983 by Peter Seabrook
Cookery text copyright © 1983 by Pamela Dotter

Book design by Patrick Leeson and Alan Hamp

Typeset by Servis Filmsetting Ltd
Printed in Great Britain by Colorgraphic Ltd, Leicester
and bound at the Pitman Press, Bath

Introduction

We all gain satisfaction from seeing a living thing growing under our care. Because of this, gardening is one of our most popular pastimes, but it offers much more besides.

Many plants are decorative and growing these gives much pleasure to the eye. Many fruits and vegetables are easy to cultivate and they provide good fresh food at modest initial cost.

There is nothing new in this because cottage gardeners have for years cultivated a mixture of flowers, fruits and vegetables in plots around their homes. The old countryman had more space, however, than many modern houses and, it is interesting to note, they had no room or time for neatly-manicured lawns. Now as paved terraces and patios are becoming a feature of many modern garden plots there is every reason to consider abandoning the lawn. The hardness of paving can be softened by growing plants of all kinds in containers and the remaining land can be tightly cropped to get the maximum yield from a small area.

The aim of this book is to help the suburban gardener to maintain a steady supply of home-grown food in an appealing way from a compact plot. Apple, pear and plum trees, for example, provide flowers and fruit. Brussels sprouts may not look very decorative in the winter but the tightly-curled green kale or purple-leaved cottagers' kale can look attractive and provide valuable winter greens. Many vegetables and soft fruits can be mixed in with purely decorative plants to serve both utilitarian and aesthetic purposes.

Where the space for gardening is limited it means less work and so more can be invested in a smaller area with the result that the returns in every sense are increased. Modern varieties have been bred to give maximum yield under today's conditions. Many are easier to grow: the near leafless pea, 'Bikini', for example is almost self-supporting. Recently introduced methods of growing also make gardening easier with cut-and-come-again lettuce and mini-cauliflowers ideally suited to the small garden. Edging borders with 'Spurt' kale and seakale beet is quite as attractive as many ornamental plants and has the added advantage of providing food. Walls and fences provide protection and the ideal conditions for growing cane fruit like blackberries, grapes and loganberries. South and west-facing fences also provide good conditions for the more tender crops like courgettes, tomatoes, peppers and beans – all good candidates for container cultivation. Even the balcony and broad window-sill are room enough to start off, following some of the suggested growing ideas.

No food is so tempting and delicious as that picked fresh, straight from your own garden. This book has been written to help you make the best of the room available to you to grow healthy and abundant plants. Once cropped, mouth-watering recipes are provided to make the best of your cultural skills as well as tips on storage, freezing, bottling, jams, chutneys and wines.

Using the book

Little space is wasted in *Good Food Gardening* on giving long and complicated instructions for soil preparation, digging, hoeing or garden planning which so many impatient gardeners ignore anyway. However, all the really basic advice is covered and easily found by recourse to the index. Soil preparation, for instance, is dealt with in the Salads chapter but the advice given there is, of course, applicable to all vegetables. Likewise, cloches and plant protection are dealt with in the Protected Crops chapter, digging and hoeing in the Greens section and so on.

In the Cookery sections it is important to remember that the recipes have been tested in both metric and imperial, and that when following a recipe it is necessary to use *either* metric or imperial measurements exclusively.

Climate Variations

Climate factors which affect gardeners in the British Isles have been dealt with in the text. As a very general guide, bearing in mind that all averages quoted are variable, the maps below will give some guide to climate conditions in terms of summer temperatures and periods of frost in Australia, New Zealand and South Africa. The guide for the chance of frost is the important factor with tender crops like tomatoes, the cucumber family, aubergines and peppers. Using cloches reduces the risk of frost damage at the critical times shown.

Australia shows great climatic variations and rainfall is extremely variable. Except for the south east, the coastal belt of New South Wales, all areas are subject to drought and even in this region irrigation may be necessary for up to two months a year. The map (right) shows average daily maximum temperatures of the hottest month of the year, usually January.

Frost is not a serious problem but the map (below) shows the period when slight ground frosts (air temperatures below 2°C (36°F)) may occur.

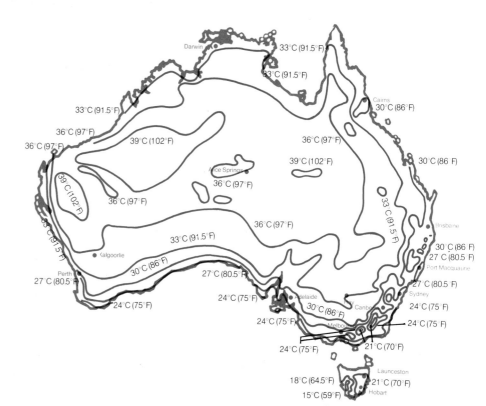

New Zealand has a generally moist climate and droughts are rare. Rain falls predominantly in the winter in the north while summer rains become more predominant towards the south. The map (right) shows average daily maximum temperatures of the warmest month of the year, usually January.

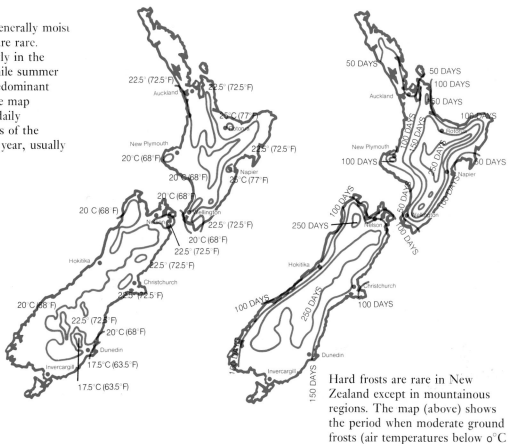

Hard frosts are rare in New Zealand except in mountainous regions. The map (above) shows the period when moderate ground frosts (air temperatures below o°C (32°F)) may occur, mainly from May to September.

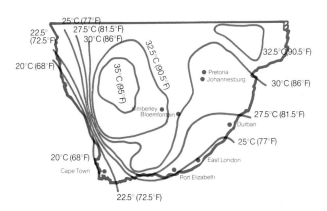

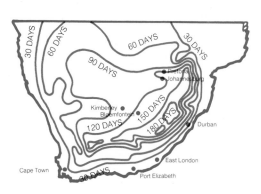

South Africa has considerable seasonal variations in rainfall. The Port Elizabeth-East London coastal belt has appreciable rainfall throughout the year, the Cape Town area has very dry summers while the rest of the country has most rain in the summer. The western side of the country is very dry. The map

(above) shows the average daily maximum temperatures of the hottest month of the year, usually January.

The inland parts of South Africa may suffer moderately severe frosts occasionally. The map (above) shows the period when moderate ground frosts (air temperatures below o°C (32°F) may occur, mainly from May to September.

Salads

All vegetables and especially salads are at their very best gathered fresh and eaten with the minimum of delay. Some grow very quickly: mustard and cress is fit to cut within seven days if grown indoors in the warm and radish can be ready to pull after six weeks when sown outside in early summer.

Chicory deserves to be much more widely grown. You can sometimes find roots offered for sale in garden centres from December to March. Potted up, these roots produce lovely fresh salad in a warm cupboard in the depth of winter. Once you have the taste for them and see how easily they force, it is an easy step to sow seed in late April to grow your own roots and produce the cheapest of all winter salad.

Impatient and less energetic gardeners, eager for quick results, can use growbags filled with fertilized peat. All you have to do is open the bag, water well and then leave for a few hours for the peat to absorb the moisture before sowing short root carrots, lettuce, beetroot, radish and salad onions.

Soil cultivation and preparation

A patch of soil needs to be cultivated, however, for the cheapest crops and pickings sufficient to stock the deep freeze. Gardeners who tend to forget to water their plants would do best to plant them in the rain-watered open soil unless some automatic system of watering is introduced for the bags.

Digging soil to the depth of a spade, or fork on stony soil, is the way to get good crops. Always mix in plenty of organic matter with this first dig, suitable materials are peat and/or well-rotted plant remains (garden compost) and/or well-rotted down animal manure. Heavy clay soil is very much easier to cultivate and the crop is better if this preparatory digging is done in the winter, preferably by Christmas. Winter weather will convert the lumpiest clay into crumbling granular soil. Lighter soils are easier to cultivate but deep spring digging exaggerates the rapid loss of water in hot weather. (See Hoeing: page 51.)

Most gardeners cannot gather up sufficient garden compost and it proves too expensive to buy all the peat and/or manure it takes to convert rapidly poor rough land into good fertile soil. The tip here is to concentrate the attack – apply compost or peat 4–6 in deep over as large an area as possible one year and then next time extend to an adjacent patch and over the years the whole garden will be improved.

A deep cover of organic matter thoroughly dug into soil will give a dramatic improvement in the first year, especially for clay and chalky soils. Gardens really are as good as the organic matter dug into them. The organic addition does so much: it helps to hold water in dry weather; it improves drainage by holding clay apart; it darkens the soil to improve sun heat absorption; it provides food for plants and beneficial soil organisms. There is little point in spending money on good seeds, plants, tools and other gardening aids if the addition of organic matter is skimped. Where money is short, gathering autumn leaves and rotting them down in a large heap over a year or two provides leaf mould, quite as good as peat for soil improvement.

Once the soil is physically improved with mixed-in organic matter it is easier to hoe, plant roots develop more extensively and more vigorously and then fertilizers – concentrated plant foods – can be applied and will have the greatest beneficial effect.

Don't waste your time with so-called miracle clay soil cures; there is no short cut and cheap option; soil improvement comes from masses of organic matter and winter digging.

Having said that, if you've got a patch of soil in spring and want to start growing vegetables right away, it is possible. Just chip up the top 4 in (10 cm) of soil with a spade, or fork it through, mixing some peat or compost as you go and easy crops like radish, lettuce, peas (which always seem to do well in soil cultivated for vegetables for the first time) and cabbage will give acceptable crops. They will need watering well in dry weather and liquid fertilizer added to the water every 14 days or so through the summer.

The only other soil additive to consider is lime. Where masses of organic matter is dug for a number of years into soil which does not contain chalk, the soil can become very acid. One good dressing of lime at $\frac{1}{2}$ lb to 1 lb per square yd (225–450 gm/m^2) in the autumn or winter will soon neutralize the acidity. It is advisable to check the acidity of your soil and the need for lime with a simple soil test kit available from all garden stock retailers, before application. Too much lime in the soil can cause as many problems as too little.

If you are not sure about the lime, don't worry about it, I've grown vegetables satisfactorily for over eight years on two separate gardens without either checking the acidity or applying lime. Potatoes and rhubarb prefer acid soils, the peas, beans and most root crops are best in neutral soils and beetroot, carrot, cauliflower, celery, leek, lettuce and onions prefer slightly alkaline soils.

Soil dug in early autumn. The top lumps are already starting to crumble as wetting and drying, freezing and thawing breaks them up.

If the soil shows acid after checking with a soil test kit, apply lime in autumn or winter.

Year round salad chart													
Crop	Sow	Jan	Feb	Mar	Apl	May	Jun	Jly	Aug	Sept	Oct	Nov	Dec
BEETROOT	Apl-July												
CABBAGE (for coleslaw)	May												
CARROTS	Late Mar-Jun												
CELERY Self Blanching	Apl-Jun												
Blanched	April												
CHICORY Forced	Apl/May												
ENDIVE Batavian	Jun-Early Aug												
CUCUMBERS – Ridge	Early May												
– Greenhouse/Window-sill	Feb-July												
LETTUCE **Summer** i.e. Suzan	From Jan-Jun												
Autumn i.e. Avondefiance	May-Aug												
Greenhouse **Winter** i.e. Dandie	Sept-Jan												
Spring i.e. Valdor	Sept-Oct												
MUSTARD AND CRESS	Year round												
ONIONS Salad	Mar-Sept												
PEPPERS Sweet Green (as for Tomatoes)													
RADISH – small	Mar-Sept												
– winter large	July												
TOMATOES – outdoor i.e. Arla	April												
– greenhouse or window-sill	Feb/Mar												

····· store roots in peat, force some each week ▆ harvest fresh ▆ store roots in peat ▆ shed stored

Cut-and-come-again lettuce. The variety here is 'Valmaine'. Note that the stumps in the foreground are starting to produce another crop.

Lettuce

Pick-and-come-again-lettuce

Lettuce leaves are the basis for most summer salads and there are two simple ways to provide a steady supply from late May through to the autumn frost. The first is to sow the variety 'Salad Bowl' and just keep picking the larger outer leaves. Even easier, and especially suited to shaded gardens where lettuce does not heart properly, is the cut-and-come-again system.

Select a strong-growing variety of cos lettuce such as 'Lobjoits Green', 'Paris White' or 'Valmaine.' Sow in a square

Eight distinctly different lettuce sown late July, ready to cut in September/ October.

metre patch of well-cultivated soil. Arrange the sowing in rows spaced 5 in (13 cm) apart, sowing a couple of rows every two weeks until the whole square is filled, starting late March/April. Thin the seedlings out so that they stand approximately 3 cm apart. Where growth is rapid in warm, damp weather, the first leaves are ready to cut in 40 days. Cut off all the leaves 1–2 cm above ground as required and leave the stump to sprout again and produce another supply of leaves in a few weeks. At least three cuts should be obtained from each plant.

Liquid feed the rows each week and water well in dry weather. Watch for greenfly and other aphids. A spray containing bioresmethrin or pirimicarb will control these pests and allow picking in 24 hours.

Upright growing 'Little Gem' and the single, well-hearted 'Tom Thumb' (foreground) with the cut leaf or oak leaf 'Salad Bowl' (centre).

Hearted lettuce

There are three main types of lettuce: the ordinary cabbage – so called 'Butterhead' varieties – a few of which have reddish leaves (eg 'Continuity'); the curly crisp lettuce often referred to as 'Great Lakes' type and the upright, long-leaved cos lettuce.

It is advisable to choose not simply the type which you prefer but, more important, the right variety for each season. The curly crisp lettuces do not grow well in Britain in winter and early spring. Therefore we sow 'Great Lakes', 'Webbs Wonderful' and 'Windermere' in spring and early summer for summer/early autumn cutting.

There are summer- and autumn-hearting cos lettuces like 'Lobjoits Green' and the dwarfer, more tightly-hearted 'Little Gem', which are also sown in spring and early summer. For early spring harvesting you should sow 'Winter Density' in late September/early October and grow under cloches to cut April/May.

Cabbage varieties offer even more choice. 'Suzan' and 'Hilde II' are good for early spring and summer to cut from May through to the frost. 'Avondefiance' is especially good for summer sowing to crop well into the autumn. Then there are varieties like 'Ambassador', 'Dandie' and 'Kloek' to sow in September in greenhouses for winter cutting and 'Arctic King' and 'Valdor' to sow outside and protect with cloches through the winter to cut April/May. (See page 33.) *Note* Where the temperature goes over 20°C, lettuce seed germination is reduced.

Lettuce will grow best in fertile soil although in poorer soils growth is much improved if the plants are given dilute liquid fertilizer every 14 days during the summer and early autumn. A really good watering seven weeks from sowing will give the best summer lettuce.

Most varieties will need spacing 12 in (30 cm) apart excepting the small but tightly-hearted and delicious 'Tom Thumb' and 'Little Gem', which can be spaced at half this distance.

Apart from an occasional hoe to control weeds, lettuce needs little cultural attention. Better blanched hearts will be produced if the large outer leaves on cos lettuce are held in with a wide elastic band. Do not fix the band too tightly, just firm enough to hold the leaves.

Lettuce sown under cloches in late September/early October with sweet peas. The lettuce are cut as the sweet peas take up all the space.

Greenhouse lettuce

While it is easy to grow lettuce outside, especially in summer, winter-maturing lettuce grown in glasshouses can be a bit tricky. It is usual to raise the seed first in seed pans or seed trays. (See pages 42–43.) Then they are transplanted singly into the greenhouse border soil or growbags. Take care when transplanting to avoid damaging the seedling leaves and never plant deeply. If the seedlings flop over on to the soil after transplanting that's fine, they will soon grow upright again.

As the lettuce starts to heart, the first two seed leaves yellow and die. These dying leaves encourage botrytis disease and if you only have a few lettuce it is worth gently pulling the brown seed leaves off. Try to keep the surface soil dry by ventilating the greenhouse well on sunny days.

Keep the glass on greenhouses and cloches scrupulously clean in the winter. Lettuce need every bit of available light during the dark, short days.

Self-hearting dwarf cos lettuce 'Little Gem', cropping in a mixed flower and vegetable border.

'Butterhead' type of lettuce grown quickly as a space filler alongside French beans.

Chicory

There are several different types of chicory, all have the characteristic slightly bitter taste. One of the simplest to grow is the cos lettuce-like type which is sown in June or July. It forms a self-hearting plant which is cut to use fresh like lettuce in the autumn and early winter. Immature leaves can also be picked to eat fresh but if you overdo the early picking the plant is denied sufficient reserves to form the heart. As well as the green 'Sugar Loaf' types there are red-leaved varieties to bring extra colour to salads.

Varieties specially bred to force in the winter are, however, by far the most valuable. There is no easier and cheaper way to get masses of winter salad leaves. They are usually called 'Brussels' chicory but try to avoid the old 'Witloof' variety because the roots need covering with sand or soil to force properly. Look for the new hybrids with names like 'Normato', 'Crispa' and 'Zoom' because they are easier to force and do not need the sand covering.

Sowing dates are important for the new hybrid forcing varieties and late April/early May is the ideal time. Sow the seeds in well dug and cultivated soil in rows 15–18 in (40–45 cm) apart. Thin the seedlings as soon as they are large enough to pull out easily to stand 3 in (7.5 cm) apart down the row. The wider the seedlings are spaced, the larger the roots will grow and the larger each individual chicon will be, but quite modest, good carrot-sized roots will force well.

Apart from an occasional good water-

Lift chicory when the leaf tips start to yellow in October, screw the tops off and store the roots in peat.

Roots are potted five to eight in flower pots and covered with black polythene. After the plump chicons (left) are snapped out a second crop of thin leaves grows (right). An example of red-leaved chicory can be seen left (foreground). These are more tender if the centres are blanched.

ing in dry weather and hoeing to kill weeds, they require little attention through the summer. In the autumn – usually late October – when the leaf tips start to yellow the whole plant is lifted with a fork, the foliage screwed off and the roots packed in layers surrounded by dry peat in a box. Do not *cut* the leaves off as cutting too close will damage the growing shoot at the top of each root.

From November or December to April a few roots are potted up each week in old potting compost or peaty soil. Five or six roots fit into an 8-in (20-cm) flower pot and the root ends can be snapped off if they are too long to go in. Remove any brown or slightly rotten leaf bases from each shoot and then water well before enclosing in a black polythene bag to

Clear blue chicory flowers grow on roots seven months after forcing if planted in the garden.

The cropping period can be extended by lifting well-developed plants with some soil on the roots in October/November and planting them in wooden trays. Placed in a dark shed they are protected from very harsh winter weather and blanch ready for eating.

Lamb's Lettuce, Corn Salad

This salad is very easy to grow. Sown outside in August and September, the young leaves can be picked for salads right into the winter. If you like the flavour this plant can also be grown in pots, in window-boxes and growbags.

Mustard and Cress

The quickest of all salad crops and both types, when germinated in very warm conditions, are ready to cut in seven days. Grow a steady supply in old 250 or 500 gm margarine tubs. Wash the tubs and lids clean and cover the base of the tub with $\frac{1}{2}$–$\frac{3}{4}$ in (1–1.5 cm) of damp peat or all peat seed compost.

Sprinkle a good covering of cress over one pot and mustard over a second pot. Syringe with water, put the lids on and place over (not on, it's too hot) a radiator, central heating boiler or hot water tank. If its warm enough the seedlings will be well up, ready for the lids to be removed, in two to three days and the tubs can be placed on a light warm window-sill to keep growing and green up.

A new lot can be sown every day to maintain a steady supply for sandwiches. Alternatively, sow several tubs for a greater supply at one cutting. The tubs ready to cut will hold for several days on a cool window-sill as long as the peat is kept damp.

One plant of endive blanched under a plastic bucket. Plant of corn salad bottom left.

Endive

A member of the chicory family, endive is quite hardy and well suited to summer sowing for winter salads. The mass of leaves, once well grown, are made more tender and less bitter by covering and blanching before use.

There are two kinds, the 'Moss Curled' which looks like a cross between cabbage lettuce and parsley and the more lettuce-like 'Batavian Endive'.

Sow the seeds outside where you want them to grow from May to July for the curled kinds and July to late August for Batavian types. Thin the seedlings out to stand 12–15 in (30–38 cm) apart and, especially in poor soils, water with dilute liquid fertilizer several times in summer and early autumn to get good big centres to the plants.

Blanching is achieved by totally covering plants with a bucket, or using black polythene over tunnel cloche wires, or just placing a square of wood over the centre of the 'Moss Curled' varieties.

exclude the light and then bring indoors in the warm.

In a week or two the new roots will form. Once formed, they will grow faster if the temperature is increased. In four weeks or so each root will have produced a creamy white chicon 6 in (15 cm) high which can be snapped off and used either raw in salads or cooked.

If the pot is re-covered and the compost kept damp a second crop of loose leaves will grow and this is fine for salads. Even after these two crops the roots are not finished because, planted out in spring in the flower border, they produce clear blue flowers in the following summer. You can also pick some of the soft, young light green leaves from the flower stems for salads.

Margarine tubs producing a seven to ten day production cycle of mustard and cress. Note $\frac{1}{2}$ in (1 cm) of peat seed compost and the lids used first to cover the tubs until the seeds germinate.

Lifting trench-grown celery, late December after the leaves have been cut back by frost.

Celery and Celeriac

There are three main types of celery which can be grown by gardeners. The most succulent and flavourful is the traditional 'trench' grown kind which is sown under glass in early spring, planted out in 6 in (15 cm) deep trenches in early summer and the leaf stems surrounded with soil as they grow. This earthing up to blanch produces the crisp white and in some varieties, pink-stemmed celery hearts.

Much easier to grow, although some say much less palatable, are the self blanching varieties which are planted on the surface in blocks fairly close together, 12 in × 9 in (30 cm × 23 cm), to get the self blanched stems. There is a choice here of creamy white to yellow stems with varieties like 'Latham Self Blanching' and the green stems of American Green varieties like 'Greensnap'. It is difficult to understand why the green is not much more popular with gardeners, it certainly deserves to be for both taste and ease of growing.

Finally we have celeriac which produces a large root of strong celery flavour.

The roots can be a bit tough and this form is best used cooked. Celeriac is raised under glass like the other celeries and planted out, once the possibility of frost is past, on the surface in rows 18 in (45 cm) apart and spaced 12 in (30 cm) apart down the row.

All celery likes fertile soil, that means plenty of peat, garden compost and/or manure to hold moisture through the summer. Let celery go short of water and it bolts prematurely to seed and is very tough.

Small domestic gardens are best served by the self blanching types. Several sowings from early spring to early summer, sufficient to plant a square yd (sq m) or so, each time, will give a succession of hearts to harvest.

The best results will be obtained where the plants are grown in cold frames, polythene and cold glasshouses or, at least, where the plants are started off under cloches. All the self blanch varieties grow very well in growbags, they love the rich peat compost and, given plenty of water, grow beautifully. Growbags have the

advantage too that the celery can be sown in early summer, planted in growbags in mid-July and grown on outside before moving into the greenhouse or frame after summer crops such as tomatoes. This will provide celery hearts to last right through to Christmas.

Once you've got the hang of self blanched celery growing then progress to the trench types. The trench needs to be dug in good time to nearly a spade's depth and 12 in (30 cm) wide. If you have more than one trench, space the trenches 3 ft (90 cm) apart. Dig plenty of organic matter into the base of the trench, then fill back half the soil, leave to settle and then plant out in a single row 6 in (15 cm) apart down the centre of the trench.

Once the plants are growing strongly and the leaves 12–15 in (30–38 cm) high, start to return the rest of the soil and keep earthing up every two or three weeks until you have 15–18 in of leaf stalk covered. Sprinkling in a few slug pellets as you earth up reduces the chance of damage to the blanched stems by this pest.

The celery is best to eat after one or two autumn frosts. It usually lasts well in the soil to Christmas and later varieties even into January.

Where stems are hollow and the plants have poor hearts, the soil may well need lime. Brown spots on the leaves are caused by a fungus called celery leaf spot. Modern seed dressings are reducing the chance of this problem but if it does occur spray with fungicide containing benomyl, maneb or zineb. Small larvae also tunnel the leaves on occasions and these are killed by spraying with dimethoate or trichlorphon.

A block of self blanching celery surrounded by other vegetables to help improve blanching of stems.

Radish

Radish for salads are one of the easiest and quickest crops to grow if the soil is fertile, damp and the weather warm. Poor soils and gardens overshadowed by trees make radish growing more tricky but with plenty of liquid feed or, in the last resort, a move to fertilized-peat-filled growing bags, acceptable crops can be grown.

You need to distinguish very clearly between the two different types of radish. The best known are usually sown from late March to October and in warm conditions are ready to pull in four to five weeks. Less common are the winter radish with either red or black skins; they grow to large turnip size and are lifted in early winter and stored as a root for use when the more common type is not easily grown.

Quick growing radish

The seed is sown in rows 9 in (22 cm) apart and ideally the seedlings thinned to stand 1 in (2.5 cm) apart down the row. The rows can be closer or the seed broadcast and just raked in but hand weeding, rather than hoeing down the rows, is then necessary.

For the best results, water diluted liquid fertilizer around the seedlings every ten days. Dust with HCH for flea beetle control.

Popular varieties include the cylindrical-shaped red with white tip 'French Breakfast', scarlet globe-shaped 'Cherry Belle' and 'Saxa', globe-shaped and white-tipped 'Sparkler'. The larger and long white rooted variety 'Long White Icicle' can be used raw in salads and cooked when it has a turnip-like flavour.

Start pulling just as soon as the first roots are large enough to eat; pulling the largest first allows more space for the remaining roots to develop. Sow a short row every ten to 14 days through the summer to get a steady supply.

A number of new varieties are being introduced to suit the poor light and colder conditions of winter. Several have so called 'small tops', making them suitable for growing in the greenhouse and under frames and cloches. 'Rota' and 'Novired', for example, sown early to mid October under glass and with a little heat are ready to pull in late December and sown in January are ready to pull March/April.

The variety 'Red Prince' (*Prinz Rotin*) produces very large roots without going hollow or pithy and grows well out of doors and under glass. If you have a greenhouse used in summer for tomatoes, it is well worth taking an early crop of radish from growbags before planting up with tomatoes. Alternatively, take a late crop of radish in the autumn, once the tomatoes have been cut down and the remaining green fruits ripened on the stem.

Winter radish

There are 3 commonly listed varieties: 'China Rose' of cylindrical shape and with

Sow a short row of radish every ten to 14 days for a succesion of crops. Here from the left are, 'Salad Mixed', 'Pink', 'Long White Icicle' and white-tipped 'French Breakfast' to illustrate the range of colour and variety available.

rose-coloured skin, and round-shaped and long cylindrical 'Black Spanish' types, both of which have unusual black skins. Certainly crops to grow if you want something different to have for winter salads.

Sow this type in July, not before, in rows 12 in (30 cm) apart and then thin the seedlings out to stand 8 in (20 cm) apart down the row. Apart from hoeing to control weeds they require little attention. The roots are lifted in November and stored in boxes of peat for winter use. They will survive outside in the cropping rows in mild winters but it is advisable to lift to be on the safe side.

The red-skinned radish variety 'China Rose'.
Left The winter radish 'Black Spanish Round'.

Cookery

Lettuce

This is the main salad vegetable that forms the base of a green salad for accompanying almost every hot or cold meal. By mixing succulent leaves of round lettuce with crunchy cos-type lettuce, it can be used exclusively. Lettuce is valuable for its vitamin C and mineral elements, particularly the outer dark green leaves which contain iron. Cook lettuce only when there is a glut and they are bolting.

To prepare: cut off the base and the outer damaged leaves and wash both sides of leaves under running water. The solid heart can be cut into quarters for washing and serving. Dry well by shaking the leaves in a salad basket or clean teatowel. If not required immediately, pack loosely into a plastic container, seal and chill in the bottom of the refrigerator. A limp lettuce can often be revived by storing in this way.

To serve: arrange lettuce leaves in a salad bowl. If large, tear the leaves to avoid bruising. Serve with a dressing to complement the food being served. The simplest dressing is vinaigrette, made from 2 or 3 parts oil to vinegar or lemon juice and seasonings. Experiment with different types of ingredients such as olive oil, wine vinegar, herbs, mustard, etc.

To store: if no refrigerator is available, pull up the plants with roots intact and place in a saucepan containing about $\frac{1}{2}$ in (1 cm) water, close tightly with a lid and store in a cool place.

To cook: braise peas on a bed of shredded lettuce or make into soup.

To preserve: lettuce leaves cannot be frozen, but surplus could be cooked and stored as a purée.

LETTUCE SOUP

An ideal soup for end of season lettuce. Add a swirl of soured cream to each bowl before serving for a special meal.

Follow the Master Soup Recipe on page 66. Cook $\frac{1}{2}$ lb (250 g) each of chopped onions and potatoes in 2 oz (50 g) butter. Add 1 lb (500 g) prepared, shredded lettuce and $\frac{1}{2}$ pint (250 ml) chicken stock. Cook 15 minutes then sieve or liquidize. Blend 1 tbsp (1 × 15 ml sp) cornflour with $\frac{1}{2}$ pint (250 ml) milk and a small can evaporated milk. Add the purée, $\frac{1}{2}$ pint (250 ml) water, salt and pepper and bring to boil.

Chicory

The crispness and slight bitterness of chicory are very refreshing and it combines well with fruit for mixed winter salads. For starters and snacks, mix chicory with fish, serving one chicon (chicory head) for each portion.

When cooked it makes a good, juicy accompaniment to fried and grilled meats. Its bitter-sweet flavour is particularly pleasing with chicken.

To prepare: do this just before it is required to avoid discoloration. Never leave chicory soaking in cold water or it will develop a bitter flavour. Trim the stalk; pull off and discard the outer leaves. Serve sliced, or pull off the leaves from the chicon. Pointed leaves make an attractive garnish.

To cook: place prepared chicons in a pan of boiling, salted water with 1 tbsp (1 × 15 ml sp) lemon juice for each pint (500 ml) of water. Cover with a lid and simmer for 15 minutes. Carefully lift each chicon out of the water, drain well, then gently pat dry with a cloth or kitchen paper. Place in a serving dish and dot with butter, or sprinkle with buttered breadcrumbs and brown under the grill. For a starter, serve cooked chicory with Hollandaise sauce.

To store: this salad vegetable must be used almost as soon as it has been harvested. Keep it dark or it will become limp and bitter – store chicory in a black plastic bag, even for the shortest length of time.

To preserve: the only method is to freeze cooked chicons. Wrap up the drained and dried chicons individually in cling film, then pack them into a freezer bag.

To serve: unwrap chicons and place them in an ovenproof dish. Leave in the refrigerator to thaw; then cover with buttered breadcrumbs and bake in a moderate oven for about 20 minutes until the top is crisp and golden.

CORDON BLEU CHICORY ROLLS

Prepare this dish in advance if you wish, then bake it when required. It can also be made with a centre of celery.

For 4 portions

Metric		Imperial
4	chicons	4
1 × 15 ml sp	lemon juice	1 tbsp
100 g	Cheddar cheese	4 oz
75 g	butter	3 oz
1 × 15 ml sp	made mustard	1 tbsp
4	large slices bread	4
4	slices cooked ham	4
2	tomatoes	2
	parsley	

1. Prepare a moderate oven (190 deg C, 375 deg F, Gas Mark 5). Trim ends of chicory and remove any discoloured leaves. Place in a saucepan of boiling salted water. Add lemon juice, cover with a lid and simmer for 15 minutes, drain and pat dry with kitchen paper.

2. Grate cheese finely. Beat butter and mustard together in a basin. Reserve half on a plate and add cheese to remainder in the basin. Beat together.

3. Remove crusts from bread and spread each slice with cheese mixture. Wrap a slice of ham and then a slice of bread, cheese side inwards, around each chicon. Place in a shallow ovenproof dish and spread each roll with the remaining butter mixture.

4. Cut tomatoes in quarters; place in dish. Bake on shelf above centre of oven for 20 to 25 minutes, until bread is golden brown and crisp. Garnish with parsley.

Note: this dish freezes well. Make up to end of stage 3: place rolls in a freezer-proof dish. Cover, label, chill and freeze. Store for up to 2 months.

To heat: place in centre of oven. Heat oven to moderate and leave for 50 minutes.

STIR-FRIED CHICORY

A crisp vegetable to serve with grilled and fried meats and fish, this is very quick to make. Prepare it in advance and cook just before it is required.

For 4 portions

Metric		Imperial
1	small onion	1
1	large carrot	1
4	chicons	4
25 g	butter	1 oz
1 × 5 ml sp	soy sauce	1 tsp
1 × 5 ml sp	lemon juice	1 tsp
1 × 2.5 ml sp	sugar	$\frac{1}{2}$ level tsp

1. Peel and chop onion, peel carrot. Wash chicory and trim off end and outside leaves; cut into rings.

2. Melt butter in a large frying pan or wok, add onion and fry quickly for 1 to 2 minutes. Grate carrot and add to pan; stir over a high heat for about half a minute.

3. Add soy sauce, lemon juice and sugar, stir well, then cut chicory into rings and add to pan. Stir the mixture over a high heat for 1 minute, then serve immediately.

Note: add cubes of garlic sausage to Stir-fried Chicory to make it into a snack meal. It can also be used as an omelet filling.

Endive

Curly endive is a useful salad vegetable when lettuce is scarce. It has a slightly bitter flavour and a crunchy texture which makes it best when eaten raw. It can also be braised and served with a cream sauce.

To prepare: trim off the thick stalk and separate into sprigs. Wash, drain and store as for lettuce. Serve the leaves whole or shredded.

To cook: blanch in boiling water for 5 minutes then drain and rinse in cold water; drain well. Fry a snipped rasher of smoked bacon with a chopped onion in 1 oz (25 g) butter, place in a casserole, top with endive (cut to size, if necessary), cover and cook in a moderate oven (160 deg C, 325 deg F, Gas Mark 3) for 45 minutes.

To store: Store prepared endive as for lettuce. Not suitable for freezing.

Mustard and cress

These quickly grown salad vegetables are useful in winter. Use in a green salad or for garnishing sandwiches and cooked dishes.

To prepare: usually, there is no need to wash, just snip off the stalks at the base as required.

To store: keep moist, cover loosely with a plastic bag and store in the salad drawer of the refrigerator.

Celery

Celery is one of the most useful kitchen vegetables. It is particularly delicious with cheese dishes, especially in salads, while casseroles and tomato dishes benefit from the pungent flavour of cooked celery.

To prepare: trim the root and remove any damaged stalks – keep those for cooking. Trim the leaves, wash and keep these for soup or flavouring. Separate stalks and scrub with a brush. Cut centre in half down the length.

To use raw: slice and mix with apple and cheese in a salad. Fill stalks with cream cheese pâté or savoury butter and cut into 2 in (5 cm) lengths for appetizers. Cut into small sticks to serve with savoury dips or herb-flavoured mayonnaise. Keep handy for slimmers 'nibbles'.

To cook: braise and serve as a hot vegetable, make into a purée soup, add to lamb, beef and chicken casseroles. Add to fresh tomato sauce and soup. Stir-fry with other crisp vegetables.

To store: pack prepared celery in a plastic bag and store for up to 2 days in the bottom of the refrigerator.

To freeze: not suitable for serving raw, but surplus can be frozen blanched or cooked or in a purée. Slice into ½ in (1 cm) pieces, blanch 2 minutes, drain, dry and open freeze. Pack in plastic bags.

To dry: spread the leaves on a tray and dry slowly in a fan-assisted oven or in the warming drawer. Crumble and store in a jar ready to add to soups, stews and tomato dishes.

Celeriac

This is like the root part of celery. It has a nutty texture and a celery flavour. The leaves can be used for flavouring soup.

To prepare: scrub the root and peel thickly like a turnip then slice, dice or grate. Place straight into water with added lemon juice or dressing to prevent discoloration.

To serve raw: cut into matchstick-sized pieces, turn in dressing and add to salads, or grate and mix into mustard-flavoured mayonnaise.

To cook: add to casseroles or boil in salted water with lemon juice added 1 tbsp (1 × 15 ml sp) to 1 pint (500 ml). Serve hot with a savoury white or a cheese sauce. Serve cold with cooked ham.

To store: trim the leaves except the tuft at the top and layer in moist sand.

To freeze: cut in dice or strips, blanch in boiling water 3 minutes then drain, dry and open freeze on a tray. Store in plastic bags for up to a year.

Radishes

Bright pink radishes make an attractive garnish for cold foods as well as adding crunchiness to salads.

To prepare: trim stalk then wash and drain. Serve small radishes whole and large ones in slices. For garnish, make radish 'roses'. Cut down from base in 3 diagonal cuts. Leave for about ½ hour in iced water until they open.

GREEN CAESAR SALAD

Choose green salad vegetables for their varied texture. Add the croûtons and dressing just before serving.

For 6 portions

Metric		Imperial
1	round lettuce	1
	endive	
	mustard and cress	
12	radishes	12
2	large slices bread	2
25 g	butter	1 oz
	olive or corn oil	
	DRESSING	
1	clove garlic, optional	1
	salt	
1 × 5 ml sp	freshly-chopped mint	1 tsp
	pepper	
1 × 15 ml sp	lemon juice	1 tbsp
1 × 5 ml sp	French mustard	1 tsp

1. Prepare lettuce, endive, mustard and cress and radishes. Shred half the lettuce and endive, slice half the radishes, cut remainder to make radish 'roses'. Place shredded vegetables and radishes in salad bowl.
2. Cut bread into cubes. Melt butter, add 1 tbsp (1 × 15 ml sp) oil and fry bread until golden; drain.
3. Peel garlic, if used; place on a saucer with 1 tsp (1 × 5 ml sp) salt. Using a round-ended knife, rub salt against garlic to crush. Place in a basin and add 3 tbsp (3 × 15 ml sp) oil, mint, some pepper, lemon juice and mustard; mix well.
4. Just before serving, add bread and dressing to salad bowl and toss to coat. Arrange leaves around edge and radish roses in centre. Serve as an accompaniment or a starter.

Salad Niçoise

SALAD NIÇOISE

For 4 portions

Metric		Imperial
250 g	French beans	½ lb
4	eggs	4
200 g	can tuna steak	7 oz
	French dressing	
4	sticks of celery	4
1	large red pepper	1
8	black olives	8
56 g	can anchovy fillets	2 oz
1	cos lettuce	1
100 g	peeled prawns	4 oz

1. Wash beans; trim ends and cut in halves, if very long. Cook in boiling, salted water for 5 to 7 minutes, until just tender. Drain and leave to cool.
2. Hard-boil eggs for 10 minutes; crack, leave to cool in cold water, then shell and dry on kitchen paper. Cut eggs in quarters. Drain oil from tuna; reserve 1 tbsp (1 × 15 ml sp) oil for dressing. Place fish in a bowl; flake with a fork.
3. Add reserved oil to French dressing then drained beans and allow to marinate, while preparing salad.
4. Wash and slice celery. Cut red pepper in half, lengthwise; discard seeds, core and white pith. Slice pepper into strips. Halve and stone olives.
5. Drain anchovies; place in a sieve and rinse with warm water. Dry on kitchen paper; cut each along centre into strips.
6. Remove and discard outer leaves from lettuce. Wash lettuce well; tear leaves into pieces, reserving a few whole leaves.
7. Just before serving, arrange lettuce in base of a large salad bowl. Place tuna, sliced celery, egg, beans, dressing, prawns and red pepper in the bowl, with anchovy fillets and olives. Garnish Salad Niçoise with reserved lettuce leaves. Serve with new potatoes or crusty French bread.

Greens

The brassica family, or as we more frequently refer to them, greens, provide a very wide range of vegetables which in the relatively mild British winter climate, we can grow to cut fresh the year round. Choosing the different varieties of each kind carefully, we can have cabbage and cauliflowers the year round, Brussels sprouts can be picked from August to April, the kales from January to May and calabrese from early summer to Christmas.

There is no other range of vegetables so varied, so easy and so productive. Their only problem is growing them to excess and getting poor crops because of the build up of pest and disease, coupled with soil impoverishment. All successful gardeners rotate their crops – that is, avoid growing the same kind of plant repeatedly year after year in the same place. You certainly need to follow this advice with green vegetables and also remember that turnip, radish, kohlrabi,

swede, wallflowers and stocks are all members of the same family.

Try to think of all the above listed kinds as *brassicas* and then group the remaining vegetables into either *root vegetables* (beetroot, carrot, parsnip, potato, artichoke, etc) and all *other kinds* (peas, beans, onions, celery, sweetcorn, etc), then you can select one from each group for every place in the vegetable garden and achieve a three year rotation. If at all possible I like the greens to follow peas and beans because the greens are hungry plants and benefit from the extra nitrogenous plant food left in the soil by the legumes.

Spare spaces in the vegetable plot can be filled with very quick-maturing things like lettuce and spinach. Do not worry too much about rotation as long as the crops are moved about from year to year as much as possible; diseases like club root on brassicas will then not be given the chance to multiply rapidly.

Raising plants from seed

Most of the greens are raised by sowing seeds outside in the open garden, in just the same way most hardy vegetables are sown. Lumpy soil is trodden under foot when it starts to dry, knocked by fork and raked to crumble it down into what we call a fine tilth.

Where the soil is hard and lumpy you can make a tilth good enough for seed sowing by chopping in peat. That is, spreading 1–2 in of peat over the soil and then cutting this into the surface by repeated short chops with the end of a spade.

The seedlings are easier to distinguish and hoe between when sown in straight rows. Use a taut line to guide either the hoe or trowel and even a piece of wood to pull out a drill. This should be 1–2 in deep, the greater depth for larger seeds. If the soil is very dry, water the base of the drill several times and let it soak in before sowing the seed.

If you hold the seed in the palm of your hand you will find the seeds can be spaced down the row by just rolling them out between thumb and index finger. Brassica seeds need spacing about 1 in (2.5 cm) apart when they are to be transplanted. If you are sowing in the cropping position, just sprinkle two or three seeds in the place you want each plant to occupy then thin back to one in due course. Generally speaking the greens do better transplanted. Lifted from the seedling row and planted quite deeply with dibber or trowel, the stems are better secured and, especially the tall-growing and over-wintering kinds, will be able to withstand buffeting by the wind.

Early crops of cauliflower, cabbage, calabrese and Brussels sprouts are obtained by raising the seeds indoors and pricking out the seedlings singly into $3\frac{1}{2}$ in (9 cm) pots or peat blocks before planting out. This practice can also be of benefit where the soil is infected by club root disease. Where the plants are given a flying start with the young roots well

Knock down clods with a fork or rake.

Draw out drill with a hoe (note right foot holds the guiding line in place) or trowel.

The foot still holds the line.

Sow seeds by rolling from palm between thumb and index finger.

Shuffle fine soil back over seeds with the feet. This also gently firms the soil close to the seeds.

Firm down the sown row with the feet if the soil is light and rather dry.

Lightly rake out footprints.

Year round greens harvest chart													
Crop	Sow	Jan	Feb	Mar	Apl	May	Jun	Jly	Aug	Sept	Oct	Nov	Dec
BRUSSELS SPROUTS early and late varieties	Mar/Apl	▓	▓	▓						▓	▓	▓	▓
CABBAGE Spring Maturing	late Jly				▓	▓	▓						
Summer Maturing	Feb-Apl						▓	▓	▓	▓	▓		
Winter Maturing	Mar-May	▓	▓	▓									
CALABRESE	Feb-Jun								▓	▓	▓		
CAULIFLOWERS	Sept, Jan-May					▓	▓	▓	▓	▓			
KALE	Apl/May		▓	▓									
SAVOYS	Apl/May	▓	▓	▓									
SPROUTING BROCCOLI	Apl/May			▓	▓								
TURNIP TOPS (picked as greens)	Sept		▓	▓									

established in a fertile and disease-free compost, they will grow to maturity even in infected soil.

Make sure all the brassicas are well firmed when transplanted. To test try and pull the plant up by a piece of its leaf. If the piece tears off, the plant is firm enough, if the plant starts to come up in your hand, it needs more firming.

Note hoed-out drill to make watering easier. The plant is firmed in by pushing soil over with the back of the trowel.

A hollow can be left when firming in brassica plants to make watering easier.

Brussels sprouts

One of the finest winter vegetables, Brussels sprouts improve in flavour with frosty weather and for this reason gardeners are best served with the long season and late harvesting varieties. The introduction of F_1 hybrid varieties makes the cultivation of tall stems packed with tight sprouts relatively easy. They do, however, require fertile soil although to some extent regular watering and feeding through the summer will compensate for poor soil.

Seed is sown under glass in February and March for the earliest crops (this longer growing season also helps produce better crops in poor soils). The general and easiest practice is to sow outside in the garden in March/April and then transplant in May/June.

Space the plants $2-2\frac{1}{2}$ ft (60–75 cm) apart in their final cropping site. While it was once necessary to firm plants in very well to get good tight sprouts, the modern hybrid varieties are not quite so strong rooting and over-firming is unnecessary and better avoided.

Once well established it is advisable to spray several times through the summer with a general garden insecticide to control caterpillars and aphids. Pay special attention to the central growing point of the plant and the undersides of the leaves. Remove the old lower leaves as they yellow and pick from the base of the plant first.

It is a good practice to line the soil on one side of each row with a layer of moss peat 1–2 in (2.5–5 cm) deep in the autumn. This reduces compaction of the surface and prevents your shoes bringing soil on to the path when harvesting sprouts in the winter wet.

Once the sprouts are picked the stems can be left to produce a flush of young shoots which can be picked to provide a tasty green vegetable in the spring. The variety 'Ormavon' not only produces sprouts but also a small 'cabbage' on the top of each plant. This cabbage is best cut in January/February because once cut, sprouts higher up the stem develop faster. Always pull the old stems up before they open flower: left to grow on they really impoverish the soil.

Left Firm sprouts pack every stem of modern F_1 varieties.

Old Brussels sprouts stems (background) left to produce spring greens. 'Talled Green Curled Kale', also called 'Extra Curled Scotch Kale', and the 'Cottager's Kale' with purple older leaves are very hardy winter green vegetables.

Kale

There are several different types of kale, all of which are very hardy and over-winter successfully in the hardest of weather. Toughest of all is the 'Cottagers' Kale' and the large older leaves turn such a bright purple in winter they are suitable for flower arrangement. The curly kales are also very attractive but stay green and young leaves are so parsley-like they can be used for garnishing. Best of all for the masses of tasty green shoots we want to gather in late winter and early spring is the variety 'Pentland Brig'.

Gardeners in a hurry can also try the recently introduced dwarf curly kales like 'Spurt' and 'Fribor'. These can be harvested as soon as the leaves are big enough to pick just as you would gather spinach. While these new varieties can be sown over a much longer period, from early spring to early summer, in rows 12–18 in (30–45 cm) apart, the traditional kales need sowing March/April and transplanted into their cropping sites from June to August. The tall kinds make big plants, best suited to the larger gardens and allotments where they need spacing $2\frac{1}{2}$ ft (60–75 cm) apart.

Sprouting Broccoli

The modern varieties of calabrese are smaller and so much quicker to develop from sowing to harvest that they are surpassing the purple and white sprouting broccoli which come in early and late maturing kinds. Like big kales they need a long growing season, sown in March/May transplanted June/July and are not ready to pick until 12 months from sowing in the following March to May period.

If you have the garden space, in all but the most exposed and coldest of northern districts, they are well worth growing. Some people compare the miniature cauliflower-like shoots produced in great profusion to asparagus and certainly picked fresh or frozen the sprouting broccolis take some beating.

Like all tall over-wintering green vegetables the young plants need planting fairly deep with several inches of the seedling stem set down in the planting hole. This helps the plant to anchor well and to support the large head it produces against the buffeting winter wind.

If you have pigeons in your garden then winter protection will be necessary. If the green vegetable patch is not too large then a fine mesh net will not only keep the pigeons off in winter but also

keep the cabbage white butterfly from laying eggs and introducing caterpillars in summer.

Pests

Swollen roots and the sudden wilting of young brassica plants in hot weather are not only caused by club root disease. If you lift the plant carefully and look at the root, even cutting open any swollen parts, you will find a small maggot is often the

One of the new dwarf curly kales which can be grown quickly for young leaves to pick like spinach. They can also be grown right through the winter to produce masses of green shoots to harvest in early spring.

cause of the damage. Where this occurs a good sprinkling of soil insecticide, for example one containing diazinon or bromophos granules, down the seed drill and around the plant when transplanting, will control it.

Purple sprouting broccoli makes a large plant but produces masses of shoots with purple flower buds which turn green when cooked.

Cabbages and savoys

Gardening can be very confusing at first sight but fortunately it has a simple logic which can be easily understood. Take cabbage for example: spring cabbage we sow in summer, autumn cabbage we sow in spring and early summer cabbage we sow in late winter!

When you are buying cabbage seed it is important to remember the group heading refers to the season of maturity. Sadly there is not one variety which can be sown all seasons to mature all seasons. Having said that, most varieties can be sown outside in March to May to transplant from May to July and the various types provide cabbage to cut from July to May.

The June gap is filled by sowing spring-maturing types like 'April', 'Durham Elf' and 'Flower of Spring' in late July/early August. The late July sowing produces seedlings to transplant in September and, if you forget to sow, then early to mid-August sowings can be made where the crop is to mature. Missing out the transplanting saves a check to growth and regains a couple of weeks, but untransplanted crops get a bit tall, what gardeners call leggy.

Nothing stays the same in gardening and now summer cabbage varieties like the super pointed hearted F_1 hybrid 'Hispi' can be sown under glass in January or February, planted out in April and it grows so fast it is ready to cut in June and early July.

The tip with July-sown spring cabbage is to plant them out 9 in (22 cm) apart, then every other plant can be cut to provide tasty, fresh spring greens in April and the remaining plants left to develop fully-hearted cabbage. These varieties, the 'Hispi' and some other fast-growing summer cabbage, will produce two crops from one stem. After you've cut the first heart, leave the old stem in the ground, give it some extra fertilizer, water well in dry weather and each stump will produce two or three more small cabbages.

Autumn-maturing varieties, like 'Winnigstadt', are good cabbages but there are so many other fresh vegetables at that time, not to mention the second crop on stumps, that I don't give them priority. Very hardy winter varieties like F_1 'Celtic Cross' stand so long in the garden – bullet hard, large round hearts ready to cut from December to late April – that they are indispensable in the year round fresh vegetable plan.

Some of the new crinkle-leaved savoys and purplish-green 'January Queen' type cabbages will also stand ready to cut for a long time. The sowing date for the F_1 hybrid savoys is quite critical; if sown

Spring-maturing cabbage growing under a polythene tunnel cloche for early crops. Every other plant is cut at this stage for use as spring greens, leaving the wider-spaced plants to mature as fully hearted cabbage.

before late May for transplanting in mid July there is a tendency for the hearts to split prematurely. Later sowing of 'January King'/'Queen' types results in smaller heads so closer planting is possible here.

Deep red to purple varieties grown to provide red cabbage for pickling and to cook fresh are sown outside in spring to mature in the autumn. Varieties like 'Ruby Ball' produce attractive crimson leaves, pretty enough to grow in the flower border.

Cultivation

Seed raising under glass (see pages 42–43) is the same as for other greens and once well established the seedlings are transplanted 18–24 in (45–60 cm) apart. The wider the spacing the larger the cabbage as a general rule, and the varieties which take six months or more to mature usually need more space and grow into large heads.

Over-wintering spring cabbage will grow better given protection of either glass or polythene tunnel cloches and they will be fit to cut several weeks earlier.

All cabbages benefit from extra fertilizer which is high in nitrogen. Hoe fertilizers like nitro chalk, sulphate of amonia or growmore in around the plants once they have rooted out into their cropping positions. Spring cabbage responds well to this extra fertilizer applied in March. Foliar fertilizer watered over the leaves will also encourage plants to grow, a useful stimulant where the leaves have gone purplish green and pale, caused either by being waterlogged and cold in winter or by dry and poor soil in summer.

It is a help to draw out a deep drill, as if for seed sowing, before transplanting all brassica plants in the bottom of the drill. This makes summer watering easier and more effective. It also allows extra soil to be drawn up around the stems in early winter to give extra support against gales.

Increasing interest in the use of raw cabbage for cole slaw and salads make the 'storable cabbage' of value. Here varieties like 'Holland Late Winter' are sown in spring and grown to maturity by November. Then the large, very hard round heads are cut and the outer leaves removed before storing in a heap in a cool shed or garage. Treated in this way, the white to cream hearts will keep to March/April. They are best stacked on a wire netting frame to allow air to circulate right through the heap.

Cabbages, showing some signs of pigeon damage photographed after severe frost in late December (red pickling cabbage; crinkle-leaved savoy; pinkish-tinged 'Christmas Drumhead'; large, white, Dutch storage cabbage; red-tinged 'January King' and 'January Queen').

F_1 hybrid cabbage are very uniform: every plant produces a tightly hearted head like this 'Minicole'.
Left After thinning (see photograph opposite) to eat as spring greens the remaining plants at 18 in (45 cm) spacing are left to produce mature heads like this variety 'April'.

Calabrese and Cauliflower

Calabrese

Green sprouting broccoli spears, commonly seen in the deep freezer chests and on restaurant menus, deserves to be more widely grown. Perhaps one reason for its absence is the name calabrese on the seed packet. Whatever name you use, this crop is much easier to grow than cauliflower and it produces more than one picking because, if left, the stump produces several lots of side shoot spears after the main head is cut.

The earlier you sow in spring the

longer the plants will continue to yield but one of the best times to sow is late June. The plants grow very rapidly in warm weather and can have hearts ready to pick in ten weeks. Cool, damp autumn weather sustains new side shoot growth on each plant and with a liquid feed they will crop right through to Christmas if the weather stays reasonably mild.

Whatever happens, keep picking any spears surplus to immediate needs: they will deep freeze beautifully and if the spears are left to flower it reduces the crop.

Seed can be raised indoors in pots and planted out for early picking, but the easiest way is to sow the seed in the cropping row from mid-spring to summer. The surplus plants which are pulled up when thinning can be transplanted elsewhere and will form their first, larger central head two to four weeks later than the undisturbed seedlings.

The wider the spacing the larger the first main head will be but, for general garden use, space the rows 15 in (45 cm) apart and thin or space the plants down the row to give one plant per square ft (900 sq cm). This should give first heads of about 6 oz weight on average garden soil.

When the seedlings emerge watch out for small black flea beetles which eat away neat, round holes in the young leaves. Repeated watering will deter them and dusting with HCH powder will kill them (when wet with dew it helps the insecticide to stick to the leaves).

Apart from sowing, thinning and/or transplanting, hoeing for weeds and spraying to kill caterpillars, there is little else to do. The occasional good watering in dry weather and the application of liquid fertilizer once or twice will considerably increase the weight of crop gathered.

Watch out for the new F_1 hybrid varieties – some will produce a larger first head but the best, in my view, are those that produce smaller first heads and masses of secondary spears.

A smaller central head on this variety but . . . .

. . . once cut the plants produce a lot more side spears. Note the attractive silver blue leaf colour which flower arrangers find useful. If you pick too many leaves too early, however, the crop will be reduced! The spears which are starting to open yellow flowers (background) are too old to eat and should be cut off to encourage new spears to form.

Plant breeders are working on biennial varieties which, it is hoped, could be sown late September/early October and over-wintered under cloches. This would provide crops to pick from April to June when green vegetables can be in short supply. The home gardener with a deep freeze will be safer, however, with the late spring/early summer sown crops.

Cauliflower

Cauliflowers are quite easy to grow on rich fertile soil with plenty of water in summer. They can be quite difficult in the average garden, however, where the soil just isn't good enough. You stand the best chance of success under average garden conditions with the long season varieties, that is the spring sown-autumn maturing types and the late spring sown-late spring (12 months later) maturing

If you are in no hurry to cut, and the curd is mature like this, it is worth bending one or two of the larger leaves over the curd to protect it from the sun so that it will remain in good condition for a longer period.

Cauliflower year round cropping chart												
Types and variety examples	Jan	Feb	Mar	Apl	May	Jun	Jly	Aug	Sept	Oct	Nov	Dec
SUMMER MATURING TYPES												
Snowball												
Snow Crown F₁												
Snow King F₁												
Dok Elgon												
AUTUMN MATURING TYPES Australian varieties												
Barrier Reef												
Kangaroo												
Snowcap												
WINTER HARDY TYPES (Broccoli)												
Leamington												
Late Queen												
PURPLE HEADED CAULIFLOWERS												
Royal Purple												
Purple Cape												

Legend:
- over winters / outside unprotected
- grow seedlings in pots under glass
- transplant into cropping position
- sow under glass (cloches, frames, greenhouse)
- sow outside
- harvest

types which used to be called broccoli and are now known as winter hardy cauliflowers. Both autumn and winter hardy varieties grow quite large and take up a lot of space.

Those gardeners who like succulent white cauliflowers but find their attempts to grow good heads of quick-growing varieties like 'Snowball' unsuccessful should switch to the mini-cauliflower growing system.

It will be seen from these remarks that choosing the right variety for each season is all important and the year round cropping chart should help you make the right choice.

Careful soil preparation is advisable for all types and this means digging in plenty of well-rotted compost, peat, etc., well before planting and feeding with liquid or powdered fertilizers when the plants are growing fast and the leaves are expanding at a rapid rate. Good weekly waterings with dilute liquid fertilizer will often compensate for poor soil and help produce reasonable-sized cauliflowers.

The quick-growing and early varieties maturing in summer can be sown under glass in late September/early October, pricked off singly into 3½ in (9 cm) pots and overwintered in a cold frame to plant outside in spring. Alternatively, sow in heat January/February and grow on under glass to again plant out in spring. The third choice is to sow outside either under cloches in early spring or uncovered in March/April.

All other varieties are sown in April/May outside and transplanted when 4–6 in (10–15 cm) high. Water the plants well before lifting to transplant and water well after transplanting because any check to growth is likely to cause premature 'buttoning': the formation of small immature cauliflowers.

Summer maturing cauliflowers are spaced 18 in (45 cm) to 2 ft (60 cm) apart and the other types need at least 2 ft (60 cm) spacing.

Mini-cauliflower

Premature buttoning is no problem here because the whole idea is to grow seedlings close together and encourage the early formation of miniature curds 1½–2½ in (4–7 cm) across. Each one is large enough for a single serving and they are ideal for deep freezer storage.

The seed of summer varieties like early maturing 'Garant' and later maturing 'Predominant' is sown in rows 9 in (23 cm) apart and the seedlings thinned out to stand 4 in (10 cm) apart. If you prefer, seedlings can be raised in a single row and then transplanted out in the cropping site at the required spacing. Transplanted seedlings are likely to crop over a slightly longer period than directly sown crops.

If several sowings are made at two to three week intervals they will provide a succession of crops. Once the small curds are cut the stumps are pulled out and the soil prepared for a different crop.

Purple cauliflower

Add variety and interest to the vegetable plot by trying a few of the cauliflower 'Royal Purple'. The curds are rich purple colour which turn green when cooked. This variety can also be cut young and eaten raw to bring a different taste and colour to salads. Sow them late May to late June for autumn cropping.

The alternative, if seed can be obtained, is 'Purple Cape', a winter hardy kind which is sown in May to cut the following February/March.

Problems – whiptail

Where the soil is acid the chemical molybdenum is in short supply and this can cause deformed plants with strap-shaped leaves. The growing tip often dies and the plant goes blind. Apply lime to acid soils to reduce the chance of this but, should it occur, water the soil with a solution of 1 oz of ammonium or sodium molybdate per gallon before sowing future crops.

Mini-cauliflowers grown at a close spacing are the easiest way to get crops on poor soils. The wider the spacing, the larger the curds. Top left in this small vegetable plot.

Cookery

Brussels sprouts

A traditional vegetable to serve with Christmas dinner, but tiny sprouts can also be shredded and served raw in salads. Pick whilst they are small and tight.

To prepare: trim off the end of the stalk with a sharp knife, cutting off the lower outer leaves. Cut a cross in the base of each. Wash in cold water. If there may be aphids on the sprouts, add salt to the water and leave to soak for 10 minutes. Rinse well.

To cook: aim to cook as quickly as possible by fast boiling and to serve immediately. A slow cooker is not suitable. A pressure cooker can too easily overcook green vegetables. Use a large saucepan and fill to 1 in (2.5 cm) depth with water. Bring to boil and drop in the sprouts while boiling on full heat. Cover with a lid, reduce heat and boil until the stalks are just tender, about 7 to 8 minutes. The sprouts should be slightly crisp and not soft and water-logged. Drain in a sieve or colander and save the cooking water to make the gravy. Serve immediately.

Microwave: best for small sprouts. Cook in a covered serving dish, without water; ½ lb (250 g) takes about 8 minutes.

To store: prepared sprouts will keep in a plastic bag in the refrigerator for up to 3 days. Sprouts can be frozen, but they tend to go rather soggy and must be boiled for a very short time from frozen when required. Or put frozen sprouts without water in a covered serving dish or plastic bag with a sprinkling of salt and cook in a microwave oven for about 4 minutes.

To freeze: grade for size: small sprouts are best. Soak ½ hour in cold salt water, blanch and cool for 3 minutes, drain well on tea towels then open freeze. Pack in freezer bags for storage.

BRUSSELS SPROUT SOUP

Make as for Cabbage Soup (see page 25).

Kale

The strong-tasting leaves of kale make a welcome winter vegetable dish. It is rich in iron. Similar to spinach in its use in cooked dishes.

To prepare: discard any damaged leaves and cut out the mid rib with a sharp knife. Wash and drain well. Tear into pieces.

To cook: as with all leafy vegetables, aim to cook as quickly as possible and to serve immediately.

Boil in 1 in (2.5 cm) depth of salted water in a covered saucepan for about 10 minutes. Drain in a sieve, return to saucepan and chop with a knife. Stir in a knob of butter and some pepper.

To store: the prepared leaves will keep in a plastic bag in the bottom of the refrigerator for about 2 days. Press out as much air as possible from the bag.

To freeze: blanch and cool for 1 minute. Drain well, chop and pack in family portions in freezer bags.

Broccoli

Green, purple and white sprouting broccoli have a central head, similar to a small cauliflower. When this has been cut, spears are produced at the side. The heads can be served as a starter with a dressing of melted butter or Hollandaise sauce. The spears are cooked quickly like other green vegetables.

To prepare: peel off the outer skin if it is tough and remove any tough leaves.

To cook: cook in a small amount of boiling, salted water for 10 minutes. Drain carefully. Serve with melted butter.

Microwave: in a roasting bag or in a covered dish with a little water and a sprinkle of salt for 8 or 9 minutes; drain.

Stir-fry: slice stalks finely then stir-fry with heads in hot oil.

To serve hot: coat with a cheese or butter sauce. Serve sprinkled with browned almonds.

To serve cold: coat cooked broccoli in French dressing, chill and serve as a starter.

To store: prepared broccoli will keep in a plastic bag at the bottom of the refrigerator for up to 3 days.

To freeze: soak prepared broccoli in salted water for ½ hour. Rinse then blanch and cool for 3 to 5 minutes, depending on size. Drain well on a cloth. Open freeze then pack carefully in rigid container to avoid damaging the heads.

Cabbage

Cabbage is the vegetable that we either love or loath, though this opinion is often dependent on the skill of the cook. It is not an easy vegetable to cook, because of the different types. Crisp, hearty cabbages need different treatment from those with soft green leaves. The crisp varieties are also good served raw as a salad.

To choose: the best cabbages are heavy for their size. Tightly-packed leaves are usually crisp and sweet. Choose loose-leaved spring cabbages that are bright and firm.

To prepare: prepare and wash cabbage in advance of cooking, but to retain the valuable vitamin C, never leave cabbage soaking in water and shred it just before cooking. Cut off the end-piece of stalk and any outer discoloured leaves, then wash in a bowl of water. If the cabbage has a firm heart, cut it in half through the stalk, then place it, cut side down, on the board and shred it finely across the stalk. If you don't like the stalk, cut each half into 3 and trim off the stalk from the centre. Alternatively, leave the cabbage in wedges for cooking. To prepare soft green-leaved cabbages, discard any coarse outer leaves, wash the cabbage, then break off the large outside leaves. Cut out the stalk if coarse. Shred the outer leaves and keep separate, then shred the heart.

To cook: aim to cook as required in a small quantity of boiling, salted water to retain the texture, vitamins and mineral elements. The coarse leaves are boiled in the water and the tender heart is steamed at the top. Fill a large saucepan to a depth of 1 in (2.5 cm) with water. Add 1 tsp (1 × 5 ml sp) of salt and bring to the boil. Add the cabbage a handful at a time, keeping the heat under the pan high so that the water does not go off the boil. Put the coarser leaves in first, then top with the tender heart (it may be necessary to cook the outside leaves for 2 or 3 minutes before adding the heart). Cover tightly with a lid, then boil on a medium heat for 5 to 10 minutes. Test by biting a piece after 5 minutes; the cabbage should be tender but still retain a 'bite'. If overcooked, it becomes soft and slimy and smells of sulphur. Pour into a colander or sieve (save the cooking water for making gravy), toss to remove excess water, then return it to the saucepan, add a knob of butter, some salt and pepper and serve immediately in a warmed serving dish.

To store: hearty white cabbage can be conveniently stored in nets in a garden shed. With so many varieties to choose from, fresh cabbage should be available throughout the year, but if your planning has gone wrong and you have a surplus, freeze shredded cabbage after blanching for 1 minute. Red cabbages are best cooked then frozen in usable amounts.

To pickle: use red or hard white cabbage. Wash, shred and layer with cooking salt in a bowl. Leave for 24 hours, then drain and rinse with water. Drain thoroughly and pack into clean jars. Cover with cold spiced vinegar, then plastic or plastic-lined lids. For a sweet pickle, dissolve ½ lb (250 g) sugar in each 1 pint (500 ml) vinegar. Use high-strength spiced pickling vinegar for best results. Red cabbage can be eaten after 2 weeks and white cabbage will be ready after 1 week.

BRAISED CHICKEN WITH CABBAGE

The cabbage keeps the chicken moist when cooked in this one-pot meal.

For 6 to 8 portions

Metric		Imperial
1.2 kg	oven-ready chicken	2½ lb
1	firm white cabbage	1
4	rashers smoked streaky bacon	4
100 g	black pudding	4 oz
1	large onion	1
2	sticks celery	2
1	large carrot	1
2 × 15 ml sp	oil	2 tbsp
1 × 5 ml sp	mixed dried herbs	1 tsp
1 × 5 ml sp	salt	1 tsp
	pepper	

1. Remove chicken giblets and place in a saucepan; cover with water and cook for 30 minutes. Rinse chicken, dry with kitchen paper, then truss with string. Prepare a moderate oven (180 deg C, 350 deg F, Gas Mark 4).

2. Finely shred cabbage; plunge into boiling, salted water in a large saucepan, return to boil, cook 2 minutes, then drain.

3. Remove rind from bacon; cut each rasher into 3. Remove skin and slice black pudding, peel and chop onion; wash and slice celery, peel and slice carrot.

4. Heat oil in a large frying pan and fry

chicken all over until golden brown; place on a plate. Fry black pudding and bacon, then onion, carrot and celery. Mix into cabbage with herbs, salt and some pepper. Spread a layer in the bottom of a large, deep casserole. Place chicken on top, then pack remaining cabbage mixture around the chicken.

5. Strain stock from giblets, measure 1 pint (500 ml) and add to casserole. Cover and cook in centre of oven for 1½ hours until chicken is tender.

6. Pile vegetables on a serving dish and arrange chicken on top.

CREAM OF CABBAGE SOUP

Follow the Master Soup Recipe on page 66. Cook ½ lb (250 g) each of chopped onions and potatoes in 2 oz (50 g) butter. Add 1 lb (500 g) shredded cabbage and ½ pint (250 ml) chicken stock. Cook 15 minutes then sieve or liquidize. Blend 1 tbsp (1 × 15 ml sp) cornflour with ½ pint (250 ml) milk and a small can evaporated milk. Add the purée, ½ pint (250 ml) water, salt and pepper and bring to boil.

STUFFED CABBAGE LEAVES

Use dark and light cabbage leaves to make this attractive dish. It is a marvellous way to serve cabbage as an economical mid-week family meal.

For 4 Portions

Metric		Imperial
50 g	long-grain rice	2 oz
2	meat extract cubes	2
1	medium-sized onion	1
250 g	minced beef	½ lb
	grated rind of half an orange	
1 × 2.5 ml sp	mixed spice	½ tsp
1 × 5 ml sp	salt	1 tsp
	good shake of pepper	
1 × 5 ml sp	Worcestershire sauce	1 tsp
250 ml	boiling water	½ pint
2 × 5 ml sp	cornflour	2 tsp
8	small cabbage leaves	8
	butter	
4 × 15 ml sp	tomato ketchup	4 tbsp

1. Prepare a moderately hot oven (190 deg C, 375 deg F, Gas Mark 5). Place rice in a saucepan, crumble in one extract cube and add 1 pint (500 ml) water. Bring to boil, reduce heat and cook uncovered until rice has absorbed stock.

2. Peel and chop onion, place in saucepan with minced beef and cook for about 10 minutes until onion is lightly browned. Add orange rind, spice, salt, pepper and Worcestershire sauce. Dissolve remaining extract cube in boiling water and add to pan. Bring to boil, cover and simmer for 15 minutes. Blend cornflour with a little cold water and add to saucepan. Cook for 1 minute, remove from heat, stir in rice.

3. Cut out the thick end of cabbage stalks. Place leaves in a large saucepan of boiling water, cover and cook 2 minutes; drain.

4. Divide meat mixture between cabbage leaves, wrap each like a parcel and place close together in a shallow 2 pint (1.25 litre) casserole.

5. Melt 1 oz (25 g) butter in a saucepan and stir in tomato ketchup. Pour into dish, then top each cabbage roll with a little butter. Cover, cook for 30 minutes.

Cauliflower

This attractive and versatile vegetable is delicious both raw and cooked. It can be broken into florets or cooked whole.

To prepare: discard the outer very coarse leaves and end piece of stalk. Cut off the more tender leaves with the stalk and shred finely.

To serve whole: cut a cross in the base of the stalk. Wash well under running water, drain.

To serve in florets: break off the florets, cutting off a piece of stalk with each. If serving raw, finely shred the stalk, leaving about 2 in (5 cm) below the head.

To cook:

Whole: bring 2 in (5 cm) depth of salted water to boil, add shredded stalk and leaves and re-boil. Place whole cauliflower in saucepan, stalk side downwards, cover tightly with a lid and cook over moderate heat for about 15 minutes until the stalk is just tender. Test by piercing with a skewer. This way, the tough stalk cooks by boiling and the tender curd is steamed gently, and both are cooked at the same time. Use a large egg slice or perforated spoon to lift cauliflower out of the water. Shake gently to remove excess water then place in a shallow serving dish and keep warm. Thoroughly drain cooked stalk and leaves. Use kitchen paper to absorb any moisture in dish then surround cauliflower with stalk and leaves. Coat with a well-seasoned thick white sauce (see below).

In florets: bring about 1 in (2.5 cm) salted water to boil. Place florets, stalks downwards in saucepan, cover and boil for 8 to 10 minutes until the stalk is just tender. Drain gently; cover with a sauce, if desired.

Front **Stuffed Cabbage Leaves,** *Back* **Braised Chicken with Cabbage.**

Microwave: place florets in a loosely-tied roasting bag or serving dish covered with a lid or cling film with 4 tbsp (4 × 15 ml sp) water and a sprinkle of salt. Cook 1 lb on high power for 10 to 12 minutes; drain.

Stir-fry: finely slice the stalk, separate florets into small pieces and stir-fry in hot oil.

To serve cooked:

With a white sauce made by whisking 1 oz (25 g) each of butter and flour with ½ pint (250 ml) milk in a saucepan over a medium heat. When sauce boils, cook 2 minutes, season generously with salt and pepper and pour over the cauliflower to coat. Add chopped parsley or 2 oz (50 g) grated cheese, if desired.

With melted butter or melted brown butter: crushed garlic or finely chopped onion can be added.

In batter: par-boil florets for 5 minutes, drain and coat in batter made by mixing 1 oz (25 g) self-raising flour with ¼ pint (125 ml) water. Deep fry until golden brown.

In soup: follow Master Soup Recipe on page 66.

In a curried vegetable mixture.

To serve raw: in florets with savoury dips, with French dressing.

To store: wash, drain and store either whole or in florets in a plastic bag at the bottom of the refrigerator for up to 4 days.

To freeze: divide into florets; blanch and cool for 3 minutes then open freeze and pack in freezer bags.

To pickle: florets of cauliflower can be pickled on its own in a sweet spiced vinegar or mixed with other vegetables such as courgettes, cucumber, French beans and onions. Soak them in brine for 24 hours then drain, pack into jars and cover with cold vinegar.

Cauliflower is one of the main vegetables in Piccalilli.

Herbs

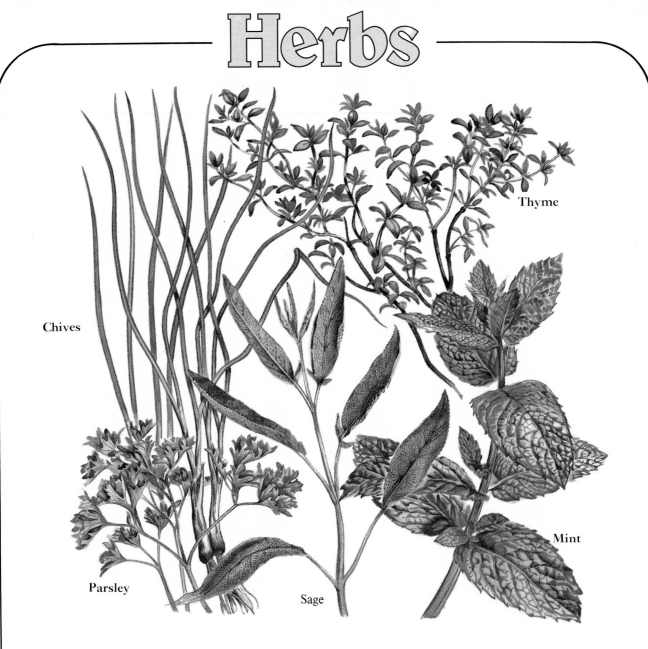

Chives

Thyme

Parsley

Sage

Mint

Complete gardens are now filled with the very many different kinds of herbs and while some are suitable for medicinal use, here we are looking at those kinds which combine culinary and decorative qualities. As a general rule all herbs do better in an open sunny place and in soils which are free draining. This produces short sturdy growth and leaves of stronger scent and flavouring. While adding sand to heavy clay soils will make them more suited to herbs, do not be put off by difficult soil – herbs will grow in all soil types.

Most of the more popular kinds can be grown in pots and varieties with attractive leaves and flowers can be planted in the flower garden. It is worth remembering to site any herb planting close to the house so that fresh leaves can be gathered easily even on cold, rainy days.

Fortunately most of the culinary herbs respond well to repeated pinching and the removal of young leaves. Indeed, the sages, thymes, parsley and mints produce compact and more attractively bushy plants, given this treatment.

While fresh green leaves can be gathered from April to Christmas from most herbs, some form of protection is needed for year-round supply. Young plants, either cuttings or seedlings, grown in pots on the window-sill or in hanging containers close to the kitchen window are the answer for December to April picking.

Several sowings may be needed of chives, parsley, sage and rosemary if a steady supply of leaves is required right through the winter.

Where to grow

A herb bed or border is by far the best way to ensure a really good supply of fresh herbs and it need not be very large. Arrange the taller kinds to the back or centre and try to plant with contrasting foliage shape and colour to give added interest. Lift a few paving slabs for example and place shrubby rosemary and sage to the centre and lower growing types around them. Parsley can be used as a very attractive edging.

Where space is limited, even where you have no garden, herbs can be grown in tower or strawberry pots, growing bags, tubs, window-boxes and plant troughs. Make sure the containers are at least 6 in (15 cm) deep if good-sized, productive plants are wanted. A mixture of half John Innes Potting Compost No 1 and half proprietary peat compost will give good results.

The thymes are attractive plants for the rock garden and for banks and can even be grown by sweeping the seeds, with a little potting compost, into the cracks between paving. Sink gardens, too, are useful for herbs, with the low thymes sited on the edge to creep over the sides.

Preserving

Where there is an abundance of fresh herbs at any one time most can be preserved by drying. Cut the leaves and young shoots when they are dry and either tie in bunches and hang up to dry right out for ten to 15 days or spread out in a tray and dry quickly over a radiator or hot water boiler. Once crisp dry, the leaves can be crushed up before storing in airtight jars.

Rooting cuttings

New young plants of all the shrubby types can be propagated from cuttings and they root most easily when the weather is warm from May to September. Choose young, *non*-flowering shoots 2–4 in (5–10 cm) long. If the bottom of the cutting is changing from soft, sappy green to a more woody mature state, so much the better.

An ornamental and attractive herb garden. The old fashioned knot garden can be imitated using lavender, sage or parsley for the edging.

Remove a few lower leaves, dip the cut end in rooting powder if you have some and then push three or four cuttings around the edge of a 3½ in (9 cm) pot filled with peat and sand or all peat seed compost. Enclose the whole lot in a white polythene bag and seal the top with a rubber band, trapping enough air in the bag to keep the polythene off the leaves. Then place it in the light on a window-sill.

A variety of herbs can be grown in tower pots outside throughout the summer and brought under cover in the autumn to extend the pickling season.

Take the bag off for an hour or two every two or three days and once the cuttings stop wilting after bag removal, leave the bag off altogether.

When the cuttings start to make new top growth they can be removed and transplanted singly in 3½ in (9 cm) pots of potting compost.

Bay

This attractive evergreen grows well in pots, can be trimmed in a variety of shapes and also grows well as a free-standing shrub. As the leaves can be burnt brown by exposure to freezing winter wind it is best to plant in a sheltered place and move the pots into the shed or garage in cold winter weather.

Where plants are trimmed to shape into balls, pyramids and standards, cut with secateurs, not shears to avoid bisecting leaves. The trimmings will provide leaves to dry for flavouring.

New plants are grown from cuttings but they are not too easy to root. The best time to take cuttings is July–August when the lower part of the shoot stem is starting to harden.

provide thick thongy roots which are shredded for flavouring. Lift the roots and retain the top four inches to re-plant and maintain supplies. Although the chances are that odd pieces of root left behind after lifting will provide all the replanting needed.

Marjoram

There are three forms of this herb, all used for flavouring, often in association with thyme and in mixed herbs. The wild marjoram grows well in chalky soils and has a perennial root which can be divided in spring and autumn. There is a small form with attractive yellow leaves called *Origanum vulgare* 'Aureum'.

Sweet marjoram is a perennial but because it is not completely hardy is best seed-raised each spring under glass and planted out in early summer. Plants can be lifted from the open ground in the

autumn and potted up to provide fresh leaves in a frost-free place.

Pot marjoram is a lovely shrub and again needs a sheltered place. It can be propagated by cuttings and raised from seed.

Chives

Repeated sowings of chive seeds into pots of seed compost indoors will provide fine tasty leaves for flavouring the year round. Seedlings planted out in the garden in spring are the most productive, however, and these plantings produce slender bulbs which grow without attention year after year. From the second summer chives produce clusters of attractive lavender blue flowers which, if left, will produce seed to provide even more young plants. However, if you let the plants flower it does reduce the amount of harvestable leaves each clump produces. Clumps of bulbs can be lifted and divided in April or September.

Dill

This thin feathery-leaved plant grows quite tall, up to 3 ft (90 cm), and fits well into flower borders. It is an annual and has to be raised each year from seed. Both the seeds and leaves can be used for flavouring. Thin the seedlings out to stand 9–12 in (23–30 cm) apart.

Garlic

Growing almost like a cross between leeks and onions, garlic is better in a corner of the vegetable plot rather than the herb

Golden variegated mint, silver variegated and green thymes, golden marjoram and a variety of different green leaf shapes make an attractive herb bed.

Right Four square pots rest in a square saucer for a window-sill display of parsley, two thymes and a mixture of two mints in one pot.

garden. Cloves, small pieces of garlic bulb, are planted ideally in October and certainly before December. The larger outer cloves are likely to produce the biggest bulbs.

They make 2 in (5 cm) growth before Christmas and are best with cloche protection over winter (see page 33). The following spring/early summer they grow to 3 ft (90 cm) and should be ready to lift in July–August. Space the planting cloves 6–8 in (15–20 cm) apart in rows 12 in (30 cm) apart, pushing them in 1 in (2.5 cm) deep in the soil.

Horseradish

No plant for the tiny plot, horseradish produces large dock-like leaves and the deep, penetrating and invasive roots can become a difficult weed if left undisturbed for several years. If you have an insatiable appetite for horseradish, then small pieces of root planted in the late autumn to early spring period will soon grow to

Mint

Again there are different forms of mint with widely varying leaf shapes and textures. Invariably they are strong growing and invasive with thick underground roots which are difficult to restrain once they really become established. Grow them in pots either free-standing or sunk in the ground to keep their growth within bounds.

New plants are easily grown from

An attractive mixture of purple sage and variegated mint.

The three-coloured sage is best kept as a young plant.

pieces of root or young soft green non-flowering tips which root quickly in water or peat and sand. Repeated rooting of young tips is the easiest way to maintain a supply of fresh leaves year round.

There are three mints worthy of inclusion in small-scale herb growing. The common 'Spearmint' for mint sauce, the white variegated 'Applemint' with more rounded leaves to boil with new potatoes and the quite large-leaved golden *Mentha × gentilis* 'Variegata' which is a very attractive plant for flower borders.

Parsley thinnings can be transplanted into a pot for a window-sill cultivation.

Parsley

Old wives' tales galore surround the cultivation of parsley. It is a biennial and best sown outside in the open soil in April/May where it will germinate and grow quite easily. Thinnings from the seed row can be transplanted into pots and seed sown in pots at any time of year for plants to grow on the window-sill.

The deeply curled leaves of the better seed strains make very attractive edges to both vegetable gardens and herb beds. Cloche cover the outside grown plants to provide fresh green leaves through the winter (see page 33).

Rosemary

The lovely pale lavender flowering rosemary can be grown from seed and by rotting cuttings in August to October. It is best considered as a small shrub or kept as a seedling in a small pot and, once picked to death, more seeds sown.

Older plants get rather bare at the base and succumb to cold winter weather and waterlogging, so it is advisable to root new cuttings every few years where this herb is grown as a shrub. Left untrimmed, it will eventually form a rounded plant over 3 ft (1 m) high and *Rosemarinus officianalis* 'Miss Jessop's Variety' has narrow upright growth.

Sage

Like rosemary, sage is ideal for the front of shrub borders and in among herbaceous plants, as well as in the herb garden. There are three attractive plants, the common *Salvia officinalis* with greyish green leaves, the purple-leaved *S. o.* 'Purpurascens' and the grey leaves, edged with purple, pink and white of *S. o.* 'Tricolor'.

After flowering in July all sages are best trimmed back to keep neat low bushy growth. They thrive in light soils and sunny positions. Softwood cuttings root easily in spring and early summer.

Thyme

Brushing past the low growing garden thyme, *Thymus vulgaris* always brings the lovely fragrance into the air. This useful herb also produces pretty mauve flowers in summer. Clip back after flowering to encourage more green shoots for culinary use.

There are several different kinds with attractive leaf forms and the golden-leaved, lemon-scented *T. citriodorus* 'Aureus' and the silver-leaved forms are recommended for decoration and culinary use in the small garden.

Cookery

Herbs

Herbs were formerly used as nature's remedies for ailments, but nowadays they are mainly valued for their flavouring properties. They are especially useful as an economical flavour-booster for bland foods, including diet foods. Herbs contain essential oils, mineral elements, and some contain vitamins, although they are not eaten in sufficient quantities to make much contribution to the diet. The oils tend to evaporate in hot sunshine, so it's best to pick herbs early in the day, especially if they are to be stored some time before use.

How to use herbs: strip the leaves from the stalks, chop them finely and add them to dishes, usually before cooking. Sprigs can be added to vegetables or meat as they are boiling in water or stock. Sometimes sprigs of herbs tied in a bunch are used in a dish so that they can be easily removed before serving. This is called a bouquet garni when bay leaves and sprigs of thyme and parsley are tied together. Sachets of these dried herbs are available in the shops; they are infused in the liquid of the dish while it's cooking.

Parsley: this is one of the most popular herbs because it has so many uses. It brings out the flavour of other foods and is valuable for adding to mild-flavoured dishes such as fish, chicken and veal. It is used as a garnish, either chopped or in sprigs. The stalks have most of the flavour, and sprigs of parsley can be quickly fried in hot fat for serving with fried foods. Parsley sauce is a traditional accompaniment for fish.

Mint: there are numerous varieties of mint, but all can be used to make mint sauce or jelly to serve with roast lamb. New potatoes wouldn't taste as good without a sprig of mint added to the cooking water, and peas and carrots also benefit from this treatment. Mint tea is a popular drink in the Middle East and mint is frequently used in Middle Eastern cooking.

Thyme: both the common garden thyme and lemon thyme are delicious in stuffings, with tomato dishes and poultry. Put a sprig of thyme in your bottle of vinegar to give the vinegar extra flavour when used in salad dressing.

Sage: roast pork needs sage and onion stuffing and strongly-flavoured meats are enhanced by it too. Cheese tastes good with sage – there is Sage Derby cheese with an attractive pale green ripple through it. If you grow your own sage, quickly dry leaves in a moderate oven, then crumble into a dish.

Chives: these have a delicate onion flavour and are used raw. A bunch of chives is often snipped over vegetables as a garnish just before serving. They can also be added to salads and salad dressings, or try them mixed with cream cheese for Jacket Potatoes.

To store herbs:

Freezing: fill ice-cube trays with chopped herbs, top up with water and freeze them. Separate the cubes and store them in plastic bags. When you need the herbs, drop a cube into the dish while it's cooking. It will melt immediately, and the flavour of the herbs will permeate the dish. You can also blanch sprigs of herbs in boiling water for half a minute, dry on kitchen paper and store in freezer bags. To use, crumble the frozen leaves.

Drying: tie small-leafed herbs such as thyme and parsley in bundles and hang them up to draw in a warm, airy place. Strip the larger-leaved herbs from their stalks and place on a wire tray. Dry them in the oven on the lowest setting with the door ajar. A fan oven is convenient for this; alternatively, use a microwave oven. Crumble the herbs between the fingers and store them in airtight jars away from direct sunlight.

CONCENTRATED MINT SAUCE

This is a useful way of preserving mint. The colour darkens with storage, but the flavour remains good. Fill small jars with finely-chopped mint, top up with vinegar, then cover with polythene or plastic-coated lids. To use, place some mint in a sauceboat, add vinegar and sugar to taste.

TOMATO AND ONION SALAD

Arrange layers of sliced onion and sliced tomato in a salad bowl. Sprinkle each layer of tomatoes with some salt, pepper, sugar and finely-chopped chives. Pour some French dressing over salad just before serving.

HERB VINEGAR

An infusion of herbs in wine or distilled vinegar is an easy way of adding flavour to salad dressings or any dish that requires vinegar. Use strongly-flavoured herbs such as thyme, chives, sage and rosemary. Place about 6 tbsp (6 × 15 ml sp) of the finely-chopped fresh herbs in a wide-necked jar, then add 1 pint (500 ml) warmed vinegar. Cover with a glass or plastic lid and leave to infuse for two weeks, shaking the jar occasionally. Taste the vinegar, and, if it is strong enough, strain through a paper tissue in a nylon sieve. Pour into tall bottles and push a sprig of the herb into the bottle to decorate and identify the flavour.

MINT JELLY

Some recipes are based on apple jelly and involve straining the juice, but this very quick method is equally good.

Metric		Imperial
	fresh mint	
500 g	*granulated sugar*	*1 lb*
250 ml	*distilled malt vinegar*	*½ pint*
25 g	*gelatine*	*1 oz*

1. Thoroughly wash some small jars with plastic-coated lids, drain well, then dry in a warm oven; leave to cool. If lids are not available, prepare covers from thick polythene.

2. Strip leaves off the mint stalks and chop leaves finely. Place in a measuring jug and press down lightly; there should be sufficient to reach the ½ pint (250 ml) mark.

3. Dissolve sugar in a saucepan with ¾ pint (375 ml) water, then bring to boil. Reserve 1 tbsp (1 × 15 ml sp) mint, add remainder to pan and bring to boil. Remove from heat and add vinegar. Cover with a lid and leave to infuse for 15 minutes.

4. Place a white paper tissue in a strainer and pour liquid through; press lightly with a spoon.

5. Place gelatine in a basin with 3 tbsp (3 × 15 ml sp) cold water. Add 3 tbsp (3 × 15 ml sp) of the mint liquid and place basin in a saucepan of boiling water. Stir over a low heat until gelatine has dissolved, then add to the rest of the mint liquid. Add a few drops of green colouring, if desired. Leave in a cool place until slightly thickened, then stir in the reserved chopped mint and pour into jars gently, avoiding bubbles. Cover with lids or polythene and store in a cool, dark cupboard for up to 6 months. Serve with roast lamb.

CREAMY HERB CHEESE

Make cheese a few days before it is required to give the flavours time to blend properly.

Metric		Imperial
1	*clove garlic, optional*	*1*
1 × 2.5 ml sp	*salt*	*½ level tsp*
250 g	*medium fat, soft cheese*	*½ lb*
1 × 15 ml sp	*chopped parsley*	*1 tbsp*
1 × 15 ml sp	*snipped chives*	*1 tbsp*
2 × 5 ml sp	*chopped thyme*	*2 tbsp*

Peel garlic, if used, and place on a saucer with the salt. Using a round-ended knife, rub salt against garlic to crush clove. Place in a basin and add remaining ingredients. Beat well together, then place in a small serving bowl, cover with foil or cling film and leave in the refrigerator for at least half a day before serving. Store for up to 1 week and serve with oatcakes or cracker biscuits.

SAUSAGE STUFFING BALLS

These make a crisp accompaniment for Christmas poultry or pork. If fresh sage is not available, use half the quantity of dried sage.

Makes 16

Metric		Imperial
1	*medium-sized onion*	*1*
450 g	*sausagemeat*	*1 lb*
1 × 2.5 ml sp	*salt*	*½ tsp*
2 × 15 ml sp	*finely-chopped fresh sage*	*2 tbsp*
100 g	*fresh white breadcrumbs*	*4 oz*
1	*large egg*	*1*

1. Peel and finely chop onion. Mix with sausagemeat, salt, a shake of pepper, sage and half the breadcrumbs. Beat egg with 2 tbsp (2 × 15 ml sp) water, add half and mix well.
2. Make mixture into 16 balls with floured hands and coat with remaining egg and breadcrumbs. (Freeze at this stage, if desired.)
3. To cook, place around a joint of pork, a duck, or goose for the last 40 minutes of the cooking time. Alternatively, cook in a separate tin in a little hot dripping, basting occasionally.

PARSLEY BUTTER

This classic herb butter is sometimes called Maître d'Hôtel Butter. Keep a roll in the refrigerator ready for topping grilled meats and fish. Other herbs can be added, but parlsey brings out the flavour of food. Add mint or rosemary for lamb and chives for new potatoes and grilled gammon.

Metric		Imperial
100 g	*butter*	*4 oz*
2 × 15 ml sp	*chopped parsley*	*2 tbsp*
1 × 5 ml sp	*lemon juice*	*1 tsp*
1 × 2.5 ml sp	*salt*	*½ tsp*

1. Cream butter until soft, then add remaining ingredients.
2. Wet a small piece of greaseproof paper, then make the butter into a roll about 1 in (2½ cm) thick. Leave to harden in the refrigerator. To serve: cut into thin slices and top grilled meats or fish just before serving.

Clockwise from the left: Creamy Herb Cheese; Tomato and Onion Salad; Sausage Stuffing Balls; Concentrated Mint Sauce; Mint Jelly; Parsley and Thyme Stuffing; Parsley Butter.

PARSLEY AND THYME STUFFING

Use this stuffing to complement the delicate flavours of veal, chicken, or fish. Fresh herbs are really best, but use half the quantity of dried herbs if none are available. Lemon thyme gives a particularly good flavour. This quantity is sufficient to stuff the neck end of a chicken or small joint of meat. Use double this quantity to stuff the neck end of a turkey.

Metric		Imperial
100 g	*fresh white breadcrumbs*	*4 oz*
	rind of 1 lemon	
2 × 15 ml sp	*chopped parsley*	*2 tbsp*
2 × 15 ml sp	*chopped, fresh thyme*	*2 tbsp*
25 g	*shredded suet*	*1 oz*
	egg or milk to bind	

Mix the dry ingredients and add sufficient egg or milk to make a soft mixture. If mixture is not being used to stuff a joint, bake in a moderate oven and cut into squares to serve, or roll in balls and coat in egg and breadcrumbs and bake around the joint.

Garlic

This pungent-flavoured herb should be used with discretion. Its flavour enhances that of many cooked dishes and salads. The flavour intensifies with freezing; either omit from dishes to be frozen or reduce the quantity used.

To prepare: pull off a clove from the bulb. The juice can be extracted by pressing a clove in a garlic press. Alternatively, peel the clove and place on a saucer with a little salt. Using a round-ended knife, rub salt against garlic to crush. Garlic cloves can be chopped or cut into slivers, depending on their use.

Uses of garlic: rub a cut clove around a wooden salad bowl or rub on toast and crumble into a salad or soup. Add to salad dressings, mayonnaise, butter and marinades. Use to flavour oil in stir-fried food. Add to tomato sauce, especially for serving with pasta. Use in stews and casseroles.

To make Garlic Butter: mix 50 g (2 oz) butter to each crushed garlic clove. Use to top steaks.

To make Garlic Bread: spread the butter on thick slices of a French loaf, re-shape loaf, wrap in foil, and bake in a moderate oven for about 15 minutes.

Protected Crops

There is quite a range of frost tender plants grown in the vegetable garden which need to be raised under glass in the warm each spring. Most, of course, are fruits but somehow they are always grouped with the vegetables, especially in the seed catalogues.

Cucumbers, marrows and melons form one section and tomatoes with their close relatives aubergine, golden berry, okra and pepper the other. The ridge type cucumbers, marrows, courgettes, certain tomatoes, aubergines and peppers can be grown outside in a warm sheltered garden but they all benefit from cloche or frame protection as young plants.

There are dwarf bush varieties of tomatoes which can be grown in hanging baskets and also mini varieties of indoor cucumber, pepper and tomato which really can be successfully grown to fruit early and late in 6–8 in (15–20 cm) pots on the window-sill.

All these different kinds thrive in fertilized-peat-filled growbags and if you have experienced difficulty growing any of them in the past, a switch to growbags and care with watering will guarantee success.

Root diseases, like verticilium, can damage virtually all these crops and for this reason growing any of them in the same soil for more than two seasons is a risky business. It is much better to either move to another site with cloches and frames or switch to the isolated, disease-free peat in growbags.

Another good piece of advice is to delay sowing; it is much better to sow a little later and get really rapid development in warm temperatures for all main crops. One check when seeds are germinating or the plants are young and very tender can affect their development for the whole season.

Protected Cropping

Most people see the greenhouse as the answer to many gardening problems. In practice putting plants under cover does give us more control of their environment but this in turn means that inattention for even a very short while – especially inadequate watering and ventilation on hot sunny days – can cause considerable damage.

I suggest you start by protecting crops rooting out into the garden soil with cloches; progress with experience to cold frame and cold greenhouse before trying the year round cropping of tender plants which is possible with a heated greenhouse.

The simplest cloche cover, for radish, lettuce, parsley and similar low-growing crops and to raise seedlings early, can be made by covering the soil with a bottom-less wooden box and putting a sheet of glass on the top. Rows of strawberries and vegetables can be covered with either polythene or plastic cloches. Glass is not included here because it is not an attractive material in small gardens where children, balls, dogs and those of us who on occasions are a little clumsy, spend time!

The cheapest cloche and one which I

Burpee hybrid type cucumber and melon 'Sweetheart' growing under two different 3 ft (1 m) long cloches.

find very practical is the polythene tunnel, which consists of no more than wire hoops stuck in the ground every yard or so to support a long strip of polythene sheet. Each wire hoop has two loops, about 4 in (10 cm) from each end of wire.

Polythene tunnel cloches are a cheap way to give protection. Note the way string is tied to loop in the wire hoop to support polythene, the ends of which are tied to stakes. The strawberries are growing through a white polythene mulch.

Push the hoops into the soil, unroll the polythene over the hoops. Secure the polythene by tying string to the loop on one side of the wire hoop, taking it over the polythene and securing to the loop on the other side. See photograph. This allows the polythene to be lifted between the sandwich of hoop and string for cultivation, watering and crop harvest. I say watering but for most of the year sufficient water will get to crop roots by

Polythene tunnel greenhouse with the whole floor area available for fruit and vegetable growing.

Corrugated Novolux sheet held in place with a wire hoop which incorporates the handle. There is a black plastic alternative to the wire.
Right Glass cloches give early crops but need careful handling.

running down the sides and moving inwards by capillary movement. The same system of 'tunnel' cover can be used with netting for strawberry and seedling protection.

Somewhat easier to handle are the corrugated plastic sheets held in semi-circular tunnel shape with two galvanized wire hoops with handles. These cloches really are invaluable to give warm soil for earlier seed germination, earlier and later growth of crops as well as weather and bird protection. Always see the ends of any kind of cloche are covered: left open-ended much of the protective value is lost and once wind gets under them they easily blow away.

Cold frames are a little more airtight than cloches and, covering a larger soil area, retain warmth longer. They do need carefully ventilating in periods of bright hot sun however, and summer shading by painting the glass with a white-reflecting material like lime-wash or proprietary glass shade, will be necessary.

Progression from cloche and cold frame to cold greenhouse is the natural step. Polythene tunnel houses with a netted section in each end door for ventilation will protect the gardener from the weather as well as the crops. These polyhouses are quite easily moved so cucumbers, melons, courgettes and si-milar crops can be grown in the border soil. After three years when the polythene sheet needs replacement the house can easily be moved over fresh soil.

Growing cucurbits

We give cucumbers, marrows, courget-tes, melons and pumpkins the group name cucurbits and they all revel in what good gardeners describe as free draining, constantly damp soil. Something of a contradiction in terms but a soil condition achieved by either heaping masses of well-rotted organic matter, be it compost, animal manure or straw, on each planting site or by growing in fertilized-peat-filled growing bags.

They are quick-growing, gross feeding plants which also need warm conditions for the best growth and most flavourful crops. The marrows, courgettes (which are after all no more than young marrows) and pumpkins are hardiest of all and do grow well and crop heavily outside and unprotected if raised first of all under cover. The ridge or outdoor cucumbers will also grow outside but do better with some cloche protection.

One or two melons, like the variety 'Sweetheart', will also fruit successfully under cloches but most melons and greenhouse cucumbers (longer, less prickly-skinned types) need either cold frames or, preferably, greenhouse protection.

While ridge cucumbers, courgettes, marrows, gherkins, pumpkins and squashes can all be grown outside, all the cucurbit seedlings are best raised under glass. The simplest system of all, is to cover seeds sown direct into the fruiting

site with a jam jar. Make a shallow hollow in the well-prepared fertile soil and fill with several handfuls of damp all-peat seed compost, so that it leaves a mound. Sow two or three seeds fairly close to-gether in late May on the top of the mound and cover them with a jam jar. Once the seedlings are through and well-established they can be thinned out to leave the strongest one.

A little more trouble, but much safer, is indoor seed raising. One seed is pushed thin side down $\frac{3}{4}$ in (19 mm) deep into a $3\frac{1}{2}$ in (9 cm) pot of well-moistened all-peat seed compost. Enclose the pot or pots in a polythene bag and place *over* (not on) a source of heat such as a central heating boiler, radiator or hot water tank. The temperature needs to be at least 65°F (or preferably 70°F (20°C)) and the seed will be up in three or four days.

Seed sown in compost (and soil) at temperatures below 55°F (13°C) will absorb moisture and, even if they do germinate, growth will be permanently checked and the total crop reduced. Soil outside is unlikely to reach the required temperature before early June but cloche cover will warm the soil up earlier. This applies not only to cucurbits but also to peppers, sweetcorn, tomatoes, French and runner beans.

At the first sign of the inverted 'u'-shaped shoot pushing through the com-post, move the pots close to the glass on window-sills and in glasshouses.

It is a good idea to have the pots only

two-thirds full of compost and then when the seedlings are developing their third (first true-shaped) leaf the rest of the pot can be filled with compost. New roots will form from the seedling stem and reduce the chance of producing tall, thin, straggly seedlings.

Late April/early May is the best time to sow. Sturdy well-established plants will be produced to put outside under cloches in late May and outside uncovered in early June, once the possibility of frost is past. It is unlikely you will have enough well-rotted-down heaps of garden compost for all these crops and while they will grow reasonably well in ordinary soil, I get better results with extra care. This entails ordinary digging first and then again hollowing out a shallow, dish-shaped hole and mounding the equivalent of half a growbag of fertilized peat in the hollow. Plants romp away in this and root out into the soil below which acts as a food and moisture reservoir. You may well ask why not just put two plants in a growbag; this certainly works beautifully but careless watering can quickly spell disaster and, grown partly in soil, the margin for error is much greater.

All the cucurbits, except greenhouse cucumbers, need pollen from male fruitless flowers to cross pollinate the female flowers and set fruits. This will occur naturally with all plants, although a little interference by manually crossing the melons is advisable. All these plants will need plenty of water during the summer to set and develop fruit properly and inadequate watering and feeding can cause poor fruit formation.

Where these plants are grown in a growing bag, I prefer to use the proprietary growing tray and wicks or a homemade equivalent to overcome the watering difficulty. The growing tray is no more than a 2 in (5 cm) resevoir of water which supports the growbag. Put

Two courgettes 'Zucchini' growing in a growbag and watered by a growtray.
Left Wicks are used to draw water up by capillarity into the growbag.

the tray down first then set the bag on it and cut two holes in the upper surface ready for planting. Water the peat in the bag well and leave for a few hours to soak in, then check with your hands to see that the peat really is damp right through, even into the corners. If not stir wet and dry peat together and water again. When thoroughly damp the plants can be knocked out of their pots and planted in the peat. Grow for a week or two in this way and, once the peat in the bag starts to dry, cut three small holes in its base, one at each end and one in the middle, and push three plant-watering wicks up into the peat, leaving enough wick sticking out to touch the base of the tray. Water the bag once more from the top to damp the peat and wicks right through and, from that point on, all watering can be achieved by keeping the growing tray topped up with water. The plants will draw up all the water they need through the wicks and you will be surprised just how much this is on hot days. Clear proof that we all too often give our plants too little water in summer.

Courgettes and marrows

Courgette varieties will produce more small fruits than varieties of marrow but where the courgettes are left uncut they will grow to marrow size and equally marrows can be cut very young to use as courgettes. If courgettes are cut when approximately 6 in (15 cm) long and 1 in (2.5 cm) in diameter, each plant will produce the maximum number and biggest yield of tender fruits.

Several courgette varieties are not only extremely productive but quite attractive too: 'Zucchini' has rich dark green fruits and silver spotted leaves, 'Gold Rush' has rich deep yellow fruits and both grow in bush form, producing large yellow male flowers. 'Gold Rush' makes a particularly attractive tub and growbag plant.

There are white, green and striped-skinned marrows in both bush and long trailing types. Bush varieties grow quite big and need a square yd (1 m²) each in fertile soil, while the trailing types grow even larger. One way of handling the trailing types in a small garden is to erect a tripod with 8 ft (2.1 m) canes. Space the legs 2½ ft (75 cm) apart and plant one marrow at the base of each and tie the trailing stem up the cane.

Ornamental gourds, pumpkins (also called mammoth gourds) and the vegetable spaghetti marrow are all grown the same way as trailing marrows and need spacing 4½ ft (1.4 m) apart in the open ground. The name squash and marrow are often interchanged and varieties with flying-saucer shaped fruits and scalloped edges are often listed under squash. 'Custard Yellow' is a yellow-skinned variety and 'Custard White' has a white skin; both are best cut and cooked while still young.

One of the golden courgettes with attractively coloured leaves in a tub with pepper, tomato, golden berry and aubergine plants also in tubs.

One of the green bush marrows with attractively marked leaves.

Children can have fun with marrows and pumpkins, they grow so quickly it retains a child's interest. Young fruits can have the skins scratched with a pin or similar sharp object marking out a name or initials. Then as the fruit grows, so the name comes up clearly in brown. Very large pumpkins can be grown if restricted one to a plant and, as well as providing pumpkin pie, they are ideal to carve out for Hallowe'en faces.

Outdoor cucumbers and gherkins

Usually listed under the sub-title ridge cucumbers, the outdoor types are easy to grow and much less trouble than the frame and greenhouse kinds, which really must have warm protected conditions. Several of the gherkin varieties can be left to grow large, rather like courgettes left to grow into marrows, and eaten as cucumber. These outdoor and cloche-grown varieties will have a slightly thicker skin and some are rather prickly. This is no serious problem because the skins can be peeled from the cucumbers. Some varieties, including 'Burpless Tasty Green', have quite tender skins and if eaten skin and all are found by some people to be less indigestible. Recently introduced F_1 gherkin varieties will produce many fruits of similar small size at the same time to make harvesting easier.

Where space is very limited, outdoor cucumbers can be trained up and tied to large mesh wire or plastic netting. If this method is used, space the plants 12 in (30

Golden courgettes are good to eat and look at.

cm) apart down the row. In the open garden and under cloches space the plants 3 ft (1 m) apart down the row.

There are one or two possible problems to watch out for when growing the cucumber and marrow family. Slugs can soon eat through the succulent stems in the early stages and it is advisable to sprinkle a few pellets (preferably based on methiocarb) around each plant. Where the plants are allowed to get dry, greyish-white mildew fungus grows on the leaves. As long as the plants are kept well watered this will not be a serious problem. Mosaic virus often attacks marrows and the leaves become mottled yellow, puckered and deformed. Infected plants are best quickly pulled up and destroyed before it is spread by greenfly. Spraying occasionally to eliminate greenfly can reduce the chances of this disease (see page 8).

Giant pumpkins are fun for children to grow.

Melons and greenhouse cucumbers

While the melon 'Sweetheart' can be grown and cropped quite easily and satisfactorily under cloches, most melons require the additional warmth and shelter provided by a greenhouse. All melons will need pollination: pick an open yellow male flower (the one without an embryo fruit behind the petals), remove the petals and push the yellow pollen-bearing stamens into an open female flower. It is best to do this in sunny weather when the flowers are dry and the pollen spreads easily.

Quite the reverse is the case with greenhouse cucumbers which must not be pollinated whatever happens. If pollen from male cucumber flowers does pass to female, the latter produces bulbous-ended, bitter-tasting cucumbers. This can also be caused by insufficient feeding. Fortunately today we have the 'All Female' varieties which never, or very rarely, produce male flowers. Do not run the risk of mixing ordinary cucumber varieties with the all female ones because this will allow cross pollination.

Apart from pollination the melons and greenhouse cucumbers can be treated in the same way. Germinate the seed in very warm conditions. Don't sow too early indoors if the plants are to be grown in a cold greenhouse – late April/early May will be soon enough. Then in late May/early June, two plants can be set out in a full-sized growbag.

There is one other choice. The comact and smaller fruited greenhouse cucumbers like 'Fembaby' and 'Petita' can be grown to full cropping size in 7–8 in (18–24 cm) diameter pots on the windowsill. These can be sown quite early, even January/February and quite late, June/July, for early and late crops respectively.

Cucumber growing and fruiting in a 7 in (18 cm) diameter pot of all peat compost on the window-sill, alongside a pot-grown green pepper.

Cucumber 'Petita' growing and cropping well in an 8 in (20 cm) flower pot of all peat compost. Training consists of removing the growing tip from side shoots after two leaves have formed. Given plenty of feeding, ten to 12 fruits will be produced.

Melon 'Sweetheart' growing and fruiting well planted on a mound of fertilized peat under cloches in the open garden.

Raise the seedlings in $3\frac{1}{2}$ in (9 cm) pots as usual and when well established pot on into 5 in (13 cm) pots and then, finally, into the larger pots, using all peat potting compost every time. Remove the first one or two fruits which form to allow the plant to get established but once 18–20 in (45–50 cm) of stem growth is made the young fruits can be left to develop. Keep the plants well watered and well fed when they are growing fast and six to eight fruits can be produced on the young plants. If heavy fruiting checks growth put a 3 in (7.5 cm) high, thick polythene collar around the top of the pot and pack more damp all peat potting compost into it. New roots will soon push out from the stem to produce new growth and more fruits.

Training

The simplest way to train is on a single main stem upwards, either tied to a cane or held by winding a soft fillis string around the stem as it grows. All the side shoots which develop where each leaf stalk joins the main stem are stopped at two leaves past the first fruit or certainly once the side shoot is 12–18 in (30–45 cm) long.

The all female cucumber variety F_1 hybrid 'Uniflora D' is self-stopping and you only need train the main stem up the cane. Under cloches the 'Ogen' and 'Sweetheart' melons will grow and fruit with no special training system.

Keep feeding and watering the cucumbers to keep producing more fruits. Melons are fed and watered until the fruits stop increasing in size and the skin colour changes as the fruits ripen. Then the amount of water needs to be reduced until the fruit end farthest from the stem gives a little when pressed with the thumb. Fruits are then ready to cut and eat. A brown, barky appearance on cracks and a delicious ripe smell on warm days also indicates ripeness of melons.

Three melons 'Sweetheart' growing in a fertilized-peat-filled growing bag. Note watering by the green growtray at the base.

Cookery

Courgettes

These are very useful for small families as they grow quickly and can be harvested daily, when about 6 in (15 cm) long. Cut 2 for each portion. They are useful in mixed vegetable dishes, chutney and pickles.

To prepare: wash and trim both ends, cut in thick chunks or lengthwise in halves or quarters. There is no need to remove the skin or seeds which are very soft.

To cook: courgettes are best cooked without additional water, though they can be steamed whole for 15 to 20 minutes. Fry gently in butter.

Buttered courgettes: melt a large knob of butter in a saucepan and add sliced courgettes seasoning between each layer. Cover with a lid and cook slowly for 10 to 15 minutes, shaking the pan occasionally.

Microwave: layer 1 lb (500 g) prepared sliced courgettes in a serving dish with seasonings. Dot with butter, cover with a lid or cling film and cook on high power for 12–15 minutes.

To serve cold: slice courgettes finely and mix with French dressing laced with chopped fresh herbs, or mix with prepared salad vegetables.

To store: whole courgettes will keep in a plastic bag at the bottom of the refrigerator for up to 3 days.

To freeze: cut into 1 in (2 cm) lengths. Blanch and cool for 3 minutes, pat dry then open freeze. Pack in freezer bags for storage.

To pickle: use in mixed pickle dishes; layer with salt to remove liquid. Use as an ingredient in chutney.

COURGETTES PROVENÇALES

Cook a small chopped onion or shallot, a crushed clove of garlic and a peeled sliced tomato in a little butter. Add 1 lb (500 g) sliced courgettes and seasoning then cover and cook slowly for about 15 minutes, shaking the pan occasionally.

COURGETTE FRITTERS

Cut courgettes lengthwise into quarters, dip in coating batter made from self-raising flour and water and deep fry for 4 to 5 minutes.

COURGETTE RAITA

Young courgettes are crisp and delicious served raw in a salad. The fresh-tasting yogurt makes a quick dressing.

For 4 portions as a side salad

Metric		Imperial
250 g	small courgettes	8 oz
	salt	
125 ml	natural yogurt	¼ pint
2 × 5 ml sp	German or Meaux mustard	2 tsp
	paprika	

1. Wash and trim courgettes. Cut into thin slices and layer with salt in a colander or sieve; leave for 30 minutes to drain. Pat dry on kitchen paper.
2. Place yogurt and mustard in a bowl; mix well. Gently turn courgettes in mixture to coat. Place in a serving dish; sprinkle with paprika.

Marrows

There are many ways of serving this traditional British vegetable. They are best when harvested young. The gigantic ones are really only suitable for showing, though they can be used to make wine. Use marrow as a vegetable, in pickles and chutneys and as a base for jam. It is low in calories and carbohydrate and can replace pasta or potato for slimmers' meals. Vegetable spaghetti marrow and various squashes are interesting varieties of marrow.

To prepare: cut off the skin, slice or cut in half lengthways and remove the seeds and centre pith. Vegetable spaghetti marrow is cooked whole, if young and up to 7 in (18 cm) long, otherwise it is peeled and cooked as for other marrows.

To cook: marrow contains a high proportion of water and it is best to either boil in the minimum amount of water or to steam. Alternatively, cook in butter or with another moist vegetable such as tomatoes. Avoid overcooking or marrow will become flabby and tasteless. Vegetable spaghetti marrow is boiled whole until tender, about 25 to 30 minutes.

To serve: drain, place in a serving dish, cut into wedges and top each with a knob of butter and salt and pepper. The seeds can be eaten and the flesh comes away in strands. If very mature, remove the seeds and scoop the flesh off the skin.

Buttered marrow: melt a large knob of butter in a saucepan, add prepared cubed marrow and some salt and pepper. Turn gently to coat in butter then cover and cook over a low heat until just tender, 15 to 20 minutes. Alternatively, cook in a moderate oven for about ½ hour or in a microwave oven for 8 to 10 minutes.

Baked Stuffed Marrow: cook rings or halves in a covered casserole in a little water in a moderate oven until tender, about ½ hour. Drain, fill with a savoury meat or cheese mixture, dot with butter or grated cheese and bake for a further 20 to 30 minutes.

To store: whole in a net in a shed.

To pickle: layer with salt, rinse, drain, and mix with other brined, prepared vegetables; cover with spiced vinegar.

To freeze: not recommended, but cooked buttered marrow can be frozen in a container.

Cucumbers

Cucumber is a valuable addition to any salad; it is also attractive as a garnish for savoury dishes. A great favourite in Greek and Middle Eastern cookery, cucumber is often teamed with yogurt for refreshing dishes or served in thick chunks with curries. Cucumbers can be cooked like courgettes and are useful for mixed pickle dishes.

To prepare: there is no need to peel cucumbers unless the skin is tough and prickly. Cut off the stalk and flower ends then slice thinly.

For garnish: run the point of a knife down the skin to remove the skin at intervals. Alternatively cut each slice to the centre then arrange as a cucumber twist or form into a cone.

To cook: as for courgettes or in soup.

To serve raw: to remove the excess of water that can spoil a mixed salad, layer slices of cucumber with salt in a colander and leave to drain for about ½ hour. Rinse, pat dry then mix into a yogurt or soured cream dressing and sprinkle with chopped fresh herbs. Use in cold soups.

To store: wrap a cut cucumber in cling film and store at the bottom of the refrigerator for up to 4 days.

To freeze: as a purée to use in soups or as chunks cooked in butter then chilled and frozen. Use as a hot vegetable.

To pickle: thickly slice, sprinkle with salt and layer in a colander, leave to drain for 1 hour then pat dry. Layer in a jar or with other brined vegetables and cover with sweet spiced vinegar (see page 123).

Gherkins

These are similar to cucumbers and are mostly grown for pickling.

To prepare: rub gherkins with a cloth to remove prickles.

To pickle: wash, drain and leave in brine for 3 days. Drain and pack in jars, cutting large gherkins lengthways, if necessary. Cover with warm spiced vinegar and leave in a warm place for 24 hours. Drain and re-boil vinegar and repeat until the gherkins are a pleasant green colour. Add more spiced vinegar, if necessary and cover. Add dill seeds to the jar, if desired.

Pumpkins

Beautiful golden pumpkins are mature in the autumn just in time to make lanterns for Hallowe'en or pies for American Thanksgiving. The cooked flesh is creamy in texture and is served mostly as a vegetable. It makes a delicious creamy soup.

To prepare: cut into wedges and remove the seeds and stringy bits. Pumpkin can be cooked in its shell-like skin or cut away and sliced or diced.

Clockwise: Courgette Fritters; Courgette Raita; Courgettes Provençales.

To cook: for use as purée in pies, soups or as a vegetable, cut into small chunks and cook in a covered saucepan over a low heat for 15 to 20 minutes. Press through a sieve or liquidize with a little of the cooking stock in a blender or food processor. To make soup, follow the Master Soup Recipe on page 66. Omit the potatoes and add 2 tbsp (2 × 15 ml sp) tomato purée.

To serve as a vegetable: cut prepared pumpkin into thin slices, fry in butter then sprinkle with onion or garlic salt, black pepper and chopped parsley. Roast small chunks of pumpkin in the meat tin around the joint, basting occasionally. Use pumpkin purée to thicken a vegetable curry. Fry the vegetables and curry powder together then add diced pumpkin, soaked beans, rind and juice of orange and water. Cook until tender and the pumpkin is reduced to a purée.

PILGRIM PUMPKIN PIE

This pie is traditionally served on American Independence day to follow the Thanksgiving turkey. It freezes well, either whole in its dish or cut into wedges.

For 6 to 8 portions

Metric		Imperial
	PASTRY	
150 g	plain flour	6 oz
1 × 1.25 ml sp	salt	½ tsp
75 g	lard and margarine, mixed	3 oz
	cold water to mix	
	FILLING	
425 ml	pumpkin purée (see note)	15 fl oz
2	eggs	2
100 g	moist brown sugar	4 oz
200 g	can evaporated milk	7 oz
1 × 5 ml sp	ground cinnamon	1 tsp
1 × 2.5 ml sp	ground nutmeg	½ tsp
1 × 1.25 ml sp	ground allspice or cloves	¼ tsp
1 × 2.5 ml sp	salt	½ tsp
125 ml	whipping cream	¼ pint

1. Prepare a hot oven (210 deg C, 425 deg F, Gas Mark 7). Place a 9 in (22 cm) oven-glass pie plate on a baking sheet.

2. Place flour and salt in a bowl, add fats, and cut in small pieces and rub in with the fingertips until mixture resembles fine breadcrumbs. Add about 6 tsp (6 × 5 ml sp) water and mix with a fork to form a firm dough. Turn out on to a floured board and knead with the fingertips.

3. Roll out to a 12 in (30 cm) circle, support pastry on rolling pin and line pie dish. Trim edge with scissors ½ in (2 cm) out from rim then turn pastry under to give double thickness; flute edge with the fingers.

4. To make filling: place pumpkin in a basin and beat in eggs with a fork. Add sugar, milk, cinnamon, nutmeg, allspice or cloves and salt; mix well. Alternatively, place all together in a liquidizer goblet or food processor and mix.

5. Pour half into lined pie dish then place baking sheet on oven shelf and add remaining mixture. Bake for 15 minutes then reduce heat to moderate (180 deg C, 350 deg F, Gas Mark 4) and bake for a further 35 to 45 minutes until filling is set 2 in (5 cm) in from edge. Leave to cool then chill if not required at once. Just before serving whisk cream and pile spoonsful around edge of pie.

Note: Make purée by baking wedges of deseeded unpeeled pumpkin for about 20 minutes in a moderate oven until tender or simmering in a small quantity of water in a covered saucepan for 20 minutes; drain well. Sieve and measure. Alternatively use a 15 fl oz (430 ml) can pumpkin purée.

Melons

Serve as a starter, with smoked meat and fish or as a dessert. Melon needs lightly chilling, but the flavour is impaired if it is served too cold.

To prepare: cut large melons in wedges and scoop out the seeds. Small melons may be halved or the tops cut off for the easy removal of the seeds then served whole. Cut a little off the base, if necessary, to stop the melon rolling over.

To serve as a starter: cut flesh from skin of wedges of melon, replace on skin, cut across into pieces and pull alternate pieces to each side. Garnish with lemon and orange twists and maraschino cherries and serve with a sprinkling of lemon juice or sugar mixed with a little ground ginger. Whole or halved melons can be served with sweet sherry or port poured in the centre. Diced melon or melon cut into balls with a special gadget can be mixed with peeled prawns, tuna or crabmeat and served on a bed of shredded lettuce. Serve wedges of melon with smoked mackerel or Parma ham.

To serve as a dessert: mix diced melon with stem ginger and sprinkle with lemon juice. Fill whole or halved melons with soft fruits and sprinkle with liqueur.

Melon Basket: use an attractive-skinned melon and cut a small piece from the base to make it stand firmly. Either cut off the top third in a straight piece or cut to form a basket handle. From the top centre of the melon, make a vertical cut 1 in (2.5 cm) to the right from centre and half way down the melon. Repeat from left of centre. Cut each side horizontally from side to vertical cut and remove the wedges of melon. Remove seeds and cut out melon flesh with a knife or baller gadget. Mix melon with soft fruits or mandarin oranges and stem ginger and pile into the basket. Chill for about 1 hour before serving.

To store: leave to ripen at room temperature; blossom end should yield gently to pressure when ripe. Store in the bottom of the refrigerator. Freezing is not recommended, but if necessary, pieces of melon can be stored in a lemony sugar syrup in tubs.

Tomatoes are the most popular cold greenhouse crop but aubergines can be grown just as easily.

Greenhouses

Choice of greenhouse will depend on the space available, the crops to be grown, the structural material preferred and the money you are prepared to spend. Polythene-covered structures will be the cheapest and are suited to the do-it-yourself enthusiast. A few pieces of 21 ft (6.4 m) long, $\frac{1}{2}$ in (13 mm) bore galvanized water pipe, which is easily bent into a semi circle, some wood and a large sheet of 500 gauge U.V.I. (ultra violet inhibited) film is all you need to build quite a large covered structure. The film needs replacing after three summers, if not before, but if crops are being grown in the soil the whole house can be moved to a fresh site before replacing the polythene sheet.

Glass is the most popular cladding for greenhouses and the weight of glass often adds to the strength of the house. There are several plastic materials like acrylic and polycarbonate sheet which are a little more expens-

ive but have the advantage of being quite easily cut, less dangerous and much stronger than glass.

Aluminium-framed greenhouses are corrosion resistant and preferable to wood and other materials. If a wooden greenhouse structure is wanted for any reason the rot resistant and relatively maintenance-free red cedar frames are best. Wood has the disadvantage of being heavier and more light obstructing than aluminum.

Greenhouses are best sited in an open space away from shadows cast by trees, hedges, fences, walls and buildings. It is important to trap every bit of winter sunlight and warmth. Some protection from strong wind is also an advantage, especially for heated greenhouses. Wind blowing over the glass will cause heat loss and, even worse, blowing between the glass overlap it literally blows the trapped heat out of the house.

A greenhouse is likely to be the largest single purchase made by gardeners and it is advisable to take time when making the decision on which model to choose. Restriction of space may dictate buying a small free-standing or lean-to model for very tiny gardens. The smaller the house and smaller the volume of air contained, the quicker it will become excessively hot and excessively cold. A reasonable size for most gardens is 12 ft (3.6 m) long and 8 ft (2.4 m) wide. I would try to avoid houses less than 8 ft (2.4 m) square, even if it means delaying the purchase for a year or two.

Where it is the intention to heat the greenhouse to extend the cropping season, then double glazed houses are great money savers. On an exposed site a double glazed house will cost as little as 40% of the heating costs for a similar-sized, single glazed glasshouse.

While heat is an advantage and allows more crops to be grown over a longer period each year, good ventilation is essential. The rule of thumb guide is one sixth of the floor area available as opened ventilators. It often costs extra to have one or two extra vents in the greenhouse but again this is money well spent.

A little help is valuable when erecting a greenhouse. Walls and ends are built separately first with most models and then bolted together. Trials with these two houses proved that the double glazed house (left) is a very efficient structure to heat. On bright days and still nights the soil and house retained enough heat to keep out frost, even on cold nights.

Erected houses with insufficient ventilation can be improved by fitting a fan in the ridge in one end of the house and louvres in the base of the opposite end. Fixing a thermostat to the fan gives accurate temperature control and avoids scorching temperatures in periods – even brief ones – of hot sun.

Ventilators unattended are of course useless and automatic opening and closing devices are essential on at least one vent. While electricity is needed to control the fan, the automatic vents work by the natural expansion and contraction of metal or wax and do not require electricity.

Additional heating can be provided by burning paraffin, gas and electricity. Without question electricity is the best, the easiest and the most efficient for the amateur's greenhouse. It is also the most expensive but as long as the heater is used carefully electricity will give full value for money. The thing to remember is for *every* 5°F (2.5°C) you raise the minimum temperature over 45°F (7°C), you double the heating cost regardless of the fuel type used.

Gas and paraffin can be used to fire burners within the house but it is advisable to use them sparingly, just to keep out frost. Burning fiercely, they release toxic fumes and excessive water vapour. To some extent this is counteracted by having the ventilator slightly open but opening the vents increases heat loss.

There is a great variety of shape, size and design of greenhouse and the best place to make a selection is at a centre which offers a range of models from

The 10 ft × 12 ft (3 m × 3.6 m) polythene greenhouse, which has withstood very severe gales and protected a wide range of crops. Ventilation is provided by netting over the top half of the doors in both ends. This netting is covered with plastic in winter when little ventilation is necessary.

different manufacturers. Pay particular attention to the door: sliding doors are less likely to get caught by a gust of wind. A snug fitting door is an essential part of heat saving and some designs have doors large enough to allow a wheelbarrow through, which can be useful.

Some models are advertised at attractively low prices but their glazing bars are very thin and they require fundamental extras such as foundations, bases and lower walls. Most makes allow easy construction but if you can enlist the help of someone who has already erected a house of similar design it will be a great help. Some manufacturers will also offer an erection service and as this reduces the VAT charge it is often a competitively-priced service and one to be recommended.

only really effective when the edges of the sheets are sealed together to prevent the heat being blown out by wind, referred to above.

The alternative to a free standing greenhouse is a lean-to, conservatory or glass-sided home extension. Where the glass-sided structure is fitted to a wall of the house then heating, especially to frost free conditions, is much easier and often quite cheap. Once again the bigger the volume of air within the structure the better and a good, south-facing wall can absorb a lot of warmth from the sun to slowly release at night.

Whatever the structure try to arrange full use of it the year round. Many gardeners do little more than raise a few seedlings in spring and grow a crop of tomatoes in summer. There are plenty of crops to grow to make full use of the greenhouse. Peach trees, for example, grow well in large pots. Leave these potted trees outside until the first sign of buds breaking in the early spring. Then bring them in to protect the blossom from frost and, because of the drier atmosphere in the greenhouse, avoid the ravages of peach leaf curl disease. Once the fruit has set and before the onslaught of red spider pests in the heat of summer, trees can be moved outside to make space for tomatoes. A lot of the hardier vegetables can also be grown and cropped in cold or slightly heated glasshouses through the autumn and winter. Self blanching celery, lettuce, radish, salad onions, spinach, even cabbage and turnip are some good examples.

Early summer tomatoes, cucumbers and peppers growing happily with flowering pot and bedding plants in a heated greenhouse.

Soil floors are an asset because they allow crops to be grown in the border soil as well as providing a humid atmosphere. Paving slabs put down on sand give a clean surface and, if damped down in warm weather, help maintain humid conditions.

Summer shading is needed over the glass in really hot weather for most crops and especially where ventilation is inadequate. White is by far the best colour because it reflects the sunlight – green shading materials increase the temperature within the house – and there are proprietary white shading materials which can be polished off easily with a dry cloth each autumn. Where white polythene sheet is used for summer shade it can also be left up for winter heat retention. Heat saving within a glasshouse by lining the inside with polythene sheet is

The border soil in a cold greenhouse cropped with lettuce through winter to cut early spring.

Raising tender seedlings

The same method is used for raising plants of aubergine, golden berry, pepper, okra and tomatoes and the seeds are similar, even if they vary a little in size. It is never worth economizing at this stage and buying the best seed and disease-free branded seed compost is essential. Use the all-peat seed compost for easy transplanting and a good root system.

Moisten the compost thoroughly before use; if it is damp enough some moisture will ooze between the fingers when a full handful is squeezed tightly. If the compost is too dry, wet and leave for a few hours to allow the moisture to be fully absorbed before use.

Loosely fill a flower pot, seed pan or a shallow plastic container, for example a plastic margarine tub, and then firm by pressing a flat surface on to the top of the compost so that it is $\frac{1}{4}-\frac{1}{2}$ in (1–1.5 cm)

below the rim. This leaves ample space for subsequent watering and if you are not too sure about watering, see that the container has a drainage hole in the base. Another easy watering check is to weigh the sown pan immediately after sowing, then when it has dried out a little and lost weight it can be watered until the original weight is regained.

Space the seeds evenly over the surface of the pan. If you find this difficult it is quite easy to lift each seed on the dampened end of a match and place it in position on the compost. Then sprinkle a little compost over the seeds and place the pot in a polythene bag. If you have several pans to sow the alternative is to cover them with a sheet of glass, to retain the moisture, and newspaper to keep out strong sunlight.

Placed over a good steady supply of warmth (65°F (18°C)) the seeds will be pushing through in a matter of days. Peppers will take a little longer than most and are slower growing, so earlier sowing for these is recommended. At the first sign of shoots pushing through the surface the covers must be removed and the pots placed in a light position. Once the first two seed leaves have unfurled the seedlings should be transplanted singly into $3\frac{1}{2}$ in (9 cm) or similar pots filled with potting compost. When transplanting – what is called pricking off – always handle the seedlings by the leaves and don't be afraid of dropping the stems well down in the hole so that the leaves are close to the top of the compost. This helps to prevent the formation of tall, thin, so called leggy, plants and additional new roots form from the buried stem.

Placed on a light, warm window-sill and in heated greenhouses, these plants will grow quickly and need to be close to clean glass to get all the available light in early spring. Where temperatures might drop rather low in the light position at night, it is worth moving the seedlings into the warmth each evening and back into full light each morning. On the window-sill a backing of silver foil will reflect light on to the seedlings and improve their growth.

When the roots fill the $3\frac{1}{2}$ in pot and the plants get a little top heavy, it is time to move them up into either a one size larger, $5\frac{1}{2}$ in (13 cm) pot or into the cropping position. It is well worth keeping tomatoes in pots up to the stage of the first flower fully opening and starting to set. If they are planted too soon in fertile compost in early spring, growth can be so rapid the first truss (bunch) of flowers does not set and fruiting is delayed. Spraying the flowers with special fruit set chemical also prevents this.

Always handle seedlings by the seed leaves, never by the stem . . . .

When pushing the soil in around the roots be careful not to press against, and bruise, the tender stem. The slightest bruising can cause stem rot.

Transplant seedlings into peat blocks and they can be planted out with no further root damage. Peat blocks are suitable for many vegetables raised under glass to plant out later in the garden.

Aubergine

The fruits of aubergine have become very popular in modern day cooking and the plants are so attractive they can be decorative as well as a useful food provider. Young plants can be set out in the open garden under cloches in late May/early June, the cloches are removed as the plants get too large to be contained and fruit from August onwards. Much heavier weight of crop will be achieved where the plants have the protection of a warm south wall, frame or greenhouse. Yields will be better too in fertile compost and growing bags.

Large green leaves with purple undersides and stems are in themselves attractive and a good foil to the mauve flowers with yellow centres and subsequent large purple black fruits. The plants can be left to develop naturally into a bush, to be supported by a cane and tie. Alternatively the centres can be pinched out when the plant is 18 in (45 cm) high and the side branches which develop trained out on strings. The latter method is better where a long cropping season is planned with early sowing and greenhouse protection for a whole season.

The several different kinds of aphids – green, brown and whitefly – are attracted to aubergines (and peppers) and a regular look out needs to be kept for these pests. Spraying with one of the many aphid and whitefly killers at the first sign of attack will keep plants clean (see page 8). One other possible trouble is the soft brown rot disease botrytis, also called grey mould on account of the fluffy grey mould which subsequently develops on the brown rot. Cold, damp conditions encourage the spread of this disease which often starts on the dying petals around the embryo fruits. I find it advisable to remove the old petals as the tiny pale mauve fruit starts to grow, particularly on plants grown outdoors where heavy morning dew can encourage rotting.

Fruit is ready to pick when large, plump and the skin really shiny – once the skin colour goes dull the fruits are past their best. In addition to the purple-fruited varieties there is a white skinned-kind with a more rounded shape.

Very similar in its cultural requirements to aubergine is okra, commonly called 'Lady's Fingers' because of the finger-like shape of the long slender green seed pods which are used to flavour soups and stews. The leaves are rich green, the flowers bright yellow and the stems green and flushed pink.

Many exotic dishes can be made from purple fruited aubergines, slender green courgettes, red and green sweet peppers with their bulbous, square-shouldered fruits, long, slender, orange-red hot peppers, lovely tomatoes, green kohlrabi and onions.

Masses of fruit developing on three aubergine plants in one growbag; three or four branches are being trained out from each plant.

Sweet pepper growing and fruiting in a 6 in (15 cm) pot on the window-sill.

Peppers

There are two quite separate kinds of pepper plant, the most commonly grown sweet pepper with rounded and hollow boxy fruits, quite as easy to grow as tomatoes and the really hot tasting chilli or cayenne peppers which need a little more heat to grow well. They both have green fruits initially and then as the fruits ripen they turn either red or, in some cases, yellow to gold. Picking the fruit green, particularly for the sweet peppers, allows the plant to produce a much heavier total weight of crop. It is for this reason the red peppers usually cost a little more in the shop, with the grower getting less if the fruits are left on the plant until fully ripe and red.

All the peppers need warm conditions to raise sturdy young plants and because the seedlings grow so much slower than tomatoes it is advisable to sow them at least four weeks earlier than you would tomatoes – usually late February/early March. Good big plants with the first flowers opening can be planted outside late May/early June and given cloche protection for three or four weeks. They form quite stiff, woody bushes and will crop well into the autumn, withstanding quite cold autumn weather. It is worth removing the first one or two forming fruits to help the plant get well established and produce a heavier yield. This will of course delay picking by several weeks.

Under glass the growing tip can be removed and three or four branches trained up strings if a good, long and warm growing season can be provided. Where plants are trained in this way and every side shoot from the main branches pinched out after one leaf, the yield can be double that of untrained bush plants.

Peppers make very good pot subjects and some of the smaller varieties can be successfully grown to full fruiting on the window-sill. Where a few early fruits, rather than a heavy yield, is the aim the very first flowers are allowed to set on these pot grown specimens. There are quite a number of dwarf hot peppers which are grown more for ornamental use than culinary purposes but they can be eaten. Varieties of sweet pepper, including 'Triton', are the best for early fruits and also make very pretty pot plants.

Patio pots and tubs are also perfect containers for aubergines, peppers, bushy early tomatoes and okra. Plants are raised indoors and planted up in the tubs in June

An aubergine and two sweet pepper plants in a growbag, outside, against a south-facing wall and providing sufficient fruits for the average family's needs.

and stood in a warm sunny place.

Given a good long growing season the sweet peppers and larger fruited hot peppers will make large plants. If they are planted in the greenhouse border soil – they do well given this treatment under polythene houses – space the plants $2\frac{1}{2}$–3 ft (75–90 cm) apart. By far the easiest way to grow them is three to each standard-sized growbag.

All plants will need regular feeding once the first fruits start to swell. Diluted liquid tomato fertilizer watered on once, and with big heavy cropping plants twice, a week will give the biggest yield.

Tomatoes

The seed packet racks and seedsmen's catalogues are packed with different tomato varieties, a bemusing and confusing number for gardeners who are often persuaded to select packets just because the names sound familiar. This is far from the best thing to do, with many old, well-known names superseded by more recent introductions with many improved qualities.

Think out where and for what purpose the tomatoes are to be grown and then select a variety which has been bred to meet these requirements. Consider first of all, the tomatoes to be grown outside where early ripening is essential; otherwise the plants will be full of green fruit with the approach of winter and there will be little chance of their reaching maturity. Bush varieties will grow little more than 12 in (30 cm) high and can be covered for the whole of their life with cloches or cloched in the autumn to ripen off the last few fruits. 'Arla' and 'Red Alert' are low growing bush varieties and very early ripening. If you can wait a few weeks longer then the slightly bigger bush types like 'Alfresco' and 'Sleaford Abundance' will give heavier yields.

'Sweet 100' has a good flavour, thin skin and produces multiple trusses of delicious small fruit.

Remove the side shoots which form above each leaf as soon as possible and be especially careful to remove the shoot below each flower truss. It will be seen that the two original seed leaves on this plant are still green and healthy, the sure sign of a good specimen grown without a check to growth.
Left **'Minibel', a good variety to grow in a pot on a window-sill.**

There are outdoor varieties too which can be tied to stakes and the side shoots removed to produce the single stem traditional 'cordon' style plant. 'Outdoor Girl' is one of the earliest and has rather unusually shaped, potato-like leaves. There are large fruited varieties suitable for outdoors, for example 'Marmande', and bush types with very fleshy plum-shaped fruits like 'Roma' so good for soups and cooking.

Some varieties have really superb flavour and the small fruited 'Gardeners' Delight' and 'Sweet 100' are two of the best. They can be grown outside and under glass, usually cordon style. The more humid atmosphere in greenhouses can encourage leaf mould disease and to avoid this, varieties with cladosporium resistance should be selected. All of the better greenhouse varieties are F_1 hybrids and some, like 'Curabel', 'Virosa', the very early 'Herald' and 'Grenadier' combine disease resistance, good flavour and high yield.

There are very compact bushy plants

are caused by erratic watering: usually letting plants get dry to the point of wilting on a hot day.

Whitefly can be a real pest of tomatoes and several other fruiting crops in glasshouses. Heavy populations cover the leaves with a sticky exudation and the black sooty mould fungus grows on it. Clean greenhouses out thoroughly after each crop to reduce the chance of this pest overwintering. At the first sign of attack on the new crop, spray every seven days with a whitefly killer like permethrin until there are no signs of their presence.

Old leaves on the base of the plant below ripening fruit will go yellow and can be removed to improve air movement and reduce the chance of disease build-up. Green fruits picked in autumn as the weather cools will ripen more quickly if placed in a cardboard box with a ripe apple. The apple gives off ethylene gas which is a ripening agent.

suitable for growing in flower pots and hanging baskets, for example 'Minibel', and somewhat larger plants suited to patio tubs like 'Pixie'. Very keen gardeners can also grow the yellow fruited, the orange and red striped and currant-size fruited varieties for added interest. Exceptionally large fruited, so called beef-steak kinds, are also good flavoured but the large flowers pollinate best under glass and in warm sunny conditions. For this reason it is as well not to sow the giant fruit types, including 'Big Boy', too early.

Complete newcomers to gardening are well advised to choose the bush types because, after planting, they need no more attention then merely watering, feeding and picking the fruit. All the other varieties grown up a single main stem will need all the side shoots removed which grow from the stem at each leaf joint. Pay particular attention to those side shoots which come from immediately below a bunch (truss) of flowers. If these 'truss shoots' are left they grow strongly and take much of the food which would otherwise be directed to the development of fruit.

While tomatoes will grow well in ordinary garden soil, even in the greenhouse borders, after several years root diseases build up and decimate yield if they do not kill the plants altogether. Commercial growers used to steam sterilize the soil between crops and keen amateurs resorted to ring culture to avoid this, but now the growbag gives the cheap, easy and heavy yielding alternative.

One or two crops can be grown in new soil but then you are well advised to cover the soil with polythene – black underneath

'Gardeners' Delight' has long trusses of the sweetest fruit, each one about 1 in (2.5 cm) in diameter. Note the larger fruit on traditional varieties on the left.

Right 'Tigerella', the unusually-coloured and very good-flavoured variety. Note the soft string support tied to the base of the plant and wound round the stem.

to supress weeds and white above to reflect light – and bring in growbags. Don't be tempted to try and change the soil: it is just too easy to leave a little infected soil behind and then all the work is of no benefit.

Place the growbags on to growtrays at the outset but stand the pot-grown plants on the bags until the first flowers are well formed. Then the peat in the bag can be well watered, the tomatoes planted out three to a full sized bag and three wicks pushed up into the peat compost with one end of each left dangling in the growtray reservoir of water. You will be amazed at the quantity of water three plants use up on a hot day when they are carrying four or more bunches of fruit, six gallons is commonplace. When the tomatoes start to form, feeding should start. Liquid feeding is easiest and can be either watered over the surface soil and peat or poured into the reservoir tray. There are a number of liquid tomato foods and most need applying at least once a week in summer and early autumn. Well fed plants will respond by having thick, dark green, tightly-curled tops.

Yellowing between the leaf veins on heavy cropping plants is usually caused by insufficient magnesium and an epsom salt solution added to the water corrects this. Black patches on the base of the fruit

Canes and stakes are used to support cordon tomatoes grown in the soil. Where they are grown in growbags the most common support system is soft string, one end tied to the plant stem just above the compost and the other fixed to the superstructure above. The string is wound round the stem in a spiral as the plant grows.

Flowers will sometimes abort – go brown, shrivel and drop off – when the plant is growing too strongly or is short of food when carrying several bunches of set fruit. Lack of light in early spring and low temperatures can also have this effect. Spraying with fruit set, improving the cultural conditions and tapping the plants to shake the pollen across in warm sunny weather, all help fruit formation.

Cookery

Aubergines

This vegetable is a staple ingredient in Mediterranean cuisine, the best known dish being Moussaka. It is served both hot and cold, but always cooked. It is served mostly as a vegetable accompaniment, but it can be stuffed and baked, which makes the meat or fish go a long way.

To prepare: wash then trim both ends. Cut in thick slices and layer in a colander, sprinkling with salt as you go. This extracts the bitter juices. Leave for 30 minutes then rinse under running water, drain and pat dry with kitchen paper.

To cook: fry in a mixture of butter and oil on both sides until golden. Drain on kitchen paper. The slices may be floured then coated in egg and fresh breadcrumbs or coated in a thin batter made from self-raising flour and water before frying. Brush with oil or melted butter and grill or bake.

To serve cold: cook whole in boiling, salted water for about 20 minutes. Peel when cool and cut flesh into chunks. Place in a salad bowl and mix in natural yogurt or soured cream and chopped lemon balm or parsley. Alternatively, mix prepared aubergine with chopped tomatoes, sliced spring onions, a crushed clove of garlic, olive oil, lemon juice and seasonings. Chill for about ½ hour before serving.

Microwave: place in a casserole or plastic bag. Cook 1 lb (500 g) for 10 minutes.

To store: aubergines store for about a week in the salad compartment of a refrigerator.

To freeze: blanch in boiling water for 4 minutes, drain, dry and open freeze. Fry from frozen or add to casseroles and stews.

MOUSSAKA

Replace lamb with minced beef, if you prefer

For 4 to 5 portions

Metric		Imperial
500 g	boneless neck fillet of lamb	1 lb
250 g	onions	½ lb
2	medium-sized aubergines	2
	salt and pepper	
500 g	tomatoes	1 lb
50 g	butter	2 oz
2 × 15 ml sp	chopped parsley	2 tbsp
1 × 15 ml sp	olive oil	1 tbsp
	SAUCE	
50 g	margarine	2 oz
50 g	plain flour	2 oz
570 ml	milk	1 pint
50 g	cheese, grated	2 oz
1	egg, beaten	1

1. Prepare a moderate oven (190 deg C, 375 deg F, Gas Mark 5). Grease a 3 pint (1.5 litre) shallow ovenproof dish. Cut lamb into small cubes, removing any excess fat. Peel and slice onions. Slice aubergines, spread on a plate and sprinkle with salt, skin and slice tomatoes.

2. Heat half the butter in a frying pan and gently fry onions to soften them, without browning. Add meat and continue frying gently, stirring, until meat changes colour. Remove from heat and stir in 2 tsp (2 × 5 ml sp) salt and some pepper. Spread meat mixture in ovenproof dish and sprinkle with parsley. Heat remaining butter and the olive oil (or omit oil and use an extra 1 oz (25 g) butter) in frying pan. Rinse and dry aubergine slices and fry on both sides, to brown lightly. (Add a little extra butter, if necessary.) Drain on kitchen paper.

3. Arrange aubergine slices on meat in dish; season with salt, then place sliced tomatoes on top, adding a little more salt.

4. To make sauce: melt margarine in a small saucepan, add flour and milk and bring to boil, stirring with a spoon, or whisk, cook for 3 minutes. Remove from heat. Add grated cheese together with beaten egg. Taste and add seasonings. Pour over layers in dish. Cover with lid, foil or greased greaseproof paper. Place on a baking sheet just above centre of oven for 1 hour. Remove lid or covering and cook for a further half hour. Serve hot with vegetables.

Note: Marrow or cucumber may be used instead of aubergines. Marrow should be peeled, sliced and seeded. Cucumber should be peeled and sliced. Fry them as for aubergines. If desired, use 2 lb (1 kg) of uncooked, sliced potatoes instead of aubergines. Start and finish the dish with a layer of raw potato slices, then top with sauce.

Peppers

These attractive Mediterranean vegetables add a delicious flavour and colour to many dishes. They are a valuable addition to salads, both for their crisp texture and nutritive value, as they are a rich source of vitamin C. They combine well with tomatoes and aubergines in many dishes.

To prepare: remove the seeds, core and white pith. Cut in rings or in half through the centre, depending on method of cooking or serving.

To cook: blanch in boiling water for 2 minutes before adding to stews and casseroles. For serving stuffed, blanch, then bake. Thread on kebab skewers and barbecue or grill.

Vegetable Gougère

To serve raw: mix with salad ingredients or serve strips with a dip. Use strips for garnish.

To store: place in salad drawer of refrigerator and store for up to a week.

To freeze: blanch slices for 2 minutes, halves or prepared whole peppers 3 minutes. Drain upside down. Pack in freezer bags and store for up to 1 year. Use frozen; not suitable for serving raw.

To pickle: soak halves overnight in brine, drain and rinse then pack in jars and cover with sweet spicy vinegar. Add peppercorns and a whole red chilli to jar, if desired.

RATATOUILLE

This mixed vegetable dish stores for up to a week in a refrigerator or up to 3 months in the freezer. Omit garlic for freezing.

For 4 portions

Metric		Imperial
2	large onions	2
2	cloves garlic	2
2 × 5 ml sp	salt	2 tsp
2 × 15 ml sp	cooking oil	2 tbsp
2	green peppers	2
1	red pepper	1
500 g	courgettes	1 lb
250 g	tomatoes	½ lb
	pepper	

1. Peel and slice onions. Peel garlic, place on a saucer with salt. Using a round-ended knife, rub salt against garlic to crush.

2. Heat oil in a saucepan and cook onion and garlic for 5 minutes without browning.

3. Cut each pepper into 8 pieces and remove all seeds and white pith. Peel courgettes and cut into ¼ in (6 mm) slices. Place tomatoes in a bowl, cover with boiling water and leave for 1 minute; drain, peel, then cut into slices.

4. Cover onions with green and red peppers, then the courgettes and, lastly, the sliced tomatoes; sprinkle well with salt and pepper. Cover saucepan with a tight-fitting lid.

5. Cook over a low heat for 30 to 40 minutes until all vegetables are tender. Turn into a warmed serving dish. Alternatively, serve cold as a starter or use to fill a savoury flan.

Tomatoes

The flavour of a freshly-picked tomato is unique. It can be used in so many ways in the kitchen; raw in salads and as an attractive garnish, as a base for soup and sauces, to serve with savoury dishes, particularly pasta, to add flavour to stews casseroles and braises and baked, grilled or fried as a vegetable accompaniment. Over-ripe, green or surplus tomatoes are useful for making sauces, pickles and chutneys.

To prepare: remove calyx, wash and cut according to use. Slice across the stalk or cut in wedges for garnish and in salads, cut in halves across the stalk for grilling and frying. Remove skins then chop roughly for sauces, soups and stews. To skin tomatoes, place in a bowl, pour over boiling water, leave 1 minute, drain then peel from the stalk end using a knife. Alternatively, spear on a fork and hold in a flame, turning until the skin splits, then it will easily peel off.

To cook: tomatoes are very juicy and need to be concentrated for use in most dishes. They are often skinned and cooked until thick and pulpy, or cooked with the skins on then sieved to produce a smooth sauce.

To grill: cut in half, brush with oil, season with salt, pepper and sugar, if desired and cook under a moderate grill for about 5 minutes.

To fry: cut in halves and fry slowly on both sides.

To bake: cut a cross in the skin of the rounded end, place stalk side down in an ovenproof dish cover with a buttered paper and bake in a moderate oven (190 deg C, 375 deg F, Gas Mark 5) for 10 to 15 minutes. Alternatively, cut off the top, scoop out the centre and mix with breadcrumbs and a savoury filling such as grated cheese or canned fish; press back before baking. Sliced tomatoes can be layered in an ovenproof dish with seasoning and chopped fresh marjoram or basil and baked with a topping of buttered breadcrumbs.

Microwave: as for baking in a covered dish for about 5 minutes, depending on quantity.

To serve cold: slice, cut in wedges or serve whole with hot or cold food. Layer with other salad ingredients such as cucumber and onion and coat with a herb or garlic-flavoured dressing.

To store: place in a plastic bag in the bottom of the refrigerator and store for up to 1 week.

To freeze: tomatoes are not suitable for eating raw after freezing, but can be cooked. Freeze as purée in plastic boxes or in ice cube trays then store in freezer bags or pack whole in freezer bags and use while still frozen. Make ketchup, pickle and chutney.

FRESH TOMATO SAUCE

Peel and finely chop an onion, fry in a knob of butter until soft but not browned. Add some celery leaves or 1 stick, chopped, 1 lb (500 g) quartered tomatoes, ½ tsp (1 × 2.5 ml sp) each of salt and ground cinnamon, 1 tsp (1 × 5 ml sp) sugar and a generous shake of pepper. Cook uncovered, stirring occasionally, over a low heat until sauce is thick and pulpy. Press through a sieve then taste and add more seasoning, if necessary. Serve with sausages, hamburgers and deep fried foods.

VEGETABLE GOUGÈRE

Choux pastry is more usually served with sweet dishes, but it is equally good as a crisp casing for a filling of vegetables and cheese.

For 4 portions

Metric		Imperial
	CHOUX PASTRY	
50 g	Cheddar cheese	2 oz
75 g	plain flour	2½ oz
1 × 2.5 ml sp	salt	½ tsp
1 × 1.25 ml sp	dry mustard	¼ tsp
	pepper	
50 g	margarine	2 oz
2	eggs	2
	FILLING	
2	medium-sized tomatoes	2
50 g	Cheddar cheese	2 oz
1	large aubergine	1
50 g	margarine	2 oz
25 g	plain flour	1 oz
125 ml	milk	¼ pint
1 × 1.25 ml sp	dry mustard	¼ tsp
	salt and pepper	

1. Prepare a moderately hot oven (200 deg C, 400 deg F, Gas Mark 6).

2. Dice cheese. Sift flour, salt, mustard and a shake of pepper on to a plate.

3. Place margarine and ¼ pint (125 ml) water in a medium-sized saucepan. Bring to boil, remove from heat, quickly stir in flour mixture with a wooden spoon and beat until mixture forms a ball in the pan.

4. Whisk the eggs together, beat into mixture a little at a time, beating well after each addition. Stir in cheese.

5. Place choux pastry in an 8 in (20 cm) ovenproof dish and, using the back of a wetted metal spoon, spread it to edges of dish, leaving a thin layer in centre.

6. Bake in centre of oven for 15 to 20 minutes until risen and light brown.

7. To make filling: place tomatoes in a bowl, cover with boiling water and leave for 1 minute. Remove skins, chop tomatoes. Grate cheese.

8. Wash aubergines, cut into small cubes; melt margarine, in a medium-sized saucepan. Add aubergines and stir occasionally until margarine has been absorbed.

9. Stir in flour and remove pan from heat, add milk, mustard, some salt and a good shake of pepper. Bring to boil, stirring continuously, and cook for 2 minutes. Stir in tomatoes and half the cheese; add seasonings if necessary.

10. Pour vegetable mixture into choux pastry case and sprinkle top with remaining cheese. Return to the oven for 10 to 15 minutes.

Onions

The onion family provide our most versatile vegetable and salad crop, used as a single vegetable both raw and cooked, with other vegetables and stuffings for flavouring, for pickling and providing young seedlings to be pulled fresh for salads.

Fortunately some are easy to grow although raising giant bulb onions for exhibition and raising from seed sown outdoors early in the year can be tricky. If you follow the rules there will be little difficulty in providing all the onion crops required the year round and beginners are well advised to start out by planting onion sets, shallot bulbs and salad onions. Once experience is gained raising the salad onions from seed sown outside, move on to raising the bulb onions and leeks from seed.

Occasionally you may hear of skilled gardeners raising exhibition-size onions and leeks from bulbils. They keep their biggest and best plants each year and grow them on to form seed heads in the second year. The mass of round greenish buds and white flowers are trimmed off each head and at the base of each flower stem small plantlets form. These plantlets with tiny bulb at the base are potted up singly and grown under glass through the winter. Quite big plants are then transplanted into the cropping site in spring to give the exhibitor a flying start.

I mention this only because so many people are fascinated by the exhibition giants and wonder how they're grown. Most of us are more than adequately served with set and seed raised plants and very large specimens can be grown from these if required.

Digging and Hoeing

Deep and thorough digging is often recommended especially for onions and other vegetables and flowers which are popular with exhibitors. In practice deep digging will encourage deeper root penetration and this in turn provides more moisture for the plants. There will, however, be ample moisture anyway in wet years and in dry years there will not be enough moisture however deep we dig, so deep digging is only likely to give fair return for the work one year in three.

That said, the effect of digging, up to two spades' depth, is quite long lasting especially if plenty of well-rotted organic matter is dug into the lower level to keep the soil open for root penetration and to retain moisture. (See page 7.)

Leeks are greedy plants and revel in damp soil which is rich in garden compost and/or manure. They produce masses of white root which will help considerably to break up heavy clay soil.

Regularly hoeing the soil also helps the plants by retaining a loose surface cover of soil and preventing unnecessarily fast evaporation, as well as killing weeds which can be a considerable drain on soil moisture and soluble plant foods.

There are three basic types of hoe, the traditional 'draw hoe' which we pull towards ourselves walking forward, the 'Dutch or push hoe' used walking backwards but pushing the hoe away in short jabbing movements and push-pull hoes which are moved backwards and forwards in the soil, also used walking backwards. The draw hoe is used to pull out seed drills, to pull up the soil in what we call earthing up, as for potatoes, sweetcorn, trench celery and blanched leeks, as well

as hoeing the surface. Because it is necessary to walk over the soil just hoed, with this tool, I only use it for weed control when the surface is caked down hard or the weeds rather big. Even when I do use it this way I like to run the push-pull hoe quickly through again to remove footprints and loosen any buried weeds from the soil. Catching the soil right, that is

just as it starts to dry out on the surface, is the easy way to garden and if a Dutch hoe or push-pull hoe is used at this time, the soil will work easily and weeds will never be a problem. Once you have a crumbly surface texture run the hoe quickly through the soil every two weeks or so to maintain this tilth and eliminate all weeds.

Working backwards with the push hoe removes footprints as you work and slices off the weeds. Note the draw hoe on the left used for working forwards on hard soil. The draw hoe is the best tool to pull soil up when earthing up potatoes and celery.

Year round onions harvest chart														
Type	Sow	Plant or thin	Jan	Feb	Mar	Apl	May	Jun	Jly	Aug	Sept	Oct	Nov	Dec
BULB ONIONS														
from sets		P. Mar/Apl												
from seed	S.G. Late Dec to Mar	P. Mar/Apl												
from seed	S.O. Mar/Apl	T. May/Jun												
Japanese or winter growing type	S.O. Aug	T. Winter/ Early Spring												
SALAD ONIONS														
White Lisbon type	S.O. Aug													
White Lisbon type	S.O. Apl/Jun													
PICKLING ONIONS	S.O. Mar- Early Jun													
LEEKS	S.G. Feb/Mar	P. Apl												
	S.O. Mar/Apl	P. May-Jly												
SHALLOTS		P. Jan-Apl												

S.G. sow under glass   S.O. sow outdoors   P plant   T thin out   ▬ harvest   ▬ storage life

Shallots

Plant on the shortest day and harvest on the longest is the old gardening adage for shallots. While weather conditions are far from conducive to shallot bulb planting on many of the shortest days they can be planted very early and are one of the first of the new season crops to go in.

There are yellow and reddish coloured varieties but all kinds are given the same treatment. Bulbs are gently pushed to half their height into well-prepared soil. Space the rows 12 in (30 cm) apart and the bulbs 6 in (15 cm) apart down the row. Do not plant too close because each bulb makes quite a clump of growth and hoeing causes damage to the young shallots when they grow out into the row.

Remember that planting big shallots produces large clumps of six to eight new shallots with relatively small bulbs, while planting small bulbs produces less bulbs but mostly larger ones. So if you are growing for pickling either buy, or select from last season's crop, big planting bulbs, but for large bulbs to be used for culinary purposes plant smaller bulbs. The larger planting bulbs will benefit from a slightly wider spacing, closer spacing will have the effect of reducing the final weight of crop.

Once the foliage starts to yellow and fall over about mid-summer they are ready to harvest. Lift each clump with a fork and leave out in the sun to get straw dry, then the old leaves and roots will easily rub off. The dry bulbs can be stored in shallow trays for almost a year. Shallots can also be pulled late spring/early summer, while still immature and with masses of succulent green leaves, to eat as salad onions.

Intercropping

One of the advantages of early maturing shallots is the opportunity to intercrop and get two crops from the one piece of land in a season. Usually when gardeners talk about intercropping they mean growing a very quick maturing crop like radish, lettuce or spinach between much slower establishing and long-term crops like trench celery, peas, runner beans, Brussels sprouts and the like.

When you sow a couple of rows of peas for example in spring the space between the rows looks enormous in March to May. By early June the full flush of summer growth certainly fills the rows and makes full use of the land. Intercropping by sowing radish at the same time as the peas allows a quick harvest of radish for salads before pea foliage blocks out all the light. (See page 13.)

In the case of shallots the principal is put in reverse: as their leaves show the first sign of yellowing, winter greens including 'January Queen' cabbage are planted among them. The dying shallot leaves gives the greens some protection from hot sun as they become established and once the greens need more space the shallots are ready for lifting and harvesting. This gives two crops not only from one plot but also from one lot of digging! Where you want to keep all the onion-type crops together for the year then plant leeks among the shallots.

Leeks

One of the hardiest of all winter green vegetables, leeks can be left in the open garden to dig as required. In the past leeks were quite widely spaced, planted quite deep and even earthed up a little to produce large thick stems with a long white blanched section of stem.

Fun to grow perhaps but not the easiest of things to handle in the kitchen and

Note small shallot sets planted foreground produce less in number but larger bulbs. Large sets in the next row produce more but each one is somewhat smaller at harvest time.

earthing up can allow soil to get into the blanched section and make for unpleasantly gritty vegetables. Some of the very latest leek varieties have been bred to supermarkets specification of smaller easily-managed stems which are self blanching. They can be sown where you want them to grow and just thinned out to produce plenty of very palatable stems.

The more commonly practised method of leek growing is to sow indoors in January/February and outdoors March/April to provide seedlings to transplant into the cropping site from April to July. The earlier the sowing the longer each leek is likely to grow. Growing to modern prepack size, varieties like 'King Richard' and 'Splendid' can be sown direct in the cropping site March to early May.

Seedlings to transplant should be of pencil thickness and the leaf tips can be shortened by up to one-third before dropping into holes made with a dibber 5–6 in (12–15 cm) deep. Just fill the holes with water after planting; there is no need to either back-fill with soil or firm. Maximum yield will be achieved by spacing the plants 12 in (30 cm) by 6 in (15 cm) – wider spacing for larger stems and closer spacing for smaller stems.

Note the great mass of root on leeks which helps to improve heavy soil.

Leeks are gross feeders and heavy watering in dry weather and several dressings of fertilizer are beneficial through summer and early autumn. The fertilizer can be either powder, hoed into the surface before watering, or dilute liquid type, but whichever is used make sure it has a high proportion of nitrogen.

Although the leeks can be left in the growing site until wanted, if you need to clear the soil ready for the next season's crop they can be lifted and just heeled in. That is, the roots and lower part of the stem buried in damp soil or peat. It is quite a good idea to have a few lifted and kept protected in damp peat in the winter, then if very hard frosts makes the soil too hard to dig, leeks will still be available to cook.

When lifting this crop leave as much root as possible behind in the soil. The great mass of vigorous white roots does much to break up clay soil and leave it in better condition for successive crops.

Indicator crop

Where seeds like leek and onion take time to germinate it is a good tip to mix in a *little* radish seed. This germinates very quickly and acts as a guide-line down the row to allow hoeing each side for weed control. The radish are pulled and eaten by the time the leeks or onions need all the space.

Onions

There can be no easier crop to grow than onions planted as sets. Almost regardless of soil type and condition these immature bulbs pushed gently or trowelled into the soil in early spring grow away quickly and produce fully grown bulbs by the autumn which will store well right round to the following early summer.

A little care in the preparation of the soil before planting, digging before Christmas and mixing in plenty of well-rotted compost as you dig, will give much improved growth and a very much heavier total yield of crop. When buying onion sets look for the smaller sizes; these are less likely to bolt, that is, form seed

Leeks are a good winter crop. Plant alongside early summer-maturing crops and then extra space will be available for leek development in the autumn.

heads prematurely, and because each one is lighter in weight you get more for your money. Where seed heads do form just snap them out as soon as you see them and use up the smaller, poor bulbs such plants produce first.

Sets have completely changed the method of onion growing and few gardeners now raise their main bulb crops from seed. Where cash is an important consideration, seed raising should not be ignored however because it remains the cheapest way to grow onions. Soil preparation is very important for spring, direct-sown seed however because fine soil and shallow drills $\frac{1}{2}$–$\frac{3}{4}$ in (12–18 mm) deep are required. Even in well-prepared seed beds they will take several weeks to grow and it will be found F_1 hybrid varieties germinate earlier and over a wider temperature range. While salad and pickling onions have to be sown in the cropping site because of the numbers required, the bulb onions can be raised from seed sown indoors. Late December early January sowing under glass is essential for exhibitors who need the longest possible growing season to build up prize-winning giants.

Even for ordinary home consumption indoor sowing is well worthwhile if you have the available window-sill, cold frame

Twist the wispy top from onion sets before planting 6–9 in (15–23 cm) apart with a trowel.

or greenhouse space. The earlier you sow the larger the bulbs are likely to be but, for kitchen use, February/March sowing is soon enough. The seed can either be sown in a seed pan and transplanted singly into small pots or a few seeds sown direct into the pots. The young seedlings are then planted out like sets 6–9 in (15–23 cm) apart in rows spread 12 in (28 cm) apart in the spring.

It is not essential to thin out the seedlings where several come up in each pot because if planted in a cluster they push one another apart to make space for each bulb. Maximum yield is likely where plant population is 8 per square ft. Another good way to raise onions is in peat blocks, once again several seeds are sown in each block and the complete block planted without thinning and without damaging root disturbance. (See page 43.)

When planting onion sets it is well worth either twisting or cutting off with scissors the wispy top left from leaf die-back. Where the strawy tip is left, both worms pulling down into holes and birds foraging for nesting material will pull them out and scatter along the row making it necessary to replant.

While the main crop bulb onions are sown late winter/early spring under glass and outdoors in spring, it is also possible to sow hardier varieties outside in the cropping site in September to overwinter under cloches. This rather old fashioned system has been overtaken by the 'winter growing' or 'Japanese' onions which are sown in August and are ready to harvest in June. These varieties including 'Express Yellow' are very hardy and continue to grow whenever the temperatures are above 40°F (4°C). Sowing dates are critical, early August in the north and cold districts, mid-August in the midlands and late August in the south of Britain. These varieties also prove most valuable for producing salad onions under cloches and in cold greenhouses through the winter. Remember to feed these winter-growing varieties in the winter; they are one of the few crops which respond to fertilizer applied at this time.

Sowings of salad onions can be made in August and from March to June to provide a steady supply of fresh young plants to pull. Small onions for pickling are either sown late, that is early summer, or pulled early when the ideal bite size has been achieved. When harvesting early just lift carefully with a fork and leave in the sun for the foliage to shrivel and the small bulbs to ripen. Onions grown for their bulbs should be left until the tops fall over naturally and start to yellow. Do *not* physically bend the tops over because this encourages neck rot diseases. If you want to speed up the ripening process for any reason just ease them out of the ground with a fork and again leave in the

Silver-skinned pickling onions, like 'Barletta' illustrated here, are lifted once the bulbs are a little larger than the desired size. They will shrink a little as they dry off in the sun.

sun to dry.

Once the tops have fallen and started to yellow it is as well to lift them because if left and exposed to heavy rain, new growth can be made and the bulbs split. This most commonly occurs with onions grown from sets. When the tops are straw dry the old outer skins can be removed and the onions stored in trays or tied in bunches in a cool place.

Varieties

The great array of onion varieties can be somewhat daunting to the first time vegetable gardener. Choice can be simplified by going for 'White Lisbon' for salads (some specialists seedsmen offer a winter hardy strain for autumn sowing; remember, though, most winter hardy varieties of vegetables have extra fibre to provide the hardiness and are therefore not quite so tasty compared to other varieties under summer conditions), a silver-skinned small onion for pickling, 'Sturon' or 'Stuttgart Giant' for sets, 'Hygro' F_1 for main crop bulb onions and 'Express Yellow' for August sowing.

Even easier is a good patch of 'White Lisbon', sown in the autumn, some pulled for salads and some left to produce bulbs for cooking. If some of the bulbs are left they will re-grow and split up like shallots to provide more spring salading 17 months after sowing. Don't leave them any longer because they will just run to seed!

Disease

There is one disease called white rot which can be a problem. Leaves on infected plants yellow and when lifted have white fluffy mould at the base of the plant. This disease survives in infected soil for many years and so, if possible, avoid planting in it. If you have infected soil I find raising seedlings in $3\frac{1}{2}$ in (9 cm) and even better 5 in (13 cm) pots of all-peat sterile compost and planting carefully so the base of the bulb doesn't come in contact with the garden soil, allows perfect disease-free crops to be grown.

Let the onion tops fall naturally before lifting with a fork and leaving in the sun to ripen completely.
The winter-growing Japanese onions benefit from additional fertilizer worked in around the plants in winter when the surface is not frozen.

Cookery

Shallots

The milder flavour of shallots is often preferred to onions, but they are mainly grown for pickling.

To prepare: pull apart from the bunch then remove the outer skin as for onions. For pickling, it is much easier and quicker if they are peeled after overnight brining.

To pickle: (see general notes page 123). Leave overnight in brine made from 2 oz (50 g) salt to each 1 pint ($\frac{1}{2}$ litre) cold water for each 1 lb (500 g) shallots. Drain, peel and cover with more brine. Place a plate on top to keep them immersed and leave for 24 hours if small, 36 hours if large. Drain well and add to boiling spiced vinegar. Bring back to boil and cook $\frac{1}{2}$ minute, pack in jars and cover with hot vinegar. Cover with lids. Ready to use after 1 month if high strength vinegar is used.

Leeks

Leeks are a useful winter vegetable which can be used in a variety of dishes. Add them to soups, stews and casseroles or serve them raw in winter salad.

To prepare: leeks can be gritty and need careful preparation. Trim off outer coarse leaves then cut off the top part just where the green leaves start to separate (reserve these leaves for flavouring stock). Cut half way through the leek lengthwise and open out. Rinse under running water to remove all soil. Cut into rings or leave whole.

To cook: cook in 1 in (2.5 cm) boiling, salted water until just tender – overcooking makes them soggy. Cook whole leeks 15 to 20 minutes, slices 5 to 10 minutes. Drain well in a colander then line the serving dish with 3 thicknesses of kitchen paper before adding leeks. Leave to drain 5 minutes before removing paper. Add a knob of butter or coat in cheese or parsley sauce.

Buttered Leeks: melt 1 oz (25 g) butter in a large saucepan or skillet for each 1 lb (500 g) leeks. Add finely-sliced leeks, cover and cook over a low heat for about 5 minutes, shaking the pan occasionally. Sprinkle with salt and black pepper before serving.

Microwave: place 1 lb (500 g) sliced leeks in a casserole with 2 tbsp (2 × 15 ml sp) water. Cover and cook 10 minutes.

To serve raw: chop prepared leeks and mix with shredded cabbage for a winter salad.

To store: store prepared leeks in a plastic bag in the bottom of the refrigerator for about 4 days.

To freeze: cut in large slices and blanch for 1 minute. Drain, dry and open freeze. Pack in freezer bags for up to 1 year.

Use cooked leeks in savoury flans or wrap slices of cooked ham around cooked leeks; top with cheese sauce and brown under a grill.

LEEK AND POTATO SOUP

Follow the Master Soup Recipe on page 66.

CREAMED LEEKS

For 4 portions

Metric		Imperial
6	leeks	6
4	medium-sized potatoes	4
4	rashers streaky bacon	4
83 g	packet full fat soft cheese	3 oz
25 g	butter	1 oz
	salt	
	black pepper	
25 g	Cheddar cheese	1 oz

1. Wash leeks thoroughly, trim off roots and any tough outside leaves; cut into rings. Peel and slice potatoes. Remove rind and bone from bacon; cut into long strips.
2. Cook leeks and potatoes together in boiling, salted water for 10 to 15 minutes, until tender. Drain well, then mash, using a fork or potato masher.
3. Add cream cheese and butter; mix together until well blended. Season to taste with salt and black pepper.
4. Turn mixture into a shallow, ovenproof dish. Arrange bacon strips on top in a lattice pattern. Grate the Cheddar cheese and sprinkle over; brown under a grill until bacon is crisp. Serve as a supper dish.

Onions

The gardener needs to keep up a supply of onions for the kitchen because savoury dishes are so dependent on their flavour. They are good eaten both raw and cooked and make useful accompaniments when pickled.

To prepare: cut off the outer skin and trim at both ends; wash then chop or cut into slices or rings.

To cut rings: hold the onion on its side; using a stainless sharp knife, cut thin or thick slices parallel with the base. Push out the slices to form rings.

To chop: the easiest way is to follow the chef's example and actually dice the onion. First cut slices, divide in half and place flat side down on board, cut lengthways then across. The finer the slices, the smaller the chop.

To cook: almost every method of cooking can be used for onions.

To boil: place prepared onions in boiling, salted water, cover and simmer until tender. Large onions, 1 hour; small onions, $\frac{1}{2}$ hour; chopped or sliced onions, 10 minutes. Onions may be par-boiled for half their cooking time before baking or roasting. For sauces, boil onions in a mixture of milk and water.

To bake: whole or sliced onions are baked in a covered casserole in the oven. They are often par-boiled, then stuffed and baked.

To roast: use medium-sized par-boiled onions to roast around a joint. Baste occasionally.

To fry: for many savoury dishes onions are first fried in fat until golden brown. This caramelizes the sugar in the onion and gives the dish a mellow flavour. When the strong flavour of onion is needed in the dish, the onion is fried gently to prevent browning. Onion rings are coated in either thin batter or milk then self-raising flour and deep fried until golden; drain well.

To sauté: place the onions with a little fat in a shallow saucepan with a tightly fitting lid. Cook over a low heat, shaking the pan occasionally until the onions are golden brown. Use this method to mix the onions with cooked ingredients when further cooking is not required.

Stir frying: onion is fried in oil, often with garlic to flavour the oil in Chinese cookery.

Microwave cooking: cook whole, quartered or sliced onions in a covered dish without added liquid. One lb (500 kg) of onions takes between 6 and 8 minutes.

To store: spread out on wire trays or hang up in nylon mesh bags. Alternatively, string them up with rope, tying in the long tops as you go. Cut onions can be stored wrapped in cling film at the bottom of the refrigerator.

To freeze: store prepared onions. Chopped onions do not need blanching; blanch sliced, floured onion rings in hot fat for 3 minutes and whole onions in boiling water for 4 minutes.

To pickle: pickle small onions as for shallots (above). For a quick-maturing pickle, choose large jars to fit the size of the onion rings then cut onion in thick slices and layer in jars, sprinkling each layer with moist dark brown sugar. Cover with spiced vinegar and store for 3 days before using. Keep for up to 3 weeks.

ONION SAUCE:

Fry a large chopped onion in 1 oz (25 g) butter until soft but not brown. Stir in 1 oz (25 g) plain flour, $\frac{1}{2}$ pint (250 ml) milk and some salt and pepper. Stir over a low heat until sauce thickens and boils. Cook gently for 5 minutes.

CREAM OF ONION SOUP

Follow the Master Soup Recipe on page 66.

STUFFED ONION DUMPLINGS

For 4 portions

Metric		Imperial
4	medium-sized onions	4
300 g	plain flour	11 oz
1 × 5 ml sp	dry mustard	1 tsp
	salt	
75 g	lard	2$\frac{1}{2}$ oz
75 g	margarine	2$\frac{1}{2}$ oz
100 g	Cheddar cheese	4 oz
198 g	small can tomatoes	7 oz
1	beef stock cube	1
	pepper	
1 × 15 ml sp	Worcestershire sauce	1 tbsp
2 × 5 ml sp	cornflour	2 tsp

1. Peel onions, keeping them whole. Cook in boiling, salted water for 30 minutes or until tender. Drain and leave until cold.
2. Place flour, mustard and 1 tsp (1 × 5 ml sp) of salt in a bowl. Add fats, cut into small pieces and rub in with the fingertips until mixture resembles fine breadcrumbs.

Add about 3 tbsp (3 × 15 ml sp) of water and mix with a fork to form a firm dough.
3. Turn out on to a floured board and knead lightly. Divide pastry into 4; roll out each piece and trim to a 6 in (15 cm) square. Prepare a moderate oven (190 deg C, 375 deg F, Gas Mark 5).
4. Grate cheese. Empty contents of can of tomatoes into a sieve over a measuring jug and gently squeeze with the back of a spoon. Place drained tomatoes in a small bowl with three-quarters of cheese; reserve the remainder for the topping. Make up juice from tomatoes to ½ pint (250 ml) with boiling water. Add beef stock cube, a shake of pepper and Worcestershire sauce; stir until the stock cube has dissolved.
5. Using a teaspoon, remove centres from onions; roughly chop centres and add to cheese mixture. Season with ½ tsp (1 × 2.5 ml sp) salt and a shake of pepper. Fill each onion cavity with cheese mixture and place 1 onion in centre of each pastry square.
6. Brush edges of pastry with water. Draw each corner of pastry square towards centre, then mould pastry around onion. Press joints of pastry firmly together and press each corner towards base of onion. Bend back points of pastry at top of onion; brush pastry with beaten egg or milk. Repeat with remaining onions and pastry squares.
7. Fill the top of each cavity with any remaining filling and the reserved grated cheese. Place dumplings on a baking sheet and bake in centre of oven for 30 minutes.
8. Place 2 tbsp (2 × 15 ml sp) of tomato stock with cornflour in a small saucepan; mix until smooth. Add remaining tomato stock and bring to boil, stirring; cook for 1 minute. Pour into a sauce boat and serve with onion dumplings.

ALE AND ONION SOUP

Brown ale gives richness to soup, and also combines well with cheese in a topping for wholewheat rolls. Add a couple of rolls to the soup to make a filling and wholesome main meal.

For 4 portions

Metric		Imperial
1 kg	*large onions*	*2 lb*
250 g	*carrots*	*½ lb*
50 g	*butter*	*2 oz*
275 ml	*can brown ale*	*9.68 fl oz*
2	*chicken extract cubes*	*2*
750 ml	*boiling water*	*1 pint*
2 × 5 ml sp	*salt*	*2 tsp*
	pepper	
100 g	*mature Cheddar cheese*	*4 oz*
1 × 15 ml sp	*cornflour*	*1 tbsp*
2	*small wholewheat rolls*	*2*

1. Peel and slice onions. Peel carrots and finely chop.
2. Melt butter in a large saucepan. Add onion and carrot, cover and cook over a low heat for about 10 minutes, shaking pan occasionally.
3. Measure 50 ml (2 fl oz) brown ale, and reserve. Dissolve chicken extract cubes in

boiling water, add to saucepan with remaining brown ale, salt and a good shake of pepper. Bring to boil, cover, and simmer for 20 minutes.
4. Finely grate cheese; place in a small saucepan with cornflour. Gradually stir in reserved ale. Place over a low heat, stirring occasionally, until melted.
5. Just before serving, prepare a hot grill. Cut rolls in half; spread hot cheese over. Place under grill for a few moments until golden and bubbling.
6. Pour soup into warmed tureen and float rolls on surface. Serve at once.

Above **Stuffed Onion Dumplings**
Below **Ale and Onion Soup**

Peas and Beans

Runner bean flower

Broad bean flower

Runner beans

Broad beans

Dwarf beans

All the many different types of peas and beans, grouped under the title legumes, are valuable vegetables for the home gardener, not just for the fresh food they provide but also for their soil-enriching capability. If you look closely at the roots when pulling up these crops you will see masses of little round nodules. These contain beneficial bacteria which are able to convert nitrogen in the air into nitrogenous plant foods. Their effect is to leave the soil with more plant food after the crop than before. While plant breeders are trying to introduce this useful bacterial combination to other plants, for the present it only occurs on legumes.

This soil-enriching quality also makes the peas and beans very useful in the rotation of crops. If possible, plant the nitrogeneous fertilizer-hungry cabbage, sprouts and other brassicas after the peas and beans to get full benefit from the plant food for free. When clearing the peas and beans I always try to snap the stems off at soil level to leave all those plant-food-full nodules in the soil.

Another useful feature of this group of vegetables is their good deep freezing quality. Fresh picked, young garden peas and broad beans freeze very well and there are now small seeded varieties of broad beans which can be grown to mix with peas for freezing. French beans too are another excellent deep freeze vegetable and the old gardening problem of too many peas or beans at any one time is really side-stepped by freezing the surplus.

Regular picking is important for peas and beans and once the pods start to ripen, harvesting every few days will give the best possible quality and the highest yield.

Support systems

Most of the peas and all of the climbing kinds of beans will need some system of support. You only need to look out from the train on to British backyards and allotments to see the variety of methods and ingenuity in constructing supports. For those with access to hedge cuttings and tree prunings, branches from elm, birch, hazel and hornbeam, take some beating for support.

Climbing beans are most easily supported by canes and the tip here is to remember just how high you can reach when putting them up and that, fully furnished with leaves and beans especially at the top, they create quite an obstruction to wind. If the beans are supported on a series of tripods or pyramid-shaped supports the wind can blow through, then if one pole or cane breaks it isn't the start of the whole row blowing over.

Wide mesh plastic netting and strings attached to a stout framework are other common means of bean support. It really does need strong, well-secured end posts if this method is used for a long row. A 2–3 ft (60–90 cm) high roll of wide mesh galvanized wire netting will give many years of service for pea support but this is usually too expensive for the taller beans.

There are a number of maypole-like and wigwam-shaped proprietary systems of bean supports which allow a neat group to be cropped in a small area. There is even a semi-circular one which can be fixed to a fence or post. Where the garden has to meet the many demands of a family it is worth growing climbing beans up a wigwam structure sufficiently big to let children play inside. They can also be used to provide an attractive and productive summer screen. Runner beans are best for this and different varieties can be chosen to give a mix of flower colour from white through pink to red.

Climbing beans grow well in the fertilized-peat-filled growing bags. The best way to support these is with soft fillis string. Tie a loop around the bag first and then take the other end up and fix above to an adjacent wall, fence or wooden superstructure. It is also possible to loop the string loosely around the stem at the base of each bean and then tie the other end to a support above; the beans soon climb up the strings. This is the system most commonly used to support climbing French beans grown in greenhouses for early and late crops.

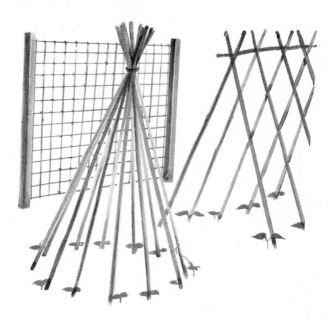

Above Bushy twigs used to support French beans. Can also be used for peas. *Below* A variety of supports for climbing beans.

Broad or Fava Beans

It might be something of an acquired taste but for me the fragrance of broad beans in flower on an early summer evening is a real pleasure. Fortunately this crop is coming back into favour, in part because it freezes so well but also because it is easy to grow and plant breeders have introduced several improvements in recent years.

There are three main types to look out for when buying seeds. First, the winter hardy 'Aquadulce' types which can be sown October/November and overwintered outside for early crops. In practice most broad beans will overwinter all right in the average winter conditions and in virtually all seasons with cloche protection but 'Aquadulce' is earlier and sets pods better.

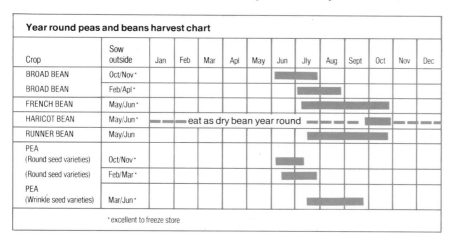

Year round peas and beans harvest chart														
Crop	Sow outside	Jan	Feb	Mar	Apl	May	Jun	Jly	Aug	Sept	Oct	Nov	Dec
BROAD BEAN	Oct/Nov*						▬▬						
BROAD BEAN	Feb/Apl*							▬▬					
FRENCH BEAN	May/Jun*							▬▬▬					
HARICOT BEAN	May/Jun*	▬ ▬	▬ eat as dry bean year round					▬ ▬	▬	▬	▬ ▬		
RUNNER BEAN	May/Jun							▬▬▬▬					
PEA (Round seed varieties)	Oct/Nov*						▬▬						
(Round seed varieties)	Feb/Mar*						▬▬						
PEA (Wrinkle seed varieties)	Mar/Jun*						▬▬▬						
* excellent to freeze store														

Next comes the long pod types which are best sown outside in early spring and in pots under glass late winter/early spring to plant out in March/April. Later cropping and much shorter podded are the 'Windsor' types for outdoor spring sowing and summer harvest.

Finally there are the smaller podded and small bean varieties like 'Ite' (formerly 'Beryl') and the winter hardy 'Polar'. The smaller broad bean seeds I find more attractive when cooked and served they are certainly better as a mixed vegetable with peas and sweetcorn. Watch out too for the seed colour on broad beans, both 'Windsor' and 'Longpod' types are available as white-seeded and green; the green-seeded again look more attractive when cooked, in my opinion.

The seeds of all are large enough and easy to sow separately where required to crop; space the rows 2 ft (60 cm) apart and the seeds 9–12 in (23–30 cm) apart down the row. They also grow well in peat pots; soak peat pots in water before filling with seed compost and then sow one seed per pot. They germinate quickly under glass and if the pots are kept damp the roots soon grow right through the peat, then the young seedlings can be planted out without either damage to roots or check to growth. Make sure the peat pot is completely covered with soil when planting; if the top edge sticks out the pots dry out.

Usually these beans do not need supporting although in very fertile soil and from early sowing some may get a little bit tall. If so then a few canes pushed in up the row and one or two lines of string each side of the beans is all they will need to hold them up.

If you are somewhat bemused by all the varieties, 'Express' is a good variety for early and heavy crops. You will have to search around for the small seeded types or go to specialist seed companies.

Always harvest broad beans while they are still young. Once the scar where bean was attached to pod turns black the beans will be very tough and starchy to taste. If you shell the broad beans under a bowl of warm water it will prevent the black staining of your fingers and thumbs.

Blackfly can be a problem pest but pinching the tops out of plants when beans have set controls them; otherwise spray with permethrin.

The extra-long podded variety 'Hylon' contains ten to eleven seeds per pod and speeds up the shelling.
Early crops will be picked from seed sown in pots under glass in late winter. Keep peat pots wet to encourage the roots to grow right through.

Heavy crops of dwarf French beans are achieved by watering once the flowers start to set.
Dwarf French beans are good plants to grow in pots.

French, Dwarf and Climbing Beans

This group of beans like it warm: sow too early and in cold soils and the germination and growth will be very poor. Much better to sow a little later and grow them fast for the biggest plants and heaviest yields. Sow from early May to mid-July. The early May to early June dates are needed if you plan to grow dried haricot beans to ripen fully and store dry, using such varieties as 'Purley King' and 'Chevrier Vert'. A good tip for cold springs is to keep the seeds in a warm, humid atmosphere for seven days before sowing. Given this treatment they will grow much better.

Fresh green or snap beans are the most popular and the best for most gardeners. Just sow the seeds 4 in (10 cm) apart in rows spaced 12–18 in (30–45 cm) apart (see page 17) and all you have to do is hoe to destroy weeds, water in dry weather *once the plants start to flower* and nothing else remains to be done save picking the succulent pods regularly. This regular picking and watering at the roots from flowering will considerably increase yield.

While the dwarf types like 'Tendergreen' and 'Loch Ness' are the most popular there are climbing types. These do really well raised in the warm in early spring and summer and then planted in greenhouses. There is even a very attractive purple-podded variety.

All types grow well in fertilized-peat-filled growing bags using the climbing varieties under glass if you have the space. A few climbing French beans in the greenhouse, alongside tomatoes, is one possibility: the beans do not have too dense foliage and by the time the tomatoes and other summer crops need all the space the French beans can be cleared, perhaps sowing another lot in July to mid-August for autumn cropping to late November, after the tomatoes are cleared.

The dwarf types on the other hand are suitable to grow in pots and bags to crop on window-sills, greenhouse staging and outside on warm balconies, terraces and patios. When growing these beans indoors syringe the foliage regularly to reduce the chance of red spider attack. This minute pest is hardly visible to the naked eye but multiplies rapidly in hot dry conditions, turning the leaves a pale green to bronze. Severe attacks will also have fine cobwebbing over the growing tips and leaves.

While all the legumes generate extra nitrogen, they do need feeding at the outset and an application of a good general vegetable fertilizer like growmore is advisable for all vegetables. In the case of French beans they will also respond to superphosphate fertilizer reasonably close to the seeds. Never apply fertilizer to the seed drill: emerging seed roots can be damaged by growing out into pure fertilizer. Always work it right into the soil so that it becomes incorporated and dissolved throughout the plant root spread. The exception with French beans is to mix some superphosphate into the soil 2 in (5 cm) below where the base of the seed drill will be.

Runner or Scarlet Beans

We are fortunate in Britain to have warm and humid climatic conditions in summer which suit this particular crop. Elsewhere the hot dry atmosphere reduces flower set and the pods develop so rapidly they go tough and stringy too quickly for culinary purposes.

They really can be the most productive and for me are one of the most delicious of all vegetables. There are several tips for good crops. The seed needs sowing when the soil is warm, 50°F (10°C), in late April under cloches and outdoors in May, even to late June, for September and October cropping. They require an open sunny site, plenty of moisture from flowering onwards when they also need liquid feeding weekly and regular picking. Picked often and while the pods are young not only gives tasty beans but also the heaviest crop.

It will be seen from the many support systems for climbing beans that a variety of plant spacing can be made. The

Runner beans grown up tripods.

heaviest yields are likely to come from a plant density of one per square ft and this can be achieved by sowing one seed every 6 in (15 cm) down two rows 2 ft (60 cm) apart. Where a double row of canes are used to support this double-sown row it is worth erecting the canes first and sowing the seeds at the base of each cane. To save money or canes you can space them 12 in (30 cm) apart and grow two plants per cane but it will reduce yield slightly. Once sown inside the double row of canes a 1–2 ft (30–60 cm) strip of polythene can be secured to the canes, burying the lower edge to hold it in place. This will help warm the soil and protect the young seedlings. Some gardeners soak runner bean seeds in water before sowing to speed germination but in practice this does more harm than good.

Where germination is a bit erratic down the row, young plants can be watered, lifted and transplanted to fill gaps. It is well worth planting a few extra seeds at the row ends to cater for this. Seed can also be sown early indoors and raised one per pot under glass to plant out in late May, early June. In my experience

One of the white-flowering and white-seeded runner beans grown in a tub. They grow equally well in fertilized-peat-filled growbags.

most people get better results from sowing direct into the crop site a little later.

It is not essential to provide supports; runner beans can also be grown pinched, which produces low bushy plants rather like dwarf French beans. This has the disadvantage that the pods rest on the soil, get splashed with mud and some may get eaten by slugs but, in spite of this, it is another very proven and worthwhile system of growing and requires no more than pinching out all the young twining tips once they get 15 in (37 cm) high. There is a low growing non-climbing variety called 'Hammonds Dwarf' and plant breeders are introducing other improved varieties which can be grown low without the need for repeated pinching out of runners.

Gardeners growing vegetables for exhibition go to some lengths digging out trenches in the soil 18–24 in (45–60 cm) wide and 12 in (30 cm) deep. They dig masses of manure and/or well-rotted compost into the base of the trench before refilling and leaving to settle before sowing. While this soil treatment does give heavy crops of very long pods, for average garden purposes we need do no more than dig in plenty of compost for the runner bean patch in the winter. The

newer varieties like 'Mergoles' (white seed and flower) and 'Pole Star' (red) have so little string that with the top and bottom of each young pod removed they can be cooked like French beans sliced but not 'strung'.

All the old favourites are delicious picked young but several of the very long-podded exhibition varieties produce unpalatable fibre in the pod quite quickly in hot dry weather. Where runner beans are grown for a quick decorative and productive screen then a mixture of red, pink and white-flowered varieties can be sown. A few seedsmen also still offer the bi-coloured runner bean called 'Painted Lady', known way back in the 1880s as 'Lancaster Runner'. Some gardeners find 'Painted Lady' and the pink-flowered 'Sunset' better setting under poor growing conditions.

Towards the end of the cropping season if the crop is too heavy and provides more than you need leave some of the older pods. These will ripen on the vine, even after frost has destroyed the leaves, and can be picked once the shell is brittle and shelled to provide free seeds for next year.

Slugs can be quite a troublesome pest eating the young shoots in spring but a sprinkling of slug pellets, preferably those based on methiocarb, will reduce if not eliminate this problem. Blackfly can also colonize flower stems and leaves, producing a black sticky deposit with heavy infestation. A good greenfly spray (if possible one which leaves the bees unharmed or alternatively sprayed late evening when the bees have stopped working) applied at the first sign of attack will prevent damage.

trenching and the organic matter provides a good moisture reservoir and regular watering and feeding once the pods start to set will compensate for the lack of trenching. Avoid watering and feeding prior to flowering unless the weather is very dry because this can give leaf and

Pink-flowered 'Sunset' and red-flowered 'Enorma' grown up a wide mesh, plastic netting support.

stem growth at the expense of flowers and pods.

A word or two on varieties even though every practised gardener will have their own strong views on the matter. For me the white-flowered varieties are invariably of good quality and do not go tough, 'fibrey' and stringy so quickly. Some of the

Runner beans grown up tripod supports and in a solid row. The tripods are less likely to be severely damaged in gales.

One of the more recent introductions: 'Selka', the half-way house between runner and climbing French beans. If picked young and sliced it tastes like runner beans but sets pods as easily as French beans.

Peas

Garden peas very often grow and crop extremely well in soil dug and cropped with vegetables for the first time. While many gardeners recommend potatoes as a first time ground-cleaning vegetable, as long as the land is reasonably free of perennial weeds, I like to include peas.

hardier because the peas have less sugar and more starch. This doesn't matter as long as the round-seeded early varieties are sown early and picked while very young. Hardy round-seeded types can also be sown in October, possibly cloche protected, to provide early picking. I find equally early crops – if not earlier – are obtained by raising the better quality

wrinkle-seeded early varieties in pots under glass in late winter/early spring and planting out in late March/early April.

Sow seed or plant to give something like eleven seedlings per square ft of garden. All but the leafless and semi-leafless varieties are best grown in rows and the taller the variety the wider the spacing between rows; 2–3 ft (60–90 cm) is usually sufficient space. Fan-shaped twiggy sticks pushed into both sides of each row will give a very neat support system and, once the main branches are pushed into the soil, the unwanted taller pieces can be pruned off level at the required height and, with other smaller branches, pushed in along the base to get the tendrils curling on and the plants growing strongly upward.

Where you are short of space and have no supports of any kind, try the leafless or semi-leafless varieties. They have far more tendrils in place of the leaves and crop equally well. The tendrils twine into one another and hold themselves up off the ground. I sow several rows across a square or rectangle, push a cane in at each corner and put one or at the most two strings around the sides. This is all the support they require.

Old gardening advice says peas do not grow well up pea sticks used a second time and this has proved the case for me. Where the sticks are strong enough to use again play safe and employ them to support hardy border flowers.

A great deal of plant breeding work is being undertaken on peas and several new varieties and types are now available. While there are a number of the traditional shelled types, 'Beagle' is early maturing and 'Kelvedon Wonder' is an early of good yield and quality. Mid-

The earliest crops of peas are grown by raising seeds five or six per 3½ in (9 cm) pot under glass and planting out under cloches.

Peas grown in a neat row with bushy branches pushed in on both sides to support them.

The semi-leafless pea 'Bikini' supported by no more than two strings around the outside of a block of plants.

There are early, mid-season and late-maturing varieties and it is worth selecting one of each or at least one early and one late variety to have a succession of pods to pick. The other thing to remember is the average temperature after the first sowing: where the weather is cold or cool, space the successional sowings wider apart. If warm weather succeeds the first sowing the second can be made in two weeks but if the weather is cool leave three or four weeks between them. This will space the harvesting over six weeks.

The early varieties of peas will be described on seed packets and in seed catalogues either as 'round' or wrinkle-seeded. The round-seeded varieties are

season to late types which are well proven include 'Early Onward' and 'Greenshaft'.

The French 'Mange Tout' type has also received the breeders attention and varieties with completely edible pods as well as peas are now widely sold. Really succulent is 'Sugar Snap' which grows a full 6 ft (1.8 m) tall and produces a pod at every leaf joint from 3 ft (90 cm) high. Heights are being reduced however and varieties like 'Edula' at 3 ft (90 cm) are convenient for the small garden; they are heavy cropping but the whole lot matures over a much shorter period. When you snap one of these pods in half the actual pod will be seen to be several millimetres thick just like a French bean and each one full of plump peas. They are equally tasty snapped in half to mix raw in salads as well as cooked whole.

The small seeded petit pois are also gaining in popularity and heavier yielding varieties are being introduced here. Small seeds also mean small pods however and while they are lovely to eat you need plenty of time to do the shelling. The very busy (or lazy!) cook will be much happier with the 'snap peas'.

If you sow earlies in early March under cloches the crop will be ready to pick late May. The second earlies like 'Greenshaft' will take 12 to 13 weeks (a week or two longer) and the main crop and late types 13 to 14 weeks to the full pod stage. Sow the seeds in 'V' shaped drills 1–1½ in (2.5–4 cm) deep. Dressing the seed with a fungicidal dust improves germination in cold wet soil.

While peas do not thrive in the heat of summer, light crops can be obtained by sowing the early varieties in June. Kept very well watered they provide lovely

What the small-seeded petit pois varieties lack in size they make up for by the number of pods.

'Edula' the pea with edible pods, quite as thick as French beans. It grows 2–3 ft (75–90 cm) high and can be eaten raw in salads or cooked.

young peas in the autumn. This crop is much more chancy under home garden conditions than the earlier sowings.

Small white maggots in the pods at shelling time are the larvae of pea moth. This pest is unlikely to be a problem with the early sowings but where it has occurred on main crop peas in the past, spray the plants in the evening after the bees have finished working, with fenitrothion seven to ten days after the start of flowering. This pest is the greatest problem with 'snap peas' where the pods are not opened before cooking! It is advisable to give these a preventive spray in areas where pea moth occurs.

Watch out too for mice when sowing peas outdoors, under cloches and in frames. They love seed peas and leave a telltale funnel-shaped hole where each pea was dug from the row. Trapping or putting down mice bait controls these vermin.

The snap pea 'Sugar Snap' requires 6–7 ft (3 m) high netting support, but makes up for this by producing many pods over several weeks.

Cookery

Beans

To cook:

Broad beans: pick these young and cook them whole in their pods, but do not attempt this if the pods are over 3 in (7.5 cm) long. If they are, then shell them and cook only the beans. Plunge the beans into a little boiling, salted water in a saucepan, cover with a lid, reduce heat and cook for about 10 minutes until the pods are tender. Drain and return to the pan with a knob of butter and toss to coat, or coat the beans with a savoury white sauce. This is particularly nice with bacon or fish. Add chopped parsley if you like. For shelled beans you will need about 1 lb (500 g) for each portion (don't waste the pods: if you haven't sprayed them, use them for making wine).

French beans: wash the beans and cut a small piece off each end with a sharp knife. Cook whole in boiling, salted water like broad beans, for about 7 minutes, or cut in chunks straight across the pod and cook for about 4 to 5 minutes.

Runner or Stick beans: cut a thin piece off the sides of each bean unless of a stringless variety, then cut diagonally into diamond shapes. Or cut down the length into strips.

Haricot beans: these are usually left on the plants to dry, but they can be harvested fresh. Cook the fresh or newly dried beans in stock or boiling, salted water for about 30 to 40 minutes. For beans that have been stored: bring the beans to boil, then leave to soak in the water for 1 hour before seasoning and serving hot or cold.

To store: Wash, drain and store in plastic bags in the refrigerator for up to 1 week.

To preserve:

Salting: this method works well for runner or French beans, though there is some loss of colour during storage. It is only worthwhile to preserve young, tender beans. Prepare them as for cooking; dry well. Use a large glass or stoneware jar (large glass jars can often be bought from sweet shops). 1 lb (500 g) cooking salt is required for each 3 lb (1.5 kg) beans. Use the special packets of kitchen salt, not table salt. Grated block salt can be used. Weigh salt carefully to avoid failures. Follow instructions in preserving section, page 122.

Freezing: use only tender, young, fresh beans. Remove strings, leave French beans whole or cut them and runner beans into chunks; remove pods from broad beans. Blanch and chill for 2 to 3 minutes depending on size (eg cut beans and broad beans, 2 minutes, whole beans, 3 minutes). Drain and pat dry, then either open freeze in a thin layer on metal trays and tip into plastic bags or boxes to store, or else pack into usable amounts in freezer bags. Store for up to 1 year.

Master Soup Recipe

SUMMER BEAN SOUP

A good way to use up mature beans, and it's equally delicious with other types of beans and vegetables. The chicken stock could be replaced with ham stock, if desired.

For 4 portions

Metric		Imperial
1	medium-sized onion	1
1	medium-sized potato	1
25 g	butter	1 oz
1 kg	broad beans	2 lb
1	chicken stock cube	1
1 × 15 ml sp	cornflour	1 tbsp
250 ml	milk	½ pint
	salt and pepper	
150 ml	carton soured cream, optional	5 fl oz

1. Peel and chop onion and potato, place in a saucepan, with butter, cover with a lid and cook slowly, shaking the pan occasionally until the onion is soft, but not browned.

2. Add beans and 4 cut-up pods, 1 pint (500 ml) water and the stock cube. Bring to boil, stirring, cover and simmer for 20 minutes.

3. Pour soup into liquidizer goblet and run machine for about 1 minute.

4. Rinse saucepan, place cornflour in pan and gradually blend in milk. Strain soup from liquidizer into saucepan and bring to the boil, stirring. Taste and add salt and pepper.

5. Just before serving, re-heat soup, remove from heat and stir in half the soured cream, if used. To serve: swirl remaining cream over surface of soup. Sprinkle soup with crispy bacon pieces, if desired.

BEAN AND SWEETCORN SALAD

At the start of the season when there's only a small quantity of each vegetable, mix them to serve as a salad.

For 4 portions

Metric		Imperial
250 g	runner beans	½ lb
2	cobs of sweetcorn or	2
200 g	can sweetcorn kernels	7 oz
	FRENCH DRESSING	
1 × 15 ml sp	wine or cider vinegar	1 tbsp
2 × 15 ml sp	vegetable oil	2 tbsp
1 × 5 ml sp	French mustard	1 tsp
	salt and pepper	

1. Wash, string and slice the beans. Cook in boiling, salted water until just tender, about 5 minutes; drain.

2. If using fresh sweetcorn, cut kernels off the cobs with a sharp knife and cook them in a little boiling, salted water for 2 minutes then drain. Drain canned sweetcorn thoroughly.

3. Place French dressing ingredients in a medium-sized basin. Add a generous shake each of salt and pepper, then whisk with a fork until thick. Just before serving, add beans and sweetcorn and stir gently to coat. Serve with cold meats, sausages or canned fish and buttered crispy bread rolls.

CRISPY MACKEREL SALAD

When lettuce gets boring, crisp up your appetite by using summer vegetables this way for a high tea salad.

For 4 portions

Metric		Imperial
1 kg	broad beans	2 lb
3 × 15 ml sp	French dressing	3 tbsp
4	large slices bread	4
50 g	butter	2 oz
2 × 15 ml sp	chopped parsley	2 tbsp
198 g	can mackerel steak	7 oz
	tomato	
	cucumber	

1. Shell beans and cook in boiling salted water until tender, about 10 minutes. Drain and place in a bowl with French dressing and a shake of garlic salt, if used; leave to cool.

2. Remove crusts from bread; cut bread into cubes and fry in butter and oil, mixed, until golden brown; stir in parsley.

3. Drain liquor from mackerel, remove skin and lightly flake fish. Arrange in a line down the centre of a serving dish. Arrange a row of beans at each side of the fish, then a row of crispy bread cubes.

4. Slice tomato and cucumber, arrange at each end of the dish.

OMELET BEAN FEAST

This Spanish-type omelet makes a quick hot or cold meal. It is also an interesting picnic food when served in wedges.

For 4 portions

Metric		Imperial
1	large onion	1
1	large potato	1
25 g	margarine	1 oz
250 g	runner beans	½ lb
4	eggs	4
	salt and pepper	
50 g	Cheddar cheese	2 oz

1. Peel and slice onion, peel potato, and cut into cubes. Melt margarine in an 8 in (20 cm) frying pan and cook onion and potato slowly, stirring occasionally until lightly browned, for about 10 minutes.

2. Prepare beans, cut into slices and cook in boiling, salted water until tender, about 5 minutes; drain, add to pan.

3. Beat eggs together with 4 tbsp (4 × 15 ml sp) water, 1 tsp (1 × 5 ml sp) salt and a shake of pepper. Pour into pan and cook slowly until just set. Meanwhile, prepare a moderate grill and grate cheese. Sprinkle cheese over omelet and place under grill until lightly browned. Serve, hot or cold, with a green salad or grilled tomatoes.

Peas

Fresh garden peas have a very special flavour which must be guarded with careful cooking. Some peas are grown to full maturity and are preserved by drying. Other varieties are cooked in their pods.

To prepare: remove pods if necessary. Use the pods to make soup. The pods of petits pois, the tiny peas, are tender and can be

cooked and eaten whole if young. Pull off the outer skin from the blossom end.

Mange Tout or Sugar Peas are eaten whole. They should be topped and tailed as for French beans.

Snap peas are cooked whole in their fleshy pods. Pull the string first from the blossom end then the stalk end.

To cook: boil peas in lightly-salted water for 15 to 20 minutes, depending on their maturity. Add a sprig of mint and a teaspoon of sugar, if desired.

Petit pois can be boiled or cooked in a covered pan in a little melted butter.

Microwave: cook in a covered serving dish without added water; stir occasionally. Cook $\frac{1}{2}$ lb (250 g) about 8 minutes.

Stir Frying: an ideal method for shelled peas or whole Mange Tout or Snap peas.

To serve raw: serve shelled peas in salads. Mange Tout and Snap peas can be sliced for salads.

To store: shelled peas keep in a closed container in the refrigerator for up to 2 days.

To freeze: blanch and cool shelled peas for 1 minute, peas in shells for 3 minutes then dry and open freeze. Pack in plastic boxes or bags.

PEA SOUP

Follow the Master Soup Recipe on page 66 using mature shelled peas or young pea pods. Strain the soup through a sieve after liquidizing. Some spinach can be added to improve the colour. Use ham stock if possible and garnish with crisply-fried bacon.

FRENCH STYLE PEAS

The fresh sweet flavour of peas is retained by cooking this way in the minimum of water

For 4 to 6 portions

Metric		Imperial
1 kg	*peas*	*2 lb*
5	*cos lettuce leaves*	*5*
6	*spring onions*	*6*
1 × 5 ml sp	*salt*	*1 tsp*

Top left **Mexican bean salad;** *bottom left* **Omelet Bean Feast;** *top right* **Crispy Mackerel Salad;** *bottom right* **Summer Bean Soup.**

1. Shell peas. Wash lettuce and onions. Trim onions so that just the bulbs remain.
2. Place lettuce in a saucepan, then peas, onions, 1 tbsp (3 × 15 ml sp) water and salt.
3. Bring to boil, cover and cook very slowly for 30 minutes, shaking pan occasionally. Add more water, if necessary, to prevent burning.
4. Pour into a warmed serving dish and serve immediately.

Roots

There can be no better method of harvesting and storing solar energy in summer for winter use than growing root vegetables. Seeds sown in spring develop rapidly in the warming summer days and store up food reserves in the root by early autumn, which provide us with a good natural food storage system.

While all the roots need to be mature for long, sound storage, the tastiest root vegetables will be those grown quickly and eaten young. For this reason it is worth making several sowings of carrot, beetroot, turnip, kohlrabi and planting both early and main crop varieties

of potatoes to get the longest possible period of pulling and lifting succulent, tender young roots. Parsnips are the exception to this rule and need to be mature before lifting and ideally lifted and left exposed to frost, to get the best culinary quality.

It should be remembered that turnip, swede and kohlrabi are all brassicas and need to be grouped with the 'greens' when working out where to sow and plant to achieve a rotation of different crop types in each patch of soil.

Storing root vegetables

Farmers and gardeners with a sizeable volume of root crops to store in the past would 'clamp' them. This involved heaping the vegetables on soil which was not likely to get flooded, covering first with straw – a good heat insulator – and then with a layer of soil to keep out frost and rain. The more severe the frost was likely to be the thicker the layers of straw and soil on the sloping sides of the heap. A tuft of straw was left at the top of cone-shaped heaps and a series of these straw chimneys were built into long clamps of triangular cross section. These chimneys allowed a little movement of air and the release of excess heat given off by a heap of stored root crops.

While few gardeners today will have the space or weight of crops to clamp their root vegetables, it is worth understanding the kind of atmosphere provided by the clamp to achieve long storage in good condition. Good storage comes from cool but frost-free temperatures, a dry, in the sense of free from rain, and yet damp atmosphere and some air movement.

Dry peat provides the most practical storage medium for home gardeners. Any kind of box, even a stout cardboard box lined with a large polythene bag, can be filled with a layer of peat, layer of roots, layer of peat etc until the box is filled. The peat always has sufficient moisture to keep root shrivelling to a minimum, it holds a great volume of air among the particles and, partly because of this, is a very good insulator against cold – and excessive heat.

While several of the root vegetables are hardy and survive frost out in the soil, lifting and storing in peat clears the soil to allow preparation for other crops and also provides a supply when the soil is frozen solid, which physically prevents lifting.

Another easy way to store root vegetables is to place a layer of peat on the soil then arrange a layer of roots and heap peat over them, repeating this several times. The peat is easily broken into, even in hard frost and once the roots are eaten the remaining peat can be dug into the soil. Storage materials other than peat include sawdust, composted bark and sand, although the latter will freeze solid if left exposed.

Where short term storage for just two months or so is all you need, thick-walled craft paper sacks are sufficient. It is better not to use polythene bags because condensation forms on the inside and tends to encourage rot. All storage bags should exclude light because light will turn root crops, like potatoes, green.

Where you have an abundance of tasty

The easy way to clamp root vegetables for winter storage. Layers of root vegetables are covered with dry peat to insulate from frost and a polythene cover used to keep the peat dry.

young roots, especially potatoes with skins which scrape, they can be stored in this condition. Lift and select only sound young tubers and place immediately in an airtight tin. Place the tin in a polythene bag to keep it clean and bury a foot or so deep. In these cool airtight conditions the young tubers retain the, as lifted, freshness for months. It is a good idea to store some roots lifted in summer for special meals like Christmas dinner.

Beetroot

The seeds of most varieties of beetroot come in clusters and the rough corky seed-carrying structure is bulky, making the seed packets appear very well filled. Once the packets are opened it will be seen there are not as many clusters as seeds of other plants. Gardeners tend to sow the clusters as they would single seeds, however, and more than one packet is then needed for the average garden row. This is unnecessarily extravagant and makes another job thinning out the mass of seedlings which grow. It is better to space each seed cluster 4–6 in (10–15 cm) or so apart down the row and then one packet will be sufficient. Red beet seed packets sell in greater quantity than any other vegetable seed, no doubt due to the misunderstanding over the clusters. If you want to sow red beetroot seed in just the same way as other row vegetables then look for 'Monodet', it has just one seed per cluster and produces globe-shaped roots.

Care should be taken when selecting beetroot varieties because there are significant differences between the various kinds. The most popular globe beets come in 'early' and ordinary types. If you are sowing before mid-April or in cold soil be sure to choose the early ones, for example 'Avonearly' and 'Bolthardy'. The ordinary varieties like 'Detroit' and 'Globe' will run prematurely to seed rather than form good roots if sown too early.

Several varieties, including 'Cylindra' and 'Formanova' have quite long cylindrical-shaped roots which are fine if you want circular slices of equal sizes to serve. Varieties with long extended and inverted cone-shaped roots, including 'Cheltenham Greentop', 'Long Blood Red' and 'Cheltenham Mono' (which has one seed per cluster) produce the heaviest yields. These large roots store well but they are rather bulky for the modern small garden and most saucepans!

There are two eye-catching beetroot varieties which are only different from the traditional globe beet in their root colour. Beet 'Albina Vereduna' has bright white roots (just the thing if you want to avoid the staining red juice of ordinary varieties) and 'Burpees Golden' has a golden orange skin and yellow flesh. Both have the added advantage that their leaves can be picked and eaten like spinach. Don't be in too much of a hurry to pick the leaves because this will reduce the plant vigour and prevent good root development. Once the roots have developed, however, there is no harm in using the younger leaves before pulling and harvesting the roots.

Bolthardy beet raised indoors in pots and planted out in April for . . .
. . . early June pulling. Note the cluster of seedlings push apart as the roots develop and seeds sown between the plantings are growing to fill space once the early roots are pulled.

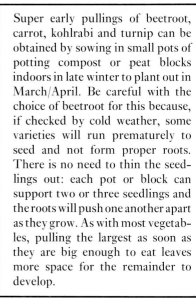

Super early pullings of beetroot, carrot, kohlrabi and turnip can be obtained by sowing in small pots of potting compost or peat blocks indoors in late winter to plant out in March/April. Be careful with the choice of beetroot for this because, if checked by cold weather, some varieties will run prematurely to seed and not form proper roots. There is no need to thin the seedlings out: each pot or block can support two or three seedlings and the roots will push one another apart as they grow. As with most vegetables, pulling the largest as soon as they are big enough to eat leaves more space for the remainder to develop.

Under the heading 'Leaf Beet' you will also find varieties grown only for their leaves, not for the root. 'Perpetual Spinach Beet' can be sown in the spring and summer to produce a steady supply of spinach-like leaves. Seakale beet, also called 'Swiss Chard', has a very attractive green leaf and bright white stem. The leaf can be eaten as spinach and the younger leaf stems cooked and eaten as you would seakale. Prettiest of all is 'Rhubarb Chard', a seakale beet with brilliant crimson stems and dark foliage. This is a good vegetable to grow in the flower garden, being both attractive and good to eat.

All the leaf beets can be sown from April to July and the seakale beets are

The crimson-stemmed variety of Swiss chard is an attractive flower border plant, useful in flower arrangements as well as a cooked vegetable.

quite hardy. June/July sowings will provide leaf and stems to harvest well into January in all but the most cold and exposed gardens.

Growing beetroot

Once you've sorted out exactly which one to grow the rest is quite easy. Sow in rows 12 in (30 cm) apart and thin the seedlings to about 6 in (15 cm) apart in well-cultivated soil. If the seedlings are thicker in the row then pull some roots to cook when they are only partly developed at $1\frac{1}{2}$ in (3–4 cm) diameter. These young roots are especially good to eat. Very early roots can be grown by sowing a cluster of seed in a small pot and raising the seedlings under glass. Plant these out without thinning about 12 in (30 cm) apart down the row. A few more seeds can be sown between each planted pot of seedlings to give a succession of roots. Once the early sowing has produced sizeable roots these can be pulled and the later sowing develops to fill the space.

The beets thrive in hot sunny positions and even quite light sandy soils but, for good root development, avoid shady sites. Seeds can be sown from early spring through to July, long beet requires spring sowing to produce their full-sized roots.

Roots for storage are best pulled in October and the leaves screwed off just above the top of each root. Old gardeners often recommend a pinch of salt along the row for good beet; the reason for this is the beets' response to sodium. This is more effectively applied in the form nitrate of soda which provides quick-acting nitrogen fertilizer as well. In general the beets respond well to quite heavy general fertilizer application in line with potatoes, at 4 oz per square yard. Pests and diseases are unlikely to be a problem with beet crops.

Attractive leaf colour on the red beets, as well as the bright white or crimson stems of 'Swiss Chard' really are good enough to be grown among flowers for decoration as well as for subsequent eating. The leaves also last well in water and are artistically used by flower arrangers. Even when sown in rows the leaves soon grow to touch and completely cover the ground to mask any sign of the rows.

Two different globe beets: one cylindrically-shaped root which is easier to slice and the golden beet grown for its roots and leaves.

Carrots and parsnips

Both carrot and parsnip roots store well and provide valuable vegetables through the winter, but while the flavour of parsnips improves with maturity and exposure to frost, all the carrots are tastiest pulled and eaten young. Parsnip seed can quickly lose its ability to germinate well and it is advisable to sow new seed each year or be very careful with seed storage from one year to the next. All vegetable seeds store best in dry, cool conditions and for every 1% increase in moisture within the seed over 5%, the storage life halves. Every 9°F (5°C) rise in temperature over 32°F (0°C) also halves the germination life and the temperature and humidity effects are cumulative. So storage in warm, damp conditions really destroys the life in seeds.

Where there is more seed in the packet than you need in a year the surplus left in the packet is best stored in an airtight tin or jar kept dry with silica gel and kept in a cool place. Seeds in foil packets have usually been super dried before packing and will hold their germination for three years unopened. Once opened the seed life is the same as that of seed sold loose in the packet.

Even where old seed, for example carrot, does germinate all right it is likely to give a lower yield than new season

One of the small globe-shaped carrot varieties suitable for growbags and early crops, but difficult to peel.

seeds of the same variety. The best practical advice is to store seeds in an airtight tin in the cool and endeavour to use up all kinds in two seasons and certainly three.

Carrots

There are very many different varieties which are usually grouped under eight headings according to root shape. Placed in order of quality, 'Berlicum' types come first, followed by 'Nantes' and the early 'Amsterdam Forcing'. The 'Chantenay' and 'Autumn King' types are likely to give heavy yields of big roots which store well. There are small globe-shaped roots for cooking whole and the very long tapering roots of varieties like 'St Valery' grown by exhibitors.

Recently introduced F_1 hybrid varieties especially in the 'Nantes' group will cost more for the seed but give very high quality roots which grow vigorously and with great uniformity. The roots are so succulent they need to be lifted carefully with a fork to avoid snapping them in half.

You may get away with sowing in

Five different varieties of carrot with different root shape. The 'finger' or 'Nantes' Type (second left) is an F_1 hybrid. The seed may cost more but grown quickly, can be pulled early and is of superb quality.

Parsnips are best lifted before they make a lot of re-growth in the early spring.

September and over-wintering under cloches but for the earliest crops sow a few seeds in pots or peat blocks indoors January/February and plant out March/April. The more accepted outdoor sowing dates are late March to July. Sow in shallow drills, spacing the seed to give seedlings about 1 in (2.5 cm) apart and space the rows 9–12 in (22–30 cm). The wider spacing produces the large roots for long winter storage.

Sowing thinly eliminates the need to thin which reduces the chance of carrot fly attack. The carrot fly homes-in on the smell released when carrot leaves are crushed. Sowing late, late May to early June, reduces the chance of carrot fly laying eggs against the seedlings and lifting in late August reduces the damage caused by carrot fly larvae eating into the roots. Dusting down the seed rows with diazinon soil insecticide is advisable for the main spring sowing where carrot fly is a problem.

Sticky leaves and white flecks on the leaves are signs of willow carrot aphis, any greenfly spray will kill this pest. Select one based on dimethoate for the best control if you can allow the necessary seven days between spraying and harvesting.

Carrots grow best in a neutral to slightly chalky soil. The roots tend to split if the soil is allowed to dry and is then given a good soaking, either by rain or hand watering. See that the soil is kept quite damp to avoid cracking and splitting.

Gardeners who wish to grow extra long roots of carrot and parsnip for exhibition make large inverted cone-shaped holes in the soil with a crowbar. These holes are filled with potting compost or finely sieved soil and a few seeds are sown over each hole. The seedlings are eventually thinned to one to produce a long large specimen root from each hole.

Parsnips

Many gardeners still sow parsnips very early and recommend early sowing to produce large roots. It is much more practical to sow in March/April and even early May, however, when the soil is warm and germination is quick. Sown a little later and the seedlings left a little closer, they produce smaller roots which are much easier to handle in the kitchen.

Two varieties which characteristically produce smaller roots are 'Avonresister' (bulbous shape) and 'White Gem' (wedge-shaped), both are resistant to the root disease canker which marks the roots a nasty brown and causes premature soft roots. Incidentally, later sowing reduces canker but manure-rich soils are more likely to encourage it.

Space the rows 12–15 in (30–38 cm) apart and thin the seedlings to stand 3–4 in (7–10 cm) apart down the row. If you have plenty of space and want the larger roots which are easier to peel and less root is wasted in the peeling, then space the rows 15–18 in (38–45 cm) apart and thin the seedlings eventually to 6–8 in (15–20 cm) apart.

Apart from routine hoeing to control weeds (see page 51), watering in very dry weather to prevent splitting and a general fertilizer worked into the soil in spring, no special treatment is required. Roots can be left in the soil all winter and lifting a few in November and leaving them on the surface exposed to frost improves their taste. It is worth lifting some, exposing to frost and then storing in peat to use when very hard frost and snow prevents lifting. Roots should also be lifted and stored in peat before excessive re-growth is made in spring. Usually it is necessary to lift in early spring anyway to prepare the soil for the new season's crops.

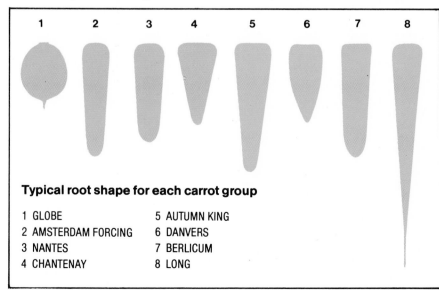

Typical root shape for each carrot group

1 GLOBE	5 AUTUMN KING
2 AMSTERDAM FORCING	6 DANVERS
3 NANTES	7 BERLICUM
4 CHANTENAY	8 LONG

Potatoes and Jerusalem Artichokes

It takes space to produce quantities of these two vegetable tubers, the more so for Jerusalem artichokes, which are members of the sunflower family and grow 6–8 ft (2–2.5 m) high. Both have their place, however, even in the smallest garden and if you like to eat either or both there are ways to accomodate them.

Potatoes are often referred to as a good ground-clearing crop and this is the case for several reasons. First, we have to dig the soil well before planting and if plenty of well-rotted garden compost, manure and/or peat is mixed in it does nothing but good for potatoes. They are a quick and strong-growing crop and the mass of foliage smothers weeds which survive the

repeated cultivation as the rows are earthed up. If potatoes are being planted as a temporary space filler and ground cleaning exercise, select one of the so called aggressive growers: 'Maris Bard', 'Wilja', 'Desiree' and 'Majestic'. It is a good tip to remember to plant the strong-growing types on poor and light, dry soils: the more vigorous and extensive root system helps provide extra moisture for the plants and heavier crops.

Ground clearing apart, it is the very early new potatoes which provide such a treat and make this crop worthwhile to the small plot cultivator. The very quick-maturing early varieties are worth growing in pots, starting them off in the greenhouse if you have one. Just one or two pots will yield an acceptable crop for cooking. It is also worth growing a few plants in the garden because, lifted early,

Planting well-chitted seed potato tubers will give earlier and heavier yields.

Early lifting reduces the chance of damage by slugs and blight disease.

they leave space to plant winter greens, leeks, and to sow crops like Chinese cabbage, kohlrabi, turnip, Swiss chard, lettuce and leeks, to name but a few.

It is always worth getting the tubers to sprout before planting, whether early or later main crop, because it will give both earlier and heavier yields. The selected and certified disease-free tubers are stood, eyes facing upwards, in one layer in a shallow tray in a light but frost-free place in late winter and early spring. The temperature should not be too warm because this can delay shoot formation, what is correctly called chitting.

Once the tubers have sturdy dark green but short shoots they are ready to plant 4–5 in (10–12 cm) deep, 12–15 in (30–38 cm) apart in rows 24 in (60 cm) apart. Late March and early April is the usual time to plant early potatoes outside, a little later in very cold parts of the country. It may be necessary to cover the emerging shoots with cloches if they push through before the chance of frost has passed. Where late frosts are forecast a covering with newspapers overnight or good watering with cold water early in the morning after the frost, will reduce the chance of damage. Even where the foliage is burnt back by frost the plants will recover, although the crop will be smaller.

Alternatively plant one to two tubers in an 8–10 in (20–25 cm) diameter pot, half-filled with old potting compost or all-peat compost in late January-February. I say half-filled because once the plants are growing strongly the pot can be topped up, to have the same effect as earthing up. This practice of pulling soil from between the rows up round each plant ensures that

all the tubers are well covered and protected from sunlight which turn them green and inedible.

It is also well worth saving a few seed tubers to plant quite late in June to provide another crop of late maturing 'new potatoes'. One of the old tips for maintaining a lovely serving of new, scraped potatoes is to lift in good condition and place the tubers with unset skins in an airtight tin. The tin is enclosed in a polythene bag to keep it clean and buried deep in the soil. As long as you remember where it's buried the tin can be lifted as late as Christmas to provide as-lifted new potatoes.

Black polythene mulch is another possible aid to small plot potato growers. Here the chitted tubers are hardly planted, they just have soil around them and are covered with a strip of black polythene which is held down with soil on both edges. A slit is made above each tuber to allow the leaves to grow through. No earthing up is necessary and the weeds are smothered under the polythene. You can even lift the edge of the polythene, pick a few of the largest tubers and then rebury the edge, leaving the remainder to mature.

Finally a word on varieties. If you are growing for earliness then 'Maris Bard' is first choice, followed by 'Pentland Javelin' and 'Home Guard'. Go for quality when planting main crop varieties (after all if you only want yield it is cheaper to buy farm grown potatoes) and my choice is 'Maris Piper' and 'Desiree'. 'Maris Piper' has the advantage of very pretty purple and yellow flowers, but pull off and compost the small, green tomato-like seed pods from all varieties of potatoes; they are poisonous and if left on reduce the tuber yield.

The two main problems with potatoes are blight disease and slugs. Both prob-

The smoother-skinned Jerusalem artichoke 'Fuseau' and an example of the sunflower-like foliage . . .

Fertile soil will produce a heavy crop similar to potatoes.

lems are kept to a minimum, if not eliminated, by growing earlies and lifting early. Blight forms brown spots on the leaves which turn black; the fungus spores are washed down through the soil in rain to infect the tubers. Spraying the foliage with fungicide and cutting the diseased foliage off and composting if the crop is close to maturity, will prevent tuber infection.

Jerusalem Artichokes

Jerusalem artichokes have none of these problems and once planted it can prove very difficult to lift every single tuber once the crop is not wanted any more. Happily no plant will survive rep-

eated and continual beheading with the hoe and this treatment will eliminate any so-called selfsets.

This crop is best used as a temporary screen, growing to its full height in a matter of weeks. The tubers can be planted at any time from October to early April, although February is the accepted time. They thrive in full sun and partial shade and in many gardens are left year round to grow as they will, with tubers dug to eat each autumn. The crop is also used to provide pheasant cover in country districts.

If you want to space them properly then plant the tubers 15 in (38 cm) apart with 30 in (75 cm) between rows. The foliage can be used as a backing to large flower arrangements but cutting the leaves in this way will reduce the yield of tubers.

On good soil each root is likely to yield 4–5 lb of tubers and if you can find the smooth-skinned variety, 'Fuseau', it only grows half the height of other varieties and is much easier to peel.

Turnips, Swede and Kohlrabi

Root crops, kohlrabi, swedes and turnip are members of the brassica family and in the sense of crop rotation (avoiding planting the same type of crop in the same soil year after year see page 17), they should be grouped with all the greens. This is important to remember when dealing with a pest like cabbage root fly. This little creature lays its eggs alongside seedling brassicas and the small white maggots produced tunnel into the roots. If you want to deal with this by not growing the crop for a year or two, remember that radish, wallflower, stocks etc will also have to be omitted.

They are all best if grown quickly, pulled early and eaten young. In this condition they are very palatable but left to grow big the fibre content increases dramatically and the roots become very hot and strong flavoured.

Kohlrabi

A rather strange-looking plant, the swollen stem develops above ground and the leaves grow out around it. There are green, usually called white, and purple-coloured varieties. Seed can be sown

Grow kohlrabi fast and pull young for the tastiest roots.

Early June sowings of swede are less likely to be affected by mildew disease.

outside from March to early August in rows 12–15 in (30–38 cm) apart and the seedlings thinned to stand 4–6 in (10–15 cm) down the row.

They take about 12 weeks from sowing to first pulling when they are 2 in (5 cm) in diameter. They must be kept growing fast by watering in dry weather and either finding fertile soil or given liquid feeding at regular intervals. Commercial growers are now producing winter crops under glass virtually all year round and a vegetable which has always been popular on the Continent is increasing in popularity in Britain. It can be grown under frames and cold glass in the same way as early and late turnips.

Swede

When we see large fields full of big swedes in the rich red Devon soil it is tempting to think this an easy crop. In practice they need fertile soil and late sowing for the best garden crops and you need a good variety. Few vegetables come more hardy than the swede which will withstand frost and often improve in flavour with lower temperatures.

All brassicas will grow best in slightly alkaline soil and liming soil in winter to reduce acidity will also cut down the spread of club root for these crops. The variety 'Marian' has been bred to include resistance to both club root and mildew, useful additions to its other qualities

root however and young roots which have grown quickly are very palatable either cooked whole or diced. Early sowings can be made in cold greenhouses, under cloches and frames from February then they can be sown outside from late March to late July/early August. Given mild damp weather the golf ball-size roots of varieties like white 'Tokyo Cross' will be ready to pull in ten to 12 weeks. July sowings will produce mature roots to lift and store in November.

There are three main types: the all white roots; the golden-skinned and yellow-fleshed 'Golden Ball' and varieties with white roots and the top of the root flashed purple or green. Grown for roots the turnip seed should be sown in rows 12 in (30 cm) apart and the seedlings thinned to stand 4 in (10 cm) apart down the row.

Flea beetles can cause havoc among the small seedlings especially in hot weather and in the dry conditions under cloches and frames. This tiny black beetle which hops when the leaves are moved, eats countless neat, round holes in all brassica seedling leaves. They are quite easy to control by dusting with HCH (formerly called BHC) preferably early morning when the dust sticks to the dew-damp leaves.

which include attractive yellow flesh retained after cooking, good texture and good flavour.

Sow the seed late May early June in rows 15 in (38 cm) apart and thin the seedlings out to stand 6–9 in (15–23 cm) apart down the row. The wider spacing will give bigger roots which are easier to peel but, if grown too large, may well become an embarrassment in the kitchen.

Watering in dry weather will increase root size but excessive watering will produce size at the expense of flavour. Working in the standard 4 oz per square yard of growmore fertilizer before sowing should be sufficient for this crop.

Turnip

A patch of soil was always sown broadcast with turnip seed in September and just raked into the surface by old cottage gardeners. The perfectly hardy turnip seedlings withstand the worst of winter weather and provide a number of useful pickings of fresh turnip leaves to eat as greens in spring. When cooked these turnip greens are very similar to spinach; rich in iron they provide a welcome change from the other over-wintering brassicas before the spring cabbage are ready to cut. If the autumn weather is mild and some seedlings really grow away strongly some leaves can be picked eight to ten weeks from sowing.

Most gardeners grow turnip for the

September-sown turnips to overwinter as seedlings and produce early spring greens.

Three main colour-types of turnip; *left to right* gold, purple-topped and white.

Cookery

Beetroot

Beetroot is a more versatile vegetable than you might think. Try them hot with a complementary white sauce – it's ideal for white and golden beetroot.

To cook: twist off tops, cover with water, boil until tender. The tiny thinnings will take about ½ hour, larger golf-ball size beet up to 2 hours. Alternatively, cook in a pressure cooker at high (15 lb) pressure for one-third of the boiling time. If the oven is being used, either cook the beetroot in a covered casserole, or wrap them individually in foil, place in a roasting tin and bake for 1 to 2 hours. Take care when testing to avoid causing them to bleed. Do this by gently spearing a cocktail stick into the beetroot; if cooked there will be just a slight resistance. Rub off the skin then serve.

To preserve:
Freezing: choose tiny beetroot up to 2 in (5 cm) in size. Wash well then cook, skin and pack in usable amounts in freezer bags. To use, reheat in a sauce, or thaw, slice and cover with vinegar.
Pickling: slice peeled, cooked beetroot and layer in a jar. Cover with cold spiced vinegar then cover with a glass or plastic lid and store for up to 6 months. For longer keeping, dice the beetroot and pack loosely in bottling jars. Cover with boiling spiced vinegar and seal the jar. Add 1 tsp (1 × 5 ml sp) each of salt and sugar to each 1 pint (500 ml) of vinegar for added flavour.
Chutney: Add some cooked beetroot to an apple-based chutney 15 minutes before the end of cooking time.

Pamela Dotter advises
Pick the tender inside leaves of the beetroot and cook them like spinach, using only the water which sticks to the leaves after washing. Drain well in a strainer and press out the water, then return to the pan with a knob of butter, some salt and a generous grind of black pepper. These leaves will taste milder than spinach and they are rich in vitamins A, B and C.

RICH RED CASSEROLE

Try this with spare rib pork chops for beetroot fans.

For 4 portions

Metric		Imperial
500 g	minced beef	1 lb
	salt and pepper	
2	beef extract cubes	2
1	medium-sized onion	1
150 g	cooked beetroot	6 oz
	oil	
1	meat extract cube	1
125 ml	boiling water	¼ pint
125 ml	stout or red wine	¼ pint
1 × 15 ml sp	marmalade	1 tbsp
	plain flour	
1	large slice bread	1
	parsley	

1. Prepare a moderate oven (190 deg C, 375 deg F, Gas Mark 5).
2. Mix meat, salt, a good shake of pepper and one crumbled meat extract cube in a bowl. Divide the meat into 12 pieces, make each into a ball then flatten with floured fingers.
3. Peel onion; chop into large pieces. Peel beetroot, slice thickly; cut into quarters.
4. Heat 2 tbsp (2 × 15 ml sp) oil in a frying pan. Fry each piece of meat on both sides until browned. Place in a 2 pint (1 litre) casserole. Add onion to pan and fry about 5 minutes; add to casserole with the beetroot.
5. Crumble the remaining extract cube into boiling water; add stout or red wine. Chop the peel from the marmalade and add. Stir 2 tbsp (2 × 15 ml sp) flour into juices in pan. Add stock gradually, stirring well after each addition. Add 1 tsp (1 × 5 ml sp) salt and bring to boil, stirring. Pour into casserole, cover and cook in centre of oven for 45 minutes.
6. Toast bread and cut into triangles, arrange around edge of dish and snip parsley over surface. Serve with rice or new potatoes and carrots.

BEETROOT AND ORANGE RELISH

For cold meat meals, dark red beetroot makes an attractive relish. Omit the vinegar to make an interesting jam

Metric		Imperial
500 g	cooked beetroot	1 lb
1	large orange	1
1	large lemon	1
12	cloves	12
500 g	granulated sugar	1 lb
250 ml	malt vinegar	½ pint

1. Skin beetroot and cut into small cubes.
2. Scrub orange and lemon, pare the rinds using a potato peeler or a sharp knife, avoiding any white pith. Shred the rind finely then place in a large saucepan. Squeeze the juice from the orange and lemon, add to rind. Bring to boil; cover and simmer for 10 minutes.
3. Cut up the orange and lemon pith, place in another saucepan with the cloves and ¾ pint (375 ml) water. Bring to boil, cover and simmer for ½ hour. Strain through a nylon sieve into the saucepan with the rinds and press out the juice lightly. Add ¼ pint (125 ml) more water to the pith and bring to boil and repeat.
4. Add sugar and vinegar to rinds mixture; stir over a low heat until sugar has dissolved, then add the cubes of beetroot. Boil on full heat for 10 minutes, remove saucepan from the heat, place a little relish on a chilled saucer and leave until cold. Push the preserve with the finger; if is has a skin forming, preserve will set. Re-boil and re-test if necessary.
5. Ladle into small heated jars, cover with plastic, plastic-lined or double polythene tops. Serve with cold meats.

BEETROOT TARTARE

Use the same rich mayonnaise-based sauce that is served with fish to complement the flavour of beetroot.

For 4 portions

Metric		Imperial
6	gherkins	6
8	stuffed olives	8
2 × 5 ml sp	capers	2 tsp
2 × 5 ml sp	chopped parsley	2 tsp
3 × 15 ml sp	thick, mild	3 tbsp
	mayonnaise	
400 g	cooked white beetroot	¾ lb

1. Slice the gherkins and olives, chop the capers and place in a basin with the chopped parsley and mayonnaise.
2. Cut the beetroot into cubes and stir in. Serve with cold meats or fish.

Clockwise from left **Creamed Beetroot; Beetroot and Orange Relish; Rich Red Casserole; Beetroot Tartare.**

CREAMED BEETROOT

Use the beetroot thinnings for a hot vegetable to accompany roast and grilled meats. This is a spectacular way to use any kind of beetroot.

For 4 portions

Metric		Imperial
500 g	*beetroot*	*1 lb*
250 ml	*milk*	*½ pint*
1 × 2.5 ml sp	*sprig fresh thyme or*	*½ tsp*
	dried thyme	
	rind and juice of half	
	small lemon	
25 g	*butter*	*1 oz*
25 g	*plain flour*	*1 oz*
4 × 15 ml sp	*salad cream*	*4 tbsp*
	salt and pepper	

1. Cook the beetroot in simmering water until tender, about ½ hour. Drain and rub off the skins. Place the beetroot in a dish and keep warm.
2. Place milk and thyme in a saucepan, add the pared rind of lemon and bring to boil slowly. Remove from heat and leave to infuse ½ hour then strain into a jug.
3. Place butter, flour and strained milk into a saucepan and whisk until sauce boils. Cook 2 minutes then remove from the heat and whisk in the lemon juice, salad cream, salt and pepper to taste. Pour over the beetroot and serve with grilled meat.

Carrots

This useful vegetable stores well and is available all year for use as a vegetable dish, raw in salads, for use in stews, soups and braises and even in cakes and Christmas pudding.

To prepare: trim off the top and tapering root. Small young carrots do not need peeling, just wash under running water. Scrape larger carrots under running water. Old carrots need peeling thinly; use a potato peeler for speed. Cut into rings, sticks or quarters, depending on size.

To cook: boil in sufficient boiling, salted water to just cover for about 20 minutes, depending on size. Serve with a knob of butter and sprinkle with snipped fresh parsley. They can be mashed or made into a purée in a liquidizer and mixed with butter or soured cream.

Steam: carrots for 30 to 40 minutes, depending on size.

Pressure cook: sliced carrots for 3 to 4 minutes on high pressure.

Slow cook: finely-sliced carrots for at least 6 hours on low setting.

Microwave: in a covered serving dish with a knob of butter; ½ lb (250 g) cooks in about 10 minutes.

Stir fry: very finely-sliced pieces in hot oil.

To serve raw: grate and serve in salad or mix with shredded cabbage in coleslaw; cut into sticks and serve with savoury dips.

To store: when entertaining, prepare the carrots in advance and store in a plastic bag in the refrigerator. Slice or grate when required to preserve the vitamins.

To freeze: it is only worthwhile to store

young whole carrots. Wash and trim, blanch and cool for 5 minutes then rub off skins, dry and open freeze. Pack in bags for storage.

CREAM OF CARROT SOUP

Follow the Master Soup Recipe on page 66. Delicious with the added rind and juice of a large orange.

Parsnips

This root vegetable is available in winter when most other vegetables are scarce. It is sweet and can be used in many mixed vegetable dishes and casseroles. The end of the crop is useful for home made wine.

To prepare: wash well, remove the tapering end then cut out the top with the point of a knife. Peel thinly then cut into rings. If the centre core is woody, remove it by prising it away with the point of a knife.

To cook:

Boil: in salted water for 20 to 25 minutes, drain and mix in some butter or mash with butter and lots of pepper.

Roast: par-boiled parsnips around the meat with the potatoes.

Steam: for about 35 minutes, depending on maturity.

Pressure Cook: at high pressure for 3 to 4 minutes.

Microwave: in a covered serving dish with a knob of butter, 1 lb (500 g) takes about 10 minutes to cook.

Fry: parsnips cut into chips.

To store: keep in a ventilated vegetable basket until required.

CREAM OF PARSNIP SOUP

Follow the Master Soup Recipe on page 66. Season carefully and serve with a swirl of soured cream and a sprinkling of grated nutmeg.

Potatoes

This popular vegetable forms the basis of our diet. Because of the quantity eaten, potatoes are a valuable source of protein and vitamins, particularly the elusive vitamin C. New potatoes are a major source. Different varieties are best for cooking in specific ways. Those with a floury texture are best for baking in their skins and mashing. Choose a waxy potato for roasting and making chips.

To prepare: tiny new potatoes only need washing before cooking in their skins. Larger potatoes can be boiled in their skins and peeled afterwards or scraped before boiling. Old potatoes must be washed then peeled thinly and the eyes removed with the point of a knife. Cut into even-sized pieces.

To cook:

To boil: place new potatoes in boiling, salted water, cover and cook slowly for about 20 minutes until tender. Test with a fork. Add a sprig of mint, if desired. Drain and serve with a knob of butter and freshly-snipped parsley. Leave to cool slightly then peel, if desired. Maincrop 'old' potatoes can

be mashed with a fork, potato masher or electric whisk. Add a knob of butter, salt and pepper and some milk. Beat until creamy. For Duchess potatoes or potato borders, sieve potato before creaming, add beaten egg and pipe on to a greased baking sheet or over a savoury filling. Brush with egg and bake until golden.

To fry: fry par-boiled sliced potatoes in shallow fat until golden on each side. To make chips, cut potatoes into slices then in thin strips. Place in a bowl of water to rinse off the starch then drain and dry in a cloth. Fill a deep fat pan one-third full with oil, lard or cooking fat and heat to 370 deg F (188 deg C). Place a single layer in the frying basket and cook until soft but not brown. Remove from pan and shake on to kitchen paper. Repeat with remaining chips. Just before serving, re-heat oil, place all the chips in the frying basket and cook until golden brown. Drain on kitchen paper and sprinkle with salt. Game chips are cut into very thin slices with a potato peeler or electric slicer then soaked, dried and fried as for chips.

To roast: par-boil potatoes for 5 minutes, drain and shake pan to make potatoes floury. Place in hot fat around the meat or in a separate tin. Baste with fat, sprinkle with salt and cook until golden brown and crisp.

To bake: choose large potatoes, scrub and remove eyes then prick with a fork. Place on a baking sheet and cook in a moderate oven (190 deg C, 375 deg F, Gas Mark 5) for about 1 hour; test by squeezing between the fingers. Cut a cross in the top, squeeze open and top with a knob of butter or soured cream. Alternatively, scoop out potato and mash with a savoury filling such as cheese or canned meat or fish.

To pressure cook: cut into even-sized pieces, place on the trivet and cook at high (15 lb) pressure for about 7 minutes. Reduce pressure under cold water.

To microwave: scrub and prick as for baking. Place potatoes 1 in (2 cm) apart. Cook 1 potato about 6 minutes, 2 potatoes 8 minutes, 3 potatoes about 10 minutes, etc. Leave for about 5 minutes to continue cooking before serving.

To serve cold: make a potato salad by boiling new potatoes in their skins, peel and slice. Mix with mustard-flavoured French dressing and leave to cool. Coat with mayonnaise when cold.

To serve in main meat dishes: use mashed potato to top meat and fish pies, sliced in flans, pies and omelets. Use potato for thickening soups as in the Master Soup Recipe on page 66.

To store: in sacks covered with straw to omit the light (potatoes turn green if stored in the light and must be discarded as they are harmful).

To freeze: small new potatoes should be blanched until almost cooked then drained, dried and packed in freezer bags or open frozen and stored in freezer bags. For chips, blanch in hot fat, cool then open freeze and store in plastic boxes.

POTATO APPLE CAKE

For 5 or 6 portions

Metric		Imperial
	IRISH POTATO PASTRY	
500 g	potatoes	1 lb
25 g	butter	1 oz
1 × 5 ml sp	caster sugar	1 tsp
100 g	plain flour	4 oz
	FILLING	
500 g	cooking apples	1 lb
	granulated sugar	
25 g	butter	1 oz

1. Prepare a moderate oven (190 deg C, 375 deg F, Gas Mark 5). Grease a baking sheet.
2. Peel and cut potatoes; cook in boiling salted water until tender. Drain and dry over a low heat. Mash with a potato masher or fork, mix in 1 oz (25 g) butter, caster sugar and flour, a little at a time, beating well after each addition.
3. Turn out pastry on to floured board and knead until smooth. Cut pastry into 2 pieces, one slightly larger than the other. Roll out each piece to a round 7½ in and 9 in (18 cm and 22 cm) in diameter. Place smaller circle of pastry on baking sheet.
4. Peel and thinly slice apples. Arrange sliced apples on pastry ½ in (1 cm) in from edge. Sprinkle apples with 2 tbsp (2 × 15 ml sp) granulated sugar.
5. Brush edge of pastry with water and place remaining circle of pastry over apples. Seal edges together. Make a small slit in centre of pastry to enable steam to escape.
6. Bake in centre of oven for 35 to 40 minutes until cake is lightly browned.
7. Remove from oven and carefully cut out a circle from top of cake, using a sharp, pointed knife; place butter and 2 tbsp (2 × 15 ml sp) granulated sugar inside cake. Replace 'lid' and return to oven for 5 minutes to allow butter to melt. Place cake on a serving plate and sprinkle with sugar. Serve hot or cold.

Potato Apple Cake.

Jerusalem artichokes

Slimmers can use these root vegetables as a replacement for potatoes because they have no starch content. This makes them useful for diabetics. Cook and serve in a similar way to potatoes.

To prepare: scrub and peel thinly. They are quite wasteful because of their knobbly form. They discolour quickly and need to be placed in water with lemon juice added.

Boil in water with lemon juice and salt added for about 20 minutes. Drain and serve with melted butter or coated with parsley sauce.

Roast par-boiled artichokes around the joint as for potatoes.

Fry in a light batter and serve as a starter with tartare or cheese sauce.

To store: Cut off the tops and store in the ground until required.

ARTICHOKE SOUP

Follow the Master Soup Recipe on page 66. Use ham or bacon stock.

Turnips

Quick-growing, versatile turnips are well worth their growing and storage space. They are an essential ingredient of many cooked dishes, as well as providing a vegetable with about one-third the carbohydrate content of potatoes.

To cook: prepare the turnips by cutting off the green tops and, if they are young and tender, save them for cooking separately. Peel the roots thickly, cutting away the fibrous layer which is easy to see. If the turnips are large, cut them into pieces.

Steaming: young turnips of about 2 in (5 cm) diameter can be placed in a steamer and cooked over gently simmering water for about 20 minutes. This is the method to use when serving turnips as a vegetable starter with Hollandaise sauce.

Boiling: place the turnips – cut in quarters, if large – in a saucepan of boiling, salted water, just enough to cover them; cover with a lid and simmer for about 20 minutes. To serve, drain turnips in a sieve; return them to the saucepan, add a knob of butter, some chopped parsley, salt and pepper. Then toss turnips gently over a low heat to coat; add a squeeze of lemon juice to the turnips if serving them with a strongly-flavoured meat or fish dish.

Roasting: par-boil the turnips for 5 minutes in boiling, salted water. Drain them well and place around the meat in a roasting tin. Baste with fat, then cook for about 45 minutes, basting every 15 minutes.

Frying: to make turnip chips, cut up large turnips and fry them in deep fat as for potato chips.

To cook turnip tops: wash the leaves well and remove part of the stalk if it is at all coarse. Place in a saucepan with just the water that is on the leaves after washing. Cover with a lid and cook slowly until tender, about 10 minutes. Drain thoroughly through a strainer and lightly press with the back of a spoon. Melt a little butter in the saucepan, add some salt, freshly-ground

black pepper and a pinch of nutmeg. Add turnip tops; stir over a low heat. Place in a warmed serving dish and top with a knob of butter just before serving.

To store turnips:

Dry storage: store in a box of peat.

Freezing: tiny young turnips of golf ball size or less can be frozen whole. Peel and blanch for 3 minutes, then cool and open freeze. Store in a freezer bag for up to 1 year. Larger turnips are best either frozen as a purée to use as a base to soups, or cut into cubes and stored as part of a mixed vegetable soup or stew pack. Tiny 'Tokyo Cross' turnips can be packed whole. To make up soup/stew packs, aim for a mixture of turnips, carrots, swede and chunks of celery. Prepare and blanch each variety of vegetable separately for 2 minutes as they become available, then open freeze and pack in a plastic box for storage. Make up the mixed vegetables when they are all frozen.

CREAMY TURNIP SOUP

Follow the Master Soup Recipe on page 66. using 1 lb (500 g) turnips. Add some top of the milk, single cream or evaporated milk before serving for a rich soup. Use this method for soup for other root vegetables such as carrot, swede, Jerusalem artichokes and celeriac.

TOMATO-STUFFED TURNIPS

Serve these as a supper snack or as an accompaniment to sausages, hamburgers or fish for a main meal.

For 4 portions

Metric		Imperial
4	large turnips	4
4	small tomatoes	4
2	large slices bread	2
4 × 5 ml sp	chopped fresh herbs (or half the quantity of dried)	4 tsp
	salt and pepper	
50 g	Cheddar cheese	2 oz
4	rashers streaky bacon	4

1. Peel turnips and cook in boiling, salted water for 20 to 30 minutes until tender; test with a skewer.
2. Place tomatoes in a basin, cover with boiling water, leave 1 minute, then drain and remove the skins.
3. Remove crusts from bread, cut bread into small cubes, then add to tomatoes in basin with herbs and some salt and pepper.
4. Scoop out centre of each turnip, taking care not to break it, add scooped-out flesh to the mixture in basin and mash together with a fork. Press mixture into turnip shells and remainder on to a serving dish.
5. Cut cheese into 4 slices and place a piece on each turnip. Remove rind and bone from bacon; stretch rashers flat with the back of a knife.
6. Just before serving prepare a hot grill and place bacon and turnips on grill rack. Cook until bacon is brown on both sides and cheese has melted. Quickly roll each rasher and place one on each turnip; place on serving dish.

Clockwise from top left **Turnip Tops; Tomato-Stuffed Turnips; Buttered Turnips; Roast Turnips; Creamy Turnip Soup.**

Swede

This is a useful winter vegetable. Serve it on its own or add it to mixed root vegetable dishes and casseroles.

To prepare: cut off the top and root then peel thickly until the yellow part is evident. Cut into slices or dice.

To cook: boil in salted water for about 30 minutes then mash with butter and add pepper. Or place in a liquidizer goblet with butter or soured cream and a little of the cooking liquor. Liquidize until smooth and fluffy. For stews, casseroles and soups, fry with onions and other root vegetables before adding stock.

To pressure cook: place on the trivet and cook at high (15 lb) pressure for about 10 minutes.

To store: store whole in a cool dry shed.

BOMBAY SWEDE

For 6 portions

Metric		Imperial
25 g	desiccated coconut	1 oz
	boiling water	
1	large onion	1
1 kg	swede	2 lb
1	large cooking apple	1
1	small green pepper	1
25 g	butter	1 oz
2 × 15 ml sp	curry powder	2 tbsp
25 g	plain flour	1 oz
1	chicken stock cube	1
25 g	sultanas	1 oz
1 × 5 ml sp	salt	1 tsp
	pepper	
200 g	long grain rice	8 oz

1. Place coconut in a small bowl; add ¼ pint (125 ml) boiling water and stir.
2. Peel and finely chop onion. Scrub and peel swede, cut into 1 in (2 cm) cubes.

Peel, core and roughly chop apple. Cut pepper in halves lengthwise, discard seeds, core and white pith; cut into strips lengthwise.
3. Melt butter in a medium-sized saucepan. Add onion, apple and curry powder; fry for 4 minutes, stirring continuously. Add swede and flour and cook for a further 4 minutes.
4. Strain coconut through a sieve over a measuring jug, discard coconut. Make coconut 'milk' up to 1 pint (500 ml) with boiling water; crumble stock cube and add to measuring jug.
5. Add stock to pan, bring to boil, stirring. Stir in sultanas, green pepper, salt and a shake of pepper; cover and simmer for 30 to 35 minutes or until swede is tender.
6. Cook rice in a large saucepan of boiling, salted water for about 12 minutes. Test by pressing a grain between thumb and finger; drain in a sieve or colander and rinse with hot water.
7. Arrange rice on a warmed serving dish, pour swede over rice and serve piping hot.

Kohlrabi

This turnip-like vegetable is useful for serving both cooked and raw. Discard any roots over the size of a tennis ball.

To prepare: wash then cut off leaves, peel thickly, as for swede. Cut into chunks or strips.

To cook: boil in salted water until tender, about 30 minutes. Serve with melted butter and snipped parsley or mint or coat with cheese, parsley or tomato sauce. Liquidize with butter or soured cream. Alternatively, mash with butter.

Braised Kohlrabi: blanch for 5 minutes in boiling water, drain. Fry a little smoked bacon with chopped onion for 5 minutes, add kohlrabi and cover with stock. Cook in the oven or in a saucepan until kohlrabi is tender, about 1 hour. Use small, whole bulbs, if possible.

Pressure cook: sprinkle with salt and cook

at high (15 lb) pressure for 10 minutes.

To serve raw: grate coarsely and mix with French dressing.

To store: cut off the leaves and store in sand or peat.

To freeze: cut in strips and blanch for 2 minutes. Open freeze and store in freezer bags.

CRISPY VEGETABLE MEDLEY

Use any mixture of vegetables that is available. Broccoli, cauliflower and mushrooms can be included, too.

For 4 or 5 portions

Metric		Imperial
	tomato sauce	
	(see recipe on page 49)	
3	small parsnips	3
2	small carrots	2
2	small turnips	2
150 g	swede	6 oz
3	small potatoes	3
4	Jerusalem artichokes	4
3 × 15 ml sp	lemon juice	2 tbsp
3 × 15 ml sp	plain flour	3 tbsp
1 × 5 ml sp	pepper	¼ tsp
1 × 1.25 ml sp	salt	1 tsp
	BATTER	
100 g	self-raising flour	4 oz
1 × 5 ml sp	salt	1 tsp
1 × 5 ml sp	oil	1 tsp
	oil or lard for deep frying	

1. Peel vegetables. Place artichokes in a bowl of water, with lemon juice, to prevent discoloration. Cut parsnips and carrots into quarters; cut each turnip into 8; cut swede into 1 in (2 cm) cubes; cut potatoes into halves.
2. Place parsnips, carrots, turnips, swede and potatoes into a saucepan; cover with water and bring to boil. Add drained artichokes, cover and cook gently for 5 minutes, until vegetables are just tender. Drain in a colander.
3. Place 3 tbsp (3 × 15 ml sp) plain flour on a large plate; stir in salt and pepper.
4. Prepare a very cool oven (110 deg C, 225 deg F, Gas Mark ¼).
5. Make batter: measure ½ pint (250 ml) water. Place flour and salt in a basin. Make a 'well' in centre of flour; add half the measured water and 1 tsp (1 × 5 ml sp) oil. Beat until smooth; mix in remaining water. Heat a pan of oil or lard to (185 deg C, 370 deg F) or until small cube of day-old bread rises to the surface and browns in 1 minute. Roll about 6 pieces of vegetable in the seasoned flour, then dip in batter. Place frying basket in oil, add coated vegetables and fry for about 5 minutes, until golden brown and crisp. Drain on kitchen paper on a baking sheet, keep hot in oven. Repeat until all the vegetables are fried; place vegetables on a warmed serving dish.
6. Reheat tomato sauce and pour into a warmed sauce boat. Serve immediately, with Crispy Vegetable Medley.

Exotics

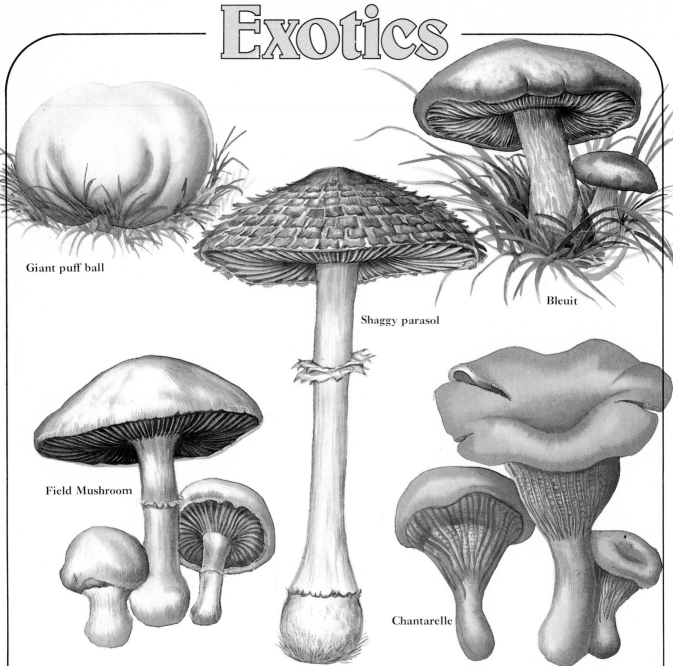

Giant puff ball

Shaggy parasol

Bleuit

Field Mushroom

Chantarelle

There are a number of less common vegetables which can be grown relatively easily in the small home garden and indoors. Some fruiting fungus may even appear without any effort on our part but only eat those you are absolutely sure are not poisonous. Even though I'm a born countryman natural caution restricts my eating to the true wild mushrooms.

Cultivated mushrooms can be home grown and aspects of the best cuisine can come from freshly-harvested home grown globe artichoke, asparagus and fennel. There is nothing to compare with home grown sweetcorn, snapped from the plant as the water comes to the boil, and eaten full of sugar sweet sap.

Even the humble spinach takes on a different guise when gathered young and fresh for immediate careful cooking. Care with sowing times, planting times, watering and soil preparation is all you need for success with these crops.

Should you have disappointing growth on these or any other vegetable just check back exactly what was done. The wrong sowing date and inadequate watering and feeding are the most common causes of failure. It is invaluable to label each sowing with the name of the vegetable, the date it was sown and I always note the source of supply. Experienced gardeners fold the empty seed packet up and wedge it in the top of a split stick to remind them what was sown. If you do this, the sowing date can be written on the packet and folded inwards to protect it from the rain. If the last fold is downwards with the glossy coloured side outwards, the seed packet will shed the rain and survive several months to harvest. Plastic labels written with lead or chinograph pencils will be much longer lasting and if you are gardening on a low budget quite acceptable labels can be made by cutting strips from the white plastic of empty washing-up liquid containers.

Mushrooms

Trying to make up your own mushroom compost and planting spawn is a very chancy business. It is much better in my view to buy one of the ready-spawned mushroom packs. Start out by thinking of the purchase as a good bag of horse manure for the garden, then all the mushrooms which come are a bonus.

Buy freshly-stocked bags: old packs which have been stored in hot shop conditions are less likely to crop well. Make your purchases well away from high summer temperatures, the mushrooms will crop best in a steady temperature around 50–60 deg F (10–14 deg C). They are no crop for the greenhouse in my view, save perhaps for an adequately heated greenhouse in winter.

Most packs come complete and just need a casing (a shallow covering of neutralized peat). This casing has the effect of trapping carbon dioxide released by the white fungus mycelium in the composting straw and encouraging the formation of fruiting heads – the mushrooms we eat.

The casing needs to be kept damp either by wicks or regular syringing over. The peat is damp enough if a small lump oozes water when picked up and squeezed between finger and thumb.

If there are holes left in the casing when mushrooms are gathered refill these with casing material or peat. Up to three separate flushes of crop are likely to come from each pack if it is kept in the dark, in a steady temperature and damp. Once cropping has finished and the cooler the temperature the longer this will take, the well-rotted compost can be dug into the vegetable plot. Commercial growers' spent mushroom compost is also an excellent soil improver. If used repeatedly over many years however it can add a fair quantity of lime – used to neutralize the peat casing – so be careful if your soil is neutral or tending to be chalky.

Sprouting seeds

Mushrooms might be tricky sometimes but sprouting seeds are childs' play if you follow the instructions. You need a large glass jar, a piece of muslin or clean cotton rag and some seeds. Put the measured amount of seeds in the jar, half fill with water, shake to wash the seeds well and then strain off the water through the muslin or cotton cloth. Where the cotton is close woven it is advisable to strain the first one or two washings off against your hand to let any particles of dirt wash out from the seeds.

Once the seeds are clean and nicely damp, but with most of the free water drained off, the jar is put in a warm place. The warmer within reason the faster the seeds sprout. Several times a day repeat the half filling with water and straining off to keep the seed constantly damp. Then in a matter of days you will have the sprouting seeds ready to eat.

Note wick to the left supplying moisture to keep the mushroom casing damp. Don't expect yields like this at every flush!

Alfalfa seeds left, Mung beans (bean sprouts) centre and Fenugreek right. Kept damp and sprouted in glass jars.

The first sprouting seed to achieve popularity was alfalfa, used in salads and sandwiches. This was followed by Mung beans always popular in Chinese dishes and then the Spicy Fenugreek. Seeds are a veritable store house of foods and vitamins and sprouting seeds retain all this goodness as well as providing succulent, tasty young growth. The only likelihood of failure comes from inadequate washing of seeds at the outset and letting the seeds actually stand in water in cool conditions which encourages wet roots. Frequent watering and straining, coupled with a warm atmosphere eliminates these problems. Also, be sure to wash the jars out well between batches.

Attractive feathery green foliage on Florence fennel with the leaf bases swelling nicely. A little soil can be drawn up around the base to improve blanching.

Fennel and globe artichoke

The common fennel is a herb where both the feathery leaves and the seeds are used for flavouring. If you wish to try growing your own seeds then sow early, that is March/April, to give a good long growing season and warm autumn weather for the seed to ripen. Grown for the leaves, seed can also be sown in May and early June.

More interest is being shown in the Florence fennel or finocchio which is grown for the swollen leaf bases used raw in salads and cooked as a separate vegetable. A warm sunny position, free draining but fertile soil is needed for the best crops. The ordinary varieties are sown in April but recent introductions like 'Sirio' can be sown as late as July because they are quick maturing and from the late sowing provide autumn crops.

It helps to blanch the base of these stems if a little soil is drawn up around them as they start to swell.

Globe artichokes are attractive and dramatic plants, certainly pretty enough to be planted in large flower borders. Large deeply-cut silver grey leaves and the flower heads, either open fresh and purple or dried and brown, are artistically used by flower arrangers.

If you have acquired the taste for globe artichoke bud scale bases, cooked and dipped in butter, then you will never see the purple, giant thistle-like flowers. The plants are not completely hardy and in severe weather like the British winter of 1962/3 they can be killed by frost.

Plants are propagated by cutting off side pieces – called suckers – in April and planting 24 in (60 cm) apart in well-cultivated soil. They need to be kept well watered if the weather turns dry until they are thoroughly established. A few globes will be produced in four or five months and the best crops are picked in the second and third year. As well as the vegetatively-propagated named varieties we also now have very good varieties

The large, purple, thistle-like flower of globe artichokes carried above the attractive and deeply-cut silver grey leaves.

which can be raised from seed like 'Grand Beurre' and 'Green Globe'. Seed is sown indoors in February and outside March/April; the seedlings are transplanted into the cropping site in summer and 18 months from sowing there will be plenty of globes to cut.

You can start cropping as soon as the first buds form and before any purpling of the bud scales can be seen. Cut them off, using secateurs, and take the big top 'king' globe first, leaving the smaller side globes to develop fully before cutting.

One to three plants should provide a sufficient crop for the average family and an open sunny position will suit them best. If they are allowed to dry out in summer the globes will be small, hard and rather wooden to eat. Winter protection of the base of each plant from frost by surrounding with dry grass, peat or similar free draining but insulating material is advisable in cold districts and in the event of very severe frost.

It is advisable to pull away the old dead leaves and dying stems before putting down the crown protecting materials. A good mulch with well-rotted manure or garden compost in early summer after hoeing in some general fertilizer will help retain the moisture and give much better growth.

Sweetcorn

The clear distinction between the vegetable sweetcorn – also called corn on the cob – and maize used for cattle food and corn flakes is the ratio of sugar to starch in the ripe grain. Maize is left on the field crops until fully ripe and converted to starch, while the vegetable corn is picked young, sappy and sugar sweet.

Plant breeders are directing their energies to increasing the sugar content, taste and yield of varieties for vegetable growing with great success. First we had the F_1 hybrids like 'John Innes Hybrid' and 'Kelvedon Glory', which gave a great increase in yield and quality. More recently the so called shrunken gene varieties have been introduced like 'Early Xtra Sweet' and these have to be grown on their own because if mixed with other varieties the super sweet quality is impaired.

All sweetcorn and especially the extra sweet ones, need to be sown in warm soil. Cold wet soils give poor germination and even those seeds which do grow seldom

Sweetcorn is best grown in a block as seen here at the top right of the photograph.

The female silks are brown here; when they turn black the cobs are usually ready to pick.

fully recover their vigour. Starch in seeds provides hardiness and resistance to cold so it will be appreciated that the very sweet kernel varieties are more susceptible to low soil temperature checks.

If you have not grown sweetcorn before it is advisable to choose one of the early maturing varieties like 'Earliking'. Sown a little later they will grow easily and quickly to mature in the late summer/early autumn warmth.

The best results come from sowing in peat blocks or small pots of seed compost under glass in late April/early May and planting out in late May. Alternatively sow under cloches where you want the plant to grow, spacing seeds two or three to each situation at 12–15 in (30–38 cm) down the rows, with rows 15–30 in (38–76 cm) apart. The wider spacing is for tall growing main crop varieties and the closer spacing for smaller early-maturing kinds.

While seeds can be sown outside unprotected there is the possibility of attack by fruit fly maggot and birds, quite apart from the possibility of poor germination in cold soils. Once seedlings are well established thin out to leave one plant at each spacing.

It is generally recommended that you plant sweetcorn in a block of several rows to help pollen distribution by wind from male flowers on the top of each plant to the lower female silks hanging from each immature cob. Satisfactory crops can be grown in a single row but it is helpful to tap plants on warm still days when pollen is falling to help the cross pollination.

Earthing up, pulling a little extra soil up around the base of each plant, also helps encourage extra root growth to increase growth and improve plant anchorage. Keep the plants well watered in dry weather and a top dressing of organic-based general fertilizer, hoed into the surface once or twice when plants are growing strongly, gives bigger cobs.

Cobs are usually ready to gather when the female silks have turned black. You can check by carefully peeling back some of the green husk and looking at the ripening kernels. I like to pick them while a white milky sap still oozes from the top grain when punctured by the thumbnail. If the cobs are still unripe just replace the husk and leave a little longer.

Picking is quite easy, with the cobs snapping cleanly away if you grasp them completely and press downwards. Yield per plant will depend on variety and richness of soil, the equivalent of one and a half per plant is a fair average, with more on the stronger varieties in a warm sunny position and fertile site.

Spinach

Warm weather and fertile soil will give spinach leaves to pick and cook in a matter of weeks. It is one of the fastest of all vegetables to grow but it is important to pick the right kind for each season.

The ordinary annual spinach can be sown from March to August; sowing a little seed every three to five weeks gives a succession of plants to pick over from May well into the winter. When the weather is hot and where the soil is poor the plants quickly change from producing the broad edible leaves and run up to form seed heads. For this reason gardeners often sow New Zealand or 'cut-and-come-again' spinach for summer cropping. It has a quite different, low and spreading habit and the plant tips rather than single leaves are picked to eat, but for spinach addicts this plant will crop right through the summer from one sowing.

Another alternative to annual spinach is the spinach or leaf beet, usually described on the packet as perpetual spinach. This is excellent for dry and poorer soils with the beet-like root producing plenty of leaves to gather and use just like ordinary spinach leaves. It is the easiest of the three different types to grow and the longest standing; it provides leaves to pick through the summer and right into the winter, being quite hardy. Sow per-

Perpetual spinach beet is an easy-to-grow and prolific vegetable.

petual spinach in April for summer use and July for late autumn and winter picking.

While large, well-developed leaves withstand winter weather they can become a little tough. Succulent new leaves can be grown on young plants under cold glass. Annual spinach, sown broadcast August/September and January/February on to a growbag in a cold greenhouse will grow well and produce

lovely crops in early winter and early spring. For these glasshouse crops choose one of the more recent hardy and fast-growing varieties with resistance to mildew disease, for example 'Jovita', 'Melody' and 'Sigmaleaf'.

Seed is sown in the garden 1 in (2.5 cm) deep in rows 10–15 ins (25–38 cm) apart and the seedlings thinned first to 3 ins (7 cm) and then to 6–9 ins (15–22 cm) apart. The second thinning provides seedlings large enough to eat. Avoid sowing in very hot weather and very wet soils because these conditions cause poor germination. All are frost hardy except New Zealand spinach which is best either sown under glass in pots in March/April to plant out late May/early June or sown where required to crop in May. This spreading New Zealand type (*Tetragona* 'Expansa') also needs more space and is planted 2 ft (60 cm) apart.

Some general fertilizer hoed into the surface once the seedlings are under way and plenty of water in dry weather is all this crop requires in return for masses of leaves.

You will see 'Broad-leaved Prickly' spinach listed in some catalogues and the word prickly refers to the unusual seed shape, not the leaves. These prickly-seeded varieties are very hardy and suited to late summer/early autumn sowing for winter harvest.

New Zealand spinach has smaller leaves and the young growing tips are picked regularly. They thrive in the heat of summer. The Swiss chard (top left) will survive well into the winter.

Left Spinach is a good quick crop to grow between slower-growing vegetables like leeks.

Harvesting needs a little care because if you pick the leaves too hard from young seedlings it checks growth and reduces the crop overall. This is especially the case with autumn-sown crops needed for winter supply. Always leave a good central group of young growth to sustain the plant and avoid allowing the outer leaves to become old and tough.

Under cold, wet conditions yellowish spots may form on the leaves, caused by mildew disease. Modern varieties are being bred with mildew resistance but should this occur it is usually easiest to strip plants out and re-sow elsewhere.

Asparagus

A luxury crop in every sense because it is slow to come into cropping, is only harvested from May to mid-June, is demanding in space with just over two plants per square yard but much sought-after for the unique taste of the tender young spears.

Success comes from a good start: the soil needs to be free draining, free of perennial weeds and improved by digging in plenty of well-rotted animal manure and/or garden compost. The one-year-old plants – called crowns – must be from selected stock, selected for both quality of the seed strain and quality of each crown. Once planted the crop is there for many years so the need for a good start really is essential.

You may see two and three-year-old planting crowns offered but there is nothing to be gained by planting these older and more expensive plants. It will be two years from planting in March/April before spears can be cut, regardless of crown age.

There is one possible short cut: seed sown under glass in January to March, grown one plant per pot and then planted out into the cropping site in June can be cut in just two years. The gain here comes from the absence of root damage at transplanting and this explains why older crowns offer no advantage over the younger plants.

Do not sow the seeds where you want the crop to grow; germination is variable and this method allows no selection of the stronger growing seedlings. Bare root crowns are planted 4–5 ins (10–12 cm) deep, 15–18 in (38–45 cm) apart down rows which are spaced 4–5 ft (120–150 cm) apart. Closer spacing than 2.25 crowns per square yard will not reduce yield but the spears will be more numerous and of poorer quality.

Some people recommend planting less deep and earthing up each winter like rows of potatoes. This is best suited to

Space out the roots of asparagus crowns when planting and avoid damaging the roots.

heavy, poorly-drained soil. Ridging up will give better quality spears but slightly lower yield.

Weed control can be quite difficult if perennial types are allowed to get established. Weedkillers like paraquat and glyphosate can be used once the asparagus stems have died down in the winter. However, for most home gardeners careful hoeing is the easiest way to keep the asparagus bed weedfree.

Cut the old yellowing foliage down to within 2 in (5 cm) of the surface soil in the autumn. This usually means just after the first frost but before the ripe berries on female plants fall. If the seeds are allowed to fall they can become a weed problem.

Once the crowns have grown for two summers in the cropping site, harvesting can begin. Cut spears for a four-week period to start with, extending to six in the fifth and future years. Always stop cutting by mid-June and allow the 'fern' to develop through the summer to build up the crowns for next year's crop.

The spears are cut when 4–6 in (10–15 cm) through the soil, just ease some of the soil away and carefully cut to the length required. Cut every two to three days to avoid having the tips of the spears opening up into foliage.

Work in some general fertilizer around the plants each spring and try to avoid cutting the foliage for flower arrangement because this will reduce future spear production.

Cut spears when 4–6 in (10–15 cm) through the surface.

Cookery

Mushrooms

A steady supply of home grown mushrooms increases your potential as a good cook. The appearance and flavour of many dishes can benefit from their addition. Pick tiny ones (called buttons) for garnish, but leave them to open slightly and grow to about 2 in (5 cm) across before using them in cooked dishes. They are called cup mushrooms at this size. When fully grown and flat, and the gills underneath have darkened, the mushrooms have the most flavour.

To prepare: trim off the ends of the stalks, then either wipe them with a damp cloth or wash gently in cold water; drain well, then pat dry with a tea-towel. Never peel mushrooms or you will lose much of the flavour. If the stalks are long, trim them level with the cap and chop them finely before adding to the dish. Or save them to use up in soup or as potted mushrooms.

To cook: cook very lightly, taking care not to overcook or they will toughen. Serve as quickly as possible after cooking. Select the size of mushrooms to suit the recipe. Button mushrooms are best in sauces, casseroles and for garnish. Choose the medium-sized cups for salads, stuffings, soups and stews or for dishes where chopped or sliced mushrooms are required. Open cups are ideal for stuffed mushroom recipes, or to fry with bacon.

To grill: brush prepared mushrooms with a little oil or melted butter and season with salt and pepper. Grill for 2 to 3 minutes on each side.

To fry: wipe mushrooms, trim off stalks level with the caps and season with salt and pepper. Place, rounded side downwards, in a little melted butter or bacon fat and fry gently for 2 to 3 minutes on each side.

To poach: cook gently in a little milk over a very low heat. For slimmers, use salted water with a squeeze of lemon juice added.

To bake: place mushrooms, rounded side downwards in a shallow ovenproof dish, dot with butter or brush with oil and sprinkle with salt and pepper. Cover with a lid or foil and bake in a moderate oven for 15 minutes.

To serve raw: mushrooms have quite a different flavour when served raw. They are very moist and tender and delicious in salads. Use button mushrooms or slice the cup variety finely. Turn them in a well-flavoured French dressing, or just lemon juice; leave in a cool place before serving.

To store: do not wash mushrooms before storing, just pile them into a plastic bag or container, seal, then store them at the bottom of the refrigerator for up to 3 days.

To preserve: a surplus of mushrooms can be preserved by drying, freezing and pickling. They can also be made into chutneys, sauces, or 'potted'.

Drying: thread the mushrooms on to strings to dry in a warm room until crisp, or on wire trays in a warm draught of air. A fan oven dries food very efficiently, or

use a microwave oven to dry the mushrooms in a few minutes. Turn occasionally during drying. Leave to cool, then pack in tightly-corked jars. To use, soak overnight, then boil in salted water until tender, or crumble the dry mushrooms into casseroles.

Freezing: see paragraph To prepare. When prepared, spread on metal trays and open-freeze for 1 hour. Pack into plastic boxes and store for up to 3 months. Alternatively, slice and cook them in a little butter with a squeeze of lemon juice and seasonings. Pack in useable amounts in plastic bags or containers, cool and freeze. Store for up to 6 months. To use: add frozen to casseroles and sauces.

MUSHROOMS PROVENÇALE

When mushrooms are plentiful, cook them this way and serve them hot or cold as an appetizing starter or special vegetable. Add some crisp croûtons to turn it into a lunch dish.

For 4 portions

Metric		Imperial
400 g	mushrooms	¾ lb
1	clove garlic, optional	1
	salt	
25 g	butter	1 oz
1 × 15 ml sp	oil	1 tbsp
	juice of half a lemon	
4 × 15 ml sp	chopped parsley	4 tbsp

1. Wash mushrooms; dry on kitchen paper and slice. Peel clove of garlic, if used, and place on a saucer with a little salt. Using a round-ended knife, rub salt against garlic to crush.
2. Heat butter and oil in a frying pan. Add garlic and fry over a low heat for 2 minutes. Add mushrooms, lemon juice and a generous shake of salt. Fry for 2 to 3 minutes, until mushrooms are just tender. Stir in parsley.
3. To serve: pour mushrooms on to a warmed serving plate.

CREAM OF MUSHROOM SOUP

Save the stalks or use the worst-looking mushrooms for soup. Open mushrooms give the best flavour but they colour the soup grey. Follow the Master Soup Recipe on page 66, using ½ lb (250 g) mushrooms instead of beans. Garnish with sliced mushrooms.

Sprouting seeds

Vitamin-rich salad sprouts are especially useful in winter when outdoor crops are scarce. Serve them raw in salads, on their own or with other salad ingredients and a French dressing. Mung beans are better known as bean sprouts which feature in many Chinese dishes. These and Spicy Fenugreek are the best sprouts to serve hot. Naturale Triticale, wheat and buckwheat can be added to bread dough.

To prepare: a light rinse under running water is all that is required.

To cook: bean sprouts and Spicy Fenugreek:

bring a large saucepan of water to boil, add sprouts all together, quickly return to boil then drain.

To stir-fry: heat a little oil in a wok or frying pan, fry a crushed clove of garlic then add the sprouts and fry quickly, for 1 minute stirring continuously.

To store: best to use them at once, but they will keep in a plastic bag in the bottom of the refrigerator for up to one day.

To freeze: blanch and cool quickly as for cooking; pack in freezer bags. To use, add frozen to cooked dishes or stir-fry from frozen.

CHINESE STYLE CHICKEN

Cook as part of a Chinese meal in just under 5 minutes, using your first crop of Chinese bean sprouts, grown from Mung beans. The spicy blend of flavours and crunchy bean sprouts are suited to most meals, so you can always vary the meat, but do remember to slice it extra thinly so that it will cook quickly.

For 4 portions

Metric		Imperial
2	chicken joints	2
1	medium-sized onion	1
1	clove garlic	1
1 × 5 ml sp	salt	1 tsp
2 × 15 ml sp	oil, for frying	2 tbsp
3 × 15 ml sp	soya sauce	3 tbsp
1 × 2.5 ml sp	ground ginger	½ tsp
2 × 5 ml sp	brown sugar	2 tsp
500 g	bean sprouts	1 lb

1. Remove skin and bones from chicken, cut meat into very thin slices. Peel and finely slice onion. Peel clove of garlic, place on a saucer with salt. Using a round-ended knife, rub salt against garlic to crush clove.
2. Heat oil in a large frying pan and add chicken, garlic, soya sauce, ginger and brown sugar. Mix together and fry for 2 minutes. Add bean sprouts and onion and fry for a further 2 minutes, stirring. Pour mixture into a large, warmed serving dish to serve with any other Chinese dishes.

Fennel

This is a popular Italian vegetable with a slight aniseed flavour. Use it raw in salads or braise the bulb. Use the feathery leaves in fish dishes.

To prepare: trim the roots at top and bottom, scrub well. Retain the stem and leaves for use in stock. Cut bulbs in halves for boiling and braising.

To cook: boil in a small amount of salted water for about 15 minutes or braise as for celery in a saucepan or a dish in a microwave oven. Serve with melted butter or grated cheese.

To serve raw: cut across into thin slices, mix with other salad ingredients, especially sharp apple, cucumber and carrots, and mix with French dressing. Serve slices for nibbles with drinks or with dips.

Globe Artichokes

The edible parts are at the base of the leaves and the heart underneath the hairy choke. The heart can be cooked on its own.
To prepare: cut off the stalk then trim the point of each leaf with scissors. Wash well then drain upside down. Rub cut surfaces with lemon juice to prevent discoloration. The choke can be removed before or after cooking. To remove, open out the top leaves then pull out the small inner leaves to expose the hairy choke. Scrape this out with a teaspoon. To use the heart only, remove all the leaves before the choke.
To cook: in a large saucepan of boiling salted water with 2 tbsp (2 × 15 ml sp) lemon juice added. Cook for 20 to 25 minutes without the choke, 40 to 45 minutes with the choke or until a leaf will pull out easily. Drain upside down.
To serve: as a starter either hot with melted butter or Hollandaise sauce or cold with French dressing. The leaves are pulled out and dipped in the sauce then the heart is eaten using a knife and fork.
To store: in the salad drawer of a refrigerator for up to 3 days.
To freeze: prepare and remove chokes. Blanch in water with lemon juice added for 7 minutes. Drain and cool. Pack in rigid boxes and store for 9 months. Cook from frozen.

Sweet corn

Serve on its own as a snack or starter or cut off the kernels with a knife and mix with other foods. Corn holders are available, or two forks can be used to hold the cob whilst the kernels are eaten. Corn fritters are traditionally served with Chicken Maryland.
To prepare: cut off the stalk and peel off the husks, remove the silks, leave whole, cut into chunks or cut the kernels off with a sharp knife.
To cook: boil whole cobs in a large saucepan full of boiling water for about 10 minutes, kernels 5 minutes. Add salt halfway through cooking time, otherwise the corn will become tough. Extra cooking toughens also, so time carefully and serve as soon as possible. Serve with lots of melted butter and salt and pepper or Hollandaise sauce. Brush with butter and cook under a grill or on a barbecue or wrap in streaky bacon. Wrap in buttered foil and bake in a moderate oven for 15 minutes, or in the ashes of a barbecue for 10 minutes. Add to casseroles for the last ½ hour of cooking. Use in soups and add cooked to corn relishes.
Microwave: melt a little butter in a serving dish, turn the prepared cobs, cover with a lid or cling film and cook 2 cobs for 4 to 5 minutes.

Sprouting seeds.

To store: cook as soon as possible after harvesting as the kernels toughen on storage unless frozen.
To freeze: blanch whole cobs 4 to 5 minutes depending on size then cool and drain well. Wrap individually in cling film. Or cut off kernels after blanching then open freeze. For cream-style corn, cut tip ends from kernels and scrape out pulp. Pack into containers.

CORN ON THE COB WITH BACON
Cook this dish for supper and serve at once to avoid toughening the corn.

For 4 portions

4	cobs sweet corn
	salt
4	rashers streaky bacon
	butter

1. Prepare a moderately hot oven (200 deg C, 400 deg F, Gas Mark 6).
2. Remove leaves and silk from cobs and trim stem end. Place cobs in a large, covered saucepan in boiling, salted water and boil for 2 minutes; drain well.
3. Remove rind and bone from bacon and

spread a little butter on each rasher. Wrap one around each cob.
4. Place in a shallow ovenproof dish and cook in oven for 20 minutes.

Spinach

Many varieties of plant produce leaves that are classed under this name, but their use in the kitchen is similar, although the cooking can vary slightly. Use spinach raw, cooked as a vegetable accompaniment, as an omelet, flan or pie filling or in soup.
Spinach is very nutritious being a valuable source of iron, calcium and vitamins A and B.
To prepare: wash well in a bowl of water, shake leaves, place in a colander, then repeat. Spinach beet has large mid-ribs which can either be cut out with a sharp knife and cooked separately or chopped with the rest of the leaves before cooking.
To cook: spinach is bulky and cooks down to almost nothing so you must allow about

3. Heat oil in a frying pan, add bacon and fry for about 5 minutes, until crisped. Remove bacon from pan and drain on kitchen paper. Place pan juices in a small bowl and add vinegar, spring onion and some salt and pepper. Whisk with a fork until well mixed.

4. Arrange spinach leaves in a salad bowl just before serving, pour over dressing and sprinkle with bacon.

MEDITERRANEAN SPINACH TARTS

These tasty little tarts make a very good supper dish or starter. The mixture can also be made in an 8 in (20 cm) flan tin.

Makes 4 tarts

Metric		Imperial
	PASTRY	
150 g	*plain flour*	*6 oz*
1 × 2.5 ml sp	*salt*	*½ tsp*
75 g	*margarine and lard mixed*	*3 oz*
	cold water to mix	
	FILLING	
250 g	*tomatoes*	*8 oz*
500 g	*spinach*	*1 lb*
	knob of butter	
	salt and pepper	
1	*small onion*	*1*
1	*clove of garlic*	*1*
6	*stuffed olives*	*6*
	oil for frying	
50 g	*Emmental or Gruyère cheese*	*2 oz*

1. Place flour and salt in a bowl. Add fats, cut into small pieces, and rub in with the fingertips until mixture resembles fine breadcrumbs. Add about 2 tbsp (2 × 15 ml sp) cold water, mix with a fork to form a firm dough. Place on a floured surface and knead lightly.

2. Divide pastry into 4. Roll out each piece to line a 4 in (10 cm) fluted flan tin or an individual Yorkshire pudding tin. Prick pastry bases with a fork. Chill 30 minutes.

3. Prepare a moderately hot oven (200 deg C, 400 deg F, Gas Mark 6).

4. Place tomatoes in a bowl and cover with boiling water; leave 1 minute, drain and peel. Prepare spinach and cook as directed, drain well. Return to pan and add butter and a good shake of salt and pepper.

5. Peel and chop onion. Peel clove of garlic and place on a saucer with a little salt. Using a round-ended knife, rub salt against clove to crush. Slice the olives.

6. Heat oil in a small saucepan. Fry onion and garlic until onion is softened but not browned, about 5 minutes. Roughly chop tomatoes and add to pan; cook for a further 3 minutes. Chop spinach and add with half the olives and a good shake of pepper.

7. Bake pastry cases just above centre of oven for 15 minutes. Divide filling between pastry cases. Grate cheese and sprinkle over tops, garnish with remaining olives. Return to oven for a further 15 minutes until cheese is golden brown. Serve warm or cold.

½ lb (250 g) raw spinach per portion. Spinach beet has thicker leaves so half that amount is required. Place the spinach in a saucepan with no added water, cover and cook slowly for about 10 minutes. Drain through a sieve and press out liquid with the back of a spoon. (Collect the liquid, season it and drink it, or save it and add to the gravy or soup – it's too nutritious to waste.) Chop with a knife. Melt about 2 oz (50 g) butter for each 1 lb (500 kg) spinach in the saucepan, add a generous grind of black pepper, 1 tsp 1 × 5 ml sp) salt and a large pinch of nutmeg. Return spinach to saucepan and reheat. Spinach beet is best cooked in 1 in (2 cm) depth of water. Both varieties can be liquidized to make a purée. Add a little of the liquid and the seasonings. Single cream or soured cream can be swirled in the purée before serving. Use well-drained cooked spinach in omelets and quiches or make soup following the Master Soup Recipe on page 66.

To serve raw: use small young leaves and serve with a salad dressing.

To store: pack washed leaves in a plastic bag and store in the bottom of the refrigerator for up to 2 days.

To freeze: blanch the leaves for 2 minutes, drain well and pack in useable amounts in freezer bags, press out air, seal and label. Cook from frozen in a little melted butter,

Front **Mediterranean Spinach Tarts;** *back left* **Crispy Spinach Salad;** *right* **Seafood Spinach Roll.**

remove lid and boil off any extra liquid before serving. Alternatively, freeze purée in plastic containers, remove, wrap the blocks in cling film and store in a freezer bag.

CRISPY SPINACH SALAD

A little spinach goes a long way when used raw in a salad. Choose young, tender leaves for the sweetest flavour.

For 4 to 6 portions

Metric		Imperial
250 g	*spinach leaves*	*8 oz*
2	*rashers streaky bacon*	*2*
1 × 15 ml sp	*oil*	*1 tbsp*
1 × 15 ml sp	*vinegar*	*1 tbsp*
1 × 15 ml sp	*chopped spring onion*	*1 tbsp*
	salt and pepper	

1. Wash spinach in several changes of salted water. Drain and pat leaves dry on kitchen paper. Remove any tough stalks.

2. Remove rind and bone from bacon; press rashers flat with a knife to stretch. Cut each rasher into 3 and then into thin strips.

SEAFOOD SPINACH ROLL

This light, savoury roll is particularly useful if you are watching your weight.

For 4 portions

Metric		Imperial
	SAUCE	
225 g	packet frozen smoked haddock	8 oz
50 g	mushrooms	2 oz
25 g	butter	1 oz
25 g	plain flour	1 oz
125 ml	milk	¼ pint
2 × 15 ml sp	tomato ketchup	1 tbsp
	salt and pepper	
500 g	fresh spinach	1 lb
	knob of butter	
	grated Parmesan cheese	
4	eggs	4

1. Cook haddock as directed on pack. Drain, skin and flake fish. Wash and slice mushrooms.
2. To make sauce: melt butter in a saucepan, add mushrooms and cook 2 minutes. Stir in flour and milk, bring to boil, stirring continuously, cook 2 minutes. Stir in fish, ketchup and a good shake of salt and pepper.
3. Prepare a moderate oven (190 deg C, 375 deg F, Gas Mark 5). Brush an 11 in by 7 in (28 cm by 17 cm) Swiss roll tin with melted fat. Draw around base of tin on greaseproof paper. Cut paper ½ in (2 cm) out from line; crease paper on line. Press paper down into tin; grease paper.
4. Prepare and cook spinach, drain well and chop with a knife. Add butter, a good shake of salt and pepper and 2 tsp (2 × 5 ml sp) cheese, mix well.
5. Separate eggs, place whites in a clean, grease-free bowl and beat yolks into spinach mixture. Whisk egg whites until stiff, but not dry; fold into spinach mixture, cutting through with a metal spoon until all the egg white has been completely incorporated.
6. Pour mixture into prepared tin, level mixture and bake just above centre of oven for 12 to 15 minutes. Test by pressing with the fingers. If cooked, mixture should feel firm.
7. Cut a piece of greaseproof paper just bigger than size of tin. Invert spinach mixture on to paper; remove paper from base carefully and spread sauce over. Roll up firmly from top with the aid of the paper. Hold gently until set, then remove paper and leave to cool.
8. Arrange reserved spinach leaves on serving dish; place roll on top and sprinkle with a little Parmesan cheese. Serve cut into thick slices.

Watercress

One of the most nutritious salad vegetables, watercress is available most of the year. It is often thought of just as a garnish but it is delicious when chopped as a sandwich filling, in salads or in both hot and cold soups.

To prepare: pick off sprigs and discard any thick peppery-flavoured stems and yellowing leaves. Wash under running water and shake dry.
To serve raw: use in salads or chop and use as a sandwich filling. A garnish for poultry.
To cook: make soup following the Master Soup Recipe on page 66.
To store: place stalks in a cup of water, cover with cling film and place in refrigerator. Store for up to 2 days.

Cooked asparagus.

Asparagus

This luxury vegetable needs careful cooking. Use the fat stalks as a starter or a vegetable accompaniment and the thin sprue in flans, to serve with grilled meats and in soup.

To prepare: wash carefully then trim the woody base, cut all stems to the same size. Scrape down the stem with a knife to remove the scales.
To cook: tie into bundles of about 10 stems with fine string. Cook upright in boiling, salted water with the stems in the water and the tips cooking in the steam above. Cook for 10 to 15 minutes.
Microwave: in a covered dish, 1 lb (500 g) will take 10 to 12 minutes to cook. Serve hot with melted butter or Hollandaise sauce or cold with French dressing.
To store: in the bottom of the refrigerator in a plastic bag for up to 2 days.
To freeze: grade into even-sized spears. Blanch thin spears 2 minutes, thick spears 4 minutes. Dry on a cloth then open freeze. Pack into rigid containers to store.

Fruit Trees

Even the smallest garden is improved by the addition of trees, as long as you choose them carefully. They provide shadow in hot sun, they can be trained to cover walls or fences and form a hedge or screen and they provide attractive leaves in autumn and flowers in spring. Fruiting trees placed carefully add height to plantings, even in the shrub border, and can make small gardens look longer.

Many people who take over a garden for the first time find fruit trees attractive but the detailed instructions to prune and cultivate cause them concern. Really there is no need to worry because all fruit trees will grow well in reasonable soil completely untended.

Apples are the easiest of all to grow, followed by the popular 'Conference' pear and 'Victoria' plum. Plums (and gages even more so) flower quite early in the year, when frost can kill the developing fruitlets. Every now and then plum trees fruit very heavily and this is often the result of a late, cold spring which has delayed flowering and so helped to avoid frost damage to the tiny fruitlets.

All the early flowering stone fruits will crop more regularly if grown and trained fan-shaped against a south or west-facing wall. Fan training is a lot more tricky than just letting a free standing tree grow away, however, and the tip for success is to train and tie in while the shoots are soft, supple and growing strongly. Once the shoots ripen into springy wood with tough bark it is virtually impossible to change and control the direction of growth and such branchlets usually have to be cut right out and a new start made with the subsequent shoots.

It is not a good idea to replant apples in soil where apples have grown before and the same goes for plums and pears. It is, however, all right to plant a different fruit, that is pears following apples or plums following pears.

Tree planting

Once a tree is planted there is little you can do to improve heavy, poor and infertile soil so your only chance to prepare the soil is before planting. So take care to dig out a large hole and mix in plenty of well-rotted garden compost, peat and good soil before planting the tree.

Trees planted with bare roots are best preceded by a stake driven firmly into the soil on the prevailing wind side of the tree. Where it is difficult to insert a stake close to a container-grown tree because of the ball of soil and root, the stake can be driven in at an angle of 45°, the head facing into the wind.

Plant all trees firmly, treading in good soil and peat around the roots. When you've finished the old soil mark, or surface of the container, should be level with the surface soil. Then secure the trunk to the stake as high up as possible, using a special plastic tie which can be loosened as the trunk swells. A pair of tights can also be used as a tie but be sure to slacken it as the tree grows.

It is advisable to keep a yard (1 metre) circle of cultivated soil around each tree. Competition for moisture by grass or weeds will severely check early growth and reduce cropping for a number of years.

Pruning – young trees

The pruning of young trees is important because if left to grow naturally they shoot upwards and quickly become too tall, producing branches and fruit which will be out of reach. It is advisable to buy two or three-year-old trees from respected nurseries or garden centres, then the correct branch foundation will already be established.

Where three or four new young branches grow out from the trunk at 45–60° rather than upright they are more strongly fixed and less likely to split off under a heavy crop of fruit in future years. A good general rule is to cut off, in winter, one half of the new growth made on the ends of all strong branches after the first year, and for at least four to seven years on all bush and taller free-standing trees.

The lead shoots at the end of each branch of all types of trained trees will also need to be given treatment to encourage short stout branches to grow and produce fruit-bearing shoots, twiggy spurs and plump buds.

Older trees will require little more than an occasional crossing branch to be pruned out to keep the fruit-bearing wood open to sun and air. If you wish your trees to produce the heaviest possible crop of large, good quality apples, pears and peaches it is easiest to learn more detailed pruning instruction firsthand from a skilled fruit grower. Established cherries and plums are best left unpruned, except perhaps for too low-growing branches which can be removed in July or immediately after fruiting. Treat these wounds with fungicidal sealant to prevent entry of silver leaf disease.

Apples

Family trees are tailormade for small gardens; they are no more than one trunk with three different varieties of apple grafted on the top. Good nurserymen will have sorted out complementary varieties so that the growth is balanced, placing the weaker ones at the top and grafting on the stronger-growing lower down. He will also choose varieties which cross pollinate each other and provide a selection of fruit which will store from September to March.

Where branches have grown into one another and compete for sunlight, prune crossing branches right out, for example the one indicated here by hands.

When you are buying any trees there are three things to watch for. First the tree should have been lifted from the nursery the autumn or spring in which you plant and container trees should have been in the pots for no more than a year. You can tell this by looking at the growth made the previous summer: check back down from the tip of each main branch and it will be 12–18 in (30–45 cm) at least before you see the growth rings showing where the older wood starts.

Next check, if possible, what rootstock

If the lead shoot is not pruned back each winter, bare sections (seen here between finger and thumb) without fruiting clusters (spurs) will form.

the tree is grown on. This is not easy because few nurserymen actually label the kind of root used. It is important because strong-growing roots produce very big trees which can be slow to fruit and the weakest types of rootstock will not do too well in poor garden soils.

Fortunately most apple trees sold are grown on roots of medium vigour called Malling Merton 106 (MM 106) or Malling Merton 111 (MM 111). They are well able to cope with the wide variety of garden soils and with dry soils that occur in summer. They are also suited to tub and large pot cultivation because the roots are better able to withstand occasional dry compost.

There are much weaker rootstocks: Malling 27 is the smallest and produces a waist high tree after ten or 15 years' growth. A little larger is Malling 9 but both need fertile soil, plenty of water in summer and secure staking for the whole of their lives. Given this, they are ideal for

Apple trees left unpruned will still fruit all right but the fruit will not be such good quality.

the small garden, either grown as a small bush or planted in a single row 3 ft (1 m) apart to form a hedge or screen in 'cordon' form.

Tree shapes

Bush trees are the easiest to grow and prune and the lollipop shape means crops can be grown under the spread of their branches. Half standard and standard trees are no more than bush trees on higher trunks. Be careful with standards as they soon grow too tall to pick.

Trained trees include the espalier type, that is a single trunk with pairs of branches growing out of the trunk in tiers (some times called tiered trees) every 12 in (30 cm) or so. They are ideal to grow against walls. Fan trees are also trained flat in one plane but the branches fan out like the spokes of a half wheel. Cordon trees have clipped branches around the trunk and are usually planted at an angle of 60° facing north. They form a good screen or fruiting hedge in the garden.

Trees grafted on to Malling 9 roots remain small and fruit early in their life, but need a secure staking.

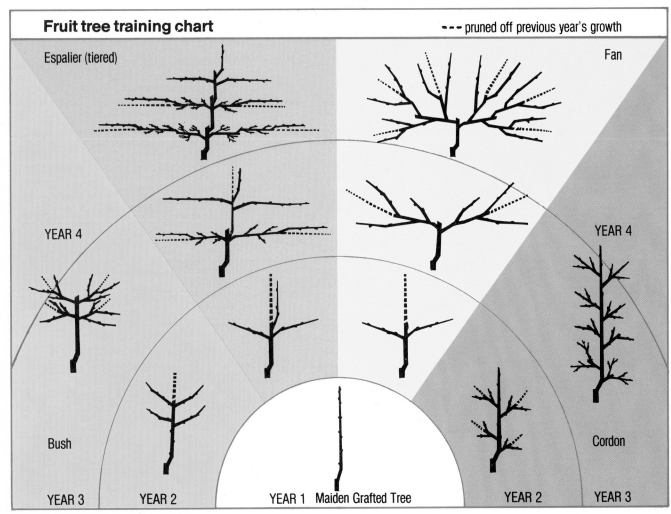

Fruit tree training chart --- pruned off previous year's growth

Espalier (tiered)

Fan

YEAR 4

YEAR 4

Bush

Cordon

YEAR 3 YEAR 2 YEAR 1 Maiden Grafted Tree YEAR 2 YEAR 3

Top fruit: pest and disease control chart (see also chart on page 109)

Problem	Spray	Feb	Mar	Apl	May	Jun	Jly	Aug	Notes
PESTS									
APHID (Greenfly) Apples, Pear, Plum, Cherry, (Blackfly) Peach	bioresmethrin or dimethoate or formothion or heptenophos or malathion or menazon or permethrin or pirimicarb or pirimiphos-methyl, or resmethrin or rotenone or diazinon				▬▬▬				Dec/Jan Tar oil.
WOOLLY APHID Apple	HCH or dimethoate or malathion or heptenophos or pirimiphos methyl				▬▬▬				green to pink flower bud stage. Before May
CAPSID Apple	bioresmethrin, or dimethoate of fenitrothion or HCH or malathion or permethrin or pirimiphos-methyl				▬▬▬				
CATERPILLAR (Winter Moth and Sawfly) Apple	trichlorphon or fenitrothion or HCH or pirimiphos-methyl								grease band apply September
CODLING MOTH Apple	fenitrothion, or HCH or malathion or permethrin or pirimiphos-methyl					▬▬▬			Also for Tortrix Caterpillar
MIDGE PEAR	dimethoate or fenitrothion or HCH or permethrin				▬▬▬				White flower bud stage
RED SPIDER MITE Apples, plum, etc.	dimethoate, or malathion or pirimiphos-methyl or rotenone					▬▬▬			DNOC/pet. February. Not a problem on unsprayed trees, natural predators control
GLASSHOUSE RED SPIDER MITE Peaches	dimethoate, malathion, pirimiphos-methyl or rotenone								
DISEASES									
CANKER Apples	liquid copper		▬▬▬						1 spray ½ leaf fall 1 spray at leaf fall
LEAF BLIGHT Quince	liquid copper		▬▬▬						
LEAF CURL Peaches	liquid copper or mancozeb thiram or zineb	▬▬							And at leaf fall 7-14 day intervals
MILDEW Apples, Quince	benomyl or bupirimate and triforine or thiophanate-methyl				▬▬▬▬▬▬▬				7-14 day intervals
MILDEW Peach	sulphur or benomyl or bupirimate and triforine				▬▬▬				as soon as seen
SCAB Apples, pears	benomyl or bupirimate and triforine or captan or thiram or zineb or thiophanate-methyl				▬▬▬				

NOTES: Do not spray with chemicals which harm bees when plants are in flower. Change choice of chemical to avoid build up of resistant strains of pest and disease. Pirimicarb is harmless to bees.

Pests and diseases

There are two likely diseases: scab which causes brown and black spots on fruits and leaves and the greyish-white, crippling mildew. Pruning out the first signs of mildew in spring and spraying with systemic fungicide will control these problems.

The main pest is codlin moth which causes maggots in the cores. Spray with fenitrothion or malathion the third week in June and again three weeks later to reduce this pest. A spray in winter with tar oil once every three years or so also helps to kill this and other pests, as well as removing the old green mosses and lichens from the bark.

Varieties

It is advisable to choose varieties which are easy to grow, have attractive flowers, fruit freely in adverse conditions and are generally disease resistant. Likely candidates are, in order of ripening:
Eating apples – 'Discovery', 'Epicure' (Laxtons), 'Fortune' (Laxtons), 'Greensleeves', 'Egremont Russet', 'Charles Ross' and 'Spartan'. 'James Grieve' is an excellent garden variety to be eaten cooked from August to October and raw from late September to October.
Cooking apples – 'Grenadier' and 'Rev. W. Wilks' (August – October). 'Bramley' is the best cooking apple but it tends to

Espalier apple tree with a pair of branches trained horizontally every 12–18 ins up the trunk.

grow too large and needs two other varieties for complete pollination. 'Cox's Orange Pippin' is the best flavoured eating apple but can be difficult to grow, especially in cold northern districts, unless given the protection of a wall.

Lovely 'Cox's Orange Pippin', but take care when picking all apples because next year's fruit buds can be easily pulled off with the apples. Lift the apple up through 180° and if ripe and ready to pick it will come away easily in the hand.

Pears

All that is said for apples goes for pears too, save rootstock and here the best for gardens is EM Quince A (East Malling Quince A) which makes a bush tree 12 ft (3.6 m) or so across and of the same height. There is the dwarfer EM Quince C but this needs good soil for acceptable crops.

The best all round pear is 'Conference' a good dessert variety which stores well

A pear tree being fan trained, it is better to direct strength to side branches first, otherwise, as here, all the growth goes to the centre . . .

...this fan-trained 'Conference' has much more evenly spread growth.

into the winter. It will set fruit on its own but such fruits are not typical pear shaped. Better crops will be achieved with cross pollination; for example, planting alongside 'Onward' or 'Williams Bon Chretien' (sold in cans as 'Bartlet'), both of which ripen in September.

The finest eating variety is 'Doyenne du Comice' but this needs two varieties for complete cross pollination of all three and a good garden combination is three cordon-trained trees of 'Comice', 'Conference' and 'Onward'. 'Comice' really is a warm weather variety and not the easiest to grow. It will need a sheltered position or the protection of a south-facing wall in all but the warmest areas.

There is the tendency to plant trees and then forget them. All will respond well, however, to regular feeding: apply a general fertilizer at 2–4 oz per square yard (60–120 gm/1 sq m). Fertilizers high in potash such as rose fertilizer are best for established apple and pear trees. Splitting the application i.e. half in August/September and the remainder in spring, will have the best effect.

Lack of water in summer in the eastern half of Britain will reduce both growth and crop, especially where the trees grow among other plants and in grass. A really good soaking in dry spells will correct this.

Where trees grow strongly and flower freely but do not set fruits, either lack of pollination or spring frost are the likely explanation. If you only have one tree and there is no pollinator in near neighbour's gardens, it is worth getting a small branch of blossom from a different variety and

placing it in a jar of water tied to a branch of your tree. There is little one can do for frost protection save covering wall-trained trees with fine mesh net.

All fruit trees which grow very strongly and fail to flower are better *not* pruned hard. Hard pruning just encourages even stronger growth. If strong, young, upright straight branches are tied over – as a boy does to make a bow for bows and arrows – this checks the flow of sap and helps produce flower buds.

Young trees which just produce a few leaves each year but fail to grow away have usually been subjected to a check when transplanted. Alternatively they may have just been 'stuck into' poor soil without sufficient preparation. Keep such trees securely staked and water the leaves with a foliar feed every 14 days through late spring and summer. This will help them recover, but where the soil is very bad it will be necessary to lift in late autumn, dig the soil and mix in plenty of well-rotted compost, peat and possibly good soil before replanting. It is often quicker and the result better if a new tree which has not had such a check is used as replacement.

Cherries, Figs, Peaches and Plums

Cherries

There are two basic types: the sweet eating cherries pruned similarly to plums and the sour cooking cherries which fruit on the previous year's growth and need treating like peaches. Pollination is tricky for most varieties excepting the self-fertile cooker 'Morello' and the eating variety 'Stella'. 'Merton Glory' will cross pollinate with all varieties which flower at the same time. It is an eating variety with white flesh.

All cherries produce attractive flowers in spring and when they set fruit inevitably attract the attention of birds. For this reason they are best wall-trained in most gardens. While walls facing any direction are suitable, 'Morello' has the advantage that it will thrive and fruit heavily if fan-trained against a north-facing fence or wall. Trained in this way they are easy to net while, on the other hand, fruit on bush trees is very difficult to protect from birds.

They need good fertile soil and the wall-trained trees will need watering well

The brilliant, shiny red fruits on 'Morello' make this a truly ornamental as well as a useful wall fruit.

during periods of hot, sunny weather. The growing tips are often attacked by black fly in summer and spraying with an aphis killer is necessary at the first sighting of curled and crippled young leaves.

Figs

Many people think of the common fig as a tender plant and yet they are quite hardy, with new growth springing from the base in the event of a really hard winter frost cutting them to the ground. The tiny fruits are produced at the tips of the branches in late summer and these are tender. They need protecting from frost over winter and then they develop further to ripen from August to October. Larger fruits growing lower down the branches seldom overwinter successfully and usually drop off in spring.

Figs are very strong-growing plants and for this reason are better grown in large tubs or in a position where the roots are somewhat restricted. Regular feeding of soil-grown plants is not usually necessary. They produce their spreading branches and large attractive leaves in all soil types but the best crops will be picked from trees grown against south or west-facing walls in warm, well-drained soils which are freely watered in summer.

'Brown Turkey' is one of the hardiest varieties with a brown skin and sweet taste. 'Brunswick' has large tasty fruits with greenish skin and orange to red flesh. The fruits are ready to pick when tiny cracks appear in the skin and a small 'tear' of juice forms in the eye of each one. They are best eaten fresh, picked warm from the tree but can also be frozen in syrup and wrapped in foil.

Gardeners with restricted space and paved areas are well advised to grow a fig

'Brown Turkey' is a good fig to grow in a tub. It can be taken into a cold greenhouse overwinter to protect the immature fruits.

in a tub. The branch tips can be wrapped round through the winter like lagged water pipes to protect the tiny fruits from frost.

Pruning consists of thinning the growth out a little in summer and removing any frost-damaged shoots in March. Take care not to prune back all the branches in spring because the branch tips are carrying the fruits. New growth will come from the base if a branch is occasionally cut back hard in spring.

Mulberries

Strange though it may seem, mulberries belong to the same family as the fig and the black mulberry (*Morus nigra*) deserves to be more widely planted. It is slow growing but, planted in a lawn, the ripe fruit can be gathered up clean as it falls on the grass. They can be grown in tubs too and the root restriction encourages fruiting in three or four years.

Peaches

It is great fun raising all kinds of fruit trees from pips and stones. Apples, pears, cherries, plums, grapes and especially peaches are easily grown from the pips taken from ripe fruit. Sow them either in pots or in the open ground in the autumn and leave to germinate the following spring.

Every seedling will be different, it is the way nurserymen breed new varieties, and most will not be as good as their selected parents. All should eventually fruit but some will make very large trees and most will take a number of years, seven to 15 is a fair average, to fruit. Keeping the seedlings in pots restricts the roots and encourages earlier flowering

and fruiting.

While it is fun to grow these seedlings, it takes time and a large garden with plenty of space is needed. Where you really want good fruit as soon as possible then buy the best quality trees of good, named varieties. Peaches 'Peregrine' and 'Rochester' are good ones for gardens and both are self-pollinating.

Bush trees will thrive and fruit in the open garden in very warm parts of Britain but they are best grown fan-trained against a south or west-facing wall. Pruning fan trees and keeping the fast-growing young shoots tied in is quite a time consuming job. After training-in the main branch framework, all the side shoots which have borne fruit are pruned hard back after picking, to encourage new shoots to grow. The flowers, and subsequently peaches, form on the side branches in their second year.

Fan-training allows the plants to be netted to help protect the flowers from spring frost and the fruit from birds. Another possibility is to grow bush trees in large pots. Leave them outside all winter, except in the hardest weather, and when buds start to open in early spring move them into a cold greenhouse to help protect the flowers from frost. Spread pollen from open flowers to flower with a feather or soft brush on warm, sunny days. After the possibility of frost has passed move the trees with their developing fruits outside. The drier atmosphere in the greenhouse in spring will help considerably to control peach leaf curl disease which affects all outdoor peaches and almonds sooner or later.

While most soils are suitable, avoid heavy, waterlogged places for peaches and, when planting close to walls, dig in plenty of well-rotted compost and/or manure to help retain moisture in hot sunny weather.

Good fruits are produced on peach trees in spite of peach leaf curl disease if foliar feed is sprayed on at 14-day intervals from late May.

Peaches fruit on the shoots which grew last year and these branchlets are pruned back after picking.

Plums

Easiest of all the plums is the lovely variety 'Victoria', which is delicious eaten raw and cooked. Other good garden varieties are the early plum 'Warwickshire Drooper' (large yellow fruit), mid-season ripening 'Merryweather' damson, the late 'Prune Damson' and the dark blue 'Marjorie's Seedling' plum. All of these are self fertile.

Two of the easier self-fertile gages are 'Early Transparent' and 'Oulins Golden Gage', but they do need warmer conditions than plums and damsons for regular crops. All these trees do grow rather large in time but a new dwarfing rootstock called Pixie should help us to accommodate more of these lovely fruits in smaller gardens in the future.

Choose damsons for the heaviest soils and once the branches are formed on young trees (see apples) little other pruning is necessary. Where drooping branches need sawing off to get under the trees, prune immediately after fruiting and paint the wounds with a protective wax to prevent silver leaf infection.

Where plums and cherries are afflicted with silver leaf disease the trees will often survive and fruit all right when given 2–4 oz of fertilizer per square yard each spring. It is important to remove *all* dead wood from infected trees by mid July. This disease spreads from spores produced on the *dead* wood.

Cookery

Apples

This favourite fruit is available for kitchen use for most of the year. There's an extended season because of the many varieties, some of which store well. Both dessert and cooking apples can be used in cooked dishes. Very ripe cooking apples make good eaters if you like an apple with a bite.

To prepare: apples go brown when a cut surface is exposed to the air. Prepare them immediately before cooking or coat in lemon juice or weak Campden solution to prevent browning. When preparing a lot of apples, drop the whole peeled apples in a bowl of water with lemon juice added then core and slice them just before cooking. Peel thinly using a stainless steel knife or potato peeler. Cut into wedges and cut out the core. To serve whole or in rings, remove the core with a special corer gadget, often on the end of a potato peeler.

To cook: there are many uses for apples and they can be cooked in many ways.

Stewing: dissolve some sugar in sufficient water to just cover the bottom of a saucepan. Bring to boil, drop in sliced apples, cover with a lid and cook over moderate heat until boiling. Remove from the heat and leave covered to finish cooking in the steam. This will keep the slices whole. If required pulped, add sugar after cooking.

Baking: remove core, score apple round centre or vertically, place in a shallow ovenproof dish and fill centre of apple with sugar, dried fruit, jam, marmalade or honey and butter. Bake in a moderate oven until just tender, about 20 minutes. Serve hot or cold. Alternatively, bake quartered apples in a covered casserole with sugar, but no water. Flavour with cinnamon, ground or stem ginger, raspberry jam or other fruit such as blackberries or currants.

To make Apple Crumble: cover sliced sweetened apples with a rubbed in mixture made from half butter and granulated or demerara sugar to flour. Bake in a moderate oven. Apple rings or quarters can be baked around a joint of pork for the last $\frac{1}{2}$ hour. Cover whole, peeled, stuffed apples with shortcrust or puff pastry and bake to make apple dumplings.

Frying: coat apple rings in batter and fry in deep fat, drain and turn in caster sugar and cinnamon. Or fry rings in butter to serve with grilled meats.

Purée: cook without peeling and coring in a little water then sieve. Mix in whisked egg whites and sugar to make Apple Snow; use in flans and pies or as a sauce to serve with desserts or roast bacon or pork.

To serve raw: blanch in boiling sugar syrup with lemon juice added (to prevent browning) then add to fresh fruit salad. Dip slices in lemon juice then add to salads. Slice unpeeled red and green skinned apples and use to decorate desserts. Serve a juicy dessert or cooking apple with cheese.

To store: Dry storage: most late season's apples will store well if perfect and unbruised. Place apples in a single layer and leave in a cool, airy place overnight. Wrap each apple separately in waxed paper, tissue or newspaper to delay the ripening process and prevent decay. Place in a single layer in boxes stalk end downwards. Cover to keep out the light then stack the boxes, but leave room for air circulation. Alternatively, layer on fibre trays, obtainable from the greengrocer or bought specially.

To freeze: blanch slices for 1 minute in boiling water, remove with a draining spoon and dry on kitchen paper. Open freeze then pack in freezer bags. Or freeze in containers as a purée, stewed or as apple sorbet.

To make jam & jelly: use on their own or mixed with other fruits such as blackberry, loganberry or raspberry. Use to extend scarce fruits or low pectin fruits. Make jelly with crab apples or windfalls and add some mint.

To make pectin stock: for adding to low or medium pectin fruits such as strawberries, raspberries, loganberries, grapes, blackberries, cherries, marrows, rhubarb. Chop up 8 oz (250 g) tart apples (including pips, core and skin) or use apple peelings and cores. Simmer (or pressure cook) with $\frac{1}{2}$ pint (250 ml) water until broken down then strain and add to each 3 lb (1.5 kg) fruit when making jam.

To make chutney: apples are the perfect base for most chutneys. (See page 122.)

To dry: cut into rings and thread on a bamboo pole or spread on a mesh tray. Dry in an oven, setting the heat as low as possible. Dry for about 12 hours, but it need not be continuous. Layer in waxed paper in a box and store in a cool, dry place. *To use:* soak before using.

To bottle: pack as slices or as a purée.

To make juice: use a food processor with a juice attachment. Add a small quantity of Campden solution to prevent browning.

To make wine: Use 6 lb (3 kg) fruit to 1 gall ($4\frac{1}{2}$ litres) water. Add 1 lb (500 g) sultanas, 2 tsp (2×5 ml sp) pectin destroying enzyme and 1 tsp (1×5 ml sp) citric acid. Core the apples, and break down in the food processor or mincer or with water in the liquidizer. Add some Campden solution to prevent browning. Ferment with a vigorous yeast starter, yeast nutrient and 2 lb (1 kg) sugar, for 5 days then strain and press out the juice. Pour into demi-john, fit airlocks and ferment until dry.

TOSSED APPLE TART

A quick and simple way of using up a glut of apples. The jam adds colour and balances the sharpness of the apples.

For 6 portions

Metric		Imperial
	PASTRY	
100 g	margarine	4 oz
50 g	caster sugar	2 oz
1	egg	1
150 g	plain flour	6 oz

	FILLING	
6×15 ml sp	strawberry jam	6 tbsp
1×15 ml sp	cornflour	1 tbsp
2×15 ml sp	granulated sugar	2 tbsp
500 g	cooking apples	1 lb

1. Prepare a moderate oven (190 deg C, 375 deg F, Gas Mark 5). Cream margarine and sugar together until light and fluffy. Beat egg in a basin, reserve a little for glaze, and gradually beat remainder into margarine mixture. Add plain flour and mix to form a soft dough. Wrap in cling film and chill for half an hour.

2. Mix jam, cornflour and sugar in a large saucepan; stir over a low heat until jam melts and thickens. Peel and core apples, cut into chunks and add to pan. Turn in jam mixture to coat; leave to cool.

3. Turn out pastry on to a lightly-floured board and knead until smooth. Cut off about one-eighth of dough and reserve. Roll out remainder to fit an 8 in (20 cm) ovenproof plate. Gather up trimmings and knead with reserved pastry. Roll out and trim to an oblong 4 in by 7 in (10 cm by 17 cm) cut into 1 in (2.5 cm) squares. Brush rim of pastry with reserved egg and arrange squares overlapping; brushing each with egg. Spread apple mixture over pastry. Place tart on a baking sheet and cook just above centre of oven for 40 to 45 minutes until pastry is deep golden brown and filling is set in centre. Serve hot or cold with custard or cream.

Pears

Freshly picked pears are firm and crunchy and their texture complements the smoothness of cream cheese in salads and starters. As they ripen, use them on their own for dessert or mixed with other fruits and sweet sauces. A pear is ripe when it just yields to gentle pressure at the stalk end. Serve it soon, because it will quickly become over-ripe and woolly. Speed up the ripening by putting it in a warm place such as an airing cupboard, slow it down in the refrigerator.

To prepare: remove stalk and use a stainless steel knife to peel thinly. Cut in halves or quarters and cut out core and stringy part between core and stalk. Turn in lemon juice to coat if not being cooked or used soon, to prevent browning.

To cook: prepare sufficient flavoured sweet syrup to cover the peeled pears, which may be whole, halved or cut in slices. Use 4 oz (100 g) sugar to each $\frac{1}{2}$ pint (250 ml) water and flavour with lemon juice, vanilla, cinnamon or replace half the water with red or white wine. Poach the pears until tender, in a saucepan or a covered casserole in the oven. Remove pears with a draining spoon, boil the syrup to reduce it then strain over the pears. Serve cold with cream or custard. Serve poached pear halves with hot chocolate sauce and ice cream to make the classic dessert Pear Belle Hélène or coat halves in fudge or mincemeat sauce. Serve slices in a lemon flavoured syrup (use a strip of rind as well as the juice) and serve

with slices of crystallised or stem ginger.
To store: use pears as soon as they are ripe.
Use hard pears in chutney or bottle them
in a light sugar syrup with lemon juice or
red wine and spices. Pears are unsuitable
for freezing and wine making. Dry store as
for apples.

PORTLY PEARS

Any type of firm fruit can be wrapped in
pastry and served in this delicious and
impressive way. Prepare them in advance
and keep in refrigerator until ready to cook.

For 4 portions

Metric		Imperial
4	*medium-sized dessert*	4
	pears	
370 g	*packet frozen puff*	13 oz
	pastry, just thawed	
	granulated sugar	
	ground cloves	
	milk or beaten egg, to	
	glaze	

1. Prepare a hot oven (220 dec C, 425 deg
F, Gas Mark 7). Wash pears, but do not
remove stalks.
2. Divide pastry in half lengthwise; roll one
piece and trim into a strip 18 in (45 cm)
long by about 5 in (12 cm) wide. Brush
pastry with water and sprinkle with a little
sugar mixed with a pinch of ground cloves.
Cut pastry into ¾ in (2 cm) strips,
lengthwise. This half of pastry will cover
2 pears.
3. Starting at base of pear, and, with sugar
side inwards, wrap pastry strips round

pears in a spiral fashion, slightly
overlapping each layer. Do not stretch the
pastry. Lightly press pastry to fit shape of
pear. Press joins of strips firmly together,
re-wetting if necessary. Repeat with second
half of pastry for remaining two pears.
4. Roll pastry trimmings together into a
strip about ¾ in (2 cm) wide; cut diagonally
across strip to make leaves, and mark each
leaf with a knife to represent veins. Brush
underside of each leaf with water and press
3 leaves firmly into position round each
stalk. Wrap stalks in a little foil to prevent
them burning.
5. Brush pears with milk, sprinkle with
sugar and place pears on a large flat baking
sheet, leaving plenty of room between each
one. Bake in centre of oven for 20 to 30
minutes, according to size and ripeness of
pears. Test by piercing base of pear with a
skewer.
6. To serve: remove foil from stalks and
sprinkle more granulated sugar over pears.
Serve hot with warmed plum or apricot
jam, custard or whipped cream.

Plums

Use large dessert plums raw or cook in
pies, crumbles and a variety of desserts.
Small dark plums such as damsons are
always cooked. They are excellent for
making jam and wine.
To prepare: remove the stalks, wash then
cut in halves down the indentation. Twist
and remove the stones. Remove damson
stones during cooking.

To cook: stew in a small quantity of sugar
syrup until just cooked. Leave the lid on
the saucepan to finish cooking in the steam.
Layer with sugar and bake in a covered
casserole without added liquid.
For pies, mix sugar with a little cornflour
and turn the fruit in this mixture. Bake
under a single crust or on a plate with a
top and bottom crust of pastry. Cook
damsons with some water and sugar. Skim
off the stones as they rise to the surface, or
sieve the fruit. Use plums in flans and
baked and steamed puddings.
To serve raw: very ripe plum halves can be
layered with sugar in a dish. Add a little
cinnamon, or add to fruit salads.
To store: pack in a plastic bag and store in
a refrigerator for up to 4 days or a freezer
for up to 1 year.
To bottle: cut in halves, remove stones and
pack into preserving bottles, cover with a
light sugar syrup ½ lb (250 g) to each 1 pint
(500 ml) – see page 124 for processing times.
To make wine: damsons and dark plums
make very good wine. Use 4 lb (2 kg) each
of fruit and sugar to 1 gall (4½ litres) water
for a rich dessert wine. Add 8 oz (250 g)
dried bananas or raisins, pectin destroying
enzyme, 1 tbsp (1 × 15 ml sp) yeast nutrient
and a vigorous yeast starter. Ferment on
the pulp for 5 days, stirring twice daily
then strain and pour into a demi-john. Fit
an airlock and ferment out.
To make jam: use equal weights of plums
and sugar. Remove stones, if possible, and
cook in a small quantity of water if
necessary, until pulped. Add sugar, skim off
the stones and boil until set. See method on
page 123.
For damson jam, use 5 lb (2½ kg) fruit and
cook in 1¾ pints (1 litre) water. Add 6 lb (3
kg) sugar, stir until dissolved then remove
pan from the heat and skim off stones with
a draining spoon. Boil until set.
To make chutney: Add to mixed vegetables
and fruits.
To pickle: damsons are particularly good
pickled. Prick the skins all over with a
silver fork or wooden cocktail stick and
cook in spiced sweet vinegar until tender.
Drain, pack the fruit into jars, reduce the
vinegar by boiling 5 minutes then pour
over the fruit. Leave over night then drain
off the vinegar again and repeat 4 times on
successive days, then seal.

JELLIED PLUM CHARLOTTE

This recipe is similar to Royal Blackberry
Charlotte (page 121). Line a ½ pint (250 ml)
basin with 6 oz (175 g) Madeira cake. Cook
1 lb (500 g) dark plums and a medium-
sized cooking apple in ¼ pint (125 ml) water
then sieve and make purée up to 1 pint
(500 ml) with water. Dissolve a lemon-
flavour jelly and 4 oz (100 g) sugar in purée
then pour into basin.

Portly Pears.

Rhubarb & Fruit Bushes

Try to find space for one rhubarb crown and a few soft fruit bushes in every garden. Even in the smallest space it is difficult to find a more fruitful and good natured plant than rhubarb.

Some soft fruit bushes are even less demanding for space, with gooseberries and redcurrants responding well to training up against a fence or wall. Redcurrants will thrive planted against north-facing walls and the more demanding dessert gooseberries like 'Leveller' benefit from the extra sun a south and west-facing fence can provide.

Blackcurrants are likely to be the most demanding for space but this fruit has no real equal for fruit pies, jams and flavouring ice cream.

Where quite a large plot is available to plant soft fruit bushes and other fruiting trees, then rhubarb provides a useful short term crop. Rhubarb crowns planted and intercropped between more woody plants quickly fill the space and can be lifted for forcing once the longer term plants need all the room. Strawberries too can be used as a three to five year infiller.

Soft fruit bushes can be planted in the spaces between newly-planted young fruiting trees like apple and plum. They will fill the space for the first four to ten years and then, when the tree branches start to meet, the soft fruit bushes will have to be removed.

When the branches do meet, small gooseberry bushes will often survive in the shade and produce acceptable crops without reducing the tree crops in any appreciable way.

Rhubarb

Even though it is good natured, rhubarb will be much more productive if planted in well-prepared fertile soil. Try to find an open sunny site (it will, however, grow in quite poor shady soil) and dig in plenty of well-rotted garden compost or manure before planting.

Three year and older roots are dug up in early spring and chopped into pieces with a spade to produce new planting sets. Each piece needs a plump pink bud at the top and a lump of root about the size of two fists one on top of the other.

Space the sets at least $2\frac{1}{2}$ ft (75 cm) apart. Plant with the bud just covered and leave to grow for one full year before starting to pull. A few stems can be pulled

the second early summer but full cropping should not be practised until the third spring.

Try to always leave a few leaves after pulling to allow the plant to rebuild plant food supplies. If you run your thumb down the base and inside edge of each stem and press outwards as you pull, the full stem will come away cleanly. Trim off the bottom thin white pieces and all green leaf and then the stems are ready to cook.

Plants will often produce a large central flower spike, especially on poorer-quality plants raised from seed and on plants pulled very heavily and in poor soil. These seed heads are better snapped out to prevent further weakening of the crown. Where you are growing several crowns then one flower head can be left and it makes a spectacular flower. Both the dramatic leaves and cream flowers are quite acceptable and decorative as well as utilitarian subjects for the hardy flower border.

Hoe some general fertilizer into the soil around each crown early every spring and mulch with garden compost or manure. Water well in dry weather and give

Well-established crowns can be lifted, left on the surface for several weeks before placing in a black polythene bag, surrounded with damp peat and (below) taken indoors in the warm, 60°–70°F (15°–20°C) to force into early growth.

Dark red stems on the quality garden variety 'Cawood Delight'.

another supplementary dose of fertilizer in early summer to encourage more strong growth and allow pulling well into the summer.

By far the tastiest and most welcome stems come from early forced crowns. Always plant more crowns than you need. Then in the third and subsequent years a crown can be lifted in late November.

Leave the big woody crown with thongy roots on the surface exposed to frost and cold. After several weeks exposed, including some frosty nights, place each crown in a black polythene bag, surrounding the roots with damp peat.

Brought indoors into the warm, it will soon be forced into early growth and ready to harvest. The black polythene is needed to exclude light and produce the best forced stems. They are ready to pull when the pale lemon yellow leaves start to darken and before the leaf edges go brown.

Once the crowns have all the leaves forced into growth they are of no more use and are best thrown away. It is also possible to cover crowns growing out in the garden with straw, dry grass and the like, held in place with a box or upturned pot to help keep them warm. They will then grow earlier and produce similar forced stems.

Each well grown crown should produce 6–7 lb (3 kg) a year from February to August. Two good varieties are 'Timperley Early', which can be forced and is a good garden variety, and 'Cawood Delight', not suited to forcing but producing stems of good red colour which retain shape and colour when cooked.

Blackcurrants

Choice of variety and the purchase of pest and disease-free stock is very important with this fruit. Given clean, vigorous bushes blackcurrants are easy to grow and suitable for most soil types.

British gardeners are fortunate in having a government administered certification scheme which ensures that bushes sold as 'Certified' are disease-free and can be relied on to give good results. Choice of variety is not so straightforward because there are a number to choose from.

Until recently the standard good commercial variety was 'Baldwin'. Now the more recently introduced 'Ben Lomond' will give up to double the yield of 'Baldwin' on similar-sized bushes. Where a really long picking season is required another relative newcomer, 'Malling Jet', should be chosen. This ripens at least a fortnight later than 'Ben Lomond' and takes the cropping well into August.

Both newcomers tend to flower later

A metal superstructure to support nets is an advantage where several fruits need protecting from birds. Black netting is less obtrusive than green in the garden and remember to remove the net, or regularly knock it, to prevent snow building up and weighing the whole structure down. Blackcurrant bushes, foreground, illustrate light brown young branches and black to grey older wood.

which helps them to resist damage from frost. Pruning systems also help to reduce the effect of frost with the flowers on older wood often setting under frosty and poor pollinating conditions, while young branches fail to produce a crop.

This rather contradicts past advice where nearly all the two-year-old, dark barked branches were cut right out after harvest. All that you need to do with these heavy-yielding newcomers is to prune out one or two of the older branches on mature bushes each autumn.

Dig the soil well and mix in plenty of garden compost and/or peat before planting. Container-grown specimens can be transplanted any time of year but other stock, lifted from the soil, is moved during the period between October and March.

Container plants will not need pruning and can be allowed to fruit the first summer after planting – you can even buy them with fruit on. Lifted bushes must be pruned back hard in the early spring following the transplanting. I really mean hard, leaving just 1–2 in (2–5 cm) of stem above ground.

Space the bushes 4–6 ft (1.2 to 2 m) apart. Where four or more are planted in one spot make the spacing in the row closer and the spacing between the row wider. Strong growth helps to increase the yield and size of currants so feed well each spring. They respond well to rela-

tively high proportion of nitrogen, such as in growmore fertilizer and this, applied at 4 oz per square yard, will give good crops.

Covering the surface of the soil around each bush with garden compost or rotted-down leaves, after flowering, improves the soil, retains moisture and improves the crop. Don't be afraid to water well as the berries start to swell if the weather is dry.

Where you have only one or two bushes it is worth picking the one or two larger berries at the top of each sprig as they ripen. The remaining fruits grow bigger as a result and you can pick fresh fruit over a longer period. Good sized bushes yield 6–8 lb a year.

Pests and Diseases

Big bud mite not only causes buds to swell up plump and round before failing to grow but it also transmits virus disease. The virus disease also called 'reversion' or 'nettle leaf' distorts the leaf shape and considerably reduces growth and yield.

Spraying with *systemic fungicides* several times when the new growth breaks in spring will help control this mite. Picking off the swollen buds and burning before the mites have chance to spread is also to be recommended. In severe cases it is worth cutting the whole bush to the ground and burning all the branches. It means no crop until the second summer but gives a completely clean start.

Gooseberries, Red and White Currants

Unlike blackcurrants, where complete older branches are regularly pruned out, gooseberries, red and white currants are shaped and pruned much more like apples. A main stem or short trunk is grown and then a framework of branches built up to carry the short fruiting pieces of stem called spurs.

Annual pruning consists of reducing the new growth made at the tip of each branch each summer by half to one third in the subsequent winter. All side growths from these main branches, made in the summer, are cut back to about 1 in (2.5 cm) long each winter.

They all prefer fertile soil and a sunny site, although the currants and cooking varieties of gooseberries will grow in partial shade and respond well to training against a north-facing wall or fence.

The skilled gardener can train these fruits up on a 3 ft (1 m) trunk like a young

Soft fruit: pest and disease control chart (see also chart on page 109)

Problem	Spray	Mar	Apl	May	Jun	Jly	Aug	Notes
DISEASES								
BOTRYTIS (Greymould) Strawberries and cane fruit	benomyl, or dichlofluanid, or thiophanate-methyl, or thiram			▬	▬			
CANE SPOT Rasps, logans and hybrid berries	benomyl, or thiophanate-methyl, or thiram			▬	▬			2 or 3 sprays at 14-day intervals.
LEAF SPOT Black, red and white currants	benomyl, or bupirimate and triforine, or thiophanate-methyl, or thiram			▬	▬			2 or 3 sprays at 14-day intervals.
MILDEW (American gooseberry mildew) Gooseberries, Blackcurrants	benomyl, or pirimicarb, or dinocap, or thiophanate-methyl				▬			
SPUR BLIGHT Logans, Rasps.	benomyl, or thiophanate-methy, or thiram	▬	▬					2 or 3 sprays at 14-day intervals. Start when shoots are ½ in (1cm) long
PESTS								
APHID (Greenfly) All soft fruit	dimethoate or fenitrothion, or formothion, or heptenophos, or malathion, or permethrin, or pirimicarb, or pirimiphos methyl, or rotenone		▬	▬	▬			tar oil Dec./Jan. all but strawberries
BIG BUD MITE Blackcurrants	benomyl, or thiophanate-methyl	▬	▬					some varieties are damaged by this sulphur spray
CAPSID Currants	malathion or bioresmethrin or dimethoate or fenitrothion, or permethrin, or pirimiphos-methyl				▬			
RASPBERRY BEETLE Cane fruit	fenitrothion, or malathion, or permethrin, or pirimphos-methyl, or rotenone				▬			
SAWFLY (and other caterpillars) Gooseberries	malathion, or bioresmethrin, or fenitrothion, or permethrin, or pirimiphos-methyl, or rotenone				▬			

NOTE: Combined sprays, for example malathion/benomyl, or fenitrothion/thiophanate-methyl in May will control most problems. Spray at the first sign of attack and when weather is still – usually evenings. Dust when dew is on plants to help chemicals to stick. Avoid using the same chemical year after year, to avoid build up of resistance.

Young bush of 'Ben Lomond' ready for picking. Green plastic netting is a rather garish colour in the garden.

Right Heavy cropping 'Careless' gooseberry with fruits being thinned to one per 1 in (2.5 cm) of branch.

tree. They can also be grown on single cordons, a column of growth 1 ft (30 cm) in circumference and 3–5 ft (1–1.6 m) high, and as two or three upright cordon stems on one short trunk. These cordon shapes make an attractive low fence or divide between plots.

Gooseberries

The easiest to grow and provide heavy cropping is the green-fruited cooking variety 'Careless'. Even heavier yielding is the new but very thorny 'Invicta'.

Note clear short trunk of first gooseberry in the row. The second had buds left on the cutting and this will grow into a mass of branches making picking difficult.

There are red-fruited kinds like 'Whinham's Industry' but by far the best, and quite as sweet as white grapes when fully ripe, is the variety 'Leveller'.

Gooseberries are generally better able to withstand chalky soils than other soft fruits but 'Leveller' will need good soil to crop well. Space the plants 4–6 ft (1.2–1.8 m) apart, and use the wider spacing for the stronger-growing, cooking varieties you plan to crop for 15–20 years.

Delay pruning until quite late in the winter because bullfinches can strip off the buds in late winter and during hard weather. Apply fertilizer each spring, using one with more potash such as rose or tomato food.

Picking can start in late May when some of the fruits can be thinned for cooking. The remaining fruits should be left spaced about 1 in (2.5 cm) down the branches to develop fully. Yields are likely to vary from 6–14 lb according to vigour of variety, size, soil and age of plant.

Caterpillars can attack these plants in April/May and quickly defoliate the whole plant. To prevent this spray with any safe caterpillar killer at the first signs of attack.

White powdery mildew disease can also affect the young growing shoots and in bad attacks cover the fruits too. Early spraying at the first sign of this disease with systemic fungicide will kill it without harming the bushes.

Red and White Currants

There can be no more attractive fruit than long strings of large ripe redcurrants. All strong-growing and healthy bushes are a good buy with varieties like 'Laxton's No. 1' and 'Red Lake' yielding 4–5 lb per bush.

White currants, for example 'White Versailles', are sweeter and better to eat raw although they crop slightly lighter. Cultural treatment for these currants is the same as for gooseberries and where the growth gets very thick and somewhat excessive, the side growths on the main branches can be cut back to just six leaves

It is essential to net redcurrants if the tasty succulent berries are to be saved from blackbirds.

Old mossy wood on soft fruit bushes and fruit trees is cleaned off by a winter tar oil spray which also kills overwintering pests.

Below Puckering and red blistering caused by yellow aphis on currants.

Blueberries

While soft fruit bushes of all kinds can be grown in amongst shrubs and perennial flowers, blueberries are the perfect dual-purpose plants. They have white bell-like flowers in late May, rich purple blue fruits in August/September and really startling red and yellow autumn leaf colour.

The autumn leaf colour certainly equals several shrubs we grow just for that quality alone. They need an acid soil, so dig in plenty of peat before planting or mix them in among azaleas and rhododendrons.

You must have at least two varieties to achieve cross pollination and heavy crops of fruit, which can be eaten raw and cooked in pies and used to add flavour to apples.

They will crop for more than 20 years and eventually reach 4–6 ft (1.2–1.8 m) high. Space them 4–6 ft (1.2–1.8 m) apart. They need no pruning for the first two years after planting. After this just thin out the occasional old branch as for blackcurrants.

There are several good varieties and 'Earlsblue' and 'Goldtraube' (mid season) give a good long picking season and have excellent leaf colour. A good sized bush will yield 10 lb of fruit, which stores well in the deep freeze.

If you have no garden these can be grown as attractive tub plants and as such will benefit from watering when possible with rainwater.

The ripening berries of blueberry in August. The rich green leaves turn yellow and crimson in September/October before they fall.

long in late July. They are then cut back to 1 in (2.5 cm) in the winter.

There are several aphid which attack currants and distortion and puckering of the young leaves is usually the first sign of attack. Any greenfly killer, preferably based on pirimcarb (which leaves the bees unharmed) will kill this pest.

Propagation

All these soft fruit bushes root easily as hardwood cuttings. Cut off healthy and strong-growing young pieces of the current year's growth in October. Gooseberries will root best if the cuttings are made before leaf fall.

Each cutting needs to be 12–15 in (30–38 cm) long and all, except blackcurrants, have the buds removed up the cutting leaving just the top three or four buds. This produces the clear stem or short trunk which makes fruit picking in future years so much easier.

All the buds are left on blackcurrants because this allows them to grow as multi-stemmed bushes. When all branches are cut off almost to soil level after planting new shoots can then grow from the below-ground buds.

Cookery

Rhubarb

January meals need rhubarb so we must be thankful that it's possible to force it in time to wake up our palates after the long months of winter stodge.

To prepare: cut off the white part near root and the leaves, wipe each stem, then cut into 1 in (2 cm) lengths.

To cook: rhubarb is very juicy and best cooked without water. Use it in pies, crumbles and desserts. To stew: layer the cut stems with sugar in a saucepan or casserole. Cover and cook over a low heat or in a slow oven until the rhubarb just boils. Remove pan or casserole from heat and leave covered for rhubarb to cook completely. A strip of orange or lemon rind or a pinch of spice adds to the flavour. Serve hot or cold with custard. For a rhubarb pie, mix prepared stems with sugar and a little cornflour to thicken the juice as it cooks. Always avoid over-cooking or the rhubarb will collapse and become stringy.

To preserve: to freeze: use 4 oz (100 g) sugar to each 1 lb (500 g) prepared stems. Layer rhubarb and sugar in a plastic container or mix and pack in a freezer bag. Store for up to 1 year. To use: cook from frozen.

Chutney: the tartness of rhubarb mixes well with spices and vinegar to make delicious chutney.

Jam: mix with fruits with good setting power such as oranges, lemons, apples, plums.

RHUBARB AND LEMON JAM

This economical jam has an unusually smooth texture. It is also delicious when flavoured with ginger.

Makes about 5 lb

Metric		Imperial
1½ kg	rhubarb	3 lb
500 g	lemons	1 lb
250 g	cooking apples	½ lb
1½ kg	granulated or preserving sugar	3 lb

1. Prepare suitable jars; wash well and place in a warm oven to dry.
2. Trim rhubarb, wipe and cut into 1 in (2.5 cm) pieces. Place in a large saucepan or preserving pan.
3. Scrub lemons, using a sharp knife or potato peeler pare rinds from half, avoiding any white pith. Shred rinds and add to rhubarb. Squeeze juice and add to rhubarb, cut up pith and place in a saucepan with pips.
4. Peel and core apples; add peel and core to the lemon pith and apple to the rhubarb.
5. Cook rhubarb over a medium heat until tender, about ½ hour. Add 1 pint (500 ml) water to pith, bring to boil, cover and simmer for ½ hour. Remove lid and cook uncovered for a further ½ hour. Strain through a nylon sieve into preserving pan and lightly press out the juice with a spoon. Discard pulp.
6. Add sugar to ingredients in preserving pan and stir until dissolved. Bring to boil and boil on full heat until set, about 5 minutes. To test, remove pan from heat, place a little jam on a chilled plate and leave to cool. If set, a skin will form on the surface which will crinkle when pushed with the finger. If not, re-boil and test again after 3 minutes.
7. Ladle jam into jars and immediately cover with waxed paper discs and cellophane tops or cover the surface with paraffin wax and cover with lids.

RHUBARB RIPPLE

This is a way of glamorizing rhubarb to make it look like an exotic soft fruit.

For 4 portions

Metric		Imperial
500 g	rhubarb	1 lb
4 × 15 ml sp	sugar	4 tbsp
1	raspberry-flavour jelly	1
1	small can evaporated milk	1

Top **Rhubarb and Orange Meringue;** *top right* **Rhubarb and Lemon Jam;** *right* **Rhubarb Ripple**

1. Trim rhubarb, wipe stalks, then cut into 1 in (2.5 cm) lengths. Place in a saucepan with sugar, cover with a lid and cook over low heat until rhubarb is tender.
2. Pour into a liquidizer goblet, break up jelly tablet and add, then run machine until mixture is smooth (alternatively, press rhubarb through a sieve into a saucepan, add jelly and stir over a low heat until jelly has dissolved). Pour into a bowl, cool, then chill until partially set. Pour evaporated milk into a bowl and chill.
3. Whisk evaporated milk until thick, then gradually whisk in all but 2 tbsp (2 × 15 ml sp) of the rhubarb mixture. Pour into a bowl, then pour in remaining rhubarb; gently cut through mixture with a spoon to swirl. Chill until firm.

RHUBARB AND ORANGE MERINGUE

Here's a way of disguising the tartness of rhubarb. The orange-flavoured custard makes a subtle blend of textures and gives a good flavour combination.

For 4 portions

Metric		Imperial
500 g	rhubarb	1 lb
1	medium-sized orange	1
4 × 15 ml sp	cornflour	4 tbsp
6 × 15 ml sp	granulated sugar	6 tbsp
2	eggs	2
75 g	caster sugar	3 oz

1. Prepare a moderate oven (160 deg C, 325 deg F, Gas Mark 3). Wipe rhubarb, trim and cut into 1 in (2 cm) lengths. Place in a 3 pint (1½ litre) ovenproof dish.
2. Scrub orange, grate rind and squeeze juice. Place rind and juice in a measuring jug and make up to ¾ pint (400 ml) with water. Place cornflour and granulated sugar in a saucepan; gradually blend in the juice mixture. Bring to boil, stirring, and cook 1 minute, remove from heat.
3. Separate eggs, place whites in a clean, grease-free bowl and beat yolks into orange mixture, then pour over rhubarb. Cook for 45 minutes.
4. Whisk egg whites until stiff, but not dry, whisk in half the sugar, then fold in remainder with a metal spoon. Pile on top of custard, spreading to edge of dish. Swirl top, then return to oven and cook for a further 20 minutes. Serve meringue either hot or cold.

Red, Black and White currants

Black, red and white currants are valued mainly for their use in cooked dishes and preserves. They are high in pectin, the substance that makes jam set. Red and white currants are valuable additions to other low-pectin fruits, such as strawberries when making jam. All currants are used in traditional summer pudding. Blackcurrants are a rich source of vitamin C.

To prepare: wash well then strip the currants off the stalks using the prongs of a fork.

To cook: stew gently with water and sugar.

If time is short, cook with the stalks on then sieve the fruit.

To store: in a shallow layer in a punnet in the refrigerator for up to 2 days.

To freeze: dry well and pack in useable amounts in freezer bags, or open freeze.

To make jam: cook 4 lb (2 kg) black-currants or a mixture of black, red and white, in 3 pints (1½ litres) water. Add 6 lb (3 kg) sugar and boil until set. Alternatively, replace half the fruit with apple or rhubarb.

To make jelly: cook 4 lb (2 kg) fruit in 2 pints (1 litre) water, strain. Leave 30 minutes then cook the pulp in 1 pint (½ litre) water for a second extract. Mix the juices, measure and add 1 lb 2 oz (½ kg) sugar to each 1-pint (550 ml) juice.

To make pectin stock: for adding to low or medium pectin fruits for jam. Cook ½ lb (250 g) fruit in ½ pint (250 ml) water for each 3 lb (1½ kg) fruit then strain. See page 98 for Apple Pectin Stock.

To make black-currant cordial: place the fruit in a bowl and crush with the hands or a wooden spoon. Add about ½ pint (250 ml) water to each 1 lb (500 g) fruit. Cook the fruit slowly over a saucepan of boiling water, crushing occasionally with a wooden spoon. Strain through a nylon sieve then through a filter paper (a coffee filter is useful). Add ¾ lb to 1 lb (300 g to 450 g) sugar to each 1 pint (½ litre) juice. Stir into the cold syrup. Store in sterilized bottles in the refrigerator or sterilize in the bottles in a saucepan of boiling water as for bottling. Use small bottles and screw or cork tops. Use the pulp to make fruit cheese.

To make fruit cheese: press cooked pulp through a sieve, weigh the purée then add 1 lb (500 g) sugar to each 1 lb (500 g) purée. Add a little cinnamon, if desired, then stir over a low heat to dissolve the sugar. Cook for about 45 minutes, stirring occasionally until thick. It is thick enough when there is no free liquid and when a wooden spoon drawn through the mixture leaves a channel. Pack in small, oiled, wide-necked jars or individual jelly moulds. Cover with waxed discs or paraffin wax.

To make wine: all varieties of currants are useful for wine. Blackcurrants have a very distinctive flavour and are best mixed with bananas or other bland flavoured fruits. For each 1 gal (4½ litres), place 2¼ lb (1 kg) fruit and 1 lb (500 g) ripe bananas in a bucket. Add 5 pints (3 litres) water and 2 tsp (2 × 5 ml sp) 2 pectin-destroying enzyme and a crushed Campden tablet. Cover and leave for 24 hours then add a fermenting yeast starter, 1 rounded tsp (2 × 5 ml sp) yeast nutrient and 2¼ lb (1 kg) sugar. Cover and ferment for 5 days stirring twice daily then strain into a demi-john, add 9 oz (250 g) red grape juice concentrate, top up with water, fit airlock and ferment out to dryness. Make red currant wine with 3 lb (1.5 kg) redcurrants, 8 oz (250 g) sultanas and 2¼ lb (1 kg) sugar.

RED FRUIT KISSEL

When the summer fruits are in abundance,

mix different sharp and sweet flavours to produce this perfect Russian-style dessert.

For 3 to 4 portions

Metric		Imperial
250 g	*mixed red fruits (raspberries, blackcurrants, redcurrants, etc)*	½ lb
2 × 15 ml sp	*cornflour*	2 tbsp
1 × 1.25 ml sp	*ground cinnamon*	¼ tsp
4 × 15 ml sp	*granulated sugar*	4 tbsp
1	*medium-sized orange*	1
	caster sugar	
75 ml	*carton single cream*	2⅞ fl oz

1. Wash fruit; remove any leaves, stalks and hulls. Place cornflour, cinnamon and sugar in a saucepan. Blend in ¼ pint (125 ml) water.

2. Using a sharp knife or vegetable peeler, peel thin strips of orange peel for decoration.

3. Squeeze juice from orange and add to pan with fruit. Bring to boil, stirring gently, and simmer for 1 minute, or until fruit is soft, but not broken. Leave to cool.

4. Divide the kissel between 3 or 4 glasses, sprinkle each with a little caster sugar to prevent a skin forming; chill. To serve: top each kissel with a little cream. Place an orange peel strip on each glass and serve any remaining cream separately.

Gooseberry

Use the hard green gooseberries for cooking, jam and wine and leave the ripe or special red varieties for dessert. Elderflowers can be added to all gooseberry dishes for an interesting flavour.

To prepare: cut off the brown flower tops and stalk end tails with scissors or nip off with the fingers. Wash well and drain.

To cook: stew in a little sugar syrup in a covered pan very slowly to avoid breaking up the fruit. A slow cooker is ideal for this. Leave to cool in the syrup for the sugar to penetrate. Alternatively, place in a casserole, sprinkle layers with sugar and cook at the bottom of the oven until almost tender. Those in the centre of the dish will still be bright green. Remove and leave covered to continue cooking then leave to cool.

To store: keep in a plastic bag in the bottom of the refrigerator for up to 1 week.

To freeze: dry well and pack in freezer bags.

To make jam: cook 4 lb (2 kg) gooseberries in 1½ pints (1 litre) water until reduced to one third. Add 6 lb (3 kg) sugar and boil until set. Add strawberries, redcurrants or rhubarb in equal proportions.

To bottle: choose small green gooseberries and nick the skin to allow the syrup to penetrate. Pack in jars and cover with a light sugar syrup.

To make wine: gooseberries make a very good crisp light table wine. For each 1 gal (4½ litres) use 3 lb (1.5 kg) gooseberries, 1 lb (500 g) sultanas and 2 lbs (1 kg) sugar. Cover gooseberries with boiling water, cool,

then crush with the hands. Add pectin destroying enzyme and a crushed Campden tablet and leave overnight. Stir in chopped sultanas, a vigorously fermenting yeast starter, yeast nutrient, a cup of tea and the sugar. Ferment on the pulp for 3 days then strain into a demi-john and fill up with water. Ferment to dryness.

To make Gooseberry Fool: mix sweetened purée with an equal quantity of lightly-whipped cream, custard or a mixture of both.

To make Gooseberry Pie: best as a double crust pie. Wash the fruit, drain then coat in a mixture of sugar and cornflour – about four tablespoons sugar to one of cornflour. Pile over the pastry, cover and bake in a hot oven (225 deg C, 425 deg F, Gas Mark 7) for 10 minutes then lower the heat and bake until the fruit bubbles.

GOOSEBERRY CREAM DESSERT

Make the first small tart gooseberries of the season into this smooth creamy mould.

For 6 to 8 portions

Metric		Imperial
500 g	*gooseberries*	1 lb
100 g	*granulated sugar*	4 oz
	custard powder	
570 ml	*milk*	1 pint
15 g	*powdered gelatine*	½ oz
150 ml	*carton double cream*	5 fl oz
1	*hazelnut*	1

1. Wash gooseberries and place in a medium-sized saucepan with sugar and 1 tbsp (1 × 15 ml sp) water. Cook over a low heat for 15 to 20 minutes until fruit is soft. Leave to cool.

2. Make up custard as directed on packet using milk, but use 5 tbsp (5 × 15 ml sp) custard powder and omit sugar. Cover and leave to cool.

3. Measure 3 tbsp (3 × 15 ml sp) water into a small basin; add gelatine and stir. Place basin in a pan of water over a moderate heat; stir until gelatine has dissolved.

4. Make a purée from fruit (press through a sieve or liquidize in an electric blender, then strain). Mix together purée, custard and gelatine.

5. Whip cream until it just holds its shape. Place a little in a nylon piping bag fitted with a star tube; reserve in refrigerator for decoration. Stir remaining cream into fruit mixture.

6. Pour into a 2 pint (1 litre) mould or pudding basin; leave to set in refrigerator for 3 to 4 hours or overnight.

7. To unmould: dip mould in a bowl of hand-hot water. Invert on to a serving plate; remove mould. Pipe the reserved cream in a whirl on top of the mould and decorate the cream whirl with a hazelnut.

GOOSEBERRY SHERBET

Make as for Blackberry Sherbet (page 121). Omit the lemon juice and add a little green food colouring.

Grapes & Strawberries

Whilst it may be fun to raise grapes from pips indoors, the fruiting of seedlings is extremely variable. Careful choice of a named variety is important if acceptable and usable bunches of grapes are to be grown most years. There is no reason why all home owners with a glass-sided sun lounge, greenhouse or home extension should not cultivate a grape vine.

Even those gardeners without glass protection can train grapes along south and west-facing walls and fences. It may be necessary to use a polythene sheet cover to ripen the fruit in a cool, sunless autumn and in the more northerly parts of the country but even in cold, poor-fruiting years they make attractive ornamental climbers.

Good named varieties of strawberries from vigorous and disease-free stocks are also needed to grow the heaviest crops of this fruit. All strawberries grow well in containers so the absence of a garden does not prevent their cultivation.

While single plants can be grown in pots, eight to 12 plants cultivated in a fertilized-peat-filled growbag will give larger pickings and prove more practical for most of us. If you can provide some protection early in the year for some plants, picking can start late May/early June and then, using several varieties, fresh fruits can be grown right through to the frost of early winter.

Heaviest crops come from the ordinary summer-fruiting kinds. The so-called perpetual or remontant types will fruit in summer but where the gardener has both it is advisable to remove the early flowers from these autumn-fruiters to increase the yield at that time of year.

Alpine strawberries raised from seed will continue to crop from summer right through to autumn, with the first year seedlings cropping from late summer onwards. They need feeding and watering well to avoid producing tiny fruits full of woody seeds.

Grapes

It is possible to grow a vine in a large tub, training one single stem upwards to form a trunk like a weeping standard rose. Such plants will need very regular watering in summer, however, to prevent the fruits shrivelling.

Vines are much easier to cultivate in the soil and deep cultivation before planting is advisable. Where they are to be grown under glass it is possible to have the roots outside and the main stem trained through the base wall into the greenhouse.

Good varieties to grow under glass are 'Black Hamburgh' and the white-fruited 'Buckland Sweetwater'. Early ripening is needed outside and suitable varieties include: 'Madeleine Angevine', a good table and wine variety; 'Brant' a strong-growing black grape suitable to eat or make wine and the very widely-planted 'Muller Thurgau' for wine. The latter requires a long growing season and plenty of autumn sunshine.

Most vines grow best in a free-draining, slightly chalky – alkaline – soil and it is worth testing the soil with a simple soil pH meter before planting. They do not thrive in heavy clay and waterlogged soils.

The vine, once planted, will grow for many years so try to get the soil right from the beginning.

Dig in deeply plenty of well-rotted manure or compost (the vine roots can go down 3 ft (1 m)), add the lime if necessary and a good base fertilizer which contains plenty of phosphates and potash. The phosphates encourage strong roots and the potash helps to sweeten the fruit.

One strong-growing variety will cover 15–30 ft (5–10 m) of wall or three weaker varieties will fill the same space. Plant one-year old container grown plants for the best results. Train up the single stem in the first summer and prune back hard in the first winter.

Any hard cuts on grapes must be made when the plant is completely dormant in December/January; if you cut once the sap starts to rise the wounds bleed and it is impossible to stop this loss of plant energy. Pinching soft new growth with the thumbnail doesn't cause bleeding.

The remaining vine stump will produce several shoots and one of these is retained and tied to a wire or similar support. Any side shoots from the main stem have the tip pinched out once one leaf is formed. The soft tip is pruned off this main stem each winter and a new shoot trained in until the rod reaches the length you require.

Untie the rod each winter and leave

horizontal to encourage side shoots along the full length of stem. Side shoots carry the fruit and the tips are pinched out of these so-called laterals two leaves past a bunch of flowers.

While this system is ideal for under glass and on walls, the Guyot system is used for wine grapes in the open garden. Here training for the first year is the same save two shoots rather than one are retained. In the second winter one of the two is pruned hard back and one left. Two more shoots are produced from behind the cut and one of these can be

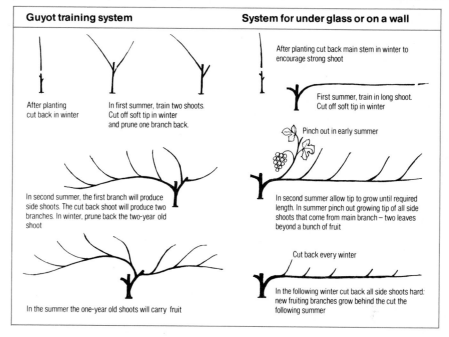

Guyot training system

After planting cut back in winter

In first summer, train two shoots. Cut off soft tip in winter and prune one branch back.

In second summer, the first branch will produce side shoots. The cut back shoot will produce two branches. In winter, prune back the two-year old shoot

In the summer the one-year old shoots will carry fruit

System for under glass or on a wall

After planting cut back main stem in winter to encourage strong shoot

First summer, train in long shoot. Cut off soft tip in winter

Pinch out in early summer

In second summer allow tip to grow until required length. In summer pinch out growing tip of all side shoots that come from main branch – two leaves beyond a bunch of fruit

Cut back every winter

In the following winter cut back all side shoots hard: new fruiting branches grow behind the cut the following summer

Garden chemicals

ACTIVE CHEMICAL	COMMON NAME	PROPRIETARY NAMES
Pesticides		
bioresmethrin (0)		Combat Vegetable Insecticide (Fisons), Combat Whitefly (Fisons)
BHC (now HCH) (14)	Lindane	Lindex (Murphy) also in Hexyl Plus (PBI), Abol X (ICI), Combat Garden Insecticide (Fisons)
bupirimate + triforine		Nimrod-T (ICI)
dicofol		in Combined Pest and Disease Spray (Murphy) (14)
dimethoate (7)	rogor	In Combat Garden Insecticide (Fison), Systemic Insecticde (Murphy)
ethioencarb		Greenfly and blackfly killer (Fison)
fenitrothion (14)		Fentro (Murphy), Fenitrothion (PBI)
formothion (7) (not on cherries)		Systemic Liquid (PBI)
heptenophos (1)		Tumblebug (Murphy)
malathion (1)		Malathion Greenfly Killer (PBI), Liquid Malathion (Murphy), in Combat Garden and Vegetable Insecticide (Fison)
metaldehyde (0)	slug bait	Many brands
methiocarb (7)		Slug guard (PBI)
oxydemeton-methyl (21)	metasystox	Greenfly (Aphid Gun)
permethrin (0)		Bio Sprayday (pbi), bio Longlast (pbi), Crop Saver (pbi), Picket (ICI), Picket G (ICI), Tumblebug (Murphy), Whitefly and Caterpillar Killer (Fisons)
pirimicarb (14)		Abol G (ICI) Rapid (ICI) (harmless to lacewings, ladybirds and bees.)
pirimiphos-methyl (7)		Sybol 2 (ICI)
resmethrin (0)		Sprayday (PBI)
rotenone (1)	derris	Abol Derris Dust (ICI), Liquid Derris (PBI or Murphy)
tar distillate	tar oil	Clean-UP (ICI) Mortegg (Murphy)
trichlorphon (2)		(May and Baker), Kilsect (PBI) Caterpillar Killer
Fungicides	grease bands	Boltac Greasebands (PBI)
benomyl (0)	benlate	Benlate (PBI)
copper (0)		Liquid Copper Fungicide (Murphy)
dichlofluanid (21)		Elvaron (May and Baker)
dithiocarbamate type	thiram (7) (do not use on fruit to be preserved)	Garden Fungicide (ICI) in Hexyl Plus (PBI),
thiophanate-methyl (0)		Fungus Fighter (May and Baker) Systemic Fungicide (Murphy)
zineb (7)	dithane	Dithane (PBI)
Wound Paint	bitumen	Arbrex (PBI)

Numbers in brackets indicate 'safe harvest interval' (that is days between spraying and picking to eat).

ALWAYS FOLLOW MANUFACTURERS INSTRUCTIONS TO THE LETTER

These lists and the help of your local specialist garden sundries retailers, who will recommend equally suitable alternative brands, should provide all the information and products you will need.

SOME USEFUL FIGURES: 1 pint = 20 fluid ounces, 1 fluid ounce = 8 drams; 8 teaspoonsful; 2 tablespoonsful. 1 pint = 568 millilitres. 1 fluid ounce = 28 millilitres. 8 pints = 1 gallon = 4.55 litres. 50 millilitres = 1.75 fluid ounces. 1 litre = 1.75 pints.

Pot-grown strawberries make attractive houseplants and each one in a 5 in (11 cm) half-pot will yield 4–6 oz of fruit.

allowed to carry fruit in the third year.

It is inadvisable to take fruit earlier than the third year because it slows down the whole rate of growth and development of the vine, affecting cropping for a number of years.

Pinch out all growing tips by late August to encourage the wood to ripen before the onset of winter. The job of pinching out the side shoots from laterals is continual throughout the summer but, if left, the vine just grows in every direction and few, if any, grapes are produced.

Each winter the laterals which have borne fruit are pruned off. They grow again the next summer on single rod vines from the stumpy spurs which develop. In the case of Guyot they grow on the two new main stems trained in the previous summer.

Once the fruits start to swell the numbers will need to be thinned out leaving no more than half if you are to have reasonable-sized fruit to eat. They can be left without thinning for wine. Mildew disease can occur but systemic fungicidal sprays will control this.

Strawberries

One of the quickest of all plants to fruit, you can plant pot-grown strawberry runners in spring and be picking fruit in a matter of weeks. Good healthy plants spaced 12–18 in (30–45 cm) down the row, in rows spaced 18–24 in (45–60 cm) apart will crop for three to six years.

Young plants are best, however, be-cause the fruit can become rather small in the fourth to sixth years, when some plants die. New stock is propagated from runners taken off healthy plants in July/August. It is important to root them as soon as possible and only choose runners from virus disease-free plants with big, green vigorous leaves.

If you delay planting runners lifted from the soil after mid August you lose one ounce per plant for every week delayed. Growing the runners in 4–5 in (9–11 cm) pots prevents any check to growth and allows much later planting.

The best advice is to buy either pot-grown runners or order bare root plants from a specialist grower for delivery in early August. If the bare root plants are not delivered until early September and growth is weak, it is advisable to pick off the blooms next spring (if you can steel yourself to do such a thing) and build the plants up for future years' heavy fruiting. Plants fruiting for the first time are called maidens and they produce earlier and larger fruits.

Runners growing on fruiting plants can be pegged into the soil between the original stock down the row to increase the plant population and subsequent yield. Growers call this the matted row system. If perennial weeds are allowed to grow in these matted rows, however, they

The seed-raised alpine strawberry sown under glass in early spring will be fruiting by late July.

can become a terrible mess.

One easy way is to cultivate the soil and then cover with heavy grade polythene – preferably black – burying the edges to hold it down. Slits are cut in the polythene mulch and one strawberry planted through each slit. The polythene smothers the weed, prevents runners rooting down everywhere, stops soil splashing up on the fruit and reduces the fruit damage by slugs.

Single rows of summer-fruiting strawberries can also be covered with cloches as the flower buds develop, until after harvest. This gives frost protection for the flowers (if the yellow centre of the flower suddenly goes black, that's destruction by frost), advances harvest by a week or two, prevents rain splashing mud on the fruits and discourages soft rots, as well as keeping the birds away. The cloches can also be moved over autumn strawberries from early September to give more bird and weather protection as well as extending the picking season.

When planting strawberries avoid setting them too deep: the crowns need to be just on the surface. The easiest method of controlling the runners is to pinch them out soft and green as soon as they are seen, except for the autumn fruiting kinds, some of which will fruit on newly-formed runners.

Varieties

There are special varieties for different purposes: 'Cambridge Favourite' is the standard type being summer-fruiting, easy to grow, of good flavour and heavy yielding. One of the best early-fruiting kinds is 'Pantagruella'; it can be planted closer because of its smaller leaves, it has a very good flavour but needs watering well if grown outside, unprotected, for the earliest picking.

Two good Dutch varieties are 'Tamella', which is very early in the first cropping year and the later cropping 'Tenira'. The latter has excellent flavour and sometimes produces a second autumn crop.

'Totem' from Canada is a variety to store in the deep freeze because it retains shape and colour after thawing. These fruits are best sliced and coated with sugar before freezing.

One of the best autumn varieties is 'Aromel'; it fruits from August to October and has excellent flavour. Another variety called 'Gento' from West Germany grows well on chalky soils (which do not suit the summer-fruiting varieties) and will crop for several years while most 'perpetual' or autumn fruiting kinds only

The large summer fruiting 'Grandee' fruiting in its first year under polythene tunnel cloches.

crop well in their first year.

Alpine or seed-raised strawberries have much smaller fruits and do not produce runners. They make a good edging to summer flower borders and grow best in partial shade. There are red and yellow-fruiting varieties which produce thimble-sized fruit if kept well watered in dry weather. Plant breeders are improving fruit size and flavour, however, and new introductions like 'Sweetheart' are much more worthwhile.

Container growing

While strawberry barrels and tubs are widely advertised, cultivation in a container which has compost more than 1 ft (30 cm) deep is difficult. The top compost tends to dry out and the bottom gets waterlogged. I much prefer growing one plant per pot or eight to 12 to a fertilized-peat-filled growbag.

Growbags and window boxes can be used by flat and balcony owners who wish to grow strawberries. If space is very restricted the tower pots with built in automatic watering systems allow 12 plants to be grown in 1 sq ft (less than 1/10 sq m) of floor space.

All these containers should be filled with all-peat composts, in which strawberries grow well. Plant up as soon as possible and leave them outside in a

sheltered place to get established. Bring them indoors in early spring for early crops; there is no point in bringing in before late February because high temperatures and restricted light will give poor crops.

The fresh, green new leaves and marguerite-type white and yellow flowers on strawberries make attractive indoor pot plants. Open flowers will need dusting over with a feather or soft paint brush to pollinate the fruit. Inadequate pollination on indoor and cloche-covered plants causes misshapen fruits.

Container-grown strawberries do not need to be fed until the leaves start to turn pale and the leaf edges lose their colour. Then give dilute liquid feeds which are high in potash, such as tomato and rose fertilizers. Plants grown out in the garden will need very little fertilizer: $\frac{1}{2}$ oz per square yard (17 gm/m²) of sulphate of potash each spring is usually sufficient for most soils. This will help to give a heavy yield of good-flavoured crops.

Greenfly can be a problem and one of the safe greenfly sprays should be applied at the first signs of attack. Sprays based on primicarb, for example, will kill aphids and not harm the bees. Leaves which are slightly sticky to the touch are sure sign of aphid attack.

Soft brown rots on the fruit and a greyish mould are the disease botrytis. It starts on the dying petals so fungus sprays, preferably systemic fungicides, should be applied when flowers begin to open, again when flowers fade and three weeks later. This disease is less likely under cloches and in dry seasons.

Cookery

Grapes

The supreme reward for growing your own grapes comes when you draw the cork from your first bottle of home-made wine. Mind you, there's a lot of work to be done before you reach that stage, but the end result is certainly worth the effort. Not that grapes will only make wine . . . think about fresh grape juice, a refreshing non-alcoholic drink, fresh fruit jellies and jelly preserves, too. Then there are the dessert grapes – usually grown under glass in this country. These are perfect for garnishing savoury or sweet dishes. If there's a surplus, bottle them in light syrup, and use the grape prunings to make Folly Wine – you'll find the recipe in most wine-making books. Or stuff the vine leaves with Dolmades, a savoury meat mixture the Greeks have made famous.

GRAPE WINE

Gather the grapes as late as possible, even after the leaves have fallen, to gain maximum sweetness. English grapes are usually too acid to use the juice exclusively; water and sugar must be added. In a sunny summer, check the specific gravity (SG) of the juice before diluting (any good wine-making book will tell you how to do this). About 15 lbs (7 kg) grapes will be required to make a gallon (4.5 litres) of juice.
To make wine from English white grapes:
1. Remove central stems but leave the small fruit stalks. Crush the grapes with the hands. Add a crushed Campden tablet, cover and leave over night.
2. Add 2 pints (1 litre) water for each 4 lbs (2 kg) of grapes and mix well. Take out a small quantity of the juice and check the SG with a hydrometer. Add sugar to increase the SG to 1.080 ($2\frac{1}{4}$ oz (65 g) sugar will raise the gravity about 50).
3. Add a vigorously fermenting yeast starter (hock for preference) and ferment on the pulp for 2 days, stirring and pressing down the cap of skins twice a day. Strain and press the pulp, pour juice into jars, fit an air-lock and ferment until dry.
4. Syphon off; add 2 Campden tablets, fit a cork to the jar and store for at least 3 months before drinking. Sweeten to taste just before drinking if desired.
To make wine from English black grapes: proceed as for White Wine adding $\frac{1}{2}$ pint (250 ml) water to each 2 lb (1 kg) grapes, but add sufficient sugar to increase the SG to 1.090. Ferment on the pulp for 10 days. Store at least 6 months before drinking.
Fresh grape juice: use the sweetest grapes to make this delicious non-alcoholic drink. If the grapes are very acid, dilute the juice with water and sweeten to taste. Place the grapes in a large saucepan and crush with hands. Add a little water if necessary and bring to the boil, stirring continuously. Boil for 1 minute then immediately pour through a scalded jelly bag to collect the juice. Taste the juice; if it is very acid, boil up the pulp with some more water, strain again. Taste, and add sugar, if necessary. Pour into sterilized bottles.

LEMON GRAPE GATEAU

The filling for this gateau is a tangy cheesecake mixture. It stores well in refrigerator or freezer.

For 8 to 10 portions
A 4-egg Whisked Sponge Cake mixture, baked in 2, 8 in (20 cm) sandwich cake tins.

Metric		Imperial
	FILLING	
250 g	*full fat soft cheese*	$\frac{1}{2}$ lb
397 g	*can sweetened condensed milk*	14 oz
100 ml	*lemon juice*	4 fl oz
	DECORATION	
100 g	*green and black grapes mixed*	4 oz

1. To make filling: beat soft cheese in a bowl, gradually beat in the condensed milk then the lemon juice to thicken the mixture (if using juice from freshly squeezed lemons, add 1 tsp (1×5 ml sp) finely-grated rind).
2. To assemble gateau: cut each sponge through centre horizontally and separate the four layers. Spread each with a quarter of the filling; leave 10 minutes to become firmer, then stack the layers. Cut grapes in halves and remove pips then arrange pairs of green grape halves with a black grape half in between, around the top edge. Arrange 6 black grape halves in the centre. Chill until ready to serve. Store for up to a day in the refrigerator; 3 months in the freezer. To freeze: open-freeze without grape decoration, then wrap in freezer cling wrap or foil.

MULLED GRAPE JUICE

Serve this sophisticated non-alcoholic drink at a party, and those who have to drive home afterwards will not feel too deprived.

For 6 glasses

Metric		Imperial
2	*strips lemon rind*	2
2	*strips orange rind*	2
$\frac{1}{2}$	*cinnamon stick*	$\frac{1}{2}$
10	*cloves*	10
500 ml	*red grape juice*	$\frac{1}{2}$ pint
2×5 ml sp	*sugar*	2 tsp

1. Place lemon and orange rinds, cinnamon and cloves in a saucepan with $\frac{1}{2}$ pint (250 ml) water. Bring to boil, cover and simmer for 10 minutes. Remove from heat; leave to infuse for $\frac{1}{2}$ hour. Strain through a white paper tissue in a sieve.
2. Return strained spice mixture to saucepan, add grape juice and sugar; heat slowly. Serve warm with slices of orange and strips of lemon rind.

Strawberry

It seems that summer has arrived when the first strawberries are picked. These luscious fruits are at their best eaten as soon as possible after harvesting. Though their elusive flavour deteriorates with storage, strawberries make the most popular jam.
To prepare: remove the hulls then wash only if necessary. Drain and dry on kitchen paper, taking care not to bruise them.
To serve for dessert: serve with caster sugar and thick pouring cream or ice cream. Flavour the cream with grated orange rind, sugar or orange-flavour liqueur such as Cointreau or Grand Marnier. Add whole to fruit salad, use in flans, tartlets and gateaux. Use as toppings for cheesecakes, pavlova and trifles. Sieve or liquidize the less beautiful or squashy berries and use as a sauce to serve with ice cream, creamy desserts or yogurt. Or make into soufflés, mousses, ice cream or sorbets.
To store: use as soon as possible. Store in a covered shallow punnet or plastic container in the bottom of the refrigerator.
To freeze: whole strawberries go mushy after being frozen, but they are still useful to add to fruit salads and trifle. Open freeze then pack in freezer bags. Serve when only just thawed. Thaw in the refrigerator. Alternatively, layer halved or sliced strawberries with caster sugar in a freezer container. Use 8 oz to 12 oz (200 g to 300 g) sugar to each 2 lb (1 kg) fruit. Leave $\frac{3}{4}$ in (2 cm) head-space to allow for expansion. Freeze as purée in small tubs or ice cube trays then pack in freezer bags.
To make Strawberry Ice Cream: separate 2 eggs and add a purée made from $\frac{1}{2}$ lb (250 g) strawberries to the yolks with 2 tbsp (2×15 ml sp) lemon juice and some red food colouring. Whisk the whites with 2 oz (50 g) icing sugar and fold in the purée with $\frac{1}{4}$ pint (125 ml) lightly-whipped double cream. Freeze in a plastic container. Warm up slightly in the frozen food compartment of the refrigerator for 2 hours before serving.
To make Strawberry Sorbet: whisk 2 egg whites then whisk in 4 oz (100 g) caster sugar followed by $\frac{1}{2}$ pint (250 ml) strawberry purée, a few drops of red colouring and 1 tbsp (1×15 ml sp) lemon juice. Freeze in a plastic container. Leave in the refrigerator as for ice cream before serving.
To make jam: pectin stock must be added or the jam will not set. Use redcurrants, gooseberries or apple to make the stock (see pages 98 and 107), or use bought bottled pectin. Cook 3 lb ($1\frac{1}{2}$ kg) strawberries in a preserving pan until the juice is reduced by half. Add $\frac{1}{2}$ pint (250 ml) pectin stock and 3 lb ($1\frac{1}{2}$ kg) sugar and boil until set.
To make Strawberry Preserve: lightly crush $1\frac{1}{2}$ lb ($\frac{3}{4}$ kg) strawberries and place in a bowl with 2 lb (1 kg) caster sugar. Leave 1 hour, stirring occasionally. Add 2 tbsp (2×15 ml sp) lemon juice and 4 fluid oz (100 ml) bottled pectin; stir then pack into small jars or plastic containers, leaving headspace if it is to be frozen. Store in a refrigerator for up to 4 weeks or a freezer up to 6 months. Once the gel is broken, the preserve softens and needs to be used soon.

STRAWBERRY FOAM CASTLE

Use up squashy over-ripe strawberries this way. It is quickly made in a liquidizer goblet.

For 4 to 6 portions

Metric		Imperial
1	large orange	1
3	sugar cubes	3
350 g	strawberries	12 oz
25 g	gelatine	1 oz
50 g	caster sugar	2 oz

1. Scrub orange. Rub the skin all over with the sugar cubes until sugar has absorbed the zest. Cut a thin slice from centre of orange, reserve for decoration. Pare a slice of rind thinly from one half of orange, reserve. Squeeze juice. Hull strawberries, reserving 5 for decoration.
2. Measure 4 tbsp (4 × 15 ml sp) cold water into a small basin, add gelatine and stir. Place basin in a pan of water over a moderate heat; stir until gelatine has completely dissolved.
3. Place sugar cubes, orange juice, strawberries, gelatine and caster sugar in liquidizer goblet, run machine until mixture is well blended. Top up to 1 pint (500 ml) with cold water. Place liquidizer goblet in fridge to chill, until mixture is half set. (If liquidizer is not large enough, pour mixture into a bowl).
4. Return liquidizer goblet to machine and run until pale and fluffy, and almost doubled in volume. (Or whisk mixture in bowl.)
5. Pour mixture into 1½ pint (1 litre) fluted jelly mould. Chill until firm.
6. To unmould: dip jelly mould into hot water for a few seconds, invert on to a serving plate.
7. Shred reserved orange rind finely with a sharp knife. Cut reserved orange slice into quarters. Slice 4 reserved strawberries into three.
8. Arrange strawberry slices and shredded peel around serving plate. Place 2 orange wedges and a whole strawberry on top of jelly. Serve with pouring cream.

STRAWBERRY WHIRLS

Try these delicious melt-in-the-mouth biscuits sandwiched with a rich creamy cheese filling and fresh summer strawberries.

Makes 6

Metric		Imperial
	BISCUITS	
200 g	margarine	8 oz
50 g	caster sugar	2 oz
200 g	plain flour	8 oz
	FILLING	
200 g	strawberries	8 oz
200 g	full fat soft cheese	8 oz
	icing sugar	
	vanilla essence	

1. Prepare a moderate oven (180 deg C, 350 deg F, Gas Mark 4). Grease a baking sheet. Cream margarine and sugar together until light and fluffy. Add flour and mix well. Place mixture in a nylon piping bag fitted with a large star tube.
2. Pipe 12 whirls on baking sheet, allowing room for spreading. Bake in centre of oven for 10 to 15 minutes until golden brown. Leave to cool on baking sheet.
3. Wash strawberries, dry on kitchen paper. Reserve 6 for decoration and remove hulls from remaining strawberries; cut strawberries into quarters. Place cheese and 2 tbsp (2 × 15 ml sp) icing sugar in a bowl and beat until light and creamy; add a few drops of vanilla essence. Just before serving, fold strawberries into cheese mixture and use to sandwich biscuits together.
4. Sprinkle the top of each whirl with a little icing sugar. Use reserved strawberries to decorate the top of each whirl.

Strawberry Foam Castle.

Cane Fruits

All the so-called cane fruits – blackberries, raspberries and related hybrid berries such as loganberry, 'Tayberry', 'Marion berry' and 'Boysenberry', freeze well. Raspberries are best grown in a row across the garden supported by wires. While all the rest can be grown in a similar way, they are more usually grown against a fence in the modern small garden.

The flowers and fruits are produced on the strong new stems – 'canes' – which grew the previous year. These plants virtually replace themselves each year, with the fruiting canes dying after the fruit ripens.

All this new growth each year means the soil needs to be well fed and kept moist when growth and fruiting are making such heavy demands on the plant.

While some people may think brambles are best left in the hedgerows, there is no doubt the modern thornless varieties are easy to grow, heavy yielding and deliciously flavoured.

Even in ornamental gardens the almost evergreen and attractively cut-leaved 'Oregon Thornless' blackberry has its place. All these cane fruits produce white flowers and pretty berries which can be trained in with other ornamental climbers.

Anyone who likes the taste of fresh raspberries, and there are many people who rank them above strawberries, should consider planting a few in amongst shrubs or border flowers. Some canes planted around a central stake can be tied in at the top, wigwam fashion.

Grown this way, they give height to a flower border, they can be tied in to keep them under control and the central pole supports a piece of net to protect them from birds when in fruit.

Blackberries and hybrid berries

Choice of cane fruit type with long stems will depend very much on personal taste but bear in mind as well the seasons of harvest. While the best known blackberry/raspberry offspring is the loganberry, a recent hybrid, the 'Tayberry', bred in Scotland is the earlier fruiting.

The 'Tayberry' starts fruiting with summer raspberries in July and produces huge fruits of brighter colour than loganberries. One well-cultivated plant can yield 10–15 lb of fruit, suitable for eating raw as well as cooking, freezing and jam-making.

Next in order of ripening comes the loganberry, usually ready to pick in late July and August. The thornless 'Loganberry LY654' is a heavy-yielding selection and the thornless stems are much easier to handle.

Blackberries end the harvest season and once again the thornless varieties are best in gardens. Older thorned varieties like 'Bedford Giant' (ripening from August onwards) and the very strong-growing and later-ripening 'Himalayan Giant' produce heavy yields but are very prickly to handle.

Parsley-shaped leaves make the 'Oregon Thornless Blackberry' attractive and the fruit has a good flavour but the yield will not be as heavy as from the thorned types. Recently introduced blackberries called 'Smoothstem' and the sister variety 'Thornfree' combine the thornfree quality with heavy yields of large fruits from late August to October.

'Thornless Boysenberry', which has fruits very similar to 'Youngerberry', is thought to be a cross between blackberry, loganberry and raspberry. It has red fruit which turn black when fully ripe and crops up to 10 lb per plant. The large fruit has small pips.

Loganberries are better in sunny sites while blackberries will grow anywhere, even on a north-facing wall although the ripening will be a little later.

Whatever your choice the soil treatment is the same. Avoid planting any of the cane fruits where cane fruits grew before. If the site cannot be changed then swop soil with another part of the garden, digging out at least a full barrow load.

Dig in plenty of well-rotted garden compost or peat before planting. All soils are suitable but on very poor sandy types it will be advisable to choose the most vigorous thorned varieties. Once planted they will grow and crop well for at least ten to 15 years.

Space the thornless types 6–9 ft (2–3 m) apart and the thorned up to 12 ft (4 m) apart. Container-grown specimens can be planted at any time of year. If bare root plants are set out from October to March it will be necessary to prune back to a few inches above ground early in the first spring.

Subsequent pruning is simple enough: just prune out the old stems completely as soon as they finish fruiting.

The cut-leaved 'Oregon Thornless' blackberry is an attractive plant, as well as fruitful.

Support and training

On fences and walls a series of horizontal wires at 3 ft, 4 ft, 5 ft and 6 ft heights are needed to tie in the new and fruiting canes. Where the fruits are free standing, very secure stakes are needed to hold the wires. A full cropping blackberry puts up a lot of wind resistance and, once up, the supports need to last the ten to 15 year life of the plants if possible.

There are several training systems: the most common is a simple fan where the new growth is tied loosely into the centre and the one-year-old fruiting stems fanned out on either side. Once they have fruited you prune them out and the young centre canes are lowered into their place, making way for the next batch of new growth.

Several other training sytems are possible and the stems can be woven in order to concentrate the most into a small area. In every case the new growth is trained up the centre and above the fruiting canes, partly to prevent fungus disease spores dripping down from the older canes.

Thornless blackberries are the most suited to small gardens and even for training against north-facing walls.

Large shapely fruits on thornless loganberry turn almost black when ripe.

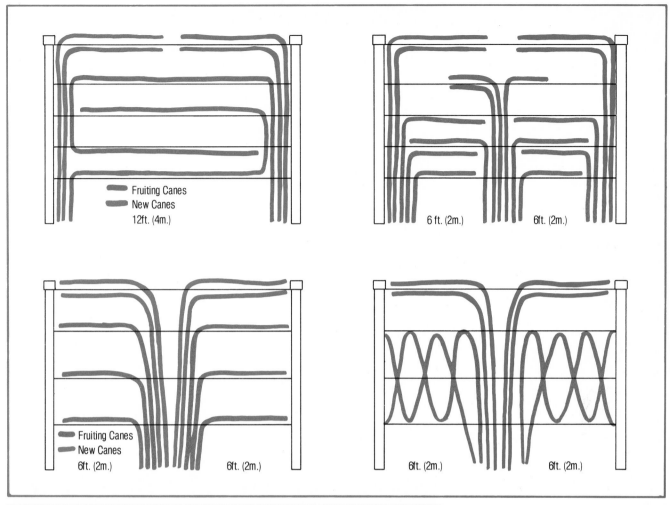

Fruiting Canes
New Canes
12ft. (4m.)

6 ft. (2m.)   6ft. (2m.)

Fruiting Canes
New Canes
6ft. (2m.)   6ft. (2m.)

6ft. (2m.)   6ft. (2m.)

Cultivated blackberries produce large fruit and ripen over a two-month period.

Aphis can attack these fruits but any of the greenfly sprays will control them. The small maggots of raspberry beetle are killed by spraying with malathion. Spray the blackberries at petal fall and loganberries mid and late June, but not when bees are active.

New plants are produced by pegging down the young tips of new canes, they soon root once in touch with the soil.

Raspberries – summer and autumn fruiting

There are two groups of raspberries which are classified according to the time of fruiting; the most important and best known being the June/July – usually called summer fruiting – varieties. The September to November fruiting, or so-called autumn fruiting, kinds are lighter cropping and need a different system of pruning. Because of the lower total yield the autumn fruiting kinds are only really suitable for the large garden. Where there is plenty of space they do considerably extend the fresh harvest season.

out and cropping will be poor. If your garden has heavy soil and is prone to waterlogging, add extra soil and compost to raise the level above that of the surrounding soil. This will drain it sufficiently for satisfactory growth. Raspberries grow quite well in light, poor, sandy soils but it will be necessary to give them plenty of water and cover the surface in summer with garden compost or lawn mowings to retain the moisture.

Make sure the soil is free of perennial weeds before planting. Once twitch or convolvulus weeds get among raspberries they are difficult to remove, so spray perennial weeds with suitable weedkillers before cultivating prior to planting. Dig in plenty of organic matter too, well-rotted garden compost, peat, manure and the like is needed. You won't have another chance to really improve the soil once the canes are established.

There is a government backed certification scheme for raspberries, just as there is for blackcurrants, potatoes and strawberries. It is the gardener's safeguard against buying canes infected with virus diseases, so always buy certi-

A 6 ft (2 m) row of raspberry 'Delight' yielding a serving for two every day for a fortnight. Notice plastic container over cane for net support.

Loganberry and blackberry trained to the fence, raspberry and blackcurrant foreground. The fence provides a good main support for the net.

Summer fruiting can also be extended by careful selection of variety. 'Glen Clova' is of good quality and one of the earliest to ripen in late June/July. 'Malling Jewel' and 'Malling Promise' are very well-tried mid-season kinds but superseded in yield and fruit size by 'Delight'. The latter is resistant to greenfly and some virus diseases as well as being a superb variety to eat fresh.

Although not as heavy cropping as the above summer varieties, 'Leo' is useful, cropping the same period as the sign of the zodiac, late July into August. All these cultivars are fine for desserts, freezing, preserving and other culinary purposes.

'September' is one of the heavier fruiting autumn varieties and 'Zeva' produces the largest berries. 'Heritage' is a strong-growing and reasonable yielding kind, while 'Fallgold' has light crops of very sweet, yellow fruits. All four crop from September to November as long as the weather doesn't get too frosty.

Raspberries will grow all right in partial shade although the heaviest crops will be picked from sunny sites. Avoid water-logged soil; raspberries with roots standing in water over winter will tend to die

fied disease-free canes from specialist growers. A few canes dug from a friend's row are unlikely to be healthy and it is not worth risking two or more years' work to get only part of the potential crop.

Planting the bare root canes can be carried out from October to March, the October planting being best as long as the new canes have stopped growing and the stems have ripened. Space the canes 18 in (45 cm) apart down the row and the rows 6 ft (2 m) apart. Firm in well after planting and see that the roots are well covered with soil. It's better to plant a little on the deep side, with roots at least 3 in 7.5 cm) below the surface.

Prune back to 12 in (30 cm) above the soil after planting. Any fruiting spurs produced can be left on these stumps but it is the new canes which grow subsequently that produce appreciable yields.

Summer fruiting varieties are not pruned after the first summer's growth and then they have all fruited wood removed after picking in every subsequent year. Autumn fruiting varieties have *all* the growth cut off every spring. New canes then grow, flower and fruit in the one year. I have managed to pick more fruits overall from varieties like 'Fallgold', however, if they are pruned the same as summer fruiting kinds. The old canes fruit twice, once in the first autumn and again the second summer before being pruned out.

Sweet autumn fruiting raspberry 'Fallgold'.

Very good crop of autumn fruiting raspberry 'Heritage'.

A 6 ft (2 m) long row of a summer variety like 'Delight' will yield 9 lb of fruit each year. All it needs for this is a good dressing of rose fertilizer each spring and plenty of water as the fruits swell and ripen.

It will be necessary to have stakes and two horizontal rows of wire at 3 ft (1 m) and 6 ft (2 m) above the ground to support the canes. With autumn fruiting kinds the new canes are tied in as they grow and after pruning with the summer ones. Tying in supports the canes against gales and a sheltered spot is best if heavy bunches of fruit are to remain undamaged in windy weather.

The main pest is the small maggot of raspberry beetle found in ripe fruit. Control this by spraying with permethrin or malathion when the first pink fruits are seen. A spray in May with a systemic fungicide controls cane spot, leaf spot and spur blight, should these occur in wet seasons.

Cookery

Blackberries

The kitchen garden should, if possible, have room for soft fruit, and blackberries justify the space because they are so versatile. Winter teas would not be the same without blackberry jam and jelly, and anyone with a store of apples also appreciates the value of blackberries as a mixer. Cultivated blackberries have a milder flavour than wild ones, and can be served either raw or cooked. Mix windfall apples into wild blackberries before stewing to make them go further and soften the strong flavour. To keep the bottom crust of plate pies from becoming too wet with blackberry juice, mix 1 tbsp (1 × 15 ml sp) cornflour with 2 tbsp (2 × 15 ml sp) sugar and add to each 1 lb (500 g) of fruit to be used.

To serve raw: if necessary, place in cold water to clean. Drain thoroughly, sprinkle with caster sugar and serve with whipped cream. For special occasions flavour the cream with a little cinnamon and sugar and decorate with strips of orange rind.

To serve cooked: for deep and plate pies, crumbles and charlottes, use them on their own or mixed with apples; mix them with other soft fruits for a Summer Pudding.

To make preserves: mix with apple (or even apple peelings) to make jelly (see recipe). For jam, use 1 lb (500 g) blackberries and apples mixed, to each 1 lb (500 g) sugar. If apples are not used, add 1 tbsp (1 × 15 ml sp) lemon juice for each 1 lb (500 g) fruit. If you want seedless jam, press the cooked fruit pulp through a sieve before adding the sugar. Elderberries or plums can be mixed into blackberries for variations of flavour. Use up to equal quantities of each fruit and blackberries, cooking the fruit separately in a little water before mixing with cooked blackberry pulp. Use equal sugar and mixed fruit.

To make wine and liqueurs: for wine, use blackberries on their own or mixed with elderberries, apples or plums. For a pleasant liqueur, infuse blackberries with gin, Bacardi or rum. Place ¾ lb (400 g) caster sugar, a strip each of lemon and orange rind, 1 lb (500 g) blackberries and a bottle of spirit in a jar. Cover, then shake the jar every day for 3 months. Strain, filter through a white tissue in a strainer, then bottle the liquid.

To store blackberries: Freezing: spread berries in a single layer on a metal tray, then freeze until just firm, about 1 hour. Pack in plastic boxes for storage. Bottling: make a thick syrup with ½ lb (250 g) sugar dissolved in 1 pint (500 ml) water. Fill bottling jars one third full of blackberries, then cover with syrup. Repeat until jar is full, then tap out bubbles. Cover with a lid, then process for 2 minutes by the water bath method or 1 minute at low (5 lb) pressure in a pressure cooker. If the apples are to be mixed in, blanch them first in sugar syrup.

Clockwise from front left **Blackberry and Apple Jelly; Blackberry Wine; Royal Blackberry Charlotte; Blackberry Sherbet.**

BLACKBERRY AND APPLE JELLY

Blackberries are best mixed with apples to help obtain a good set. If you prefer a strong blackberry flavour, use blackberries for the total weight of fruit and cook them with pectin stock made by boiling 250 g (½ lb) apple peelings with a covering of water for ½ hour, then straining through the jelly bag with the rest of the fruit. For the best set, boil up the jelly as soon as possible after straining the fruit. See Redcurrant Jelly page 125.

For about 5 lb (2.2 kg) jelly

Metric		Imperial
3 kg	mixed blackberries and cooking apples	6 lb
1.5 kg	preserving or granulated sugar	3 lb

Wash blackberries only if absolutely necessary. Wash apples, remove any bad parts, then cut up without peeling or coring and place in a preserving pan with the blackberries and 2 pints (1 litre) water. Cook slowly until the fruit has become pulpy. Strain through a jelly bag and leave to drip for 1 hour. (If the fruit contains 3 lb (1.5 kg) or more of apples it can be returned to the saucepan and boiled with an extra 1 pint (500 ml) water for ½ hour, then strained again.)

Measure the juice, then place it in the rinsed preserving pan. Add 1 lb (500 g) sugar for each 1 pint (500 ml) juice. Boil and pot as for Redcurrant jelly.

BLACKBERRY WINE

This dry table wine is rather like Beaujolais. Serve it chilled in summer. Add a handful of scented dark red rose petals if you can find them.

For 1 Gallon (4.5 litres)

Metric		Imperial
1.2 kg	blackberries	2½ lb
250 g	sultanas	½ lb
2	Campden tablets	2
	Beaujolais wine yeast	
2 × 5 ml sp	pectolase	2 tsp
2 × 5 ml sp	yeast nutrient	2 tsp
1 × 5 ml sp	citric acid	1 tsp
1 kg	granulated sugar	2 lb

1. Place blackberries in a sterilized plastic bucket and crush with a potato masher.
2. Wash sultanas in warm water then place in a liquidizer goblet with 1 pint (500 ml) warm boiled water. Run machine until sultanas are chopped then add to the blackberries. Crush one Campden tablet and add to the bucket with 4 pints (2.2 litres) cold water. Cover with a lid or a sheet of plastic tied down with string and leave overnight.
3. Meanwhile, make up the yeast starter as directed on the packet of yeast.
4. Add the fermenting yeast, pectolase and nutrient, citric acid and sugar. Stir well and leave in a warm place to ferment for 6 days, stirring vigorously twice each day. Keep the wine well covered.
5. Strain the wine through a nylon sieve into a sterilized 1 gallon (4.5 litre) jar. Top

up with cold water, fit an air-lock and leave to ferment in a warm place until the wine has cleared and stopped bubbling.
6. Siphon off the wine into a clean jar, fit a cork and leave in a cool place for at least 3 months before drinking.

BLACKBERRY SHERBET

This frozen dessert is lighter than a water ice and easy to make because it only needs whipping once. Use the same method for sherbet using other fruits as they come into season.

For 6 portions

Metric		Imperial
250 g	blackberries	½ lb
125 g	granulated sugar	4 oz
1 × 15 ml sp	lemon juice	1 tbsp
1	egg white	1

1. Turn refrigerator to coldest setting.
2. Place blackberries in a saucepan with 1 tbsp (1 × 15 ml sp) water and cook over a low heat until pulpy. Press through a sieve into a basin.
3. Place sugar in a saucepan with ¼ pint (125 ml) water. Stir over a low heat until sugar is dissolved, then boil quickly until the syrup registers 110 deg C (220 dec F) on a sugar thermometer. Alternatively, boil syrup on full heat for 4 minutes. Remove saucepan from heat and place a little syrup on the back of a teaspoon; press with another teaspoon and pull apart. If a thread forms between the spoons, the syrup is ready. Add the syrup to purée with the lemon juice, then chill in refrigerator.
4. Place egg white in a clean, greasefree basin, whisk until stiff. Gradually whisk in the blackberry syrup. Quickly pour into an oblong plastic container, cover with foil and place in the frozen food compartment of the refrigerator or a freezer until mixture is firm.
5. To serve: scoop into glasses and serve with sugar wafers.

ROYAL BLACKBERRY CHARLOTTE

Blackberries and apples are perfect partners for this quickly-made dessert. Try it with raspberries and plums, too.

For 4 to 6 portions

Metric		Imperial
4	trifle sponge cakes	4
250 g	blackberries	8 oz
250 g	cooking apples	8 oz
1	raspberry-flavoured jelly	1
100 ml	double cream	4 fl oz
1 × 15 ml sp	milk	1 tbsp
1 × 15 ml sp	lemon juice	1 tbsp
1	green-skinned eating apple	1

1. Line the bottom and side of a 6 in (15 cm) 1½ pint (75 ml) capacity soufflé dish with thin slices of cake, cutting them to fit where necessary.
2. Reserve 6 blackberries for decoration, place remainder in a saucepan. Peel and slice cooking apples, add to pan and cook slowly until fruit is thick and pulpy; press through a sieve into a basin.
3. Rinse out saucepan, return purée to pan and add jelly. Stir over a low heat until jelly has melted. Pour into a measuring jug and make up to 1 pint (500 ml) with hot water; pour into lined dish and leave to cool. Place in refrigerator until chilled and jelly has set.
4. To serve: dip the soufflé dish into hot water, loosen round the edges with a knife, then invert on to a serving dish. Whip cream and milk together until cream forms soft peaks. Place in a nylon piping bag fitted with a large star tube and pipe 12 stars around the top edge of the charlotte. Place lemon juice in a saucer, cut the green-skinned apple into thin slices and dip each side in lemon juice to prevent browning. Arrange 6 slices of apple, skin-side uppermost, radiating from centre, with two stars of cream between each slice. Arrange remaining slices of apple on the dish around base of charlotte and decorate with the reserved blackberries. Chill until ready to serve.

Loganberry

Loganberries are best harvested when dark red and then used at once. They are very juicy and will deteriorate quickly. They freeze well and their tart distinctive flavour makes them a delicious addition to many hot and cold desserts. Use as for raspberries.

Raspberry

This favourite fruit can be used in many hot and cold desserts and preserves. If wet, the berries deteriorate very quickly and become mouldy. The hull and plug is generally removed when the fruit is picked.
To prepare: wash only if necessary. Place in a single layer in a colander and gently swish in a bowl of cold water. Drain well then tip onto kitchen paper to dry.
To serve for dessert: thick pouring cream and sugar is all that is necessary, but they can be added to fruit salads, used in flans, tartlets and yogurt and used as toppings for cheesecakes and desserts. The pips are often disliked and the fruit can be either cooked or liquidized then sieved. Use raspberry sauce over creamy desserts, in mousses and fresh fruit jellies and milk shakes. The classic dish Peach Melba is made by coating the peaches with raspberry sauce and serving with ice cream.
Add to apples in pies and puddings.
To store: in a shallow punnet in the refrigerator for up to 1 day.
To freeze: open freeze then pack in plastic boxes or freezer bags. Thaw slowly in the refrigerator and the fruit will be indistinguishable from fresh berries. Freeze as purée in small tubs or in ice cube trays then pack in bags.
To bottle: use a syrup from 1 lb (½ kg) sugar to 1 pint (½ litre) water. Fill jar one third full of fruit, cover with syrup and repeat. Best to use small jars.

To make jam: boil 6 lb (3 kg) raspberries until pulped and the juice is reduced. Add 6 lb (3 kg) sugar, stir until dissolved then boil until set. For economy, replace up to half the amount of raspberries with fruits rich in pectin such as apples, gooseberries or redcurrants or add pectin stock (see page 98) then reduce weight of raspberries by 1 lb (500 g).
To make jelly: make as for Blackberry Jelly (page 120).
To make Raspberry Preserve: make as for Strawberry Preserve (page 112). *To make Raspberry Ice Cream and Sorbet:* make as for Strawberry (see page 112) omitting lemon juice and colouring.

RASPBERRY MERINGUE MOUNTAIN

Simple but effective, this gateau can be assembled in minutes. Make the meringue in advance and store in a tin, then select the fruit of your choice.

For 8 portions

Metric		Imperial
	MERINGUE	
3	egg whites	3
175 g	icing sugar	6 oz
125 ml	double cream	¼ pint
125 ml	single cream	¼ pint
250 g	raspberries	8 oz

1. Heat oven to lowest setting. Line 2 baking sheets with non-stick baking parchment. On one sheet, draw a 7 in, 6 in, 5 in and 4 in (18 cm, 15 cm, 12 cm, and 9 cm) circle and invert paper.
2. Half fill a saucepan with water, bring to boil, remove from heat. Place egg whites in a clean grease-free bowl and sift icing sugar into bowl. Place bowl over pan of water and whisk until mixture leaves a trail when whisk is lifted. Remove bowl from saucepan and continue whisking until mixture is cool.
3. Divide two thirds of the mixture between the 4 circles, spread inside the marked lines and smooth tops. Place remaining meringue in a nylon piping bag fitted with a medium-sized star tube. Pipe meringue stars on remaining baking sheet.
4. Place meringues in oven on centre shelf and just below; leave for 3 to 4 hours, when meringues should lift off paper easily. When meringues are cold, store in a tin until required.
5. Place creams in a bowl and whisk until cream just holds shape. Place one third of cream in a nylon piping bag fitted with a small star tube. Reserve half of raspberries and fold remainder into cream.
6. Place the 3 largest circles of meringue on a board, divide the raspberry mixture between the circles. Place largest circle on a serving plate and stack remainder on top, graduating in size.
7. Pipe stars of cream around each layer on to filling and place a meringue star and whole raspberry alternately on to cream stars. Pipe a large whirl on top of gateau and top with meringue stars and raspberries to complete decoration.

Preserving

Well preserved

Surplus produce can be stored by drying, salting, freezing or bottling. Add sugar to make jams and jellies and vinegar for ketchups, pickles and chutneys.

Drying

Use for apples, pears and plums, mushrooms, peas and herbs. For fruit, prepare and cut fruit into rings or quarters, remove stones from plums. Spread on a mesh tray, dry in a very low oven – a fan assisted cooker is best. Leave for about 6 hours or place on the tray of a microwave oven and heat untl crisp. Test by pressing between the fingers. There should be no apparent moisture. Leave 12 hours then pack in single layers with waxed paper between, in a cardboard box. To use, soak overnight then cook until tender.
Vegetables need blanching (as for freezing) before drying. Pick herbs for drying before they flower and early in the day before the sun evaporates the essential oils. Small-leafed varieties can be hung upside down in bunches in a warm dry shed. Large leaves can be stripped and dried on a mesh tray or in the airing cupboard. Crumble and store in jars, mixing your own blend of herbs.

Salting

Salting is an ancient but effective method of preserving vegetables, such as beans and cabbage. The moisture in the vegetables forms a brine with the salt. Use an earthenware or glass jar (not metal) with a wide neck.
Salt: use only cooking salt or sea salt, not table salt which has chemicals added to keep it free running. Use 1 lb ($\frac{1}{2}$ kg) salt to each 3 lb (1$\frac{1}{2}$ kg) vegetables.
Vegetables: choose only fresh, good quality vegetables free from blemishes. Runner beans are particularly successful preserved this way, wash beans and drain well, then slice.
To pack the jar: place a thick layer of salt on the bottom, cover with a thick layer of prepared vegetables, then another layer of salt. Add vegetables when they become available, but always finish with a layer of salt. Place a saucer on top of the vegetables with a weight to press them down and keep them under the brine as it forms. When the jar is full, remove saucer and weight, cover jar with waxed paper and secure well.

Storage: store container in a cool, dark place for up to 6 months.
To use: remove as many vegetables as required and re-seal jar. Rinse vegetables well under cold running water, then leave to soak in fresh cold water for 1$\frac{1}{2}$ to 2 hours. Rinse, then cook as usual, omitting any extra salt..

Chutney

Ingredients: use up windfall apples and end-of-season crops of fruit and vegetables for making chutney, but make sure you remove all the bruised and damaged parts.
Equipment: the finer the fruit and vegetables are chopped the better. An electric mincer or food processor is worth buying if you plan to make a lot of chutney. Use a large non-stick or aluminium pan or a preserving pan. A large pressure cooker could be used. Keep a long handled wooden spoon especially for chutney making.
Jars: save plastic-topped coffee jars and pickle jars during the year. Don't use large jars, as once opened the chutney will begin to evaporate. If you don't have enough plastic screw-tops for jars, a double thickness of strong plastic secured with an elastic band will do.
When is the chutney ready? Unlike jam making, there is no definite temperature at which the chutney is ready. The vinegar evaporates slowly during the cooking and the chutney should look thick with no free liquid when it is ready. Chutney thickens on cooling.
Storage: ensure the jars are well sealed, otherwise the chutney will evaporate and shrink during storage. Store the labelled jars in a cool, dry, dark place. Chutney should be stored several months before using to allow the flavour to develop.

SPICED RED TOMATO CHUTNEY

Makes about 3 lb (1.5 kg)

Metric		Imperial
2 kg	*ripe tomatoes*	4 lb
250 g	*shallots or pickling*	
	onions	$\frac{1}{2}$ lb
25 g	*salt*	1 oz
25 g	*mustard seeds*	1 oz
1 × 15 ml sp	*allspice*	1 tbsp
6	*peppercorns*	6
250 g	*granulated sugar*	$\frac{1}{2}$ lb
400 ml	*distilled malt vinegar*	$\frac{3}{4}$ pint

1. Collect together suitable jars and plastic-coated or plastic lids, or a piece of thick polythene for covering. Wash and dry jars and lids thoroughly; place jars in a cool oven or warming drawer, to dry out completely before filling.
2. Place tomatoes, 2 lb (1 kg) at a time, in a bowl, cover with boiling water. Leave for

1 minute; drain, then peel and roughly chop. Peel and finely chop shallots or pickling onions. Place, with salt, in a large saucepan or preserving pan.

3. Place mustard seeds, allspice and peppercorns on a piece of muslin; tie up with cotton or fine string and add to pan. Cook, uncovered, over a low heat, stirring, until juices are released. Increase heat to moderate and cook, stirring occasionally, for 30 minutes until tomatoes are reduced to a pulp.

4. Add sugar and vinegar; stir over a low heat until sugar has dissolved. Quickly bring to boil, lower heat and continue to cook, stirring occasionally, for about 20 to 25 minutes, until chutney thickens. Remove from heat and leave to cool for 10 minutes.

5. Remove muslin bag; ladle chutney into warmed jars. If using plastic-coated or plastic lids, cover chutney while hot; if using polythene, leave until cold, then cover with double-thickness circles of polythene and secure with elastic bands. Wipe jars clean, then label them giving variety and date of making.

PICKLING FRUIT AND VEGETABLES

Vinegar is used to preserve food this way. Use good-quality high-strength brewed malt vinegar to make sure the pickle keeps well. High-strength spiced pickling vinegar is available but you can make your own using the brown malt vinegar or the colourless distilled vinegar. Wine vinegar or cider vinegar can also be used for pickling.

Preparing spiced vinegar: this should be made at least 24 hours in advance if possible. Use 1 tbsp (1 × 15 ml sp) whole pickling spice to each 1 pint (500 ml) of vinegar.

Method: place vinegar and spices in a basin over a saucepan of cold water, cover basin with a plate. Bring water slowly to the boil; simmer 15 minutes. Remove basin and leave vinegar overnight, still covered. Alternatively place spices in vinegar bottle and replace lid; leave 3 to 4 weeks, then strain vinegar before using.

Fruit and vegetables: these are first salted or brined to extract some of the liquid which gives the vinegar a chance to penetrate the vegetables or fruit, and also prevents dilution of the vinegar. Salt also draws out some of the starch from the vegetables and keeps them crisp. Use block or household salt, not iodised table salt.

Preparing the vegetables: cut the washed vegetables into chunky pieces, cubes, or leave whole if small.

Brining: firm vegetables, such as onions, are placed in a brine solution made by dissolving 2 oz (50 g) salt to each 1 pint (500 ml) cold water. Place a small plate on top of the vegetables to ensure that they are all immersed.

Layering: vegetables with a high water content, such as courgettes and cucumbers, need to be layered in a bowl with salt. Leave overnight or for 24 hours in the brine or salt, then drain in a colander; rinse well under cold running water and drain well.

Preparing the jars: use wide-necked jars that have plastic screw tops, or use a double thickness of plastic and secure it with an elastic band. Thoroughly wash and drain the jars.

Packing the jars: pack the vegetables or fruit as tightly as possible into the jars without bruising them. Use the handle of a wooden spoon to fit them in. Cover with vinegar to within 1 in (2.5 cm) of rim of jar. Gently tap bottom of jar to release air bubbles. Cover jars with plastic tops. Label and store in a cool, dry, dark place for several weeks, to allow the flavour to develop, before using.

MASTER JAM RECIPE

Use this method for soft and juicy fruits that contain plenty of acid and pectin to make the jam set. See the following recipes for the ingredients and method for jam from fruits that need further preparation and do not set so well. Various types of fruit can be mixed in a jam or jelly, but they are best prepared and cooked separately.

Makes about 5 lb (2.25 kg)

Metric		Imperial
1.5 kg	raspberries	3 lb
1.5 kg	granulated or preserving sugar	3 lb

1. Collect together suitable jam jars; wash and rinse thoroughly. Place jars in a very cool oven to dry out completely.

2. Wash raspberries only if really necessary; place in a preserving pan. Cook over a low heat until juice begins to run. Bring to the boil and cook gently, stirring occasionally, until fruit is tender and juice has reduced slightly, about 10 minutes.

3. Add sugar and stir until dissolved; bring to boil and boil rapidly on full heat until setting point is reached. Test for setting after first 5 minutes, then at 5 minute intervals if necessary. If you increase the quantity, boiling time will increase in proportion, eg boil for 10 minutes if using double quantities of fruit and sugar. Use one of the following methods for testing the set of the jam or jelly you are making.

TESTING FOR SET

A. *Temperature test:* a thermometer marked in degrees to at least 110 deg C (230 deg F) should be used. Place thermometer in very hot water, stir jam, quickly dry thermometer, then place in jam. Make sure that it is sufficiently immersed to give a true reading – the bulb should not touch the bottom of the pan. When jam has reached setting point, the temperature should be 105 deg C (220 deg F). It is a good idea to combine this test with one of the following tests.

B. *Cold plate test:* remove pan from heat. Place a scant teaspoonful of jam on a cold plate; allow to cool completely. If setting point has been reached, the jam will crinkle on the surface when pushed with a finger.

C. *Flake test:* remove pan from heat. Stir with a wooden spoon, then lift spoon and turn in the hand to cool jam slightly. Allow

jam to drop. If setting point has been reached, jam will partially set on spoon, so drops run together to form flakes, which break off sharply.

4. Remove from heat and skim, if necessary. Ladle into warmed jars. Fill jars right up to the top as the jam will shrink slightly on cooling. Place well-fitting waxed discs on surface of jam. Wipe jars with a clean cloth. Cover each jar with a transparent cover, which has been wiped with a damp cloth, so that it will become taut when dry. Secure with an elastic band. When cold, label jam, marking its kind and date. Alternatively, you can use screw tops, covering jam with melted paraffin wax. Store in a cool, dry place.

BLACKCURRANT JAM

Use this method also for fruits that are hard and need cooking, such as gooseberries, plums and apricots (see the proportions given below).

Makes about 5 lb (2.25 kg)

Metric		Imperial
1 kg	blackcurrants	2 lb
1 litre	water	1½ pints
1.5 kg	granulated or preserving sugar	3 lb

1. Collect together suitable jam jars; wash and rinse thoroughly. Place jars in a very cool oven to dry them out completely.

2. Strip blackcurrants from stalks. Wash blackcurrants, if necessary. Place in preserving pan with water. Bring to boil, reduce heat and cook gently until fruit is very soft, 45 minutes to 1 hour.

3. Continue as from step 3 of Master Jam Recipe.

Gooseberry Jam: wash, top and tail fruit. Cook 2 lb (1 kg) fruit in ¾ pint (400 ml) water and add 3 lb (1.5 kg) sugar.

Plum Jam: remove stones if possible. Cook 3 lb (1.5 kg) plums in ½ pint (250 ml) water and add 3 lb (1.5 kg) sugar. Skim off stones before potting if necessary.

Fresh Apricot Jam: remove stones, crack some and remove kernels. Blanch and skin these like almonds and add to fruit. Cook 3 lb (1.5 kg) fruit in ½ pint (250 ml) water and add 3 lb (1.5 kg) sugar.

Damson Jam: cook 2½ lb (1 kg) fruit in 1 pint (500 ml) water and add 3 lb (1.5 kg) sugar. Skim off all the stones after sugar has dissolved.

STRAWBERRY JAM

Strawberries are low in acid and pectin and need to be mixed with a fruit rich in acid and pectin for a good set. Blackberries can be mixed with apples in a similar way.

Makes about 5 lb (2.25 kg)

Metric		Imperial
250 g	redcurrants or gooseberries	½ lb
250 ml	water	½ pint
1.5 kg	strawberries (prepared weight)	3 lb
1.5 kg	granulated or preserving sugar	3 lb

1. Collect together suitable jam jars; wash and rinse thoroughly. Place jars in a very cool oven to dry out.

2. Wash redcurrants or gooseberries; place in a medium-sized saucepan with water. Bring to the boil, cover and cook gently for 15 to 20 minutes. Press through a nylon sieve, reserve juice. Wash strawberries, if necessary; place in preserving pan. Stir over a low heat until juice begins to run. Bring to boil; cook, stirring gently, for about 10 minutes, until juice is reduced by half.

3. Add redcurrant or gooseberry juice and sugar. Continue from step 3 of Master Jam Recipe.

REDCURRANT JELLY

Makes about 4 lb (2 kg)

Metric		Imperial
2.5 kg	redcurrants	5 lb
	granulated or	
	preserving sugar	

1. Place a jelly bag or a square of clean sheeting in a saucepan of water. Boil for 10 minutes, to sterilize; drain, rinse with cold water and wring out. If using a jelly bag, suspend from a hook and place a large bowl underneath. If using a square of sheeting, use string to tie the corners firmly to the legs of an upturned chair or stool; place bowl underneath on seat of chair.

2. Wash redcurrants and place (still on stalks) in a large saucepan or preserving pan with 1½ pints (1 litre) water. Bring to boil and cook slowly, uncovered, until tender, about 45 minutes. Mash well with the back of a wooden spoon; ladle into jelly bag or sheeting.

3. Leave to drip for 15 minutes; put pulp back into pan and add 1 pint (500 ml) water. Bring to boil, stirring, reduce heat and cook slowly for 30 minutes. Ladle back into jelly bag, cover with a cloth or polythene bag and leave to strain for several hours or overnight, until dripping has stopped. (Do not squeeze or disturb the fruit, as this will cause the jelly to become cloudy.)

4. Collect together suitable small jars with lids (honey jars are ideal) or jars with jam pot covers. Wash and dry the jars and lids thoroughly; place jars in a cool oven to dry out.

5. Measure fruit juice and return to clean saucepan or preserving pan. Add 1 lb (500 g) sugar to each 1 pint (500 ml) of juice and stir over a low heat until sugar has dissolved. Bring to boil quickly; boil rapidly for 10 minutes, then test to see if setting point has been reached. To test, see methods described in the Master Jam Recipe.

6. Skim jelly, using a large spoon. Using a jug, pour jelly into warmed jars. Cover jelly with circles of waxed paper, then with lids or jam pot covers. Do not tilt or move jars, until jelly has set. Label jars, giving variety and date. Store in a cool, dry place away from strong light.

Bottling

Fruit has a long storage life if it is cooked and sterilized in a glass bottle. This kills the yeasts and moulds; then the bottle is sealed to prevent contamination. The tart fruits that need long cooking are often better preserved by bottling than by other methods, like freezing. Bottling can in fact improve the flavour of some fruits like peaches, apricots, gooseberries, rhubarb, plums. Vacuum bottling jars with tops that seal securely are best for preserving fruit, but jam jars or coffee jars can be used as an alternative with a cover of special fruit preserving skin on top.

Follow the golden rules –

1. Use fruit that is in tip-top condition – firm and ripe with no blemishes or bruised parts.

2. Check that there are no cracks or chips in the bottle and that the rubber gasket is not damaged or perished.

3. Label jars and use in date order.

4. Store jars in a cool, dark place as both heat and light spoil the colour of the fruit and can make the syrup turn cloudy.

5. Check jars occasionally – if any change occurs, open and use at once.

6. Bottle small fruits whole. Peaches and large plums are bottled more easily when halved and with the stones removed. Soft fruits and tomatoes are delicious bottled in their own juices.

7. When bottling tomatoes, make into purée, adding 2 level tsps (2 × 5 ml sp) citric acid per 1 pint (500 ml) of purée.

PREPARATION OF FRUIT

Wash jars thoroughly. Leave in hot water until required.

Sugar syrup: dissolve 4 oz to 8 oz (100 g to 200 g) sugar in each 1 pint (500 ml) of water. Boil for 2 to 3 minutes; leave in saucepan. Spiced syrups are delicious with peaches and pears: add 4 cloves and a 2 in (5 cm) stick of cinnamon to each 1 pint (500 ml) of syrup during boiling. Strain the syrup carefully before pouring on to fruit. Prepare fruit according to type. Place apples and pears in brine immediately after peeling to prevent browning. To make brine, add 1 tbsp (1 × 15 ml sp) salt and 1 tsp (1 × 5 ml sp) lemon juice to each 1 pint (500 ml) of water. Also, cut fruit into suitable sized pieces to fit into jars. Sterilize jars by filling with boiling water – don't dry. Pour boiling water over tops. Pack fruit tightly into jars using the handle of a wooden spoon. Rinse fruit that has been soaked in brine.

Oven method:

1. Prepare a cool oven (150 deg C, 300 deg F, Gas Mark 2).

2. Cover jars loosely with foil or tops, but don't press down. Arrange jars on a baking sheet and place in centre of oven. Cook extra fruit in a covered casserole to top up jars if fruit reduces during cooking.

3. Cook pears and apples for 1 hour, halved peaches, apricots, plums, gooseberries, cherries and tomatoes for 45 minutes and soft fruits for 30 minutes.

4. Remove jars from oven and place on a wooden board. Fill jars with extra fruit from casserole, to within ½ in (1 cm) of top. Bring syrup to boil. Fill each jar to the brim with syrup, seal jar and leave for 24 hours.

To check seal: remove screw rings – lids should remain secure; plastic skin should be taut and dipped in the centre. Tops should 'ring' when tapped. Label jars and store in a cool, dry place.

Water bath method:

1. Line base of a large saucepan or preserving pan with a thick layer of newspaper, or place a wooden board or trivet on base.

2. Bring syrup to boil. Fill each jar to the brim with syrup; seal jars, then loosen rings to allow for expansion during cooking.

3. Place jars in saucepan and fill pan with cold water until necks of jars are covered. Heat slowly so that water takes 1½ hours to reach simmering.

4. Simmer apples, gooseberries and tomatoes for 15 minutes, apricots, plums, peaches, cherries and pears for 30 minutes and soft fruits for 10 minutes.

5. Remove water from pan with a ladle or jug. Using a cloth, carefully lift out jars and place on a wooden board.

6. Press caps, pull the skin tightly or tighten screw bands. Cool for 24 hours. Check seal as for oven method.

Pressure cooker method: Use only special bottling jars. Place jars on a pad of newspaper or the inverted trivet. Close lid and check that jars do not block safety valve or steam vent. Fill jars with fruit and top up with boiling syrup: close lids, then loosen the screw rings one quarter turn. Pour water to a 1 in (2.5 cm) depth into cooker and bring to boil. (Add 1 tbsp (1 × 15 ml sp)) of vinegar in hard water districts to avoid discolouring the pan.) Close the lid, then bring slowly up to low (5 lb) pressure. This should take 5 to 10 minutes. Maintain pressure for 1 minute for berries, currants, gooseberries, rhubarb, whole stone fruits and citrus fruits; 4 minutes for purée, solidly-packed apples, halved stone fruits and pineapple. Remove from heat and leave for 10 minutes before opening. Remove jars and tighten screw bands. Check seal as oven method.

Freezing food

To blanch or not to blanch

If you intend to store vegetables for more than three weeks it is necessary to blanch them. This process retards the action of the chemical substances, called enzymes, which spoil the vitamin C as storage progresses. To blanch vegetables: use a saucepan that can hold at least six pints of boiling water, leaving enough room for the vegetables. No more than a lb of prepared vegetables should be blanched at one time, because the water in the container must be brought back to the boil within one minute. Time blanching from the moment the water comes to the boil. After they have been blanched for the required time, plunge the vegetables into a container of cold water and ice cubes for the same number of minutes as they were blanched. A wire basket, pressure-cooker separators or a large piece of muslin, in which the vegetables can be tied loosely, eases the transferring of the vegetables from one container to another. The blanching water can be used for about six consecutive batches of vegetables. Drain vegetables well and pack closely in freezer bags or containers.

Basic method for freezing vegetables

Freeze only young, fresh vegetables. A possible exception is a soup or stew-pack of raw or cooked vegetables to avoid waste. Chill until ready to freeze. Operate the fast-freeze switch for over 1 lb (500 g) of food.

1. *Preparation:* prepare according to kind, and cut into even-sized pieces.
2. *Blanching:* to inactivate enzymes spoiling colour and flavour, the vegetables must be blanched in boiling water. Only a small quantity can be done at a time; the boiling water must regain its temperature quickly. Omit blanching only if storing less than two weeks.
Prepare a large saucepan about three-quarters full of boiling water. Place 1 lb (500 g) or less of the vegetables in a wire blanching-basket. Improvise, if necessary, with a nylon bag (as used for straining wine) or the separators from your pressure cooker. Lower the vegetables into the water and time from where it returns to the boil (see chart). Cool in ice-cold water for the same time; then spread on clean tea towels and pat dry. The blanching water can be used about six times.
3. *Freezing:* open-freeze vegetables on trays, or pack in plastic boxes or freezer bags in amounts suitable for the most usual servings. Press out any air with the hands, or use a pump; close with a wire tie; label. Place on a freezing shelf or in the fast-freeze compartment.

Basic method for freezing fruit

If you are planning to freeze more than 1 lb (500 g) of food, operate the fast-freeze switch. Choose firm, ripe fruits. It is not worthwhile to freeze any but the most perfect, unless intended for jam, chutney or wine. There are three methods of freezing fruit:

1. *Loose or open freezing*
Use this method for free-flow packs. Choose raw fruits that do not discolour. Those with hard skins, like black and red currants, plums, damsons and gooseberries, can be packed dry in freezer bags. Wrap oranges for marmalade individually in self-clinging plastic; then pack in a freezer bag. Fruit for jam can be packed in a freezer bag as it is. Label it, giving weight and intended use. Freezing destroys some of the pectin, so pack an extra 4 oz (100 g) of fruit for each 2 lb (1 kg). Soft fruits must be spread in a single layer.

2. *Syrup*
Make syrup using 8 oz to 1 lb (250 g to ½ kg) for each 1 pint (550 ml) of water, and

chill. Use about ½ pint 250 ml) for each 1 lb (½ kg) of fruit. Leave 1 in (2 cm) of the container unfilled to allow for expansion during freezing. Cover, label and chill; then freeze. Use this method for fruits that need cooking, or ones that discolour, like apples, apricots and peaches. As an extra precaution against discoloration, add some lemon juice

or vitamin C to the syrup. To keep the fruit under the syrup and prevent the top layer discolouring, place a ball of greaseproof paper on top. If containers are limited, remove the frozen block, wrap in self-clinging plastic, and store in a freezer bag. Alternatively, line a cardboard box with a freezer bag; fill; freeze; then remove the box.

Vegetable blanching chart

Vegetable	Preparation	Blanching and cooling time		Freezing method
asparagus	Grade for size	thin	2 minutes	Pack into
		thick	4 minutes	containers
beans:				
broad	Shell, and grade for size	small	2 minutes	Pack in freezer
		large	3 minutes	bags
French	Trim ends; cut in chunks if desired	whole	3 minutes	Open-freeze;
		cut	2 minutes	pack in bags
runner	String, if necessary; cut into chunks	2 minutes		As French beans
broccoli	Grade for size; soak 30 minutes in cold salt water	3 to 4 minutes		Open-freeze; pack in boxes
Brussels sprouts	Grade for size; small sprouts are best. Soak 30 minutes in cold salt water	3 minutes		Open-freeze; pack in bags or boxes
carrots	Freeze only small, young carrots; scrub and trim	5 minutes		Rub off skins; pack in bags
cauliflower	Break into florets	3 minutes		Open-freeze; pack in bags
courgettes	Cut into 1-in (2-cm) lengths	3 minutes		Open-freeze; pack in bags
mushrooms	Wash and dry; cut in quarters if large	(a) Fry in butter (b) Do not blanch		(a) Pack in containers (b) Open-freeze
peas	Shell and grade into sizes	1 minute		Open-freeze
peppers	Wash; cut in halves; remove seeds and membrane; slice	2 minutes		Pack into bags or boxes
potatoes:				
new	Choose small potatoes	Until almost cooked		Pack in bags
chipped	Fry until almost cooked but not browned	Cool quickly		Open-freeze; pack in bags
spinach	Prepare as for serving	2 minutes; stir		Pack in bags
mixed vegetables	Prepare each vegetable separately; then mix	Blanch separately		Pack in bags

Freezing fruit

Fruit	Preparation	Freezing method	To use
apple	1. Peel, core, slice into salted water. Place in muslin bag or perforated container; blanch 2 minutes; drain 2. Make a purée	In dry sugar	Stew from frozen Thaw for pies
		In containers	Thaw
apricots	Remove stones; poach in syrup to prevent browning	In syrup	Thaw
bilberries blackcurrants redcurrants	Wash only if necessary	Dry in bags	Stew from frozen Thaw for pies
cherries	Wash only if necessary; remove stones	In syrup	Poach if necessary Thaw
gooseberries	Top and tail	Dry in bags or in syrup	Stew from frozen Thaw for pies
grapefruit and oranges	In segments Juice	In dry sugar In tubs or ice trays	Thaw Thaw
melon	Peel; remove seeds; cube	In syrup	Thaw
peaches	Dip in boiling water; remove skins and stones; cut in halves or slices	In syrup with lemon juice or vitamin C	Thaw
pears	Not worth freezing. During a glut, peel, core, and cut into slices	In syrup with added lemon juice or vitamin C	Poach
pineapple	Peel, core, and cut into slices or cubes	In syrup	Thaw
plums	Avoid washing, if possible. Stew if very ripe	Dry in bags	Stew from frozen Thaw for pies
		In containers	Thaw
soft fruits (blackberries loganberries raspberries)	Avoid washing if possible	Open-freeze on trays; then pack in bags or boxes	Thaw very slowly in refrigerator
strawberries	Only suitable for cooking, as they collapse. Best as purée	Best in syrup As purée, in containers or ice trays	Thaw very slowly in refrigerator
tomatoes	Leave whole, to be used for cooking since they collapse. Cook and make into purée	Whole, dry in bags. As purée, in containers	Grill or fry from frozen Thaw or heat

Index